SHARDS

MARY RODENBURG

PAGE PUBLISHING
Conneaut Lake, PA

First originally published by Page Publishing 2022

ISBN 978-1-6624-8279-3 (pbk)
ISBN 978-1-6624-8278-6 (digital)

Printed in the United States of America

This book is dedicated to my Mom, "Spoons" and Isaac.

THE POOR FARM

The poor farm of Broome County, New York, housed a long, gangly structure built in the late 1800s, and it sat on acreage that was farmed by the people staying there. The house was massive, total capacity being fifteen hundred, which it filled to the brim during parts of its history. But by the 1950s, economic factors in America changed considerably, and the poor farm population dwindled down to a maximum of three hundred people.

The roof consisted of three dilapidated layers of shingles that were peeling from decades of the wear and tear of brutal New York winters. A red brick well house stood about twenty feet from the back porch. About fifty feet behind the well house crouched a long and low chicken coop of peeling white bead board siding. There were half a dozen other outbuildings beyond the chicken coop, including two garages for farm machinery.

The property adjacent to the poor farm held a two-story brown-stained cedar house with a gray tin roof. It was owned by Mr. and Mrs. Clark. Behind this house, there was a shop with no doors and only open spaces where windows might go. It was Mr. Clark's automobile repair shop. It was large enough to fit three vehicles side by side with plenty of room in front for the long work benches. Behind this shop, there was a well house, a garage for two personal vehicles, and a shed for two tractors—a John Deere and a Farmall—as well as a small red barn for two retired plow horses.

Mr. and Mrs. Clark had adopted four boys—Jarob Connor, Bela Sovine, Jeremy Snow, and Fulton A. Fuller. Mr. Clark and his sons were very adroit mechanically. As in Mr. Clark's case, the boys were able to repair just about anything that had a motor or moving parts, but the majority of their business was automotive repair and body work.

They boys baled hay also. They sold some of their hay, and the remainder was kept for the Clarks' two plow horses. The boys harvested two hundred acres of hay each year.

* * *

Ms. Sherry Hamilton had heard about the poor farm from a prostitute in New York City with whom she had stayed for a few weeks. The girl told Sherry that her boss had found her and taken her from the poor farm back to the city. The boss eventually kicked Sherry out of their hovel, and Sherry took residence underneath the subway train tracks with some other homeless folks. She panhandled for money nearly every day and received a pittance.

Once, Sherry reached the door of a convent and rang the bell. She begged for money so she could go home. The nun at the door asked her where home was.

"Schenectady, ma'am," Sherry responded, knowing she had no intentions in going there.

The nun gave her a glass of water, a loaf of bread, and a ten-dollar bill. Sherry thanked the nun profusely, drank the water, and left with the bread and money.

Back at her place beneath the subway train tracks, Sherry handed out cigarettes she had bought from one of the nearby shops. Everybody under the tracks smoked and talked and laughed until well into the night. When the first few of them awoke in the morning, they noticed that Sherry was not among them.

The first place she went to was a secondhand store downtown. She bought an ecru cotton short-sleeved dress for a quarter, a pair of tan socks for ten cents, a twenty-cent straw hat to keep the sun from her face, plus a five-cent tan sweater. She wanted to be inconspicuous, and the shades of brown she picked did the trick. She changed into her "new" clothes and put her old ones into a brown shopping bag.

Sherry started her journey afoot from New York City, toward the wild, dry countryside of Broome County, where there was the poorhouse in which she assumed she could stay for a while. She had no idea where she would eat, rest, or sleep. She had neither pillow nor blanket. She just trusted fate. She knew hitchhiking was an option. She was accustomed to hitchhiking. It was the way she had gotten from her home to New York City.

BELA

Sherry was fortunate enough to catch a ride from a family going in her direction, about ten miles outside New York City. They were the epitome of Okies from *The Grapes of Wrath*—impoverished, jobless people (Mom, Dad, son, daughter) traveling to America looking for seasonal work. Sherry rode in the back of their pickup truck on top of some hay that had been spread out. She leaned her back against the back of the truck cab. The open back window spewed heat from the front seat of the truck. She slept most of the way to her next destination.

She had about three miles to go after being dropped off that lonely two-lane, roughly paved forest road onto a dry, dusty road that seemed to start, go, and end nowhere. She gave the driver of the vehicle five dollars and thanked him for the ride. He tipped his hat to her.

The shade of the trees, which were mostly saplings, was a pleasant reprieve from the deep, eighty-degree sunshine. Sherry took a slow pace to save energy. She wore her hat to save her face from the sun. Her feet felt great since she had had a huge break during that long ride.

Walking along the dirt road, Sherry took note of a huge cloud of dust coming toward her. It obscured everything behind it. And the dust did not settle down quickly. It just remained an airborne trail of whatever was coming her way.

It was a light-yellow Cadillac convertible, and it appeared to be flying up the road. But when one of the inhabitants took note of Sherry, the car slammed to a halt. The dust was obnoxious. It made

4

her cough and gag. She covered her mouth with her sweater and turned away from the car.

"Damn, Connor, you're choking the poor girl," someone said to the driver of the Cadillac.

That someone jumped over one of the back doors of the car and approached Sherry, who was standing off the side of the road in a dry brown meadow of scraggly weeds beneath a tree.

The young man took her forearm and asked, "Ma'am, are you all right? It is just so dry and dusty. We're having a bad spring season, no rain and everything. I'm so sorry. Excuse my language too. Are you okay?" There was something soothing about his touch and his voice.

He had to bend his head down and look into her eyes because her head was down.

But she lifted her head, and he lifted his. Their eyes met—brown hers, gray-green his. He was very slender and stood over six feet tall in his boots, quite a bit taller than Sherry's five foot six. He wore Levi's overalls and a white T-shirt. His untied boots covered bare feet, which impressed Sherry right away. He released her arm as gently as he had taken it.

"Yes, thank you. I'll be fine." She coughed a few times, and the someone took her arm again.

"Please excuse me, but it's unusual for a lady to be walking out here in the country by herself. Is there somewhere you are headed?"

Should she answer? Who were these guys? There were four of them, and three of them sat in the car watching Sherry and the someone. They didn't look unruly or unscrupulous, but there was no way for her to know what kind of men they were. She kept her reticence handy so they couldn't read her face.

Sherry looked ahead in the direction of her destination.

"Oh!" said the someone. "Let me introduce myself. I'm so sorry. My name is Bela. Bela Sovine."

"So *fine* as the girls call him!" came the words of Fulton in the back seat. He had a freshly young face, light-brown eyes, and short medium-brown hair.

Jarob turned around and said, "Shut up, peanut gallery." Jarob was the driver. Taller than the others, he had a long face, a salient nose, blond hair, and captivating blue eyes.

Indeed, Bela was usually the favorite of girls wherever he and his brothers went out and about. He had a charm and intelligence that flowed without effort. He was a natural entertainer.

Bela just sighed. "I apologize, miss. We live about three miles back near the Broome County poor farm. Have you heard of it?"

Sherry kept her face straight as she looked at Bela.

I guess I might as well take my chance, she thought. "I'm heading in that direction actually."

"Oh! All right. I wonder—I mean, I don't know if...if you would like a ride, miss? It's really dang hot out here. You have no water, I see. If you could see your way to trust me, I'll make sure you get to your destination safely. If you prefer not to ride in the car, I'd be honored to accompany you on foot."

"But you must have plans to be somewhere. I wouldn't think of making you change your plans," she replied pragmatically.

Bela looked at Jarob.

"We'll walk," he said. "I'm going to walk with her. You fellows just go on, and I'll see you at home tonight."

"You sure?" asked Fulton.

"Yup, I'm sure. Go have a grand ol' time. I want to see this lady safely to her destination."

"Okay," said Jarob doubtfully. "Good night, Bela. The town girls are going to ask about you. Good night, miss."

"Good night, miss," repeated Jeremy, seated next to Jarob. He was obviously the youngest boy of the group. He was skinny with very dark-brown hair and eyes.

Sherry nodded to Jarob and Jeremy and smiled slightly. She was not entirely comfortable with any of these guys, who seemed to have appeared from nowhere.

The Cadillac took off slowly at first. About two hundred feet later, the accelerator was punched down to get the dust flying again. The dust was far enough away to miss Sherry and Bela.

"May I have your name?"

"Sherry."

They shook hands, a little longer than she expected they should have. He had a friendly, firm grip. He looked at her slightly quizzically. He wanted to ask questions, but she had the feeling he would not do it.

"Okay, Ms. Sherry, where shall I take you?"

"Down the road please. I will let you know when we're there, if you don't mind, that is."

"My pleasure," said Bela, and he nodded once.

Friends, Sherry thought. *I might be able to be friends with this Bela.*

As they sauntered those three miles down the road, Sherry and Bela engaged in small talk—the dry season, the rain that usually drenches everything and turns dormancy into lush happy fullness of life in the world of crops. He talked about his job fixing machines and his other job baling hay. He told her he was a World War II veteran who had spent his time stateside as an automobile mechanic and a driver for commissioned officers at the Great Lakes Naval Academy. He named all the occupants of the yellow Cadillac, among them Jarob, who also had been a stateside World War II soldier as an automobile mechanic, at basic training camps all along the southern parts of the United States.

"We're all adopted," he said. "Brothers with individual last names. Kind of weird, but we were allowed to choose either our new parents' last name or any name we wanted when we grew up. We all kept the names we were given. Mr. and Mrs. Clark are good people. They adopted me way back when I was a little peeper of a year old."

"Oh my," said Sherry.

Bela smiled. "My mom and dad came to the poor farm with me. They stayed about a month. They decided it would be a better life for me if I had more stable parents. My mom and dad traveled a lot—*a lot*. They were among the last of the troubadours, if you know what I mean."

"Yes, musicians," Sherry replied.

"I'm impressed!" Bela said with another smile.

Then he said to her, "My parents are from Romania."

"Wow. New York is an amazingly long way from Romania."

"Well, yes, indeed."

Along the way, they chatted about many things. When they stopped at the mailbox of red peeling paint on top of a bare wood post, Sherry looked at Bela and said, "I presume this is where I need to stop."

Bela, surprised, said, "Oh, Sherry, if you don't want me to accompany you any longer, I understand. It's not my place to know where you're going."

She said, "I'm going to the poor farm, right here." She nodded her head toward the poorhouse.

Bela looked sad. "I…um…well, Sherry, let me take you there. I can introduce you. They won't mind. They're good enough neighbors."

"Neighbors?"

"Yes," said Bela, "I live down *that* driveway," and he showed his driveway with the short wave of a hand. "My parents and I stayed at the poor farm until they left me to Mr. and Mrs. Clark, who took me in and adopted me almost immediately."

This is all so odd! Sherry thought. *This whole landscape, those guys in that car, the ugly farmhouse where some Romanians gave up their baby to some Americans, me being here among strangers. I don't know what to do.*

She sighed and decided to tell Bela. "Bela, I'm not comfortable. This is all so new to me. I came from a small town and then ended up in New York City. I've not seen such an imposing large house in the countryside. Is it really safe there? The place looks like a lunatic asylum." Her heart felt as if shards of glass were poking it in the center. They were shards of anxiety.

"Oh yeah, no problem at all. Occasionally, there are a few people staying there who have a mental defect of some kind, but they're never violent. Just imbeciles."

Sherry nodded in understanding. "Oh, I can handle that." She had met plenty of folks under the tracks in the city who would be considered imbeciles by a lot of people.

"Then shall we?" asked Bela.

He had pep in his step, and she decided to match it and to keep up with him. He was impressed by her. He wore a glad look on his handsome face.

She had been so busy with other thoughts she had not had time to notice much about Bela other than his eyes. Now she paid attention. His hair was shoulder-length and black as pitch. His skin was a combination of brown from the sun and olive from being Mediterranean. He had a slender face; sharp, small nose; bright white teeth; and full lips, the bottom being fuller than the top. He was slender, but she could tell by the muscles of his arms and hands that he was strong. There was something light and disarming about his personality.

Eventually they reached the front porch of the poorhouse. They went up four steps and stood in front of the black wooden screen door. There was a shrill ring when Bela pressed the doorbell button. Mrs. Woodfield—five foot eight, light skinned, wearing a red and black checkered apron over her dress—approached the door, looking severe.

"Hello, Mrs. Woodfield," greeted Bela. "I have the pleasure of introducing you to a young lady. This is Ms. Sherry."

Mrs. Woodfield relaxed her face slightly and opened the door to let them in.

"Well, thank you, Bela. Did you find this little waif along the road?" she said.

"Yes, ma'am, I actually did. But we had a good walk and some grand conversations. I will leave you two ladies now. Ms. Sherry, it's been wonderful to have met you. Perhaps we can sit and chat again sometime. Watch for me as I wave from under the hood of some Ford or Edsel." He grinned at her and bowed.

She smiled at him and shook his hand warmly, firmly.

"Bela, so good to know you. Have a wonderful day. I'm sorry you missed out on going with your brothers."

Bela waved his hand in friendly dismissal of the idea.

"They were on their way to who-knows-where, probably a cinema or something. I'm all right not going."

"Chasing girls again, I presume?" said Mrs. Woodfield.

9

"Oh gosh, no way to know, Mrs. Woodfield. I think the fellows are more talk than action if you know what I mean."

"Yes, I do, and I hope you're right. You have excellent parents. So far, you are all doing them quite proud, I must say. But you worry me the most, young man. You're devilishly handsome. Please be careful. Don't let some loose girl snatch you up before you want to be!"

Sherry looked down demurely.

Bela smiled at Mrs. Woodfield. "Well, that's kind of you, Mrs. Woodfield, and now I'll be going. Have a wonderful night and the same to you." He looked Sherry square into those beautiful brown eyes after she looked up, and she was glued to his gaze for too long as far as she was concerned. She looked away when Mrs. Woodfield uttered a light clearance of her throat.

Bela exited the house.

"Well, Sherry, is there anything I can do for you? Would you like to get freshened up a bit? I must say though, you look fine, not like someone who has traveled the highways and byways of New York State."

Sherry explained the luck she had had with the Okies.

Mrs. Woodfield took her upstairs to a huge room, one of the many rooms up there. It was to be her private room until there was a need to share it. It had copper-colored walls with scalloped crown molding and dark-yellow patterned drapes. It was stifling in there. Mrs. Woodfield went to the windows and closed all the drapes to keep the sunlight from the room. On the floor, there was a large, wool Oriental-styled area rug. It smelled moldy, as if it had never been cleaned. One large closet loomed in a far corner; it was empty except for a pillow. There was one large walnut dresser. No other furniture.

Sherry was accustomed to sleeping on just about any surface. She did not mention the lack of a bed. Mrs. Woodfield did not mention it either.

They went back downstairs after Sherry put her stuff into the closet.

"Well, feel free to tour the grounds. Everyone is nice here. They'll say hi if they see you. Tomorrow, we'll get started on what work you might be good at. You look good and strong, but I won't make you work beyond your strength. There's Charles for that. He's a *big* man. You'll meet him in time too."

"Yes, all right, ma'am," Sherry replied.

"You may call me Mrs. Woodfield. Ma'am is too formal for me." She grinned at Sherry and put the palm of a hand gently upon Sherry's back for a few seconds.

"Have a good day, hon," said Mrs. Woodfield. "Supper is soon. I will ring the supper bell. Unless you're five miles away, you'll hear it. Oh, by the way, I'm afraid I must know your full name."

"Sharon Indigo Hamilton," Sherry replied. "Please call me Sherry."

Mrs. Woodfield nodded her head once and turned and walked out of the room.

Sherry had no idea what to do. She did not know the property lines, so she did not feel right about roaming the grounds. Maybe Bela could help her.

She descended the front steps and looked to her left. There was the cedar house not even two hundred feet away, And Bela *was* there, under the hood of an automobile. How was she to approach him? In the 1950s, it wasn't customary for a lady to just come out and shout, "Hey, Bela, what's up! Wanna take a walk with me?" That would be considered rude and certainly unladylike. So she just stood there wondering what to do.

Did he notice her from his peripheral vision? Nobody knows, but he popped his head up and looked right at her. They looked at each other for almost too long as far as Sherry was concerned. He put down his tools, stood up, and just looked at her. She continued to look back, shrugging her shoulders and motioning with her hands that she was bored. He seemed to understand the gesture. He raised his first finger as if to say, "Wait." He left the shop.

Five minutes later, Bela was strolling over to Sherry. He wore clean overalls and T-shirt.

"Well, hello, my new friend," he greeted. "Sorry, I wanted to get the greasy clothes off."

"What are you working on?" she asked.

"Um, a car?"

"What kind of car?"

"Some wealthy fellow's prized possession, I'm told. I'm not to ding or dent any part of it. When I'm done fixing the driveshaft, I'm to wash, shine, and wax it so it looks pristine."

"Oh my," said Sherry, "sorry to hear that."

Bela looked at her and laughed.

"Actually, it's a Model T, and it's a piece of junk."

"Oh!"

"Yeah. Hey, wait a second, you know something about cars?"

"Maybe a bit, not much, just a little."

"You want to help me sometime?"

"Wow, Bela," said a surprised Sherry. "I did help my dad once in a while, but that was mostly with construction equipment. He was unusual in that he trusted me even though I have a female mind."

"You don't say!" Bela was delighted.

* * *

Whenever Sherry got a break from mopping floors and scrubbing walls, she spent time in the shop with Bela. He was an enthusiastic and knowledgeable teacher. She got to know the names of all the tools in the shop, as well as parts of automobiles. She became his assistant, holding flashlights, screwdrivers, drills—whatever he needed. He found her a pair of overalls that fit her loosely. Mrs. Clark found her an old T-shirt of Mr. Clark's. Mrs. Woodfield gave her an old pair of work boots.

Sherry tried to stay clean by wiping grease and grime onto old cotton rags that used to be shirts. She took them back to the poor farm and washed them on an old washboard on the back porch, and she dried them on the clothesline. If it rained, she hung them up just about anywhere in the shop. Mr. Clark found out about Sherry laundering the rags. He went to a secondhand appliance store and took home an old wringer washer. Sherry could not believe it—a wringer washing machine for *her*!

That gave her an idea. She got permission from Mrs. Woodfield to do laundry for people. She used two wringers and a clothesline at the poorhouse. She saved up her money, and after paying fees to the poor farm, she was able to purchase two electric dryers found by Mr. Clark, as well as an iron and an ironing board.

Sherry's laundering business took off. She saved her money. She handed it to Bela for safekeeping every time a customer paid her. Sometimes she took barter—a nice dress or some fashionable ladies' slacks or a hat or shoes, or even pretty costume jewelry. In this manner, she accumulated a small but neat and tidy wardrobe that needed no mending. They became her Sunday attire. When she was not at church on Sundays, she wore the attire at Sunday dinnertime. She enjoyed looking nice. Bela and his brothers were happy to compliment her every time they saw her in her Sunday best.

Laundering with a wringer washer was hard work, and it took Sherry most of the workday to keep up with the task. She acquired strong arms. Bela and her brothers teased her by competing against her in arm wrestling. Occasionally, Sherry was the victor.

Even in her work clothes and overalls Sherry was a lovely sight. The barrette, pulling her hair back, showed her chestnut-brown eyes and revealed her beautiful tan face.

Sherry decided to surprise Bela one Sunday afternoon. She changed from a dress and hosiery into her overalls and T-shirt and boots and met him in the hay field where the guys were baling hay. She spent the afternoon helping them with the same strength as the strongest person there. No teasing this time though since the work was grueling, and the guys appreciated her help greatly. After that, Sherry ended up helping them whenever time enabled it.

A few days later, on a hot and dry morning, Bela passed by Sherry as she was hanging up clean wet rags onto the clothesline with clothespins at the poor farm. Bela stopped, turned around, and approached Sherry.

"Good morning," she greeted him as she continued her work, not stopping to look at him.

"Sherry."

"Hmm?" she said absentmindedly.

"You know, a longtime ago, I asked Mrs. Woodfield your full name."

"Yes?"

"If you don't mind telling me, why is your middle name Indigo?"

Sherry turned around to look at Bela. She smiled.

"My middle name is Indigo because my mother claimed I had blue eyes when I was born. Lots of babies have blue or gray eyes, but she insisted my eyes were a vibrant blue. Hard to believe since now they're the color of chestnuts, huh?"

"My thought exactly. How very rare a change."

There was a short pause.

"But a lovely name it is nonetheless. And although your eyes aren't indigo any longer, they complement your hair and your face just fine."

"Bela, that is so kind of you. I'm just a plain ol' jane, but I'm happy with myself."

"Oh, that's being unfair to your natural beauty, Sherry. At any rate, Indigo is a lovely name. You have a great day, okay?"

"Thanks, Bela, you too," she replied.

"Perhaps we can do some work in the shop soon if the sun isn't so hot—that is, if you're up to it."

"Okay," she replied. "No problem, Bela. You'll have to feed me my extra meal though. Don't forget I eat four meals a day. Mrs. Woodfield is trying to fatten me up."

"Oh, Mrs. Clark will fix you up just fine, I'm sure, if I ask her."

Sherry chuckled and wondered why Bela didn't offer to cook her a meal. *Maybe it's women's work in his opinion,* she thought and wasn't surprised. "Okay, soon then."

"Yes, ma'am," Bela replied, and he sauntered back home.

Bela made her think. *Indigo. Maybe one day in the far, far future, I shall name my child Indigo.*

Bela's Loft

There was an old abandoned barn across the field from the Clarks' place. The wood siding was now just faded red, white-washed from decades of rain and snow and sun and wind. The barn stood alone, any outbuildings now gone with a hint here and there of a foundation laid long ago.

It was one of Bela's favorite places. He drove over trailers full of hay bales to spread upon the floor of the loft so he could sit or lie there comfortably. He liked to lie on his back with his hands clasped under his head of long black hair and just listen. Maybe there were birds outside the barn. Or grasshoppers by the thousands in the tall weeds. Or thunder. Or wind. Or rain. Or maybe no sound at all. Whatever was out there, Bela took close note of it. He stayed up there for hours sometimes. He might doze off and then awaken realizing he might as well spend the night there. The season made no difference. He loved spending spring and winter days there as much as he enjoyed summer and autumn nights.

One night, he decided to stay in the loft overnight. He notified his parents. He donned flannel pajama pants, sweatshirt, socks, and his favorite work boots (untied as usual) and headed down the driveway with a lantern in one hand and a wool blanket slung over his shoulder. He happened to spot Sherry sitting on the front porch of the poorhouse. She was in a plain brown skirt and sweater and tan flats. Her knees were up, and she was rocking slightly back and forth while smoking a cigarette. Bela decided to approach her.

"Good evening, Sherry, how are you?"

"Hello, Bela, oh, I'm all right, not dandy, just all right."

"Do you want to tell me?" he asked. He stood in front of her and watched her face as she talked.

"I had a talk with my parents. They say they miss me. But I'm not missing them that much, especially my mother. I should miss my father more than I do too."

"Do you know why you don't pine for them?" asked Bela.

"I'm not certain," said Sherry. "My mother isn't my real mother. She met me after my real mother passed away when I was about two years old. She befriended my dad in church. I believe my dad married her to get some assistance in raising me, but I accept that. I don't dislike my stepmother. She's a good enough person."

Bela replied, "It's not a requirement to love someone even if they *are* blood relatives. It can't be coerced. And love has so many levels, from miniscule to magnanimous, don't you agree?"

She nodded her head, exhaled the last of the cigarette, and tossed the butt out beyond where Bela was standing. The ember died in a few seconds.

"Hey," he piped up," I want to show you something. I want to take you where I go when I want to be alone. It's one of my favorite places. It's the barn out across the field. Have you noticed it?"

"Yes, many times. I don't go there though because I don't know on whose soil I would be tramping. I'm saving up money for a Brownie camera. I'd love to take some photographs of it sometime. If you're there with me, I'll feel safe."

"Oh! You take photographs? That's wonderful."

"Just for fun, not for art. I'm not that good. But I miss taking photos. I have a Brownie at home where my parents live."

"Come," said Bela. He took her hand and helped her get up from the porch step. He held her hand all the way across the field, and it made Sherry feel warm from her head to her toes.

"I say, Sharon Indigo, you are a most unusual, interesting young lady. You're up to any adventure, and I love that. And you're a better mechanic than most men I know! You might not understand how much the boys and I appreciate your help in the shop *and* the hay field."

She looked at him with a serious face. "Thank you. I think."

"Oh yes, it's a great compliment. You're not like most of the young women we know. You're on a higher level to be sure."

It was a brief walk through a field of a large variety of weeds, the crops having left no trace of having ever been planted. It was a pleasant meadow, except for the annoying grasshoppers that jumped in front of them on their way to the barn. Sherry and Bela swatted at them. When they got close to the barn, Sherry stopped and gazed at it for a moment. The surrounding colorful meadow plants and the barn seemingly pressed against an azure sky void of clouds impressed her as beautiful. Oh, to have a camera at this moment. She could take some lovely photographs for sure.

"Yeah, beautiful here, isn't it?" Bela must have read her mind. "Come inside."

They entered the barn through a large opening where double doors could be opened and closed. Bela never closed the doors because he always wanted to see what was out there.

"There's a ladder we must climb," he said to her. He followed her up the ladder to the spacious loft. The fragrance of the hay was evident. Bela had laid it down thickly.

He invited her to lie down beside him. She did. They put their hands beneath their heads and looked up at the huge beams that held up the massive barn. There were remnants of block and tackle that had been used to hoist up straw and hay during the barn's working years. Bits of daylight peeped through small openings in the weather-worn roof shingles. The openings were so small only a heavy rain could penetrate them, and then it was just tiny drops that would fall into the loft.

They talked about many things. Sherry felt very comfortable with Bela. He mentioned his "gypsy" parents who had left him with the Clarks. He had no memory of his biological parents, and he held no bad feelings about them either.

"I'm happy to be with my adoptive family, even my brothers who are such a pain in the ass sometimes," he said.

Sherry bathed herself in Bela's voice. It was beautiful to her when he spoke and when he sang songs while playing the accordion that his parents had left him. It was of a shiny silver with black-and-white keys and black buttons. Sometimes Bela blasted out old Romanian ballads. Occasionally, his voice was somber and brooding. Sometimes he even ad-libbed songs. It was all very entertaining. He was a natural musician.

She was very attracted to this black-haired young man. Some folks might have considered him too old for her, but she did not think that way. She had been trying to be stoic about her feelings, trying to be just a friend and coworker in the shop. But up in his loft, these nice conversations they were having—well, they overwhelmed her.

"Sherry, I've never had a lady friend quite like you," Bela said to her. "I don't think I ever shall. What's the best word for you? Besides gorgeous, that is. *Eclectic*. That's it. You're unique."

"You're so kind to say such things to me," Sherry said.

"You think so?" he replied. "They're just real feelings."

"Thank you, Bela, so much. I have no other words to say."

"Well, that's just fine by me," he said.

They shifted their bodies so they were pressed against each other. As they lay in each other's arms, he gave her a most luscious, long, thoughtful kiss. She responded enthusiastically.

From his pajama pocket, he removed a two-by-two-inch black-and-white photograph of his biological parents and showed it to Sherry. The father wore a faded suit coat over a ruffled shirt. He held a black-and-white accordion on his lap. The mother, who was standing beside the father, wore a floor-length, multishade linen skirt and a white frilly blouse. In her hand, she held a tambourine.

"They're both beautiful," Sherry said. "You are your mother's twin."

"That's what I hear."

They removed their boots and shoes. Bela deftly but gently removed Sherry's underwear. Then he gave her gentle kisses between her sensitive thighs and awakened in her a passion she had never experienced. He introduced her to an entire new world of sensations. She was spellbound. She did not want it to end. He was warm and moist and carried her to an end she never had dreamed of attaining.

SHARDS

They made love for hours. When they finally fell asleep, Sherry snored very gently. Bela breathed evenly and peacefully. Soon enough, an obnoxious bird of some kind would shatter their peace with its arrival in the loft with its loud squawking sound.

The awakening occurred at 5:00 a.m. before any other birds were out and about. The squawking sound made Bela jump just about out of his skin. He shouted, "Damn you!" Then he looked down at Sherry looking up at him.

"Oops, sorry, darlin', I just hate those crows. Please excuse my language."

"No problem," Sherry replied. "They *are* obnoxious."

"How come they didn't scare *you* half to death?" he asked her.

She replied, "I was already awake. I heard them coming."

Bela helped Sherry get up. He planted a short kiss on her lips.

"Good morning, Sherry."

"Good morning, Bela."

"Wonderful night it was anyway, don't you think?"

She replied, "I had an awfully nice time, Bela. Thanks for sharing your loft with me."

"The pleasure was all mine!" he responded.

They made their way back to their respective homes—holding hands, conversing softly, both covered up by the blanket—and parted at the driveway to the poor farm. They slipped into their respective sleeping quarters and went to sleep immediately.

At about ten in the morning, Sherry was outside the poorhouse at its clothesline. She spotted Fulton trotting toward her. He stopped in front of her and handed her a piece of folded white paper.

"My nitwit brother asked me to deliver this to you. I did not read it. I'm guessing it's as goofy as he is. He's all smiles today. You must have cast a magic spell on him or something."

Sherry smiled. "Nice thought, Fulton, but no magic spell. Here, I can read it to you if you—"

Fulton put a palm up into the air and said, "Oh no, thank you though."

"Well, thanks for bringing it to me."

19

"You're entirely welcome. I'll be getting back now. See ya." He turned, and then he went on his way.

Here is what the note said:

> I hereby request another reservation with your wonderfulness some night soon.
>
> We shall meet under the mist of the moon and share a moment of cool, fresh air
>
> Before we dive into that softness of the bed in the loft.

B.

> PS—I know this poem will not ever win any Nobel Prize, but it is yours. It belongs to only you. Thank you.

Sherry got a little chuckle from Bela's little poem. *He could have had any number of girls up in his loft, perhaps girls from town. But he picked plain old me,* Sherry thought. She was a bit overwhelmed by his masculine beauty. She hoped he would make love to her again sometime, but she also wondered if she had done the wrong thing! Would he lose respect for her now? Many tiny shards of fear pricked her heart on and off for the rest of the day, interfering with her gladness.

Indeed, they would have other opportunities to make love in the loft. Sherry knew she was taking a chance getting attached to a man as handsome as Bela. He probably was not a one-woman man. But he was so warm and considerate at the same time being experienced sexually. Sherry could not help herself. She would never refuse Bela's advances.

THE NEWS

The black desk phone at the end of the hallway at the Hamilton residence rang at about 4:00 p.m. Sherry's stepmother answered it with a polite, "Hello?"

"Mrs. Hamilton, hello, this is Mrs. Woodfield from the poor farm in Broome County. Your daughter Sherry is here with us as a runaway."

"Yes, she mentioned that to us some time ago. Is everything okay? Does she need money?"

"Oh no, ma'am, she's doing quite well on her own. She's quite the entrepreneur. No, I'm calling because I'm afraid I'm going to have to ask her to leave. She's going to need a more suitable place to stay. You see, the poor farm is in terrible disrepair. It's actually slated to be on the chopping block in the near future. I'd like to see Sherry move to a nicer place."

"Oh? Okay, but you don't need our permission. She's twenty years old after all."

"Mrs. Hamilton, I'll just cut to the chase here. You might not know Sherry is pregnant. We don't know who the father is, but I have a very strong feeling that she knows. I'm looking into relocating her to a home for unwed mothers. Do you have any objections?"

Sherry's stepmom took the phone away from her ear for a few seconds. She was shocked.

"Now what do we do?" she asked Mrs. Woodfield.

"I would like your permission to talk to her about this. I hope she will call home so she can discuss things with you and Mr.

Hamilton. There are obvious options, and some options that are not so evident. I don't know if you understand."

"Well, no, not entirely."

"She has told me she'll talk to her father immediately, but it might take some time for her to be comfortable enough to talk to you."

"Well, there has been a lot of friction between Sherry and me during this past year. She is stubborn and independent and not willing to listen to reason."

"Sherry definitely has an independent streak," Mrs. Woodfield agreed. "But there are more important things to consider for the time being. So I would like to try to get her to either call you or send you a letter. Is that okay?"

"Why, yes, of course. I'd like to know what's going to happen to her and the child."

"She's very early on, verified by a physician at our infirmary here. She's very healthy, but I've been trying to put pounds on her because she's so darned slim because of working so hard. Maybe a baby will help that a bit."

"I feel as if I'm going to be sick, Mrs. Woodfield. Would you mind if we talk some other time? I'm a schoolteacher, and I'm usually home by this time."

"No, I don't mind, Mrs. Hamilton. So expect to hear from Sherry soon. I'm so sorry I have to call you under such circumstances. She's going to need someone to talk to and someone to give her advice. I hope you have a lovely evening, ma'am, and please be sure to tell your husband I called."

"Most certainly. Goodbye."

* * *

At about 5:00 p.m., Ed Hamilton arrived home from work, moving slowly, slightly bent forward from hard labor. He put his hard hat onto the kitchen table and went to find his wife. She was in Sherry's bedroom, sitting on the bed.

"Hi, dear," he said. "How was your day?"

"Oh, the children were as obedient as always. How about you?"

"Too much bending over wide open chasms where machinery must fit. Why are you here?"

She sighed and lightly slapped her knees with the palms of her hands. "Our daughter is being sent away from the poor farm. She's no longer just a runaway. She's with child. She's very early on. I feel sick about this."

"They're kicking her out? Where are they sending her?" Ed felt unsettled.

"To a place that houses unwed mothers."

"*Where?*"

"Mrs. Woodfield, who runs the poorhouse, is checking out locations. I think she might have some connections."

"Oh damn," Ed sighed. "What the hell next?"

"Why *us*? That's what I want to know. We did raise her right. I know we did."

"Dear, she's twenty years old, not two. She has her own mind and obviously an active sex life."

"I don't even know where to begin thinking about this. Mrs. Woodfield told me that Sherry will be contacting us soon, either by telephone or letter. I guess I must just wait and try to be patient until she calls."

"And try to be patient *when* she calls."

"This shakes my whole world, not just hers. How could she think so much of herself and so little of the rest of us?"

"That's not how it goes when you're in the throes of romance, dear," said Ed. "I'm guessing she didn't do much thinking at all."

"I'm surprised the poor farm doesn't keep better tabs on its residents."

"Well, if they're adults, there's nothing much the poor farm can do. And Sherry is almost there, at twenty years old. Shame she's pregnant though. She has some hard choices in front of her."

"That's what Mrs. Woodfield told me. I don't understand."

"Come now, don't be so naive. Do I have to spell it out to you? What's one choice she could make?"

"There's adoption."

"There's abortion too, and although it's illegal, I expect some girls turning to abortion given what their families put them through."

"Oh, dear God, abortion is practically a death sentence for the mother. I don't want that for my daughter, regardless of how disappointed I am in her." Sherry's stepmom shivered. "Please let us talk her out of abortion."

"Well? There's also the choice of keeping the child, and if I know my daughter, I can safely say she hasn't ruled that out."

"Mrs. Woodfield said Sherry might not be ready to talk to me yet."

Ed patted her on the knee gently. "That's okay. I'll talk to her. Do you know when she's going to contact us?"

"Nobody knows," she replied. "It's completely up to Sherry. She won't be at the poor farm much longer, so we might have to wait until she lands somewhere else. Dear Lord, pregnant and traveling around all by herself."

"I never did teach her to be wary of strangers and such. I kept her environment so safe. That's a fault of mine, I guess."

"I'll pray for her," said Sherry's stepmom.

"I will too."

"Are you ready for dinner and a cup of coffee?"

"Yes, dear, that sounds wonderful."

Hi, Dad

About a week later, the phone in the hallway at the house of Sherry's parents rang at about 6:00 p.m.

Her mother approached the phone from the kitchen, wiped her damp hands upon the front of her apron, and picked up the receiver.

"Yes, hello?" said Mother.

"Are you willing to accept a long-distance call from Sharon Hamilton?" came a stranger's voice over the phone.

"Yes, I'll accept the call," replied Mother.

"I want to come home." It was Sherry.

"Who is it?" Dad hollered from the kitchen. He was pouring his usual after-supper coffee that he always slipped slowly as he spent his remaining daylight hours seated at the kitchen table.

The coffee was jet-black, fresh from the stove-top percolator with the clear glass top.

"It's your daughter!" Mom hollered back. "She wants to come home!"

"Well, *let* her!"

"Not so fast, Ed!

"Sherry, what do you want? Money? I can get you some. You just don't belong here. You're a most selfish, disrespectful girl. You have broken my heart."

"How is that possible, Mother?" asked Sherry.

"I'm not interested in going back into the past, Sherry."

"Do you mean why I ran away? Because I'm going to have a baby?"

Mom did not respond. Sherry did not understand. It made her sad.

"Where's my dad? May I speak to my dad please?" Sherry said.

A long pause, followed by her stepmom's sighing. "Ed! She wants to talk to you, not me! Of course."

Ed took the phone and motioned for his wife to move out of earshot. She did begrudgingly.

"Sherry, how are you?"

"Hi, Dad. I'm all right. Good to hear your voice. What was your day like?"

"Same. Nothing to write home about. More roads to build. More houses to destroy in order to build those roads. It's a shame sometimes Americans have to make such sacrifices for so-called progress. Anyway, what's up?"

"Dad, I hate this place. If I knew I'd be dumped into some orphanage after running away from my stepmother, I might have reconsidered. We sleep on the floor. The rugs are filthy. Doesn't anybody regulate these places?"

"I don't know, honey. They're supposed to help you girls get back on your feet."

"Well, I can get into another home if Mom doesn't want me. She has ideals that are poles apart from mine anyway. And now that I'm older, I don't believe I can adhere to her way of life, especially when it comes to women."

"Well, Sherry, you're hardly older at twenty, but you do seem ahead of your time when it comes to the ways of the world."

"There are other homes for unwed mothers, hopefully, nicer ones. I swear I could be happy in some tiny town like New Berlin or Auburn or Sherburne! I'll milk cows. I'm good at that now. And at the poor farm, I was fixing cars and working on tractor motors—"

"As it stands, in American society now, you will be more readily accepted if you remain a lady. Please try to think of your mom."

"I know. I know. Cook, clean, laundry—I did all that too. In fact, I was taking in laundry from people and getting paid to do it. City people pay good money to have their shirts and slacks and dresses cleaned by someone else."

"Oh my god, Sharon," Ed sighed. "Strangers' dirty clothes." He was disgusted.

"I believe I've saved enough money for a good start toward a business in the future, Dad, something I can own without any man. I want to be strong enough to survive if I need to—you know, if I never get married and am on my own all my life. It's not rebellion, Dad. It's common sense. I'm sure you've noticed that since the end of World War II, more American women have been joining the workforce. And if men would admit it, they just might be happy having someone help carry the financial burdens. Moms can make money out in the workplace *and* stick to old-fashioned values at home. Look at Mom. She's a working housewife."

There was a long pause. Ed looked around but saw no hint of his wife.

"When do you want to move again?"

"As soon as I can. I promised the lady here I'd get her started with some customers for a laundry business that the girls can run. It shouldn't take more than a couple weeks. The lady has to see if she can find a few dollars for a couple more old wringer washing machines. If she's successful, it will be such a help to her financially."

"You're only twenty years old. You sound like an aged lady."

"Let's say I'm learned. I'm not going to go off the deep end and join militant women's rights groups, but I really want to start my own business, and I have to get serious about how to get started from the ground up."

"Borrow money from me, your dad."

"No, not if I don't have to. Thank you though. You're so kind to me."

"You're my child. It comes with the territory."

"Okay, so I'll do my best to check out foster homes near Albany or Rochester. I think it would be a good transition for Mom if I went to a home before *coming* home."

"Now, Sherry, answer this question please."

"Yeah, Dad?"

"What's the father's name?" His heart sank in fear that she would refuse to answer him.

"He's a good man. We're dear, dear friends, but we're not talking about getting engaged. He and I discussed the baby before I left the poor farm."

That was a lie. Bela had no knowledge of the baby.

"Discussed," said Ed, "in what way? He's not going to marry you? It's his *obligation*. Don't you see that?"

"Well, if I keep the baby, he's pledged to support me, so I don't have to work any hard jobs. And he's promised to send child support every month until the baby's eighteen."

It was another lie.

"Don't be so stupid, Sharon," Ed said crossly.

Tears welled up in her eyes, and they interfered with her speech for a few seconds. When she recovered, she said to her dad, "I have no money for a lawyer. This is the best I can do for my baby and myself. I trust him. He's not just a kid. He's twenty-seven years old."

A long pause ensued.

"His name is Bela. Bela Sovine. His biological parents are from Romania. He was born in the United States."

Ed rolled his eyes upward.

"His parents left him at the poor farm when he was small, and a nearby family adopted him. Well, anyway, Dad, I guess I'll be in touch in the next couple weeks, after I've finished my obligation at this unwed mothers' place."

"I don't know what to say. People ask about you all the time—family, neighbors, former school buddies…"

"Well, there's no need to say I ran away from home. I'm old enough. You can tell them any story you want to. Just say I want to get a taste of the big city after being a bumpkin all my life. I really am glad I did too. I never want to live in New York City. Upstate is home to me. I actually miss Schenectady. Have a good night, Dad, I love you."

"I love you too. Do you want to talk to your mom?"

"No, we can talk later, once I get into the other home."

"All right, dear."

"By the way, Dad."

"Yup?"

"How is your back feeling these days?"

"The same. Can't be fixed. I need to work for a living, and the work is hard unfortunately."

She sighed. *Pragmatic Dad. Typical American male. Works hard on massive machinery for inconsequential wages.*

"Rest your back whenever you can."

"Okay, good night."

"'Bye, Dad."

* * *

Ed's wife was in the kitchen. She was standing with her back against the countertop when Ed got there.

"She didn't want to talk to me anymore?"

"Nope," sighed Ed. "Sorry."

"Oh, it figures. I'm not surprised."

"She does know the name of the father of her child. Bela Sovine of Romanian heritage."

"*Romania*? For god's sake, he's not even American."

Racial and cultural prejudice were commonplace in those days all over America, despite so-called advancements in racial relations. The State of New York and the City of New York were no exception. Most of the time, prejudiced words were spoken without shock value because it was so commonplace. Even decent people, such as Sherry's dad, wore prejudice inside himself, not realizing it was harmful.

"I'm so frustrated and hurt, Ed."

Ed put his arm around her shoulder. "Let's make sure she finds a home for unwed mothers first."

"How would we even know where to find one? It seems as if they're available through word of mouth only."

"The woman running the current home no doubt knows of other places. I'm confident they will search until they find a decent one. I'm not worried about that. Sherry will be sure to be far enough away to prevent a connection between her situation and us. Personally I prefer some place closer to home, say Albany, so I can visit her once in a while."

Mom sighed and asked Ed, "But what will we say when it's obvious she's not living home anymore? What will we say to those people who are bound to be blatantly nosy?"

"Tell them nothing, honey" was Ed's response. "If she returns, all will become obvious in the end. The nosies will figure it all out on their own. It will all be up to Sherry, not us."

"That's sound advice, dear," said Mom. "Okay. May I warm up your coffee for the night?"

"That would be lovely, thank you," replied Ed.

TORNADO

Sherry and Bela were sitting under an apple tree in the Clarks' front yard. A warm wind was blowing from the south. From the old radio in the living room, there loomed a voice warning everyone in the area to seek shelter from a tornado that was grinding its way across farm fields just a few miles away. Sherry and Bela kept their eyes on the southern sky. It was an ominous green, and the clouds rolled rapidly in a huge circle about a mile from them. Then the wind started to roll, sounding like thunder that wouldn't stop. Stronger and stronger it grew, and soon, Sherry and Bela realized everyone who had been outside was gone, having fled for safety.

They looked at each other. *Should we stick it out?* they both wondered. They had recently begun to notice their ESP (extrasensory perception) toward each other. It was a joy to them. But this time, the ESP was in the form of fear. *Can we wait longer?* They both looked back at the house and gauged how long it would take them to hightail it back there.

There occurred the loudest crash of thunder they had ever heard, and the purest white flash of lightning they had ever seen split apart a tall evergreen tree just forty feet away from them.

They both shouted in fear and bolted toward the front door of the house, his hand gripping her hand. The wind groaned like some infinitely large door coming unhinged from the sky. Sherry and Bela were tossed and turned, fighting the force of the wind so they could get to the house.

"Get the hell down into the basement!" Jarob cried from the front room. "I'm coming too!"

The Clark family and Sherry hunkered down in the basement for half an hour, hovering in corners and beneath heavy objects, subjected to enormous amounts of rain pounding the roof of the house, howling wind, thunder, and lightning.

"It's right over us, and it's just stalled there," observed Mr. Clark.

"Anybody secured the horses?" asked Fulton.

"Yeah, I did this afternoon. I was listening to the radio. It sounded bad pretty early on," replied Jarob.

Outside the area was almost black. Nothing out there was visible except giant flashes of vertical lightning that made an eerie s sound as it hit the ground with a simultaneous massive boom of thunder that shook the house. This occurred so many times no one could count them all.

Finally the wind died down, and the storm rolled away, dissipating along its journey to the northeast. Mr. Clark and the boys were the first inhabitants to brave the elements.

In a few minutes, Fulton hollered down the basement stairs, "Okay, ladies, come on up!"

Sherry and Bela said nothing as they toured the property and surveyed the results of the tornado. None of the outbuildings were damaged, but the roof of the garage lost half its shingles.

The Farmall tractor had been picked up and plopped down on its side fifty feet away. Automobile windows were smashed. Entire trees were uprooted—tall, healthy trees. All the lights were out in all the buildings on the property.

"Wow," sighed Bela. "You and I have just experienced a finger of God."

"That's true!" Sherry replied.

"It's okay," Bela said. "We're all okay."

"I hope nobody got hurt in this one. Some folks don't have radios, so I hope they were eyeing the sky."

"Yeah, let's hope. Come, we'd better get you back home."

They held hands all the way back through the hay field, across the chicken area, and around the outbuildings, across the side yard adjacent to the Woodfield side yard, across the twin driveways and up the front porch. The orange sun was starting its descent. Mr. and Mrs. Woodfield, the Clarks, Charles and Mazie, a middle-aged African American woman from the poor farm, were standing around with their arms crossed, discussing the tornado. The scene would have made a perfect painting.

Mr. Woodfield sighed. "Jesus, girl, nobody knew where you were! We were searching for you in this crazy tornado!"

"Mr. Woodfield, please, please don't make that kind of effort for me if it puts you in danger," Sherry pleaded. "I was under the apple tree next door with Bela, watching the storm come in. I'm sorry I worried you."

"Well, I eventually ordered everybody to stop searching and climb down the ladder to the basement. It's just a dirt floor down there, but it's safer than upstairs. We could feel air getting sucked out of the cracks in the basement walls. I thought we were goners. Anybody else think so?"

"I think it crossed our minds," replied Mr. Clark.

"I guess tomorrow we'll all pool talent and resources together and see what kind of cleanup needs to be done," Mr. Woodfield suggested.

"Excellent idea. Let's all get some food and some rest and try to get up early tomorrow, shall we?" said Mr. Clark.

There were words of agreement from everyone else there. The group dispersed. Bela walked with Sherry to the edge of the Woodfield property where the driveways go side by side, and he took her hands into his. He looked at her face and studied it to make sure she was all right. Then he favored her with a most warm, assuring, loyal, long, long kiss. She held on for dear life and felt warm from the top of her head to the soles of her bare feet.

After the kiss was finally finished, they hugged each other tightly. He kissed her on the cheek and whispered, "Good night, Sherry." He stepped back a foot or two and reached into his overalls pocket. He held on to a folded white piece of paper with writing on just one side of it. "I know you're going somewhere," he said to her. "Nobody had to tell me. I just know. You have shown a tiny sliver of doubt in your beautiful brown eyes. Doubt about what, I'm not certain. Hopefully, not about me."

Sherry shook her head no. "Please trust me, not the tiniest doubt about you. There's a trip I must take, and I have to do it alone." She stroked his gorgeous black hair and pulled it back into a ponytail, holding it in her hands. His face, more visible with the hair aside, was striking in its nature. She noticed—as if for the first time—his sharp cheekbones and deep-set eyes, the five o'clock shadow that he wore almost all the time. He was so handsome.

"Sherry," he said, holding her face in the palms of his strong, slender, dark hands. His deep, gray-green eyes met her brown eyes. "Perhaps this wonderful tornado has told us something about ourselves. You still have some personal troubles to overcome, maybe with your family. I'm not certain. Perhaps there will be a divine path for you and me some day. Here."

He pressed a four-fold letter into her hands gently. "I hope you read this sometime." He grinned a wide one, and she responded with a hearty laugh.

"God, you're a good man," she said to him, almost amazed, as if she had just discovered that about him.

"My Sherry Hamilton," signed Bela. He turned away from her and walked to his house, skipped up the porch steps and opened the front screen door. He entered the house, not looking back. She, on the other hand, stood still and watched every move he made until she no longer saw him.

She entered the poorhouse and bounced up the steps to her bedroom. Sitting on the blanket she shared with him in the loft, she opened the folds of the letter and read it.

My dear Sherry,

I hope you know how much it means to me to have met you. Bless Connor and his damned convertible with the dust bowl behind it.

You are warm, funny, adventurous. I rarely meet anyone as open and nonjudgmental as you are. It's refreshing. I love your knowledge of books, and your knowledge of cars is amazing! It is our society that dictates only men may work on cars, but you have the intelligence of any man in the world, and you are not trying to rebel against society. Working on machines is just something you enjoy doing.

Sherry, it is in my heart that we meet again someday. Do you think that would be possible?

I wish for you a safe journey. You are one of the bravest persons I know, but danger does pop up when we least expect it to sometimes. So please be aware of the sights and sounds around you. Take the time to read the faces of people offering you help. Do not hesitate to say no to anyone.

If you could see your way to it, Sherry, I would appreciate word that you have arrived at your destination safely. It has been magical getting to know you. Bon voyage, young and beautiful lady. I am happy in my heart.

Yours,
Bela Gregory Sovine

BELA'S DISCOVERY

One warm, humid day after Sherry had vacated the poor farm, Mrs. Woodfield took over a large glass bowl of fresh strawberries to the Clarks' place. Bela answered the knock on the door. He appeared a bit thinner than he was the last time she had seen him, and when he smiled at her, she noticed a slight dryness in his eyes.

"Come on in, Mrs. Woodfield," he greeted her. "Hot day, huh? Strawberries. Oh boy, what a treat! You're so kind, I must say."

"Well, Mazie picked a ton of these things yesterday. I can barely keep up with her. We're freezing most of them, but with some of them, we're taking advantage of homemade biscuits and strawberries. So here are some fresh ones for your family."

Bela gracefully took the bowl from Mrs. Woodfield and walked it back to the kitchen where he placed the bowl onto the table. He returned to Mrs. Woodfield, who was still standing just inside the doorway.

"Would you care to join me and sit down for a few minutes?" Bela invited her. "It's my break time from the shop, and I'm just kickin' back on the couch looking across at the meadow. Come, please sit."

They turned and entered the living room, in the front of the house. She settled into a large stuffed chair and sank a bit too far for her comfort. She ended up raising her arms quite high to rest them on the armrests. She chuckled—embarrassed—but stayed put. Bela plunked himself onto the brown leather couch. The couch was across the doorway from the chair. Both faced the large picture window from which the meadow was visible.

Bela turned to Mrs. Woodfield and said, "I surely do miss Sherry Hamilton, Mrs. Woodfield. Maybe this is out of line, but I came to know her as a good coworker and a friend. I hope she gets back home in one piece. A young lady out there who's hitchhiking all alone—it sounds dangerous to me, even if she is a brave girl. She wanted her journey to be a private one."

"Son, do you know what happened?" Mrs. Woodfield asked Bela. "You don't, do you? She didn't say anything to you about it. Bela, we asked her to leave. She needs a better place to stay. She's expecting a baby. She's very early on. I couldn't tell by looking at her, that's for sure. She's so darned slender.

"She no doubt by now has found a place that takes in unwed mothers, a more appropriate place to be. I'm sorry she didn't tell you about the baby. I'm sure it's a very embarrassing situation for a single girl to handle. She admitted it to me because she had no one else to turn to. Her stepmother knows now, but she is not approving at all. Oh, Bela, I'm so sorry."

"She's pregnant," said Bela. "No, ma'am, she did *not* tell me. I just figured she was going home."

"No, dear, she's not going home. Her mother won't have her. But I don't know what town she's in or which home for unwed mothers she's staying at. I wish I could tell you!"

"Even if I knew, Mrs. Woodfield, I would understand the secrecy. Her life is no business of mine."

"Oh. But, Bela, I'm certain you are the father of that baby! She spoke of no other man in her life. Trust me. I have a woman's intuition. That baby is yours."

He lowered his head and sighed and then looked up at Mrs. Woodfield.

"But what can I do? She may even be out of state for all we know. I'm not her husband. I'm not even her boyfriend. What rights do I have? I'm not sure how we would manage things. I'd like to find her nonetheless. I want to raise the child if it's mine. I'm twenty-seven years old. I know I'm capable."

Nevertheless, Bela felt his heart pounding with anxiety. He hardly knew Sherry. Could he grow to love her? If not, would they be able to get along well enough to raise their child right?

"Bela, I will do everything I can to locate her. It might take a while. Perhaps her parents know where she went. I'll start with them. The least she owes you is a chance to talk to her."

"Maybe she thinks a baby would be a burden to me. She might even wish to give it up for adoption. I can understand that. Give herself a chance to start life over again."

"It's all so up in the air, isn't it? Scary for you too, no doubt."

Bela nodded his head. "I'm actually sad right now too."

"I'll help you find her. You don't deserve her silent treatment, even if she is thinking of you first. It's the 1950s, not the *1850s*. Couples should be open to communication. Give me a few days, all right? I'll start with her parents. And God bless you for being a real man, Bela."

They arose from the furniture. Mrs. gave Bela a big hug.

"I can't thank you enough," he said. "I'm so grateful for you."

Mrs. Woodfield just smiled and exited the house.

Now to tell Dad, he thought, *might as well be now. I wonder how angry he's going to be. I guess I'll just steel myself for it.*

OH, DAD

About fifteen minutes passed before Mr. Clark located Bela in the living room, on the couch, his elbows on his knees, gazing out toward the meadow.

"Son, you coming back to work?" Mr. Clark asked.

Bela broke from his reverie and turned to look up at his dad.

"Bela, you look as if you've just aged ten years."

Bela sighed. How to explain all of this to his father? It was not good news. It was actually embarrassing. Bela felt like a fool, letting some girl get pregnant. It was not cool to be young, unwed, and a parent in the 1950s. *Shit!* he thought. *Can I forget about her and let the whole thing go, never try to find out where my baby is? No doubt the baby will get a good home eventually. Sherry will definitely see to that.*

"Dad, I think you might want to sit down to hear what I have to say."

Mr. Clark shrugged his shoulders and sat in the chair recently vacated by Mrs. Woodfield.

They looked at each other. Bela had no idea about how to begin. He felt scared and stupid. He sighed again.

"Dad, you know Sherry Hamilton left the poor farm. She went to find a nicer place to live according to Mrs. Woodfield."

"I must say, I can't blame her, Bela. That place is falling apart, not worth fixing."

"Yeah, but Mrs. Woodfield told me something else about Sherry. We don't know where she is right now."

"None of my business, son," said Mr. Clark.

"It might just be mine though. Mrs. Woodfield is certain Sherry's pregnant and that I'm the father. Me. Of all the stupid things for me to do, getting some homeless girl pregnant."

"What's your plan for this baby of yours? There are options, you know—marriage, adoption, abortion…I don't want this to ruin your life. Shall we get your mother in here?"

"God no, not yet! Not until I figure out what the hell I'm going to do."

"Smart move, son."

"My first plan is to find her."

"And then what?"

"This must hurt you too, Dad, and I'm sorry."

"Not as badly as it will hurt your mother. She misses Sherry, and she will miss a little baby as well if Sherry never comes back here. Why can't the girls just leave you alone? You never seem to ask for trouble."

Bela chose not to respond to those remarks.

"I have the idea of asking her to marry me, essentially so I can keep my baby in the family. I would hope Sherry and I could grow to respect each other. She's an extraordinary girl, Dad. I'm actually very fond of her."

"Yes, marriage is a good idea for the baby. I don't want any illegitimate families hanging around here. It's not respectable. People *love* to pry, and people *love* to judge."

"I know," said Bela, dejected.

"So how do you intend to find her?"

"Mrs. Woodfield is going to question her parents. Pray to God they know where Sherry went. Otherwise, we're at a loss."

"I think she wanted to ensure you a good, normal life. She's letting you off the hook."

"But I don't know if I want to leave my child behind, Dad. In any case, if she decides to keep the baby without me, I'm obligated to support them. I have a college education, and I can make good money if I need to. It's always an option for me. I can go back to teaching."

"Right," sighed Mr. Clark. "Okay, why don't you come on back to the shop and get back to work and try to clear your head for a while? This problem won't go away immediately. You know how to reach her parents?"

"I don't, but Mrs. Woodfield does."

"It will be okay, Bela."

Bela followed his dad through the kitchen, out the back door, and into the shop.

"Damn, Sovine," said Jarob, "long enough break."

"Yeah, yeah, don't be jealous," Bela replied.

"Why not?" asked Jeremy.

"We'll talk about it later. I just want to get back to work. Rich people want their cars fixed on time."

That comment seemed to satisfy the guys for the time being.

About an hour later, they all decided to take a break. They went into the kitchen and sat at the table. Luckily, Mrs. Clark was not in the house. Bela's brothers were waiting with eagerness for information from Bela.

Mr. Clark announced, "All right, boys. Bela and I have some news for you. Ms. Sherry Hamilton is pregnant, and Mrs. Woodfield swears Bela is the father of her baby."

Mr. Clark turned toward Bela.

"Well, Dad, I believe Sherry is telling the truth. She's not the only girl I've been with, but the others aren't pregnant, thank God."

"Oh, Christ," uttered Jarob. "I should have known by the way you were so solicitous of her the day we all met her."

"Oh, Jarob," Bela replied. "There were no feelings then. I didn't even know her."

"Do you love her?" Jeremy asked.

"I never thought about it. We get along famously. She's a great friend. She makes me laugh, and I'm attracted to her physically. I guess that's as good as love."

Fulton mused aloud, "I wonder why she went away without a word."

Jarob responded, "My guess is that she's ashamed and doesn't want Bela to look down upon her for getting knocked up."

"Maybe," said Mr. Clark. "Girls do get the blame when they get pregnant. After all, they should know how to say no."

"It wasn't like that," said Bela. "I never tried to force myself upon her. We didn't really talk about it. Oh shit, nobody needs to know the details of my sex life."

"I agree," said Mr. Clark. "Just let this be a lesson to all of you about how easy it is to get a girl pregnant and the potential tribulations it can cause."

"So," piped up Jarob, "how do we find her?"

"I have a plan," said Mr. Clark. "It involves the help of Mrs. Woodfield. She's going to try to contact Sherry's parents to ascertain Sherry's whereabouts."

"Sounds good," said Jarob.

"Fair enough," replied Bela. "I hope to marry her if she keeps the baby. I'd like to make my baby legitimate."

"Good man," said Jarob. "You're going to grow up mighty fast, my brother."

"Yeah, I know," Bela sighed.

"Okay, everybody, let's get back to the shop," Mr. Clark announced.

Chairs were scooted back. Mr. Clark and the boys went out the back door.

On the way to the shop, Mr. Clark announced, "By the way, after supper, Bela and your mom and I are going to have a serious chat in the kitchen. Eavesdrop if you must, but keep yourselves out of sight!"

"You *know* we are going to listen?" said Jarob.

"Yes," replied Mr. Clark. "You're all a bunch of nosies. I know Bela and I will not be able to keep this situation under wraps with you guys around."

TELLING MRS. CLARK

Mrs. Clark was back home within the hour. Mr. Clark was seated at the kitchen table waiting to talk to her. She sat down beside him as soon as he motioned her to do so. She looked puzzled.

"News to tell you. Might as well come right out and say it. We're going to be grandparents."

There was a short pause while they looked at each other.

"Grandparents?" asked Mrs. Clark. "Please tell me how this has come about."

"Well, you know our Sherry. She's pregnant, and she's gone off to some unwed mothers' home to have the baby."

"Okay? So far so good."

"Oh, but there's more. One of our sons admits to being the baby's father."

"Oh, dear Lord, you're serious, aren't you?"

Mr. Clark nodded a few times.

"Shall I bring in the guilty party, or do you want to make a guess first?"

"Well, I pray it's not our little Jeremy."

"No worries, it's not Jeremy." Mr. Clark turned his head toward the living room and hollered, "Bela, please come into the kitchen! Your mother's here with me!"

Bela bounced into the kitchen, held his mother's face in his hands, and gave her a big kiss on the cheek.

"Yes, Dad?"

"Your mother knows about Sherry."

Mrs. Clark said nothing.

"Okay, well, that's good. I think."

"Do you intend to raise this child with her or what?" Mrs. Clark asked. She was a little angry. She took this pregnancy as an affront, as something disrespectful to her and all society.

"I would like to. But she took off without any word as to where she was going. Only Mrs. Woodfield was privy to her leaving, but even she doesn't know where Sherry is. The evening after that tornado, I just knew something was pushing her away from here. She didn't tell me about the baby. She just said she had to do something alone."

Mrs. Clark cleared her throat to kick back some tears and said, "I talk to Mrs. Woodfield almost every day. She kept it from me—all of it. Why would she keep such a secret from me? Doesn't she respect me?"

"Don't think badly of her, dear," Mr. Clark said. "She was just acting according to Sherry's wishes. Now there's the problem of finding Sherry and talking to her."

"What do you mean finding her? Didn't she go home to her parents?"

"No, Mom, some place for unwed mothers. I want to talk to her. I want her to know I'm here for the baby—and for her."

"Here for her—how?" asked Mrs. Clark.

"Well, whatever a mom and baby need. I'm not interested in abandoning her, Mom."

"Whatever you choose to do, your father and I are behind you one hundred percent. You're still young enough to fall in love and get married to someone else and have children."

"Well," said Mr. Clark, "our Sherry is an independent, head strong girl, yes? We can talk to her, but the final decision about that baby is hers alone. You understand, Bela? You have no rights."

"I get it, Dad. I'm prepared to take over the responsibilities. I don't want any child of mine to go through the torture of peer pressure from being illegitimate."

"Good thinking, son. Now the thing is—how do we find her?"

"Let's try to consult with Mrs. Woodfield tomorrow," suggested Bela. "I believe she has the Hamiltons' phone number."

"The who?" asked Bela's mother.

"Hamiltons. Sherry's last name," replied Bela.

Mrs. Clark held her head in her hands. "Yes, of course, I know that."

"Anything we can do, Bela?" asked Mr. Clark.

"No, thank you. I've got this. I think I do, anyway. Dad?"

"Yep."

"I'm scared."

"The unknown can be very frightening," replied Mr. Clark.

"Well, I need to get my work done. We'll have to see what Mrs. Woodfield says tomorrow. I love you, guys, very much, and thank you for not yelling at me or cursing me. I feel stupid enough as it is." He left the kitchen, went out the back door, and made his way to the shop slowly, sadly.

"Grandparents," remarked Bela's mother, "this is going to take some time to absorb."

"For certain, dear," replied Mr. Clark. "Can I do anything for you? Smelling salts? A bucket of cold water over your head? A sleeping pill?"

"How about a nice cup of coffee?"

"Comin' right up, straight from the stove-top percolator, still piping hot too."

THE SEARCH BEGINS

The next day, Mr. and Mrs. Clark paid a visit to Mrs. Woodfield. They all discussed the situation, and Mrs. Woodfield offered to call Sherry's parents to find out where Sherry was. She called Sherry's parents while Mr. and Mrs. Clark stood in the poorhouse kitchen.

Ed answered the call. He did not have to accept the charges. Mrs. Woodfield paid for the call. But he did wonder what she wanted. He figured Sherry was out of her life now.

"Mr. Hamilton, I have some news for you. The father of Sherry's baby wants to get in touch with her. He wishes to talk to Sherry, to make sure she's okay. Do I have your permission to contact Sherry?"

"Well, she's never made any mention of trying to avoid Bela. I think it would be okay for him to talk to her by phone or letter in the mail. He has to let Sherry decide the next step after that. What are his plans for the future?"

"He is more than willing to take on the responsibility of Sherry and the baby, even if they don't get married. But he is also willing to marry her."

"He sounds like a mature young man. I suppose he doesn't love her though."

"Well, that's a good question. I believe he is very fond of her. He's no child. He's twenty-seven years old. For all I know, he's had his fill of girls. He treated Sherry well—always."

"If he's willing to take care of Sherry's needs, that's a good start. If she wants to marry him or not, that's her business. Same if she chooses other routes."

"I understand."

"I'll give you the address and phone number to the place in Albany. But have him call or write soon. She plans to move to another place, and we don't know the address or phone number for it."

Ed gave Mrs. Woodfield the information.

"They don't take collect calls," said Ed. "Bela will have to pay for it himself. I assume he has a job."

"Oh yes, he works for his father as an automobile mechanic. He does excellent work. Mr. Hamilton, thank you for your time today."

"You're most welcome. I can't tell you what Sherry will do with correspondence. She will make up her own mind about the timing and substance of their correspondence."

"I understand, Mr. Hamilton."

"Call me Ed."

"Thank you, Ed. I hope you get to meet Bela's parents, Mr. and Mrs. Clark. They are good people. They adopted four boys as their own. Bela will do right by Sherry. You have a pleasant night, Ed. Goodbye for now."

"Thank you for calling. Goodbye."

Mrs. Woodfield handed Mr. Clark the paper with the Albany address and phone number on it and said, "Mr. Hamilton is very protective of his daughter."

"I'll give the paper to Bela right away," he said. "He wants to get in touch with Sherry in the worst way."

"Would you like me to let her know that he's going to get in touch with her?" Mrs. Woodfield asked.

"Oh no, thank you though," Ed replied. "He's got to handle this on his own. You've done enough. You've been very kind and helpful."

Mrs. Clark did not speak the entire time.

* * *

When they all said their goodbyes, Mrs. Clark merely nodded her head toward Mrs. Woodfield and smiled. She did not know what to say. She was embarrassed on account of her son getting a homeless girl pregnant. She thought, *I shall have to try to get over this embarrassment, especially if Sherry becomes part of our family.*

Sherry and Bela kept regular mail correspondence between each other. Long distance telephone calls were too expensive.

Bela did not visit Sherry. No one did. She felt self-conscious and did not want them to see her huge round belly. But she kept up written correspondence with Bela as well as her parents and the Clark clan. Even though Bela kept writing regularly, Sherry was aware that she was pregnant and unwed. It just did not feel right to be in his presence. There was a twinge of shame around her at all times, even during happy moments. And there were shards of doubt and fear that seemed to scrape at her heart every day. She prayed for wisdom, and she thanked God for the good people in her life.

Bela worked seven days a week. He did it because he was so busy, but he appreciated the work because it kept his mind from wandering far away to Sherry. He was shadowed by doubt and fear all day long, with regard to his future with Sherry, wondering if they could be compatible. But beneath those feelings, there was a desire to be with Sherry and their baby, as a husband and a daddy.

* * *

Sometimes when Bela felt saddled with Sherry and this baby she was carrying, he made his way into town with his brothers. He chatted with the ladies and sang to them and got very friendly with them. He made some of them comfortable enough to give themselves to him sexually. He was very cautious. There was no way he was going to be tied down by anyone else. He would not have any sexual relations with them without protection. He did not respect any of the ladies enough to make any of them his girlfriend. He wanted fun and freedom. Once in a while, a young lady would intimate that she wanted him all to herself. He made sure to never socialize with her again.

Mrs. Clark purchased a beautiful white cotton blanket with which Sherry could cover the baby. Mrs. Clark decided not to shop for baby clothes. She guessed it was going to be a boy, but she was not sure enough to spend a bunch of money on boy clothing. She still held out hope that Bela and Sherry would make the best decision for Bela, even if that meant they would not be together, even if it meant the child would be put up for adoption, and Bela would never have to be reminded of the mistake he made.

Mrs. Clark wanted Bela to have a clean slate and the freedom to choose what his future would look like without an out-of-wed-lock woman and unborn baby pressuring him. But she said nothing to him about how she was feeling. He was a grown man and would make the proper choice hopefully. It was extremely common for girls to give their babies up for adoption at birth. It was a clean slate for the mother too. But while she was carrying the child, it was more common than not that she would stay away from home, perhaps with relatives far away. There were also kind folks who took in these unwed mothers and helped them give birth, all without any harsh judgment. But some of those homes were run by people who believed the unwed mothers were sinners. The girls were not treated so kindly there. Regardless of the way they were treated, the final act was almost always adoption. Some girls chose not to look at their babies after they were born. It was a way to separate their emotions from the newborns.

Letters

September 1953

Dear Bela,

I heard that Mrs. Woodfield has given you the address to this house in Albany. I must advise you to write soon if you want to contact me, as I am planning on moving to another home.

Yes, I am pregnant, and yes, you are the father. I do not expect you to drop everything and become father to my baby, and I do not expect you to give up your freedom of socializing with other girls.

Please feel free to write to me as much or as little as you wish.

Sincerely,
Sherry

PS—Enclosed is a photograph of me. Please free to keep or discard it. I'll leave that up to you.

September 1953

Dear Sherry,

I hope this letter finds you in good spirits and good health.

Thank you for the picture of yourself and the home where you are staying. You are so slender; it's hardly evident you are pregnant! I used to be so shy saying that word, but I'm getting better at it. I can't imagine you looking any lovelier than you do in the picture.

Mr. and Mrs. Woodfield are all doing well. Mazie the negro woman took over your job of scrubbing the floors of the poorhouse.

Charles is doing well too. He's a great help to me when I'm swapping car engines. Is he ever a strong man!

My brothers and parents are doing fine.

I miss you every day. You are the strongest woman I have ever met, in par with my own mom Mrs. Clark who I admire greatly.

I'll sign off for now. It's late, and I need to get some shut-eye before going back at it tomorrow. Please take care of yourself.

Fondly,
Bela

Getting Ready for Rochester

A few weeks before she vacated a home in Albany, Sherry sat on the white wooden porch steps of the small house she was calling home. She decided to smoke a cigarette, something she had not done since before leaving the poor farm. In the 1950s, there was a big push toward attracting women to cigarettes. Posters sported smiling young ladies dressed in fashionable clothes, holding a cigarette between two fingers. There was no scientific concern about harming the unborn baby.

One of the other pregnant girls opened the front door and sat beside Sherry. Sherry handed her the cigarette, and the girl inhaled deeply, after which she exhaled silently. She handed the cigarette back to Sherry.

"I hear you're leaving this place," the girl said. "Good for you." She had become Sherry's closest acquaintance at the home. Her name was Clara Norman. She stood about five foot two, was blonde and pretty, and fifteen years old. Many a night she and Sherry would stay up in one of their rooms upstairs talking until the sun rose the next morning. Clara was not going to keep her baby. It was extremely rare in the 1950s for an unwed girl to keep and raise her child by herself. Most girls who kept their babies were shunned by family and strangers alike. It was a dismal way to live.

She said, "Sherry, honey, I'm not keeping the baby. I'm just too frightened to even think about it. I would have nowhere to go, nobody to help me out. My family would disown me."

"There's a terrible stigma attached to girls like us, Clara. I'm afraid too many girls turn to either prostitution or abortion to solve the problem. The way we're treated is bullshit."

"I'm scared," Clara said with tears in her eyes. "I can't talk to anyone about this except you. And you're going away! The ladies here keep hounding me—am I going to name the baby? Do I have names picked out yet? They drive me nuts!"

"They just want to know so they can notify the prospective parents, that's all. But he's still yours, and yours to name."

"What about you, Sherry?" Clara asked. "Are you going to keep your baby?"

"Well, actually I am," Sherry replied.

"God bless you!" cried little Clara. "You are older and stronger than most of us here. You will have his world figured out, and you will keep him safe from prejudice and pain."

"God, Clara, that's extremely kind of you to say such things. Thank you."

They silently shared the rest of the cigarette until Sherry tossed it out beyond the porch steps.

Sherry advised Clara, "Don't go home if you're afraid your father or stepmother will hurt you."

Clara replied, "I have nowhere else to go. Things will settle down. I'll go back to school. I'll ignore the boy who raped me, and hopefully, he'll leave me alone. Maybe I'll switch schools."

"Things will be different for me too," Sherry said. "The world will expect me to wear a scarlet letter," referencing a novel she had read about a priest who got a young lady pregnant.

That night, Sherry lay on the sleeping bag, her hands clasped beneath her head. She thought about Bela, having tiny ideas of seeing him. But she was going to be big and unattractive soon. Besides that, she was the girl who did not say no to Bela. He was much better off not having this baby in his life. And he deserved a wholesome girl, not Sherry.

Soon, Sherry would be on a train headed to the Rochester Home for Girls, a huge place built in 1895. It provided doctors and nurses to assist "unfortunate and erring young girls," as it advertised itself. While Sherry was there, the place would be renamed Rochester Maternal and Adoption Service.

Welcome Home, Leora

Leora Indigo Sovine was born at 7:00 a.m. on Saturday, February 6,1954, seven pounds even, twenty inches long, a small and lovely creature of God with indigo eyes, and a full head of straight black hair. She was welcomed by the nurses at the Rochester home.

"My little ray of brightness," Sherry said to her baby. "Welcome home, Leora." To the nurse, Sherry said, "*Leora* means 'brightness.' Her name has Greek origin."

"I didn't know that," said the nurse cheerfully. Everything had gone well, and she was pleased with the mother and the baby. Labor had been eighteen hours, with the most intense portion being only a few hours, and Sherry had handled them with strength and courage.

Many new moms in America in the 1950s decided not to nurse. It was not a popular thing to do, and many doctors discouraged it for some reason. But Sherry was of a different cloth. She began to nurse Leora as soon as the baby was handed to her. Lee caught on immediately and was content with the nutrients and the close contact with Sherry.

The nurse remarked, "She's gonna be one of those good babies, not a screamer."

"Hmm," said Sherry, "how can you tell? She's a newborn."

"I've been doing this for over twenty years," replied the nurse. "Trust me."

"Okay," Sherry chuckled, "I will."

"Just let me know when you want me to take her off your hands."

"Oh, please no, I want her in my room with me, not in the nursery."

"Well, that's highly unusual," the nurse said sternly.

"I understand, but you know I'm keeping her, right?"

"I assumed so, although that's not set in stone yet. We still have to have a conference with the doctor."

"In the meantime, may I please keep her with me?"

"Well, I'll ask the doctor about it. He's the one to decide such things."

"Thank you, Nurse, thanks so much." Sherry knew she was playing a game of humility, and she wondered how well she was doing. There was no way to know until the word came back from the doctor.

As Sherry held Leora, she gave thanks for such a wonderful, beautiful baby.

An hour later, the nurse was back in the room to take Leora. The doctor instructed the nurse to keep the baby in the nursery for the first week, during which time Sherry was expected to stay mostly bedridden. Thereafter, Leora would be allowed to sleep in a cradle beside Sherry's bed, and Sherry could get up and around. Sherry acquiesced.

After the nurse took Leora, there was a polite knock on Sherry's door. Clara stood in the doorway looking sheepish.

"Clara! My god, come in! Did you see her? She's in the nursery. They're going to keep her there for a week, and then I get to have her here in a cradle. They're being nice to me for some reason."

"I heard them talking—the nurse and the doctor. They believe you're going to keep Leora, so they figured you might as well get used to each other. But they want you to get some rest for a week or so before making the arrangements to have her here with you."

Sherry heaved a sigh. Maybe there was not going to be a battle over her baby after all.

"She's so pretty, Sherry. Most babies look like aliens!"

"Thank you." Sherry chuckled. "She looks so much like Bela's biological mother, which reminds me that I need to post a note to Bela to let him know he's a father."

"I'm so proud of you. I didn't hear any yelling or screaming, and I was on the other side of your door many times!"

"Oh, that's funny, you sneaky little thing!"

"You're so brave. I hope I handle childbirth as well as you did."

"You will, Clara, I'm sure of it. By the way, how did you get here?"

"I begged my father to let me come here because I know you, and everyone else at Albany is a stranger to me."

"Yes, and your number will be up soon."

"How accurate were they on your due date?" asked Clara.

Sherry laughed. "Two weeks off. Oh well, the baby's the only one who knows the due date, right?"

"Absolutely. So what were you going to name your baby if she had been a boy instead?"

"Edward Hamilton Sovine, after my dad and Bela."

"Sounds sophisticated."

"Maybe I'll reserve it for another baby someday. What do you think?"

"Yes, it's a great name!"

"Okay, I'll do that. In the meantime, have you picked out names yet?"

"Yes. Benjamin for a boy. Olivia for a girl."

"Beautiful. Hope it's twins so you can use both names."

"Oh my god, heavens no!" replied Clara.

"Just kidding. They'll let you know by now. You've got just one tiny baby inside that little belly of yours."

"Will they let me see him or her when it's born?"

"It's up to the doctor, honey. Be *really* nice, and he might just say yes. You have to play the game here, you know."

"I understand. I can do that."

"Good girl," said Sherry,

"Well, you get some rest. I'll come by later."

"Thank you, dear."

They gave each other a hug and a kiss on the cheek. Clara left the room.

February 6, 1954

Dear Bela,

The baby was born without complications. Her name is Leora Indigo Sovine. I hope you aren't offended by her having your last name. I can change it to Hamilton if you wish. She is a beautiful baby. She has a lot of your features, hardly ever cries. I'm such a lucky mom.

I look forward to hearing from you, but only if it's your wish to do so. The phone number is 585-555-0198.

Sincerely,
Sherry

Bela Calls

As soon as he was finished with Sherry's letter, Bela jumped up from the couch and made a beeline for the phone on the wall in the kitchen. He paid for the long distance call.

Clara answered, "Yes, hello, Rochester Home."

"Hello, my name is Bela Sovine. I'm trying to reach Sherry Hamilton. I'm the father of her baby."

"Oh!" Clara responded. "Of course! I've heard so much about you! One moment. I'll fetch her for you."

Bela waited only a moment, and then there was Sherry's voice. "Hello? Bela?"

Bela sighed with relief.

"Sherry! I miss you so much. And I miss our daughter even though I haven't met her. I would like to know if I may pay the two of you a visit."

"It's a long drive to Rochester, isn't it?"

"Jarob can help me drive."

"Does he know about Leora? Does everybody know?"

"Yes, the whole family knows. Jeremy wants to kick your behind and then drag you and me to the nearest church and make us get married. Of course, there's more to it than that—getting a marriage license and all."

"Good ol' Jeremy. How is everyone else?"

"We're all fine, Sherry, waiting for word from you."

"Oh, Bela," Sherry said, "I'm keeping her. The home wants me to let her go for adoption, but I have put my foot down. She's too beautiful to give up. I love her so much."

"Okay," sighed Bela. He was happy but nervous about being a father.

"I'm going to need lessons on being a father."

"You'll do fine. Just copy Mr. Clark. He's a great dad."

"Sherry, when may I pay you a visit?"

"Any time you like. I'm here all the time. All they need is a day's notice."

"I am so nervous. What if I drop her when you give her to me?"

"Oh, silly, you won't drop her. If that's a concern, we'll just have you sitting down."

"All right, Sherry, that sounds good. I'm going to let you go for now. It's suppertime here. I will call you as soon as I know when Jarob and I are going to head over to Rochester—one day's notice."

"Good, Bela. It's so good to hear your voice. Take care now."

"Okay, Sherry, bye for now."

"Bye."

Everyone was at the dinner table at the Clarks', listening to Bela talk on the phone.

Jarob asked, "When do you want to go? It's up to Dad as to when he can spare us."

"Oh, go on," said Mr. Clark. "Go see that baby of yours. And take that Brownie camera with you so Sherry can take photographs of her."

"Okay." Bela chuckled. "The home needs one day's notice. I'm so damn nervous. I don't even know if I can talk to her right now."

"I'll do it," Jarob volunteered.

"No, thank you, brother. Time for me to grow up. I'll call her after supper."

Bela looked at his dad. Mr. Clark nodded a couple times. Then Bela turned toward Mrs. Clark and put his hand on top of one of hers.

"We'll get through this, Mom. Don't worry."

Mrs. Clark replied, "I know, son."

To keep her mind from the situation, Mrs. Clark made half a dozen peanut butter and jelly sandwiches and put them in a picnic basket for Bela and Jarob. Then she placed half a dozen bottles of grape soda pop in a red and black checkered cooler, so the guys could have a drink when they became thirsty.

JOURNEY TO ROCHESTER

About halfway into the journey, Jarob decided to stop at a filling station and park the car away from the gas pumps. He did not need gasoline, but he was hungry for one of those sandwiches!

Bela decided to take the wheel for a while. Before they knew it, they were in Rochester, looking for a home for unwed mothers. They felt stupid because neither one of them had bothered to get the address of the place. They stopped at a local library of all places, and a librarian gave them the address and directions. She tried to flirt with handsome Jarob, and he grinned at her. Bela gave Jarob a wink. Jarob just smiled in response.

Bela kept up his bravery with Jarob at his side when he rang the doorbell. A tall, older, dark-haired gentleman answered the door and asked politely, "Yes, gentlemen, may I help you?"

"Hello, sir," Jarob responded. "Sherry Hamilton is expecting us here today. Jarob Connor and Bela Sovine."

"I see," said the man. "Would you please stay outside and wait here while I get her for you?"

Momentarily, Sherry was at the door. She wore a white linen dress with a tan sweater over it, ankle socks, and black flats. Her hair was past shoulder-length and tied back in a loose braid to contain it. Bela looked directly at her. She looked as if she had gained a few pounds, and they were becoming of her. Her face was lovely, a little fuller than he had ever seen. She was beautiful.

Sherry opened the door and said, "Jarob, Bela, my god, it's good to see you two. Please come in. There's a parlor where we can sit in private."

The guys followed her as she walked down a central hall and then turned right and entered a Victorian-styled parlor, poshly decorated and furnished. White lace curtains covered the large windows.

"Please, you guys, sit anywhere."

"Sherry," Bela said, "I have missed you so much. May I hug you?"

"Well, it's frowned upon, hugs between unwed parents, but I think that would be nice."

Bela took Sherry into his arms and kissed her directly on the mouth for several seconds. Then he gave her a few quick kisses on the lips; after which, he sat down on a red upholstered sofa.

Sherry smiled at him. She was entirely glad to see him, the man she had abandoned because she had thought she had done a terrible thing and did not want to ruin his life. And there he was, seated on a plush red sofa, waiting to meet his baby.

Jarob sat down beside Bela. Sherry remained standing. She said, "I'll go get Leora. I believe she's awake. Hold on a moment, okay?"

"Yes, sure," Bela replied, but he was nervous. It would be the first time he would lay eyes on Leora. What if she did not look like him at all? There was no DNA technology in the 1950s to show paternity. There was blood type, but Leora's blood type would match millions of men's.

Bela's doubt was submerged the second he saw Leora. She looked so much like his biological mother it was uncanny; she hardly looked like Sherry except for those indigo eyes that Bela had seen in photos of Sherry as a baby.

"Hello, little Leora," Bela said. He remained seated as he took the baby from Sherry. "You look like me. Poor thing."

Sherry and Jarob laughed.

"I'm glad you think that's a joke," Bela remarked.

"Sherry, she's gorgeous," said Jarob as he leaned toward Bela to look at the baby.

"Is there something I need to sign to acknowledge she's my child?" Bela asked Sherry.

She replied, "Yes, I'm keeping her no matter what. Don't feel as if you *must* sign it. You're here for a visit today, and I'm so happy to see you. This might be a lot for you to take in at once."

"Where do I sign?"

"I can get the house mother in here. This place doubles as a hospital, so the signature is legal. Bela, please—"

"Don't," Bela interrupted. "You can't pull me away from her, and you can't push me away from you. I want us to try to be a family."

"Okay," Sherry said softly, "I'll go get her."

A few minutes later, a tall, silver-haired elderly woman entered the parlor with Sherry. She sat next to Bela, and they spoke in whispers. Jarob and Sherry could not hear their discourse. The woman offered Bela Leora's birth certificate for Bela to sign. He signed it. The woman shook his hand and congratulated him. He thanked her. She gave Sherry the document and left the room.

"That seemed easy enough," said Jarob lightly.

"Yeah," Bela sighed with relief that it was finished.

Jarob asked her, "Sherry, would you like a peanut butter and jelly sandwich made by Mrs. Clark and a bottle of grape Nehi soda pop?"

Bela gave Jarob a sideways glance. "In this fancy room?"

"Hell, yeah, why not?"

Sherry laughed. "Yes, let's do it. If we get caught, we'll just go somewhere else."

"I'll be right back," Jarob replied.

In a moment, Sherry was chowing on a sandwich and sipping Nehi grape soda pop. "Delicious! I don't get these luxuries here. This is wonderful."

Leora started to fidget in Bela's arms. He looked up at Sherry as if asking for help. Sherry smiled and took the baby.

"She's tired. I'm going to put her in the cradle. Be right back."

After she left the parlor, Bela said, "Hell, I was afraid she was going to open up her dress and feed the baby right here! I'm sorry, brother, but I am *not* ready for that!"

"I'm sure she knows that," Jarob said. "I must say, though, she looks even lovelier than I remember her to be. I think motherhood and nursing are doing her well. What do you think?"

Bela blushed at the word *nursing*, but he replied, "I'd like to be back at my loft with her if you know what I mean. Nightfall coming on, the two of us curled up under thick blankets…yeah, she's lovely all right."

"Are you ready to stop chasing girls now that you have Sherry and Leora? You have a lot of fun with the girls in town. Will you be able to turn them away, Mr. Romantic Romanian?"

"Oh *pff*, I'm not all *that*."

"*Bullshit*, you're not. I'm serious. Those days are over if you stay with her. Completely."

"Well, hopefully, Sherry and I can grow together to tolerate and be kind to each other and raise our baby together."

"Take your time," Jarob advised. "You and Sherry can stretch out the time and get to know each other to see if you want to be married."

"I have so much respect for her. She's made some difficult decisions. She's come away from all of this with her head held high."

"Indeed, she has."

"It's now or never." Bela decided.

"You're a bright, friendly, smart, and handsome young man. You must know she will be totally proud of you."

Bela just chuckled. "And *you* keep your *clothes* on. Don't start a family this way."

"I'll do my best," Jarob said with a chuckle of his own.

"I *mean* it," Bela admonished.

"I *know* you do, brother. I appreciate the advice. You know how much I love to chase girls."

Sherry reentered the room. She surprised both men by squeezing herself between them on the plush red sofa. "You two feel like home to me," she said. "It's been a long time. I'm happy."

The three of them sat on the sofa for about an hour, laughing, joking, talking about Mr. and Mrs. Clark, the brothers, Mrs. Woodfield, Charles, Mazie, and a host of other things—fun, casual conversation. They took photographs of each other with the Brownie camera, using a new flashbulb for each picture. Jarob treated Sherry to a second sandwich and soda pop. It was so delicious, this food from home. She missed spending time at the Clarks' place. She wanted to lie down in a bed somewhere next to Bela and Leora and sleep like a rock.

But the visit came to a close about half an hour later. House rules. Sherry and Leora walked Jarob and Bela out to the front door and said goodbye after hugs and kisses, after Bela took a couple photographs of Sherry and the baby. Bela did not want to let go of his girlfriend holding his daughter, but he finally did after Sherry started trying to wrest herself from his grip. Bela gave Leora a loving kiss on the forehead and said, "Goodbye for now, my love." Lee looked up at him, and he smiled at her. Then he gave Sherry a final kiss goodbye—a nice, long one.

Jarob said, "All right already, Bela, let's get on."

So the guys left the Rochester house for unwed girls, on their way back home to Broome County, their parents, their brothers, and all the things they were going to say to everybody. It had been an excellent day.

THE INTERVIEW

"What did you name her?" asked the doctor in his characteristically irascible tone. They were seated in his mahogany-paneled office, with a large mahogany desk between them.

"Leora because she is my brightness. Indigo because of the color of her eyes. Sovine because that's her daddy's last name."

"Has he come to claim her?"

"Yes."

"Still and all, we don't recommend you name the baby. There's a great chance the father will not ever return. Nine times out of ten, the man walks off and never comes back."

"I trust Bela," said Sherry. "I'm the one who walked out on him. He searched for us and found us. He went back to settle things for us. I haven't told him I might have other plans."

"And what might they be?" the doctor asked sarcastically.

"I have money saved, and my father has promised me a loan to start a small dry-cleaning business. I'd rather live near my parents, but if he balks at that, I'll go along with his plan to live with his family—for a while."

"Do you think Bela will be a good father?"

"He will do his utmost best. This is all new to him, and he's a man. It won't come naturally. But I believe in him. And he will have his parents and mine to give him all the guidance he will need."

"Is he happy with Leora's name?"

"Oh my, yes, he's excited as could be."

"Who does Leora look like?"

"Mostly her father and her paternal grandmother—skin tone, facial features. Her eyes are mine though."

"You seem sure of yourself and your situation. Please know that you are welcome to come back here if you want to give Leora another home—a home with two married parents, you know what I mean. You're a smart girl."

"I've already signed her birth certificate. And Bela has signed the acknowledgment of paternity."

"You really do trust him, don't you? Was he embarrassed or angry or upset with you?"

"No! He is going to do fine, Doctor. When I leave here, you won't ever see Bela or Leora or me again. I promise you that. I have family support too, Leora's other grandparents, my folks. We can't go wrong. And she'll be at my side whenever it's possible. When I start my dry-cleaning business, she can go to the shop with me."

"All those chemicals. Is that safe for a baby?"

"I'll keep her safe from the chemicals, Doctor, trust me."

The doctor sighed. "Well, you still have a couple weeks before we release you and Leora. Take the time to think of all the scenarios you can, okay? This is a huge leap."

"I'm twenty years old, Doctor. I'm not a child like some of these poor girls here. My mind is made up. Thank you for your time though. I appreciate it."

Sherry reached over the desk and shook hands with the doctor. Leora slept in Sherry's arms. The doctor got up from his chair and took one look at Leora. Then he left his office.

About twenty seconds later, Clara sneaked into the room. "Sherry," she whispered. "I heard it all. I listened from the doorway. God bless you, Sherry. Leora has a great mom."

Sherry said, "You crazy little sneaky thing, you. Give me a hug."

After Clara left the room, Sherry shed a tear for the poor girl. If she were even a few years older, she would not have to follow some adult's order to get rid of her child. But she really was a child, afraid to be a single mom. *Maybe she's safer that way, and giving up her baby won't hurt so badly,* Sherry thought before she let out a huge yawn.

She looked down at little Leora and smiled. Then she took Lee into their room and settled into an hour-long nap; after which time, Lee gently announced she was hungry.

The Beginning

Sherry and Bela were married two weeks later in the County Courthouse in Rochester. In attendance were Bela and Sherry, the Clark clan, Reverend Dr. Johnson from the Rochester home for unwed mothers, Leora (being held by Clara who sat in a pew-like seat), and a judge.

Conspicuously absent were Sherry's parents. Given the opportunity to attend the ceremony, Ed had spoken for his wife and himself by saying, "Thank you, Sherry, but maybe someday you can have a real wedding. That would make your mom so happy. You know, renew your vows someday."

"Okay, Dad, I'm sorry to hear this, but I understand," Sherry had replied.

The ceremony took about ten minutes. Mr. and Mrs. Clark were honored to sign as witnesses. Reverend Dr. Johnson gave Sherry and Bela a short Christian pep talk about love and honor and commitment.

"Now that we're all here," said the reverend doctor, "shall we baptize the baby?"

Sherry responded, "Oh, thank you, Dr. Johnson. I believe it's Leora's right to decide the date of her own baptism. I don't believe she inherited any of our sins."

The judge's jaw dropped. So did Reverend Dr. Johnson's. Johnson was a holier-than-thou man, and he had judged Sherry to be a whore because of her pregnant, unwedded status. Now she wanted to leave her baby wallowing in the sins of her parents' past.

He wondered if he should push the issue, but he knew he would not win against Sherry. So he let it go. He was angry. He left the little courtroom quickly. Everyone else turned to watch him go. No one said a thing about the baptism. They all knew better.

Mrs. Clark said to Clara, "Let me see that beautiful baby."

Clara arose and took Lee over to Mrs. Clark, who clutched her firmly and lovingly into her arms. Lee looked into Mrs. Clark's eyes. Lee had serious eyes, as indigo as the bird itself. Mrs. Clark said to Sherry and Bela, "Thank you for giving me my first grandchild. She's special, a special little girl."

"Thank you, Mom," said Bela humbly.

"So where do we all go from here?" piped up Clara.

Mrs. Clark handed Lee back to her.

"We're all going back to Broome County," replied Mrs. Clark. "The kids are going to stay with us while they do a search for a place to live."

"Are you going to work, Sherry?" asked Clara. "Moms usually stay home, I guess."

"My father has offered me a loan to start a dry-cleaning business."

"Bela, are you in on this?" Mr. Clark asked him.

"Oh yeah, you bet. I applaud her for doing it."

"We're all packed, folks," said Mr. Clark. "We'll leave tomorrow morning as soon as we get up. We're all going to stay in a small hotel just outside of town here tonight."

"You'd better get your own room!" Clara chided Sherry and Bela.

"Yes, indeed, young lady, that's already arranged," said Bela. He was a happy young man. He was terribly proud of his wife. *She used to bale hay with the best of us,* he recalled. Yet she was that familiar feminine creature with all the physical wonders Bela admired.

"Bela is going to continue working for his dad for now," Sherry said to Clara. "But with his degree in mathematics, he might go on to tutor college students or even try for assistant to a professor."

"Bela, stop with working on the cars already," said Jarob. "With your four-year degree, you can make better money working at a college."

"Oh, but I love working on cars, don't I, Sherry? Sherry understands that. She doesn't want to take me away from my favorite kind of work. I can tutor or assist the professor part-time. That's my plan anyway."

Sherry reached toward Clara and took Leora into her arms, all bundled in the white cotton blanket brought by Mr. and Mrs. Clark.

"All right, folks, if that's all there is—" said the judge.

They all turned to him. They had forgotten he was there. They all smiled and nodded at him. Sherry and Bela walked up to him and took turns shaking his hand. The judge handed Sherry the marriage certificate. She looked at Bela. He gave her a two thumbs-up with a bright, beautiful grin that warmed her heart.

They took leave of the courthouse and dispersed into various vehicles. Bela and Sherry, Leora and Clara rode in Bela's pickup truck, all packed into the bench seat. Bela drove about an hour from the courthouse to a one-story, average-looking red brick motel with an empty swimming pool in front of it.

The brothers took one room. Sherry, Bela, and Leora another, the Clarks a third, and Clara one by herself.

Jeremy offered to keep Clara company. Clara looked at Sherry, who looked at Mr. Clark, who gave Jeremy permission to stay in Clara's room until she was asleep. Clara was grateful and smiled widely at Mr. Clark. "Thank you, sir, I'm not used to being alone much."

Jarob said, "Pardon the rudeness of it all, but if you start having a baby, call *us*. Don't count on Jeremy to get you through it."

"Connor, that's cold," said Jeremy.

"But true," said Mr. Clark.

Clara blushed.

Everyone disbursed toward their respective rooms. As he passed by Bela and Sherry, Jeremy looked at both of them and whispered, "She's cute."

"She's not keeping the baby," Sherry said to him in a low voice.

"Even better. A fresh start. Now *I'm* the one being cold. Can't help it. She seems like a nice girl no matter what happened to her."

"She just turned sixteen," said Sherry. "Remember that."

"Okay, I will. I'm only twenty-two after all. Good night, you two."

"'Night, Jeremy," they said simultaneously. There was no need to worry. Jeremy was a good man. He was not going to take any advantage of young Clara.

Leora did not sleep through the night. She woke up every two hours demanding to be fed. Sherry was shy about it a couple times, but after that, she decided not to hide her breast from her husband. She bade him to see how nursing works. Bela was fascinated. It was completely natural, and Sherry provided all the vitamins and minerals that were needed.

Sherry and Bela were lucky enough to sneak in consummation of their marriage. They kept their voices down so the folks in adjoining rooms would not hear them. He removed his clothing and then removed Sherry's, and then he lay beside her. He caressed her breasts and kissed all those wondrous and familiar magical areas of her body.

She responded saying, "Thank you, thank you, my handsome husband!"

And he allowed her to pleasure him in kind. He laid his hands gently upon her inner thighs and opened her up to more desires. Sherry had been told by one of the nurses at the home that she could not get pregnant while she was nursing Leora. Sherry had no fear of having wonderful, loving sex with her husband. Although Bela was never going to tell Sherry about his recent trysts with ladies from town, he told himself that he was through with them forever. Sherry was a cut above all of them.

He said to Sherry, "I pledge myself to you and Leora for the rest of my life."

Sherry shed a tear of happiness and responded, "I give myself to only you for as long as I live."

GOODBYE, CLARA

Clara and Sherry had a tearful goodbye at eight o'clock the morning after the wedding. Bela, Sherry, and Baby Leora took off in Bela's Chevy pickup truck first. The Clarks rode home in Mr. Clark's Ford pickup truck. Jarob drove his Cadillac. He had volunteered to take Clara back to the home in Rochester. Jeremy walked Clara up the front steps of the home, opened the front door for her, gently put his hand on her back and said to her, "You're going to be fine, Clara. You're a bright, brave young girl. You've got a fresh start coming up. I know you'll make a great future for yourself."

Clara blushed and sighed and looked up into Jeremy's kind eyes.

"Thanks again, Jeremy, you've been a true friend."

"Stay in touch if you want to. I'd love to know how you are getting along. I know it's not customary for a girl to write to a boy, but hell, we Clarks aren't stick-in-the-muds. I mean, look at my brother Bela. He married Sherry *after* the baby was born. They ended up together. It wasn't customary, but it's a good ending—no, a good beginning—for them."

"Jeremy, are you boring Clara with one of your Jeremy Snow diatribes?" Jarob chided from behind the steering wheel.

"Oh, you just never mind, Connor," replied Jeremy. But he turned to Clara and gave her a kiss on the forehead. "So long for now. Good luck."

"Thank you, Jeremy. Bye." She turned and entered the house.

Jeremy turned toward the car and shrugged his shoulders at Jarob. He skipped down the steps and plopped himself into the front seat of Jarob's car.

"So what did you kids do all night? Or dare I ask?" said Fulton.

"We talked as much as she could. She was asleep within an hour. I slept on the floor. She's not going to keep the baby. Once her baby is adopted by other parents, Clara may not contact the parents. She may not visit the baby ever. It's as if the baby will have vanished. What an empty feeling that must cause sometimes," Jeremy said sadly.

"Yeah," said Fulton. "She seems like the type to have a broken heart over it."

"I agree," said Jarob.

"I wonder if Sherry is going to keep in contact with Clara," Jeremy mused.

"What about you, Mr. Stars in His Eyes?" asked Jarob.

Jeremy merely said, "She's a good kid. I hope she stays friends with Sherry. Because someday, Clara will have another baby, and Sherry will be a good mentor."

"Sounds nice," said Fulton.

"Yes, it does," Jarob agreed.

DINNER AT THE CLARKS'

It was dinnertime at the Clarks' place. Mrs. Clark prepared a spread of ham, mashed potatoes, green beans, dinner rolls, and butter. Everyone was eating with gusto and complimenting her on her talent for making food taste so yummy.

Mrs. Clark asked Sherry, "Have you heard from your friend Clara?"

"She wanted me to say hello to everyone, by the way, especially to *Jeremy*. She wants to pay us a visit in a couple weeks. I hope you guys can pick her up at the train station."

Jarob teased, "You and Clara were like two little peas in a pod, Jeremy. And you behaved yourself that night in the motel room. Is she special?"

"She was pregnant, Jarob. I wanted to make her comfortable. And she wanted to talk, and I didn't mind. Sherry, did she keep her baby after all?"

"No, sadly, but she did what she believed was best for little Olivia."

"Well, I for one am looking forward to seeing her," Jeremy said with his head held high, "no matter what you all think I'm up to."

"I think Jeremy's got a crush on Clara," Fulton teased with a straight face.

Jeremy remarked, "I *told* you she was cute. But right now, I hear Leora crying."

Bela was up in a second, pushed back his chair, and made a beeline for the living room. Lee was lying in a bassinet. He scooped her up gently and took her back to his chair at the dining table. He sat with her in his arms. She quieted down immediately.

Mrs. Clark asked, "How's Daddy going to eat with a baby filling his arms?"

"Oh, he can wait," Bela replied, looking down at little Lee.

"I'll take her. You go ahead and eat your meal," Sherry suggested. She took Lee into the living room and nursed her. Lee fell asleep after she had her fill. Sherry burped her anyway and then lay her down gently onto her back in the bassinet.

When Sherry returned to the kitchen, Jarob asked her, "Ready to have another one yet?"

"Hardly, Connor," Bela interrupted. "She's just barely born. I want her walking and talking before I will even *think* about another one."

Sherry blushed. No one took notice except Mrs. Clark. She said softly to Sherry, "It's okay, honey. It will be a decision made by both of you."

Sherry nodded in relief. Siblings! It had never occurred to her that Bela would want more children! She had better watch her cycles to make sure she didn't get pregnant too soon. Sherry did not know if he would take part in raising his children, or if he would just assume it was Sherry's job. It upset her to think of these things when she was still getting to know her husband. Sudden doubt entered her brain. Maybe she and Bela weren't even compatible. Would Lee be the only thing they would have in common? Usually a couple gets acquainted *before* having children. Bela and Sherry had done it all backward.

"Mrs. Sovine, are you all right?" Bela asked Sherry.

She looked at Bela.

"Sherry, you're pale. Are you feeling ill?"

"No," she replied, "I'm fine."

"Come to the living room and sit with me for a while, please."

"Okay," said Sherry, and to Mrs. Clark, she said, "Please excuse us."

"Of course, dear," replied Mrs. Clark.

Sherry followed Bela into the living room. They plopped themselves onto the couch.

"Are you sick, honey?" Bela asked her.

She looked at him and said, "I have a confession to make. I don't know how many children we're going to have, and I admit I'm scared the job will be all up to me, and you will just work and be home only occasionally. I don't know if I'll even be a good mother to one child, let alone a whole slew of them."

"Well, it *is* customary for the woman to do the rearing of the children, but you're a unique woman, Sherry, and I don't expect you to be saddled down with kids with no life of your own. I'm only going to work as hard as I need to support us. Above that, you and I are going to have a life together, whether we have one baby or ten babies. Is that what you were worried about?"

"Yes, Bela, and I'm embarrassed to feel that way. I feel like a fool now."

He gave her a kiss on the cheek and held her hand. "Let's take it one day at a time, one baby at a time. I'm in no hurry. We've both got a few years to figure that out."

Sherry sighed gently. "Thank you for understanding."

"I wish she was awake. I have the urge to play the accordion."

Sherry laughed. Bela squeezed her hand gently with his hand.

"I'm going to see if Mrs. Clark needs help cleaning up," Sherry suggested.

"Okay. I'll keep an eye on the baby while I repose here. Don't be surprised if I end up falling asleep."

* * *

"All better?" said Mrs. Clark upon seeing Sherry back from the living room.

"Yes, thank you. All I needed to do was talk to Bela. He makes things all right."

"He's a good boy," said Mrs. Clark.

"Yes, ma'am, he is."

"Looks like Mr. Clark and I raised him right after all. You know, parents have their doubts sometimes."

She and Sherry cleared the table, and then Mrs. Clark told Sherry to go on ahead and sit in the living room with Bela and Lee. Sherry plunked herself onto the couch again. Bela put one of his arms over her shoulders, and they both dozed peacefully for an hour or so.

BELA FOUND A HOME

Bela found a three-bedroom house that used to be someone's cottage. It was in Kingston. It sat high on a bluff in the midst of deciduous trees and tall conifers. There was a view of the foothills from the kitchen window. The furnishings were outdated—mostly from the 1940s—but he did not care. It was fully furnished, which meant he and Sherry could move in right away and concern themselves with updating the place later.

He called Sherry as soon as he had made an inspection of the place. "It's ours if we want it. The realtor is eager to get rid of it. I think I can strike a deal. It's small with three bedrooms and one bathroom, but it's in a very nice setting. It sits among a lot of trees on the top of a hill. I think you'll like it."

"That's wonderful!" Sherry said.

"Do you trust me?"

"Absolutely. Make your offer."

"Okay. I'll be home before you know it so we can get to a lending institution. I love you, Sherry. We're going to be happy here."

In addition to teaching math at Kingston Junior High School, Bela took a job driving an eighteen-wheel semitruck on weekends for a teacher he had met at the junior high school. Sherry was not happy when he told her about it, but she kept her thoughts to herself. She did not want to spoil anything. She let Bela be the man of the house.

He and Sherry got approved for a mortgage right away and were in their new home within a month. Their first guests were Jeremy and Clara. Sherry took Clara aside and shyly asked her about sleeping arrangements. Clara proudly said that she and Jeremy were a couple. That's all Sherry needed to know. Clara enjoyed little Lee. "She's such a good baby!" she complimented. Little Lee took to Clara right away. She warmed Clara's heart.

Now that Sherry had a permanent home, she asked Bela if she may start her dry-cleaning business. Bela was supportive. She decided to take that loan Ed had offered so long ago. Sherry had the good fortune to buy an existing dry-cleaning building that had gone out of business. It took a couple months to upgrade and update the place. She kept little Lee with her at the shop. Her business hours were 9:00 a.m. to 5:00 p.m. so she could get home and make dinner for her family. Bela freely complimented Sherry on her dedication to her business and to him and Leora.

MATRIMONY—1958

After being engaged to Clara for two years, Jeremy called Bela on the phone. He paid for the call.

"I guess I can't wait. Clara and I haven't had sexual relations, and it's high time we did. We're going to get married next week. We want you and Sherry to be there."

"Just name when and where," Bela replied, "we'll be there."

* * *

One week later, Jeremy and Clara were married in a small church in Broome County. In attendance were Sherry and Bela, little Leora, the Clark clan, Mrs. and Mrs. Woodfield, and a minister. Jeremy was very handsome in a black suit and tie, white shirt, and black leather shoes. Clara was lovely in floor-length cream-colored chiffon, and off-white pumps. It was an expensive outfit that Jeremy had lovingly purchased for her. Jeremy announced that he intended to spoil Clara whatever that might take. That met with approval from everyone there. Pretty Clara just blushed.

All the guests cheered after Jeremy kissed the bride—a nice, happy peck on the lips. The guests shook hands with the newly married couple. Women gave each other hugs.

Little Leora said, "I'm glad you married Uncle Jeremy!" even though she probably did not know exactly what that meant.

* * *

There was a party later that month when everybody could get time off to visit the Clarks, where Jeremy and Clara were residing while they searched for housing. They had a lovely two-tiered white cake and champagne for their reception. Little Lee was mesmerized by the sparkling gift boxes.

Jeremy and Clara continued to pay regular visits to Sherry and Bela and little Leora. And they made the announcement to Sherry and Bela first when they discovered Clara was pregnant. Clara was positively aglow, and Jeremy could barely wait to become a daddy. It was a privilege to see those two together. They were such good friends in addition to being a happy husband and wife.

Clara asked Jeremy if they could name the baby Benjamin Alan if it was a boy, and Jeremy was agreeable to that. Alan was Jeremy's middle name. Neither of them knew what a girl would be named—perhaps another Olivia in honor of her sister. It made Clara sad to think of the daughter she would never meet. Jeremy always knew when she was sad, and he always gave her a hug and a light lecture about good attitude. It always relieved her pain. It was similar to the way Bela elevated Sherry's moods when she was down.

LITTLE LEORA GOES RIDING

When Leora was seven years old, Bela decided it was time for her to get used to the horses at the Clarks' place. These horses were retired work animals. He put Lee on top of one of the horses and told her to hang on to its mane. There was no saddle. The horses were docile and accustomed to being handled and manipulated. Bela had seen Jeremy and little Benjamin on one of the horses during a previous visit, so he figured Lee was old enough to try her hand at it.

They went out to one of the fields and practiced plowing so Lee could get an idea of what it was like to ride atop a very tall horse. She looked back at her daddy a few times. She wanted to make sure he was still there. Her ride lasted about half an hour. Bela figured that was long enough for Lee's initiation.

He reached up toward her and caught her when she hopped from the horse.

"Gosh, you're getting to be a big girl! Your dad won't be able to catch you much longer. How did it go? Were you scared?"

"No! Daddy, it was so fun to be up in the air taller than people. I could see far away up there. Can we ever go fast?"

"Why, yes, of course, we can. We'll go without the plow. You want to go now?"

Lee nodded her head.

"Okay, girl, I'm going to put you up on the horse again as soon as I take off the straps and the plow. Give me a few minutes."

She sat on the grass and watched Bela unhitch the horse. He led one out to pasture and kept the other one behind, the same one Lee had ridden.

Bela scooped up his little daughter and plunked her onto the back of the horse. Then he jumped up behind her. He snuggled with her for a moment. He could not help himself. He had to take advantage of those opportunities before she got too old to be hugged by her dad.

Bela directed the horse down the driveway. Once upon the road, he ordered the horse to canter. Lee felt as if she was flying.

"Go, go!" she cried to the horse.

And go it did. They rode at various speeds, and then they went back to the Clarks' place. Bela jumped from the horse and caught Lee hopping from it again. They led this horse out to pasture.

"So you weren't scared?" he asked his daughter.

"Not at all, Daddy. I loved going fast and faster."

Bela whistled as if to say my, my. "Okay, we'll do this again sometime. You can ride with Mommy too. She used to ride the plow horses. Your mommy is a very strong woman."

"Yes, Daddy, she is. I love her a lot."

"Well, guess what, kiddo? I love her a lot too."

Lee smiled up at her daddy. She was the image of Bela including the eyes that had changed from indigo to a magical gray-green. To him, she was an angel.

Growing Up

Leora enjoyed her childhood. During spring and summer, she and her girlfriends stomped through the forests around the neighborhood, stopped and sat near the brooks and streams for hours, listening to the traveling water. Later on, they sat by the brooks and streams, writing poems in the little journals they took with them. They sat and read to one another.

Whenever Bela, Sherry, and Lee visited the Clarks, there was the opportunity to ride the horses. Sometimes Bela accompanied her, and during other rides, it was Sherry who went with her. Lee became talented at riding bareback. Her parents were glad for her and proud of her. During an occasional weekend, Lee stayed behind and had a sleepover at either the Clarks' place or Mr. and Mrs. Hamiltons'.

Sometimes there were skating parties at the roller rink with her friends, doing the hokey pokey and the limbo and having a grand time skating and dancing to the organ music for hours.

Often on summer days, Lee and her girlfriends sought somebody's backyard and sunned themselves until they were a healthy-looking golden brown. They played Lee's little black transistor radio, listening to rock 'n' roll on the a.m. station. There were lots of chatter and laughter among the girls, talk about their summer fun and about what some of boys were going to be like next school semester.

Prior to school beginning again, Bela and Sherry took Lee on a vacation or two. Sometimes it was just a weekend away in the magnificent Finger Lakes region. Other trips spanned the widths and depths of the United States. Lee usually took her best friend, Sandy, along for the vacation. These were grand times for the family. Sherry and Lee took lots of photographs, and Lee made a note to herself to take her own children on trips in the future.

Autumn was time for gathering colorful leaves and ironing them between two sheets of waxed paper, for decorating the house for Halloween and dressing up in a costume for a day at school and exchanging candy with the other students. It was time for wool sweaters, cider and donuts, pumpkin carving.

Lee's favorite season was winter. She and her friends made snow angels and snowmen, had snowball fights, slid down Sherry and Bela's steep driveway on wooden sleds, landing just short of the road to Sherry's horror and Bela's delight. They skated on nearby frozen ponds. Lee was lucky enough to get rides with Sherry and Bela on a sleigh drawn by the two horses at the Clarks' farm. It was freezing cold but exhilarating to her. Each ride was followed by hot chocolate prepared by Mrs. Clark. On birthdays and Christmases, she was spoiled with gifts from parents and grandparents.

Lee was a good student. She put heart and soul into her classwork and homework assignments. She loved English and ended up in an independent study class. She had to read three books from the same author, compare and contrast the plots and the people in the stories. Her worst choice was Ernest Hemmingway. She decided, after all the work was done that she did not like his main male characters.

"Too macho," she said to her parents when they asked her why. "And the damsel was always in some sort of distress. And despite not liking each other, they ended up falling in love after fighting and scrapping. It's silly."

Sherry had to agree based on what she knew of Ernest Hemmingway. Sherry had read a few of his novels.

When it came time for Lee to attend junior high school, she was a bit nervous. She said to Bela, "There are going to be kids from other grade schools. What if they're super smart or don't like me?"

Bela replied, "I'll always be around. Come and knock on my classroom door any time you encounter trouble or just want to feel safe. I've got your back, my lovely daughter. I've arranged for you to take math from me anyway, so for at least an hour a day, I can assess how you're doing. I have the feeling you're going to excel. You're smart and beautiful and naturally friendly."

Lee smiled at Bela and gave him a hug.

"Thanks, Dad."

"Any time, honey."

Lee's friend Sandy had the same feelings Lee had. Lee reiterated to Sandy what her dad had told her. Sandy felt more at ease knowing there would be a safe zone for her in Bela's classroom; as a favor to Lee, Bela had arranged for Sandy to be one of his math students as well.

Junior High

Lee's junior high years went by in a proverbial flash. She had sleepovers with a myriad of girlfriends. Sherry was always a good hostess, and Bela was willing to embarrass Lee by hauling out his accordion and Lee's concertina. After the initial session of blushing and saying, "Dad! Really?" she was always won over by him. Sometimes a friend or two jammed with them. Sometimes it was a cacophony, but other times, there was a nice blending of notes, particularly when Adrian joined them on his baritone saxophone, her tall friend Jim played his trombone, and Lee played her concertina.

Sherry's place was sometimes packed when there were jam sessions. Afterward, there might be a dozen giggly girls spending the night there. There were 8mm-movies and popcorn and all-night girl talks. Lee spent the night at her girl friends' homes as well. She was very popular. The boys timidly told other girls how pretty Lee was, and when she heard this, she blushed. Another thing that made her so popular was the cute math teacher, Bela. The girls said he was very handsome, and the boys told her that he was a cool guy. It took her a few weeks to get over the blushing, but eventually, she admitted that her dad was a great teacher.

Chemistry in junior high took on a new life for Lee. It was much more difficult than the perfunctory lessons in grade school. She studied hard to get good grades. Her best friend Sandy was her lab partner. Sandy was a serious student and worked hard too. Jim whose lab table was across the aisle from theirs was *not* a serious student. He did not have to work or study hard to get excellent grades. He offered comic relief to Sandy and Lee when they needed it.

Jim was popular with girls. He could often be spotted in front of a locker with a plethora of girls surrounding him. He cracked quips about the teachers and made the girls laugh. They flirted with him openly. When the bell rang for the next class to begin, the crowd disbursed in a happy mood.

Band was fun. Lee and Sandy sat first chair in the clarinet section. Jim sat first chair trombone along with his friend Darrell. Adrian was the only baritone saxophone player. It was great having a teacher with a fresh approach to music—pay attention, work hard, get good grades, and "you will be able to goof off once in a while." *Goof off* meant "eating snacks and listening to music on the teacher's record player." Rock 'n' roll, symphonies, and Renaissance music were Lee's favorite genres. The teacher, Mr. Washington, was quite fond of Lee and Sandy because they were serious students. He was harder on some of the boys, including Jim and Adrian, chiefly because they tended to talk too much during practice. But it was a fine band, and many of the students—including Lee, Sandy, Adrian, and Jim—did well at solo and ensemble festivals.

Lee did well in gym. She was excellent on the parallel bars, the balance beam, and the trampoline too. When it came time to perform a routine for a grade, she paired up with Sandy. Sandy was a lovely, shy girl. She was popular with the boys too, but she would not approach them. If a boy paid attention to her, it was a tough task for her to stay attentive because her mind was bent on escaping the situation. But with Lee at her side, there was no problem conversing with boys. Lee did not mind helping out Sandy. She was Lee's best friend after all. Initially, Adrian and Jim were the only boys with whom Sandy felt comfortable, but by the time junior high was all over with, she had come out of her shell and was not fearful of engaging in small talk with boys. Adrian asked Sandy to go to school dances with him, and she said, "Yes," gladly. With Lee being Jim's date at the dances, the four of them had a blast on and off the dance floor. Other boys asked Lee and Sherry to dance, and they felt comfortable enough to go along with it. Jim and Adrian had fun teasing the girls about being so popular with the boys.

THE VISTA CRUISER

When Lee was fourteen years old, her father drove home a used Vista Cruiser.

"It's yours if you want it. But you have to help me get it roadworthy."

"Cool, Dad!" was Lee's response. It really was a beautiful car, with a third seat that faced backward, long horizontal windows on the sides of the car, and a sunroof.

"I picked it up for a bargain, so there might be some major issues. But we'll work them out, right, honey?"

"Sure thing, Dad, just let me know whenever you want my help."

So every evening for a week, Lee and Bela worked on the car. They washed and polished the car inside and out. They installed new tires. She spent time with him, changing the plugs, points, condenser, and exhaust system. She helped him bleed the new brakes and check all the interior lights and signal direction's lights and headlights. She helped him change the oil, antifreeze, and transmission fluid.

When they were sure it was good for the road, they took Sherry with them on a cross-county day trip. They stopped for gasoline and then took to any road they thought would be interesting. The Cruiser took the foothill grades just fine, and when Bela opened it up on level ground, the car went to ninety miles per hour in a hurry and purred the entire time.

They stopped at ice cream joints and drive in restaurants. Bela stopped the car once to let Sherry have a chance at it. She was more conservative with the speed. Lee was not going to be able to drive it until she turned fifteen with a driver's permit, but Bela promised her plenty of time behind the wheel prior to getting her driver's license.

It was nightfall by the time they arrived home from their road trip. Everyone was tired but in a good mood. Lee hugged her dad and her mom.

"Working on the car was actually fun, Dad," she said.

"I think I'll put in a good word for you in school so you can work on cars in the automobile shop class. It's closed to girls, but I think you should be their exception. What do you say? Okay with you? You know more than most boys your age already."

"I might be embarrassed!" Lee protested.

"*Pff*, nah, get over it, kid," Bela teased.

"Tell you what, Dad, if you can pull it off, I'll do it. I'm sure there's a lot more I can learn."

"You're on, darlin'," Bela said.

Bela had an "in" because he was a teacher for the school district. When he visited the high school principal and turned on his charm, he won over the principal. Lee was an "in" for automobile shop. She ended up being one of the top students every school year.

How Brad Met Leora—
Early September 1971

He had just left the office building, looking all handsome in black cotton slacks, a medium blue button-up cotton shirt, and a black leather jacket. He stood over six feet tall in his hiking boots. He was looking down at his class schedule and a map of the campus.

Leora happened to be on the same sidewalk, headed in his direction. Noticing that he was not paying attention to where he was going, she decided to stop.

He bumped into her. *Then* he looked up.

He looked down at her. "I am *so sorry*. I wasn't paying attention to where I was going," he said. "Are, are you all right?" He touched one of her forearms lightly with his hand, sending a slight shock wave through her body.

"I'm fine," Lee said with a smile and a glint of humor in her eyes.

"I'm Brad Adams. This is my first day here."

"My name is Leora Sovine. I'm on my way to the office. Nice to meet you, Brad." They shook hands. "And don't pay any attention to that map thing. It's a confusing mess. I can help you find your class. May I see your schedule?"

Brad held onto the schedule so he and Lee would have to be head-to-head to read it. She felt such a rush of warmth that she could hardly contain herself. He felt the same way, and he hoped she took no notice of it. There was something special between them from the very start.

She looked up and pointed to a building situated about a hundred feet to the east. "That's an auto shop. There are some nice guys in that class. You'll get along fine."

"Thank you, Leora," Brad said, "and it's been a pleasure running into you."

Lee let out a chuckle. "Oh, you're welcome. I hope you enjoy Kingston High School!"

He did not want her to leave, but she made her way toward the office building. Her skirt swished side to side as she walked. Was she doing that on purpose? He continued to watch her. She turned around and looked at him quizzically but did not stop. Then she turned toward the office building again with a wave of her hand. He waited until she was inside, and then he heaved a sigh of contentment as he practically skipped over to the auto shop building.

Lord, please let me see her again some time, he prayed in all seriousness.

He did see her again. It was at lunchtime when Adrian from the auto shop took him to the table where there was a group seated and introduced him to the students there. Everyone in the group greeted him. Lee simply turned toward him and gave him a coy smile as if to say, "Yeah, yeah, I know who *you* are." Brad did not know what to make of her. She was pretty, not bleach-blond pretty but a natural beauty with soft olive features and black hair. Her eyes were the most striking feature, a unique blend of gray and green.

Lord, here I am again, he prayed. *Please let me speak to her some time.*

It was a week or so before they had a conversation. It was during lunch at the table. They dabbled in talk—their school classes, what they were going to do when they graduated (Lee wanted to work in a hospital, but Brad was undecided). Lee wanted to press him for personal information about where he came from, but she sensed his reticence. She did not pry.

Brad joined the baseball and football teams. He made fast friends with Darren, a star athlete on both teams. Brad and Jim made friends as soon as Jim mentioned a cattle farm nearby that might need help if Brad was looking for a job. Brad smiled at Jim and said, "The Warners'?"

"Yeah, yeah! The Warners'," replied Jim. "I work there once in a while."

"They offered me a job a few weeks ago. I stay there part-time when it's too late to go home at night. Small world, huh?"

"Surely is," Jim replied. "If you ever need help, I'm your man any time at all."

They chatted a bit about the cattle and horses. Their friendship took no time at all to solidify.

Two Weeks After Brad's Arrival—Rita

A lovely blonde girl arrived in the cafeteria on a Monday during lunchtime. She stood about five foot seven with a slender build. She was from Massachusetts, staying in nearby Kingston with relatives on their horse farm. She was a 4.0 student from one of those prestigious high schools near Boston. She looked the part in her plaid pleated skirt and white cotton blouse. Her dad was a millionaire. And she stood at the front of the cafeteria, lunch tray in her hands, looking befuddled.

Darren noticed her and motioned to Collin and Darrell with a nod of his head. They turned around and looked at her. Collin left his seat and plopped his feet onto the floor. He approached the pretty girl cheerfully and said, "Hello. My name is Collin. I'm with a group of folks over there," and he turned and pointed to the table, which was toward the back of the cafeteria, just in front of a candy machine. Then he turned back to the girl. "Would you like to join us?"

The girl smiled and looked left and right as if trying to decide where to sit.

There was a short pause.

Collin looked back at Darrell and made a slight shrug of his shoulders. He returned his eyes to the girl.

"Yes, that would be nice," she finally said. "Thanks so much. I'm new here. Nobody knows me."

"Well, come on, after me, please."

Everybody in the group scooted over to make room for her. She sat to the right of Leora. Her waist-length platinum-blond braid was quite the contrast to Lee's short obsidian-black bob.

"Hi, what brings you to our school?" Adrian asked the girl.

Her voice was friendly and pleasant. "My father wants me to see 'how the other half lives,' as he proposes it. He's demanding of me full emersion into the lives of the other half to see how horrible it is to live without millions of dollars." She ended her explanation with a polite smile as if she had just finished a lovely little synopsis of a perfect little life.

The group looked 'round the table at each other. Some of them wondered if she was a spoiled rich girl who whose father was exaggerating things. Or maybe she *was* trouble, and he was trying toughness to rein her in from the dark side.

I don't know if I'm going to like this girl, Connie thought.

"Wow," said Collin. "And your father chose the illustrious Kingston High School." He was playfully sarcastic.

"Yes, he did," Rita said with a wry grin. "He chose this school."

A few-second pause ensued.

"Why?"

"Collin, you are so rude," said Connie, who was Collin's cousin, older by only a few months. They shared head and facial shape. They wore their hair one length, just long enough to contain it behind their ears. Both of them had soft brown eyes and blond hair.

Collin apologized to Rita.

The group cast a look upon Rita. Several seconds followed. They waited…

"Oh no, you're not rude," Rita replied.

"Oh okay, whew!" Collin wiped his brow.

"My name is Rita Armstrong. I'm from Massachusetts. I'm staying with relatives while I attend school here." She stood up and started shaking hands 'round the table. Collin and Darrell were impressed! They looked at each other in wonder.

Rita had eyed Brad as soon as she had joined the group. So when he stood up, he shook her hand and said, "Brad Adams." He nodded politely without smiling and had direct, deliberate eye contact with her—as if studying her during their quick introduction; she was taken aback. She saw his skin as a hue of brown that defied description, with cheeks round enough to lend him the look of someone a few years younger, eyes a dark and mystical blue, hand and arm muscles thick from physical labor, hair—tight, black curls—as shiny as obsidian, neatly trimmed mustache the same color as his hair. Rita was delighted to meet him. She was happy that *karma* (a word she had learned recently) put her in the path of such a handsome young man.

Then her eyes turned to Darren. He introduced himself as they shook hands. He was polite but indifferent. It could be because he had a girlfriend from another town. He seemed oblivious to Rita's beauty and the way she practically gawked at him. Rita, on the other hand, barely contained her excitement and almost dropped her jaw. Her eyes opened widely for about two seconds. She considered him to be beach-boy beautiful, so different from Brad—the bright blue eyes, the thick and short blond hair with the long shock of bangs on his slender forehead, light-brown stubble that he had not bothered to deal with that day, lean arms and hands. He appeared to be at least six foot four. She had never seen such a handsome blond guy in all her life, and she was *surrounded* by good-looking blond guys back in Massachusetts!

A rush of gladness slid down from her face to her toes. *I am going to actually have fun here,* she thought. *I wish Bonnie and Sara could be here to see these guys!* Bonnie and Sara were her best friends back in Boston.

Rita's upbringing had ingrained strong self-confidence in her, so she wasn't shy. Therefore, she was able to hide her amazement to most of the group. But Brad and Jim looked at each other with poker faces for a few seconds. They had caught her nuances while she gazed at Darren.

Darren was strong, physically fit, and nicely filled out with good musculature. He was deadpan and intelligent. Contrast that to his identical twin, Darrell—happy Darrell with his ability to hide his intellect behind silliness—who was quite slender. He made no effort to possess the masculine look sported by his brother.

While Darren was busy scoring touchdowns at the football games and pitching shut-outs in baseball, Darrell was offering his support by playing the trombone in the pep band that stood up in the bleachers, with Lee and Sandy on their clarinets and Adrian on the baritone saxophone, as well as a host of other students. Otherwise, Darrell was Darren's teammate on the basketball court.

Connie decided to give Rita a chance; Rita's upbringing was her strongest influence. Was she merely swinging her pendulum too far? Would there be middle ground for her someday after she got her fill of life with *the other half?* Connie had no idea. She hoped so. Rita seemed like a smart girl but not savvy, not aware that there are truly dark sides out there in society. Her pride might sting some people. She seemed physically frail, and Connie hoped Rita hadn't been exposed to real physical danger at the hands of personal adversaries.

None of the guys in the group kept a list of top 10 babes, but—guaranteed—as Rita became a familiar person at Kingston, boys who kept a list would start kicking other girls off the top 1 spot.

"Rita," asked Adrian, "do you have siblings?"

"Yes, I have two sisters and one brother. Ingrid is twenty-three years old. Enid is eight years old, and Austin is seven."

One of the students said, "Gosh, you know, the name Ingrid Armstrong sounds so familiar. I subscribe to equestrian magazines. Would she have been featured in one?"

Rita replied, "Yes, Ingrid trains and rides horses for special parades and events. Right now, she is on an assignment training horses for a swashbuckling God Bless America lollapalooza down in Alabama this year. She gets publicity frequently."

"That must take a tremendous amount of time and talent and hard work," Connie commented.

"Weeks, sometimes months, depending on the number of horses. She has to train the riders too, of course."

"She must be amazing," said Leora.

"She's the best there is. We rarely see her."

"Is her job something you aspire to do as well?" Connie asked.

Rita smiled politely. "No, Ingrid is beyond me in that regard!" She continued, "I love jumping and barrel racing, that's all."

That's all? thought Darren.

Can we say conceited? thought Connie.

"Rita, do Enid and Austin ride too?" asked Adrian.

Rita chuckled. "Well, right now Enid is just starting competing in the 4H stuff. Austin? He's something else altogether. He's heavily into fly fishing."

"Fly fishing?" some of the group said.

"There's tremendous talent required for that too, isn't there?" asked Connie.

"Yes, well, he's a natural." Rita paused. "I feel as if I've just drained you all with so much bragging. I apologize."

"Oh no!"

"No, that's okay."

Things of that nature were said in reply to Rita.

No, Darren and Connie thought sarcastically and simultaneously.

"Rita, tell me," Darren said seriously, "do your siblings look like you?" He folded his arms against his chest. *As gorgeous as you think you are, in other words?* was his thought.

Rita tilted her head ever-so-slightly as she looked at Darren quizzically. He wasn't going to faze her, but he wanted to. He kept her gaze though.

"Geez, Darren," came from Darrell, "you take the word *succinct* to a new level."

"Oh gosh, Darrell, that's fine. I don't mind," Rita said, her eyes still on Darren. She thought, *I wonder how hard it would be to make him uncomfortable. Not now. Be polite.* Rita replied to Darren, "Ingrid and I aren't much alike. Her hair is a bit shorter and darker than mine. She's almost five-foot-ten-inches tall, and her eyes are brown instead of blue like mine."

Darren nodded and smiled. "Thanks, Rita, that was nice of you."

"Oh, you're welcome, Darren."

"And the other siblings?" Connie said.

"Enid is a spittin' image of my mother," Rita said. "Austin is too actually, but Enid's hair is straight and blond. Austin's hair is dark-brown and very curly."

Brad had been listening intently while looking casual. Truth was, he was familiar with Ingrid Armstrong. Her family, Mr. Warner, and Brad's uncle Bruce were all acquaintances. It was about two years ago that Brad and Ingrid had met each other. She was at Bruce's horse farm visiting with her father and Mr. Warner. The father had wanted Ingrid to see Bruce's fantastic white stallions. Ingrid and Brad were introduced to each other. Then the adults left them to themselves. He spent some time showing her around the farm, and they rode and groomed two of the six white stallions that Bruce was preparing for auction. There transpired talk about his life as a horse trainer and her developing career. Brad was wholly impressed by her. At about dusk, they went up to the second floor of Bruce's house and spent some time in Brad's bedroom. Ingrid was just a fling for Brad, much like half a dozen other girls he had had in his bedroom. He was not emotionally attached to any of them.

Several months later, Brad and Ingrid met again at Bruce's place, and Brad was perfectly cordial to Ingrid but definitely not interested in having more sex with her. And Ingrid never questioned this. She was not a child. It had not been puppy love or any other kind of love.

But that wasn't the final encounter between Brad and Ingrid. In the near future, they were to see each other again under surprising circumstances.

A TYPICAL STUDY HALL
WITH THE GROUP

It was just another study hall, right after lunch. The group was seated 'round a big table much like the tables in the lunchroom—boring steel gray made of hard plastic components.

Darrell sneezed with vigor, covering his mouth with his hands. He looked from one hand to the other hand, wondering what to do next. He decided to wipe them on a clean piece of his notebook paper.

"Damn it, Darrell," Collin whispered, looking down at his book.

"What the heck did I do?" Darrell demanded in a whisper. He looked at Collin without raising his head.

"You sneezed on my damn textbook. And you gave me a shower. Gross!"

"Well, *geez*!" Darrell exclaimed, too loudly to be ignored. "I'm so sorry!"

"Guys, you're not studying" came a warning from Mr. Jenkins. He was seated at the front of the room in one of those massive wooden desks that only teachers are allowed to inhabit. "You're going to be holding up the wall again if you don't cool it. You know how much fun holding up the wall is."

Holding up the wall was *not* fun. To do it, the offending student stood with his back to the wall, with his hands behind him, palms pressed against the wall. It was painful to the hands and arms.

Darrell mumbled, loudly enough to be heard at the table, "Now that you've mastered the *obvious*…"

Then everyone else at the table raised their heads and took a look at Mr. Jenkins as he trained his eyes on Collin and Darrell. They could not tell if Mr. Jenkins had heard Darrell.

"Gosh," said Lee softly, "I hope you fellas are finished with your feud."

Connie suggested in a low voice, "Perhaps we should warn Cornell about these two children."

After that, everyone at the table spoke in normal tone of voice.

"You're kidding, I hope," said a girl who was at the table with the group. "These two are going to the same university?"

"Indeed," Connie replied, "and they've managed to get permission to stay in the same dorm room."

Collin and Darrell had been accepted to Cornell immediately upon graduation from high school. They chose the same major—medieval music, literature, and theater.

Darren said, "Unfortunately, together, they comprise one brain."

"That's if they're lucky," Stickman (Jim) pitched in.

"Perhaps we should provide them some brain food," Connie suggested.

"But what would that be?" asked Sandy.

After a short pause, Adrian piped up, "Oh, I know! Soylent green!"

Cheers and hand clapping were intertwined with several of the group exclaiming, "Gross!"

Adrian—who had arrived at school that day sporting a tie-dyed T-shirt with a PEACE sign sewn onto the front of it and who had coiffured a blue mohawk—lightly tossed his orange sunglasses across the table, and the glasses grazed the side of Collin's head. Adrian offered Collin an angelic smile. Collin frowned at Adrian and said, "You might be holding up the wall one of these days too, my hippie friend."

Adrian replied, "Never have, dude. And I never will."

And he never did.

Darren mumbled to no one in particular, "I wonder what it would cost me to hire someone to erase my brother from my existence."

Lee and Rita smiled at him. He did not see them. Collin and Darrell rolled their eyes upward. A silent truce had occurred between them, their little feud already forgotten.

"All right, children, that's enough," Connie admonished.

Everything simmered down, just as Mr. Jenkins was considering paying the table a visit. He stood up, and then he sat back down.

"And Adrian?" Mr. Jenkins said from his desk.

"Yes?" Adrian responded.

"That hair of yours won't be blue tomorrow."

"You must mean Monday," Darrell corrected him.

"Yes," added Collin, "today is Friday."

"Monday then, smart-ass" was Mr. Jenkins's retort.

Everybody at the table went back to studying until the bell rang.

"Well, we dodged another bullet, my buddy," Darrell said to Collin as they gathered their books and papers. They gave each other a high five.

Students flooded the hallways before the next hour of classes began. There were huddles of various numbers of students hanging around near classroom doors and in front of lockers. Lee and Sandy stood at the door of their next class, Eighteenth-Century American Fiction. It was an advanced class, relegated to students with grade point average of 3 or higher. Lee and Sandy chatted about their grade point averages. Sandy's stood at a respectable 3.8. Lee carried a 4.0.

"I hate that Stickman!" Sandy complained. "He never studies, and he carries his GPA around as if it were as light as a feather."

Lee thought Sandy was serious about hating Stickman—for about five seconds. Then they had a good chuckle.

As luck would have it, Stickman appeared in the hallway. He combed back his blond hair with his fingers as he approached Lee and Sandy on his long legs and his big feet that were covered with high-top tennis shoes.

"What's up, ladies?" He stood between the girls.

"Sandy hates you, that's all. No big deal," said Lee.

"Oh, she's just jealous of my ancient Greek appearance and my superior demeanor. I am the epitome of high quality, am I not?" He held up his chin. "Okay, don't answer that."

"Okay, that's enough bullshit," Sandy said lightly.

"Yes, James," added Lee, "are you quite finished with your superlatives?"

Sandy complained to Stickman, "Ol' Sandy here, I have to study hard for my 3.8 GPA. You never study, and you carry a 4.0. I'm jealous of the latent ease with which you're skipping through high school. I suppose it's been that way all your student life."

"Oh, that," said Jim, "*pff.*" He waved his hand in friendly dismissal. "You're doing great, Sandy, keep it up." He playfully rubbed the top of her brown-haired head, and his eyes looked down into hers, which matched the color of her hair. She was five foot six. He was six foot two.

"Have a most wonderful day, ladies," he said with a bow. Down the hallway, he sauntered, not looking back, on his way to his locker and a waiting crowd of female admirers.

Sandy put her hand over her heart. "Isn't he dreamy?" she joked.

Lee and Sandy looked at each other for a few seconds, and then they had a hearty chuckle. They hooked arms and entered the classroom.

If only you knew, Sandy, Lee thought. *Jim's the guy for me. I'm in love with him, but I haven't told anybody, not even Jim.*

CLEANUP IN AISLE 3

The science room was Mr. Jenkins's domain. He was an enthusiastic instructor, but he was stern as well. The classes he taught were for the accelerated students, of whom Leora and Stickman were two. Mr. Jenkins, known by the group as Mr. Biology, had drafted Lee and Stickman in the beginning of the school year to set up the classroom on special occasions.

When Mr. Biology had first approached Lee and Stickman about this task, he was reminded by Lee that they would be cutting into time with Mrs. Flannigan's Algebra class. "Oh, I don't give a rat's butt about that," Mr. Biology had said. "Let me talk to her."

So today at 10:00 a.m., Lee and Stickman were busy preparing materials for the next class. They talked about just about everything imaginable, Stickman doing most of the talking. Then they got to goofing around; Stickman held a flask over Lee's head. She dared him to pour the contents out onto her head. They knew he had put only water in the flask. They were just having fun.

He started to pour the water onto her head. She stepped back to avoid it and tripped on a rung of one of the stools. "Oh no!" he exclaimed as he grabbed her to steady her. But she lurched forward toward him, turned somehow, and landed on her tummy on the table, her arms and upper torso splayed out in front of her.

Everything on that table that was not bolted down was swept over the end of the table and onto the shiny wood floor. *Crash! Bam! Thunk!* Flasks, graduated cylinders, bacteria-laden petri dishes, slides, and test tubes—everything, joined by two microscopes.

Then there was silence for what seemed about a year.

Stickman was the first person to comment. He put the palm of one hand over his mouth and said, "Shit! What the hell are we going to do?"

Lee covered her mouth similarly and said, "Shit, I have no idea!" Her gray-green eyes were as wide as could be.

His mouth was still covered. "You just cursed. You *never* do that."

Her mouth was still covered too. "I know!"

"Mr. Biology is going to have our heads," said Stickman after removing his hand from his mouth.

"*That* would be correct."

To their relief, it was only Connie entering the room. She said, "Stickman, you have no idea how much trouble you two are in."

"Please," Stickman said, "let us tell Mr. Biology ourselves. A little fiction might just be the trick here in saving our lives."

"This looks like something Collin and Darrell would do," Connie commented.

Stickman replied, "Connie, you have no idea. What the hell are you doing here early anyway, my dear?"

"I came to study and to prepare for class."

"Oh!" said Stickman. "How nice."

"I feel sorry for you two. Mr. Biology isn't exactly a bundle of laughs even when he *tries* to be funny, which he won't do when he sees all this. You can imagine what I'm imagining."

"Oh yes, I see," said Stickman as he ran his fingers through his blond hair.

Lee walked to the front closet. Stickman followed her. Together, they fetched a broom and dustpan, some large rags, a mop, and a bucket, and lugged all the stuff to the tables.

Connie grabbed the two fallen microscopes. "I'll see if they're damaged. Many hundreds of dollars from your pockets if they are."

Stickman moaned, "This is just great." He sat on the floor on top of all the glass mess, put his knees up and hugged them. Lee giggled.

Connie looked at him with a straight face. "We have to get serious here. Class starts in less than an hour."

"Gosh, Con, you're such a buzzkill," said Jim as he looked up at her from the floor.

Lee had that sparkle in her eyes. She knew Mr. Biology might want to have their necks, but he would probably go easy on her. She knew he had a gentle side for her. Lee *was* awfully cute. Nobody could deny that.

They decided to wet mop the glass from the floor. It worked. The mess was stuffed into a large black plastic garbage bag and set into the closet with the cleaning items they had borrowed. Stickman wet wiped the table with one of the large rags, and then he tossed the rag into the little sink at the middle of the table.

"Take *that*," he said to the rag.

"Microscopes area all good," Connie announced from kitty-corner.

"Geez, thank God," said Stickman.

"Thank you for helping us, Connie," Lee said in her even-tempered voice while polishing the tabletop shiny with a clean, dry rag.

"No problem, honey," Connie replied. "Well, now we have the problem of stocking the tables."

Stickman spoke first. "There's no other way around it. We have to let this table borrow from other tables."

"*Splendid* idea," Connie said, "And you're right, it's the only way. Just be assured that Mr. Biology is going to figure it out that all the tables don't have the required amount of slides and flasks and cylinders."

"Yes, I know," said Stickman, running his fingers through his hair again. "He will notice right away."

As the three of them stood pondering this for a moment, who should quietly enter the room but Mr. Biology himself. He stopped just inside the room and cleared his throat.

Lee and Stickman looked each other in the eye. Jim's heart felt as if it had sunk to the bottom of his belly.

"Oh, for God's sake, *now* what?" he demanded as he approached Lee and Stickman. He ignored Connie. Mr. Biology wore slightly baggy ecru-colored cotton khakis, a pale-brown Henley shirt, and faded patent leather shoes that had cost him a fortune when they were new. His thick brown hair was simply piled on top of his head and combed down over his ears. His eyeglasses had gold-colored wire frames. He was not overweight actually; perhaps he was just a bit out of shape. Neither classically handsome nor unpleasant-looking, he wore a simple gold wedding band on his left ring finger and a simple Timex watch on his left forearm.

"I can't see what you've done. You've done away with all the evidence. Jim, you might as well tell me." He put his hands into his pants pockets and stood up straight.

"Well?" said Stickman.

Pause.

"Yeah?" said Mr. Jenkins impatiently.

Jim cleared his throat. He raised his hand to comb back his hair but thought better of it. "I made a blunder when I slipped on the floor. To be honest, Mr. Jenkins, some stuff was broken, and some the slides are contaminated from hitting the floor."

"Stuff. Important stuff?"

Stickman said, "There are items enough to go around as long as two table share materials."

"Hmmm" came from Mr. Biology. He had a hard look on his face. "I suppose you can't get to a science supply store fast enough since most of the *stuff* that we get for this classroom comes from a mail order catalog."

"Well, I presume I cannot," said Stickman.

There was a short pause.

"I can't apologize enough, can I?" he asked Mr. Biology

"Nope, you can't."

Lee looked up at Stickman and in a small voice said, "Are you quite finished?"

He looked down at her quizzically and mouthed, "Huh?"

Mr. Biology and Connie were quite taken by surprise too. They looked at Lee.

"I fell onto the table after I stumbled against one of the rungs on one of the stools. I'm the one who caused all the items to fall."

"Lee, you don't have to cover for him," said Mr. Biology.

"I know, but I'm not. I'm telling the truth."

"Jim?"

"Yes, Mr. Jenkins, it's the truth."

"Oh."

"It all started when I tried to pour a beaker of water onto her head."

"A what—"

"A beaker—"

"Of water, yes, I know, I was being rhetorical. So it's *your* fault then. Okay. Here's what we need to do. Leora, when this next class is finished, come on back here, and the two of us will make a shopping list, look up the prices in the catalog, and calculate the amount of money you and Jim will be spending. Sounds reasonable?"

Lee said, "Yes, more than reasonable. You're being very kind."

Mr. Biology nodded his head once.

"Connie, what do you think?" He had his back to her.

He surprised the heck out of Connie, shocked her in fact. She had no idea what to say, but she replied, "Sir, I wasn't here when the stuff—materials—were broken," she replied to his back.

"Okay, but do you think Leora and I have a fair deal?"

"Oh my goodness, yes, Mr. Jenkins," Connie replied.

He cheered up a bit. "Nothing deliberate here, I'm sure. But, guys, this is fragile and expensive stuff. We need every bit of it. Watch the hell out will you from now on? This is your first infraction. Please make it your final one. How are the microscopes?"

"All good, Mr. Jenkins," said Connie.

"Okay then. Thanks, Connie. And Leora, I'll see you when this next class is finished."

"Shall I let Mrs. Haner know I won't be in typing class?" Lee asked.

"Oh crap, I suppose so. No, never mind. I'll do it."

"Thank you," Lee said to him.

Stickman rolled his eyes upward. *Oh, brother, here we go again,* he thought. *Why doesn't he just adopt her? He spoils her anyway.*

"Yes," Stickman said to Mr. Biology, "thanks so much."

"Okay, children, carry on. Connie, I'll see you next hour?" He still had his back toward her.

"Yes, I'll be here. Actually, I'm here early to get prepared."

"Good. I'm off to see Mrs. Haner." He turned on his heel, glanced at Connie who did not look back at him and exited the room.

After he was gone, a collective sigh was uttered by Connie, Lee, and Stickman.

"Damn!" was all Stickman could think to say.

"Glad *that's* concluded!" said Connie.

"Thanks, you guys," Lee said humbly.

"Dear, you saved your lab partner from a doomed fate of some mysterious kind," Connie said to her.

"Lab partner. I like the sound of that," Jim mused. He cupped his chin in his hand. Then he looked at Lee and gave her a rough hug around the shoulders. She laughed. "Yes, Lee, we are partners, hopefully for always, especially after this scare today. We can survive anything! Whatta ya say?"

"Partners in *crime* is more like it," Connie commented.

"You've done it now!" Stickman said to her. "Time for *you* to get a hug." He had to chase her around the room to catch her, which he eventually did just as she got to the door. He hugged her gruffly and shook her gently up and down a few times. She laughed heartily. Then he released her.

For the rest of the hour, Lee and Stickman readied the tables as thoroughly as they could. Connie kept to herself. She made a short, temporary absence of herself when Lee and Stickman prepared her table. When they were finally able to leave the room, they made their exit without bothering Connie.

"Well!" Stickman said cheerfully as they strolled down the hall. "What's next—more destruction? How about all those vintage cars in the auto shop?"

Lee replied, "I think we should stick to something tame, such as deflating all the basketballs."

"'*Splendid* idea,' Connie would say. Shall we ask her to join us?"

Lee just rolled her eyes upward.

"Aw hell, let's crash an advanced English class. Maybe they need someone to read to the students."

Leora did read to students actually—ninth graders who were behind in their studies. She tutored reading and spelling. She was pleasant and patient. She had a 100 percent success rate in getting her students up to grade level.

THE OLD MARE

Rita and Brad ended up talking about horses one day while they waited in line outside the gym for an assembly to begin. It was a Friday afternoon, two hours before the day's dismissal. Brad had had an unfortunate encounter with an old mare when he was about ten years old. The mare had deliberately spilled Brad from the saddle, landing him on his head on a large rock, causing an instant, excruciating headache. The leader of the horses had stopped to check on Brad. He had taken Brad back to the stables on the leader horse, towing the offending horse behind them. The leader had encouraged Brad to give the offending horse a lecture, which he did. After he had finished, the offending horse was licking his hand sheepishly.

Rita enjoyed the tale of Brad and the mare. So as they continued to wait in line outside the gym that Friday afternoon, Brad asked, "Would you like to get together sometime? I work at a farm that has horses for recreation. They're all very good, well-trained horses. They get exercise regularly."

"That would be great," Rita replied. "Is it far from here? My driver would have to take me to and from the place."

"No bother," said Brad, "I can get you there and back. I assume you won't mind riding on the back of my motorcycle."

"Motorcycle?"

"I have a Harley." Brad saw her eyes go wide with excitement.

"Oh, cool. It will be my first time. Should I wear a leather coat?"

"Do you have any leather?" he asked seriously.

"Sadly no. But I can purchase some."

"I have enough for both of us. It really keeps you safe."

She nodded her head in acknowledgment.

"I have to get permission from my uncle unfortunately. He's in charge of me since I'm not living home right now since my father... oh, who cares about him? How about Monday?"

"Monday then," said Brad, "provided you get permission. I really don't want many people to know about me."

"Great," said Rita. "I get to play the part of the bad girl on the back of some dark guy's Harley. I've always wanted to do this. Wait until I shock my father with this."

"Rita, I tell you it won't be all that exciting. I'm a good, careful driver. And if it's all the same to you, I'd like it to remain moot, especially when it comes to your family."

"Oh. Okay, how come?"

Because I had sex with your big sister, little girl, Brad wanted to say, *and your uncle knows all about it already. No need for* you *to find out.*

What he actually said was "I don't like most folks to know who I am or who my friends are. I'm a private person. Nothing against you or anyone else."

A short pause.

"You know," Rita said, "that's cool. So if I ever want to run away, you will be able to drive me somewhere incognito?"

Brad sighed. *Thankfully for the entire world, she can trust me. No way I'm getting involved with* this *little girl.*

"*Not* such a good idea" came Connie's voice from right behind them. She stuck her face between Brad's and Rita's heads. "Hi, kids." She had been listening to Brad and Rita the entire time they had been talking. "Brad, dear, I'm sorry to butt in. I'm being rude."

"You're fine, Connie," Brad replied as he looked at her. "What's up?"

"I normally wouldn't say anything," Connie said, "but, Rita, dear, Brad's a very cool-headed guy. He's not the bad boy some girls think he is. He doesn't flaunt his motorcycle for anybody. It's not his nature. You must take him as he is because as he is, he's perfect!"

"All right, Connie, I understand, thank you," Rita said, nonplussed but allowing her social training to shine through.

Connie continued, "I'd hate to be the one to beat your butt if you ever went against his wishes for privacy, know what I mean?"

Rita was caught off guard but took it well. She did not blush or flinch.

"*Okay*, all you *buddies*, let's just breathe in a nice long one, shall we?" That was Stickman coming from right behind Connie. He had been listening since Connie had nudged her face between those of Brad and Rita. Stickman put the palms of his hands upon Connie's shoulders.

"Damn, Sticky-man, I'm kidding," admonished Connie.

"Didn't sound like it to me, Con," replied Stickman.

Rita was speechless. *Who* are *these people?* she wondered. *They're constantly listening to each other's personal discourses, and it doesn't even faze them.*

"Rita," said Connie, taking Rita's hands into hers, "there's no way I meant what I said about kicking your behind. Forgive me if you can. I'm such a babysitter. I worry about everybody in the group. I feel like everybody's big sister."

Rita gently squeezed Connie's hands for a second. She sighed. "Good. Because honestly, you scared the dickens out of me."

"Dickens!" cried Stickman. "If you truly want to be a bad girl, that language has got to go. I'd be honored to tutor you. You won't learn bad language from Brad here. He thinks it's against his religion to cuss in front of women."

Leora, who had been standing right behind Stickman all this time, looked down and grinned at Stickman's description of Brad.

Rita opened her mouth to speak, but Stickman stopped her by holding up the palm of one of his hands. "In due time, my dear, learn to sport the leather first. Ride the Harley. Language later."

Rita grinned. "Agreed. My apologies to Brad and Connie."

Brad and Rita grinned at Stickman. He gently nudged them and Connie into a small group hug that lasted about five seconds. Rita and Connie were not ready to be buddies with each other yet;

that was for sure. Rita lightly patted Connie's back. The sensation was barely perceivable. Connie just rolled her eyes upward.

As this little group was getting back into place in line, Brad noticed Lee standing behind Stickman. She had been her nonintrusive self. Brad eyed her directly, but she did not notice him. She was paying attention to Stickman. Stickman eased one of his arms over Lee's shoulders—Stickman the protector. He was sure Lee had heard every word between Brad and Rita. And one of those tiny shards inched its way to press against Lee's heart for about three seconds. But it caused very little pain.

Was it reassuring to have Stickman nearby? It certainly was. She was definitely enamored of him. Any sign of affection from him was welcome.

"You okay?" Stickman asked into her ear softly, knowing that Brad was eyeing them carefully.

Lee smiled up at Stickman and nodded.

"Good enough for me. Now let's hope this assembly isn't outrageously boring. Of course, if it is, the group will be on hand to help it out!" He gave Brad a friendly wink, and Brad gave Stickman one nod of his head.

It was an interesting assembly actually. A man on the gym floor, with a microphone, directed differing groups of students to make noises that simulated a thunderstorm. It started with a group who merely snapped their fingers, to simulate the start of the storm. Next, another group clapped their hands to make it sound like harder rain. A third group gently tapped the toes of their shoes against the bleacher steps to imitate faraway thunder. Finally, the big thunder came from students who stomped on the bleacher steps. For about five minutes, the director of the storm changed the dynamics by pointing to a group to stop making sound or to make louder sound. Gradually, the director had the storm dissipate by having all the students easing up on the noise level. The final sound was the beginners snapping their fingers very lightly. It was fun. Even the group got into the action with enthusiasm.

Meet Your Uncle?

On a dull gray day, Brad and Rita sat on the grass near second base in the ball field as usual. They sat with their legs crossed, looking up at the cumulonimbus clouds.

"The clouds are coming at a fast clip," Rita observed.

"Yes, too fast to drop any precipitation upon us."

"I wouldn't mind getting wet, would you?" she asked.

They looked at each other.

Brad said, "And ruin that Rita-perfect hair?"

"I didn't realize my vanity about my hair."

"Of course, you're vain. It's simply beautiful."

"Yes, it is, isn't it? Say, Brad, I've been thinking it's time for me to meet your uncle."

"Oh boy," sighed Brad, "I've been waiting for this moment."

"It's been a long time since we started riding together. Destiny says it's time to take it to the next level."

They both laughed, knowing she meant nothing romantic.

Two days later, they got off Brad's motorcycle, put their helmets and black leather jackets on the seat, and approached a waiting uncle Bruce, standing just outside a horse yard in front of his log house. It was a large two-story home with three dormers and a wide front porch. On the porch, there were half a dozen yellow Adirondack chairs and three matching round tables.

Rita was impressive in her tight pink jeans, white halter top, and new white cowgirl boots. Her hair was pulled back in a loose

French braid. She beamed a smile at Brad just as they stopped in front of Uncle Bruce.

"Good afternoon!" Bruce greeted them cheerfully. Looking at Rita, he said, "You must be Rita. I've heard some very nice things about you."

Rita was the first one to extend a hand. Her handshake was firm but polite.

"It's a pleasure to finally meet you, Bruce."

"Bruce," said Brad, "I thought we'd get Stallion out for a run."

Bruce—who was five foot eight, more stout than his nephew, hair as black as obsidian—removed his black baseball cap to reveal a receding hairline. Other than the height and hairline difference between uncle and nephew, the family resemblance was obvious.

Bruce was wearing a dark-green cotton button-up shirt, blue jeans, and hiking boots. Brad was dressed in the same fashion.

"Stallion?" Uncle Bruce said. "Um…well, I suppose that would be fine. No offense, Rita, but it's been a few weeks since Stallion has had anyone on him. But I have the feeling you've ridden your fair share of horses in your lifetime."

"I've been riding since I was three if that helps you," Rita said very nicely.

Brad said, "I'll give him one of my horse lectures. That will help him behave himself."

That was true.

Brad and Rita rode Stallion together. They stayed out for two hours, just taking it easy with the horse, allowing him to saunter through Bruce's fields. Brad did make Stallion canter and gallop from time to time to get the restlessness out. Stallion was a retired stud and was not gelded. He was still frisky at times. But he obeyed Brad, and Rita was elated to be riding this horse with Brad.

But that day's cumulonimbus clouds did turn into rain at Bruce's ranch, and soon, Brad directed Stallion to the barn. Once they dismounted, Brad and Rita removed Stallion's saddle and blanket, bit and bridle and brushed him down for about half an hour while they chatted about many things.

A short while later, Bruce met up with Brad as Brad was walking from the barn to the house. Rita was already getting freshened up in Brad's bathroom upstairs.

"You're nuts if you're not crazy about that girl," Bruce said to his nephew. "She's stunning. She's every bit as beautiful as her sister Ingrid."

"We're just friends," Brad replied.

Bruce's jaw dropped, and he looked at Brad with eye wide. "You can't be serious."

"Yes, I'm serious. It will never be romantic."

"Have you and Rita ever discussed the friendship clause of dating?"

"It never crossed my mind," said Brad. "In fact, she's enlisting my help in getting my friend Darren to notice her."

"And how do you plan on doing that?" Bruce asked with a grin.

Brad shrugged his shoulders. "No idea."

"Is he a playboy?"

"Oh, he gets plenty of attention at school, but he has a girl-friend in Binghamton."

"Has he noticed Rita?"

"Oh yeah, but he has his head about him because of the girlfriend."

"Well, I like Rita, and she's welcome here any time, even if you're gone."

"Yes, she can be trusted on any of our horses."

There was a short pause.

"And she's serious about my friend Darren."

"Well, I wish her luck. As for you, nephew, if Rita hasn't tick-led your fancy, might I know who does? She must be quite the competitor."

Brad shrugged his shoulders again. "I don't think of her that way."

"So there *is* someone!" Bruce exclaimed gladly.

"I'll have you meet her someday. She's not like Rita, who was born with a million-dollar spoon in her mouth. Not many girls are as fortunate as Rita, the rich girl."

"Well, I promise I won't treat your friend based on Rita's background."

Brad smiled politely. "I didn't think you would."

That was the end of the subject of Brad and his female friends.

Party at the Thrift Store

Some of the group was on their way to a Salvation Army thrift store one Saturday morning. Leora drove them in her Vista Cruiser.

"I intend to have fun today," piped up Rita. "I've never been to one of these places except to drop off some of our used items."

Connie and Darren rolled their eyes upward.

Oh, brother, Darren thought, *she thinks she's being magnanimous.*

It was almost two hundred miles to Syracuse from home. About halfway there, Leora pulled the Vista Cruiser into a filling station. Everyone in the car pitched in a dollar for gasoline. The attendant topped off the gas tank with regular. He washed the back and front windshields and told Lee he would check the oil.

"It appears you're a quart low, ma'am," the attendant said to Leora who was seated behind the steering wheel. The attendant wore a gray cotton shirt with TEXACO embroidered in red on the right side of the shirt, and RON in red on the left side.

He showed Lee the oil dip stick. Lee just smiled at Ron. It appeared the car was low on oil because the oil was still hanging around the engine parts, not yet settled back into the oil pan. Bela had taught Lee about that ruse before she was behind the steering wheel of a car. She merely nodded at Ron and said, "Thank you."

Lee stayed in the Cruiser. Everyone else in the group had piled out of the Cruiser to use the restroom or to purchase potato chips and candy bars.

"Hey, Lee, you want a soda pop?" Darrell hollered from the station doorway. She turned toward him. He put a quarter into an upright red cooler that had Coca Cola embossed on the front. He opened the cooler door and pulled out a green Sprite bottle from its holder, popped the top off with the bottle opener attached to the cooler, approached Lee, and handed her the ice-cold bottle. She glugged the Sprite. It felt fantastic—the chill and the fizz together were refreshing.

The rest of the journey to Syracuse was full of people singing rock songs to the a.m. radio, talking, laughing, and smoking pot from the orange baby bong. The Cruiser sailed smoothly along Highway 81 to its destination. As soon as Lee got the car parked in the store lot, Adrian bolted from the car and made a beeline toward the front door of the store. He immediately made his way to the footwear department, which took up the entire back wall of the store. There was every sort of footwear imaginable there. It was Adrian's favorite department.

Instantly he spotted a pair of nearly new brown cowgirl boots small enough for Lee's feet. "Lee," he called to her once she had entered the store, "got something for you, honey, come on back here."

She approached Adrian. He handed her the boots. "Perfect for you. Try 'em on." He smiled at her brightly.

"Lee," said Rita, who had followed Lee to the footwear department, "I have a pretty ecru cowgirl hat at home that would fit you. You would look lovely."

Lee, holding on to the boots, looked at Rita and then at Adrian.

Adrian looked at Rita and said, "Gosh, thanks, Rita, that's really cool of you. Sweet."

Lee was speechless. Rita was a stranger essentially and the assumed subject of Brad's romantic intentions. Taking a gift from Rita seemed strange.

"I'll bring it to school sometime so you can try it on, okay?" Rita broke Lee's reverie.

"Surely, Rita, thanks so much!" was Adrian's contribution since he sensed Lee holding back. "Okay, Lee, honey, try on the boots." He had two wishes: (1) break Lee from her stupor and (2) make Rita, the rich girl, go away.

Lee slipped out of her Birkenstocks and slipped on the boots. It was a perfect fit. She walked up and down an aisle to get the feel of them. They felt as if they had belonged to her all along.

"They look lovely," said Rita.

"Thank you," Lee replied.

"Three bucks, Lee," Adrian piped up. "I can give you the money if you don't have it. You really should have these boots!"

But Lee was frugal. She had plenty of money that day—twenty dollars made from tutoring the students.

Connie had observed all this from the circular rack of winter coats nearby. She wondered if Rita would ever fit in with the crowd of less fortunate. Rita didn't have to be so formal and polite to the group. Maybe she would figure that out eventually. She seemed like a nice enough girl—not 100 percent full of herself, as she had seemed on day 1 of her meeting the group.

The group stayed and shopped for about an hour. Then the Vista Cruiser headed home. About halfway there, they stopped at an A&W root beer stand to get burgers and soda pops, served on platters that hung onto the top edge of the car's windows that were half lowered.

The Vista Cruiser made its way back safely. Lee parked it in the school parking lot to let her passengers out so they could get to their vehicles. They all said goodbyes 'round the group.

"Thank you for letting me go along with you today," Rita said to everyone else.

The response was "Oh, no problem, Rita. I hope you had fun," from Connie.

"Yes, I did."

She got into the waiting black Cadillac, and the rest of the group found their ways home in their own cars.

Darren drove his car with Darrell and Collin as passengers. He had a silver, eight-cylinder Pontiac GTO that he had resurrected in Kingston High School's auto shop.

"Gosh, Rita really behaved nicely today," Darrell remarked. "Maybe she's coming around."

"Don't know, brother," Darren responded.

"I think she likes us. We're good folks," said Adrian.

"That we are," Darren replied.

"I was concerned she would try to outwit us with her wealth and beauty," said Adrian. "I guess I was wrong. I'm glad."

Darrell said, "Truth is though, she's still on most guys' top 10 babes list."

"Ah, let her be there. She deserves it," Darren responded casually.

"Yeah, you're right. Right beside Leora," Adrian mused.

Brad Extends an Invitation

It was near the end of the school week, a few months after Brad had arrived at Kingston High School. Leora was at her car, her hand on the door handle, when she heard Brad's voice close by, "Hi, Lee, do you have a moment? May I speak to you?"

Lee was ready to get home, have a little supper, and hit the books until late at night for the big microbiology exam the next day.

He approached her. They stood facing each other, Lee standing inside the doorway of the car.

"I would like to know if you would join me at Mr. Warner's farm sometime so we can ride horses. I'd love it if you would say yes."

She was surprised by the invitation. She had always thought Rita was his only equestrian companion and possibly his girlfriend as well. So she did not know what to say. She blushed.

"I'm sorry," he said right away. "Am I too forward?"

She quickly regained composure and smiled at him. "No, no, you're fine. I just didn't know you were interested in riding with me. It's been a long time for me."

His heart sank a bit. *She doesn't want to go,* he thought.

"But if you can be patient with me, yeah, I'd like to do that," she said.

He sighed lightly, happily.

"Thank you, Lee. I'll be as patient as you need me to be. I've taught kids how to ride over the years, and with kids, you must be patient. It's a requisite, and I know you'll behave better than any kid I've taught."

She grinned at him.

"When can you come over?" he asked.

"Well, I have lots of homework tonight, and I want to call my grandpa. But any other afternoon would be okay. What about you?"

He grinned. *ASAP!* he thought. But he replied, "Tell you what. Whenever you're available, just let me know. I'll make the time for you."

"Well, tomorrow is the biology exam from Hades. I might feel like letting loose a little bit after that. How about after school tomorrow?"

He was delighted. Was he going to be able to put a soft rope around her heart? *Here's hoping,* he thought.

"I'll meet you right here in the parking lot. I'll have my cycle, of course. You can just follow me over there or ride with me, your choice. In any case, it isn't far. It's just south of here about ten miles."

Lee smiled. "Okay. All right. Sounds great to me. Thank you, Brad, you're awfully kind to invite me."

"Lee, it's my pleasure. I'll see you tomorrow."

"Okay."

Next to Lee's Cruiser was a big black Cadillac sedan with tinted windows. Inside the Cadillac, in the back seat, sat Rita. She had asked her driver to hold off leaving until she could see the entire course of action between Brad and Lee. She was satisfied when it was finished, so she ordered the driver to back out and leave the parking lot. On the way out, Rita pushed the button to lower her window and waved to Lee, who had just turned to notice the Cadillac moving. Lee smiled and waved to Rita, but she was puzzled as to why Rita would extend a friendly gesture to Lee after just seeing Lee with Brad.

God, maybe I should hold off going riding with him, Leora thought as she climbed into the Cruiser. She had a crush on Brad—a real crush, the kind that gives you pressure inside your chest. Though she would probably never tell him about it, she felt it nonetheless. She felt as if she were hanging in amorous purgatory. Brad was just too beautiful and handsome and kind to pass up. She wanted dearly to see where the crush would take her. Unfortunately, it would probably have to be up to Brad to move it along. What if he wasn't interested?

Leora feared the shards of disappointment and pain. They were lurking at the surface of her heart.

When Leora got home, she plopped her school books onto the dining table and called for her mother, who answered from the bedroom where she was lying down reading.

"Mom, I won't be home right after school tomorrow. I'm going horseback riding!"

"Oh my, that's a blast from the past, isn't it?" Sherry called.

"I'll say! Wish me luck that I don't fall on my ass and make a fool of myself!"

"Good luck, dear!"

"You must be reading a good book, Mother!"

"It's excellent! Sorry, I'm not coming into the kitchen!"

"No worries, we'll talk later?"

"Sure thing, honey!"

Good enough for Lee. She decided to relax by taking a hot shower, and then she climbed into comfortable pajamas in which she would study for the rest of the night. She called her grandpa Ed and had a short chat with him, and when they were finished talking, she started studying for the biology exam.

At about 9:00 p.m., Lee broke from her studying to call Jim on the phone.

He answered, "Hello!"

"It just occurred to me, Jim," Leora greeted him, "that you never mentioned the microbiology exam that's going on tomorrow. Please tell me you've studied at least for a couple minutes."

She cringed just awaiting the answer.

"I thought about you tonight, studying all by yourself the way you always do," he said in a somber voice. Then he perked up. "Want a tutor? I'm free all night."

"You didn't study at all, did you?"

"Ummm, no?"

"Ugh, I'm doing okay. I expect I'll get a 4.0 on it."

"Well, there you have it. I'm coming over anyway since you don't need to study any longer."

"But it's late."

"*Pff*, late schmate. I'll be there in a jiff."

He hung up the phone.

So there she was, getting ready to spend time with her favorite person while at the same time feeling as is if she could hardly wait to meet up with the other guy tomorrow. Would she be able to pull it off—keep the two guys from knowing about each other? Why wasn't Jim enough for Leora? She loved him truly. But Brad attracted her in a way no boy ever had. He was dark on the outside, and she sensed a bit of darkness on the inside as well. It pulled her into her shy curiosity.

PONY, ROAN, MARE

"Okay, Lee—pony, roan, mare," said Brad. Brad, Lee, the horses, and the pony were outside in the paddock, where the animals were hanging around waiting for a treat of grain. Brad entered the barn. Lee followed him. He grabbed an empty bucket and dipped it into a barrel of grain. They walked back to the paddock where he emptied the bucket into a small trough for the animals to have a treat, which they enjoyed with loud crunches. Brad figured he would have Lee start riding on the pony first.

"Okay," said Brad, "let's get the pony's saddle for you." He grabbed a beautiful brown one with white bead trim. It was the pony's best saddle.

"Can you carry this to the pony?" he asked Lee as he handed her the blanket and saddle. She took them and carried them with ease. Brad was impressed.

"Let's get her saddled up," he said.

Lee approached the pony. The pony did not move. She was very accustomed to having people roaming about her.

"You know how to put it on, or do you need help, Lee?" Brad asked.

"I'm okay," she replied and gently flopped the blanket and saddle onto the pony's back. Then she tightened the cinches on both sides. Brad handed her the bit and bridle, and she slid them on with ease. She moved the reins over the pony's neck so they rested on the saddle horn.

"Good job, Lee," said Brad. "Hell, we might as well get started. Can you get a foot in the stirrup, or shall I help you?"

"I think I need a boost unfortunately," Lee replied.

She placed one cowgirl boot into his cupped hands, and with his help, she hoisted herself up onto the pony's back. She took hold of the reins.

To the mare, Brad commanded, "Dandy, stand." Brad jumped onto Dandy's back. There was no saddle. Brad was going to ride bareback. Bit and bridle were already on the horse. He took hold of the reins. "Dandy, walk. Penny, follow."

Dandy and Penny cooperated. Dandy took the lead. They stopped at the meadow gate. Brad reached way down and unlatched the gate. After everyone entered the pasture, Brad bent down again and relatched the gate. They sauntered through the sixty-acre pasture that was shared with the cattle. Lee learned that Penny was a quick-witted pony with a sense of humor, obedient but playful too.

"Don't be surprised to be on your way over a wide stream or a huge hole in the ground or a worn-down barbed-wire fence," Brad said to her. "But that's only if you're not paying attention to the reins. Make sure to have them firmly in your grip—not tight—firm. Rita's been caught flying over the little stream in the orchard. She actually had fun, but it's better if you stay in control. Know what I'm saying? I know you can do it." He smiled at her.

Tiny shards of jealousy pinpricked her heart at the mention of Rita, but Lee said, "I'm a bit nervous. I'm afraid she's going to lurch forward and take off without me."

"Well, you won't be going solo for a few days. In that much time, you and Penny will figure each other out. And I'll be right with you—right *beside* you if you need me. But I don't think you're going to need me."

Lee sighed and smiled nervously.

"Come on," said Brad. "Let's go to the apple sapling orchard. It's really nice there."

The walk through the sapling orchard was indeed pleasant under the azure sky of only a few high cirrus clouds. They talked about anything that crossed their minds.

After about half an hour, Brad led the horses back to the paddock, side by side, voice-commanded, cooperative. Then Brad had

Lee practice mounting the pony without using the stirrups. Lee did this half a dozen times, and then Brad announced she passed the test.

"I think you're ready to be on your own," he said to her. "You really don't need much instruction. And I can tell Penny likes you by the way she leans upon you when you're standing next to each other."

"Thanks, Brad," Lee said. "You're too kind."

"Wait until I have you jumping her on command. The two of you are going to have a blast. Rita trains horses to jump, and she already has Penny going over the meadow fence! Naughty, naughty."

The pang from a surprise—a tiny shard—left a pinprick on Lee's heart at another mention of Rita. The pang was gone within a few seconds.

"So are you ready to wash them up and give them a good grooming?" Brad said cheerfully.

"Yes," Lee replied happily.

They had more conversations about a variety of subjects. When Brad was finished brushing down the mare, her jet-black coat was as shiny as obsidian. It was extraordinary. Penny had a beautiful brown coat, and Lee brushed her down very well. When Brad put Penny and Dandy out to pasture, Lee noticed Brad standing beside Dandy. Brad looked positively gorgeous in his hiking boots and dark-blue Henley shirt and blue jeans, deep blue eyes, and dark-brown skin. He grinned at Lee. When he got closer to Lee, he asked her if she had had a good time.

"Yes, very much so," Lee replied. "Thank you so much for thinking of me."

"No problem, Lee," Brad said brightly.

They went into the house. Brad showed her the bathroom on the first floor where she freshened up her face and hands. Then he walked her out to her car. They said their goodbyes with smiles on their faces. Brad was already wondering if she would ever ride horses with him in the near future. They waved to each other as soon as the Cruiser was out onto the road. It had been a great time for Lee. She hoped Brad would invite her over again sometime. The crush she had on him was growing stronger every day, and on this day, it was powerful.

DARREN'S QUESTION

Often, during free times at school, Brad, Rita, and Darren could be seen sitting on the grass just behind second base, engaged in chatter and laughter. It had started with the boys practicing pitching and catching the baseball. Darren was a first-rate pitcher, and Brad was an all-star catcher. One day, Rita had decided to amble into the ball field, and Brad had spotted her. He had stood up and waved her toward home base. The boys stopped practicing. That was the beginning of a three-way friendship.

Nobody interfered with their time and space. Leora did not seem to mind. At least, she showed no expressions. Who knows what she really felt? It was not in her nature to talk badly about anyone else, and she was not going to burst upon the scene and confront either Brad or Rita.

But when she admitted it to herself, Leora felt a shard of pressure against her heart when she saw Brad with Rita. She decided to avert her eyes to save herself any pain. She and most of the rest of the school students who were paying attention had figured Brad would eventually snag Rita for sure.

Rita, on the other hand, was in her glory trying to impress *Darren* of her beauty and humor. She used her impeccable English language. She flirted with him by touching his forearm lightly with her fingers when he made her laugh. She brushed pretend-dust from her skirt when she got up from the ground, making sure the skirt wiggled in front of Darren.

Darren did not mind any of this, of course. But he still had his girlfriend Suzette in Binghamton; he had some thinking to do. This kept him from acting upon impulse, but he was definitely intrigued by Rita, the rich girl.

A couple weeks after Rita had joined the boys on the ball field, Darren crossed his arms over his chest and said boldly, "Now, Ms. Rita, you must give us a synopsis of the wayward ways that led you to Kingston High School. We're all friends now. Out with it."

Rita stared at Darren for a few seconds. *Karma,* she thought. *I had the feeling today would be his day to ask me about this.* She sighed. "Okay. It's nothing swashbuckling. I made a mistake, and it cost me my friends and my education at my school for at least one term. Are you sure you want to know? It's boring, believe me."

"Oh, I'm asking, aren't I?" replied Darren seriously.

She looked at Brad. He looked back at her and merely shrugged his shoulders. "Your decision."

So she sighed again and started. "I call it Rita's Escapade."

RITA'S ESCAPADE

Rita was with her friends Sara and Bonnie in Boston one day. They had taken Rita's brand-new Mercedes Benz. They were on their way to the car from a shopping center when they were approached by two young men. The taller one asked for a ride.

Rita said, "Hop in."

This shocked the other girls. This was not usual behavior for Rita. Rita merely shrugged her shoulders at her friends.

The taller guy asked Rita to take them to Mansfield, a suburb of Boston. He directed Rita which way to go. He introduced his friend and himself as Robert and Herschel. Bonnie told the guys the girls' names. Herschel asked what school the girls attended.

Bonnie merely said, "A private school."

Herschel told the girls that he and Robert had dropped out of school in their senior year.

Go figure, Bonnie thought. She prayed to God that the guys weren't doing anything illegal by taking this ride in Rita's car. The guys wore old, faded blue jeans and shirts and old, worn-out tennis shoes.

Herschel piped up, "Does anyone want any hashish? It's very potent, great stuff."

Bonnie replied, "Please don't bring that stuff out. I don't want any trouble with the police."

Herschel shrugged his shoulders. "Okay."

Suddenly, *crash*! Rita's Mercedes rear-ended a brand-new red Mustang convertible. The driver of the Mustang motioned out his window for Rita to get onto the shoulder of the road. She did, but she was afraid to get out. She made her window go down with the push of a button.

The Mustang man was handsome. He had brown hair, brown eyes, tan face. He had Ray Bans pushed back onto his head. He instructed Rita to meet him at the next exit that had a filling station and that the police would be there to take a report. She followed the Mustang man there.

Bonnie, seated beside Rita, said to her, "Tell him who your dad is. Give him one of his business cards. Your dad's a prosecuting attorney for the state of Massachusetts. It will help."

Rita looked at Bonnie and at Sara, in the back seat. "Really?"

"Yes!" everybody else in the Mercedes replied.

So she did. "Please call my father. I can pay for the damages without getting the police involved."

So as Mustang Man was calling Rita's father on a pay phone, the occupants of the Mercedes were ordered out of the car. Herschel gave the cop the account of the collision, and the other occupants agreed with the details.

The cop wanted to search Rita's car. Rita, crying, gave him the keys. The cop found nothing amiss in the trunk, just a huge amount of shopping bags full of expensive stuff. But in the back of the car, on the floor behind the front passenger's seat, there was the hash Herschel had mentioned. The cop took it and told Herschel he was going to get frisked. Nothing was found. Then the cop searched Robert and found a pipe made of nuts and bolts. It had thick resin in it. The cop suspected Herschel of having left the hash in the car, so he arrested Herschel to the sound of Herschel cussing and hollering, "You can't pin that on me!"

The cop arrested Robert for having the pipe on his possession but promised to go lightly on Robert. "You seem more of a sidekick than a criminal," the cop said.

The cop took off with Herschel and Robert. Then Mustang Man told Rita he and Rita's father had struck a deal. Rita would use a bit of her large trust fund to pay for the repairs to the Mustang.

"*Thank* you!" Rita said to Mustang Man.

But all was not well. Rita arrived home. The maid greeted her at the door.

"Rita, your father is in his study waiting for you."

"Thank you." Rita placed the shopping bags at Greta's feet.

Rita entered the study. It was a large room with dark oak wainscoting and one big window that looked out upon one of the horses pastures. The desk was dark oak as well, as were the two desk chairs. There was a large television mounted onto the wall across from the desk. In front of the television, there was a burgundy leather sofa and a table with a lamp on it.

"Greta said you wanted to see me, Father?"

"Yes, I did," he replied as he indicated the chair for her to sit. "I'm taking you out of school here for a while. You're going to live with your aunt and uncle in Kingston."

"What? Why?" Rita fought hard not to cry.

"You could have put Bonnie and Sara in danger. You had no idea what kind of men those two were. You're lucky you didn't get arrested along with them. I want you to see how the over half lives, the half who can't afford to brush their troubles away aside with money and connections. And no talking to Bonnie or Sara until I say it's all right. You've embarrassed me to their parents, and they want their girls to take a break from you."

There was a short pause.

"I can get you into Kingston High School next week. Your uncle's driver will take you to and from school. I don't want you accepting rides from any of the students there. Do you understand?"

"Yes, Father, I understand. And I apologize for being foolish. I thought I was just helping someone get a ride."

"No need to apologize to me. Some day you might want to apologize to Bonnie and Sara for putting them into potential harm."

"Yes, I'll do that. May I go now? I want to put my new clothes in the cedar closet and get ready for dinner."

"Of course, I'll see you at the dinner table."

"Thank you."

Dinner was a somber affair for Rita. Luckily her father did not mention the incident. He did not want her siblings to know about it. Her mother already knew from an earlier conversation with Mr. Armstrong. Her mother eyed her with a look of disdain. Rita tried to ignore it. She ate her dinner quickly and asked to be excused. Her mother nodded her head, and Rita left the table. She went to her bedroom and started packing for an extended stay at her uncle's horse ranch. She went to bed that night with a heavy heart.

BRAVO!

"Bravo!" said Darren as he clapped his hands after he heard "Rita's Escapade."

"Rita with a rap sheet," he said. "Now that's something I would like to see."

"I am sorry to disappoint you, Darren, but I highly doubt I will be in any more trouble than I am now—being forced to attend Kingston—no offense to any of you! I won't be getting any points on my driver's license since the Mustang guy and I struck the hush-hush deal. I'm actually relieved. I would be embarrassed by points on my license. I probably do deserve some though. I've been caught speeding a couple times, and the policemen were gracious enough to let me go, probably knowing I'm the worst driver around."

"Oh, that's classic," remarked Darren. "Get it into your little noggin that you're gorgeous, and that's why they let you get away with it. Consider yourself lucky to have such good looks."

"I don't take my looks for granted. I don't use them to benefit me."

"I don't mean to offend you. I'm just telling you the truth."

Rita replied, "Thank you, I think."

Darren asked her, "Did you ever find out the rap sheets on those two guys?"

"Oh my, yes, breaking and entering, attempted burglary, unarmed robbery, possession of marijuana, drinking underage…you name it, they've probably done it. The stuff thugs are made of. I just hope they get their act together in prison—you know, get an education, get out of there ready to settle down, and get a real job. Hard to tell. I don't know anything about their upbringings."

"Yes, the way we are raised can be so impactful," said Darren.

"I have good parents. I think my dad went overboard with me, but I can't stop that. I do miss my girlfriends though. Sara's my best friend, but Bonnie is my protector. She's like an older sister."

"What does Ingrid think of your little outing with the juvenile delinquents?" Darren asked.

Rita sighed. "Oh, I suppose she thinks I'm tainted now. She has a superiority complex, I believe. But I can't change how she feels about me. If she doesn't like me anymore, so be it. I can have my so-called sisters who aren't blood-related. My brother and other sister don't know what happened with those thugs and me. Probably never will. I don't intend to tell them. It's an embarrassment."

Poor Rita, thought Darren. *She really is sheltered. I hope it doesn't ever cause her emotional damage.*

"Well, Rita," he piped up. "I appreciate you for telling us what happened. You will get over it. No worries. You have friends here, you know. We will make your stay at Kingston as pleasant and fun as possible. Clean fun if need be."

Promise? Rita thought. But to Darren, she said, "Thank you, Darren, that means a lot to me. I know I can trust you."

"Of course, you can," commented Brad. "Darren here is top-notch." He thought, *Ingrid is another story. I can imagine her getting her digs in on behalf of Rita's mistake. Well, my lips are sealed.*

Rita grinned very widely and touched Darren's arm with her fingers. He grinned back at her. No words. Darren did have the sense to remember his girlfriend, Suzette, in Binghamton. Darren had told his girlfriend about Rita, the rich girl, and Suzette had remained neutral. She was not jealous. He liked Suzette very much and admired her intelligence (4.0 GPA). She did not attempt to change his personality or to cling to him. He appreciated her not expecting to see him every night of the week. It was a pleasant, if void of passion, relationship. Rita affected him differently. Her flirtatious nature offered Darren the mild allure of sexuality.

FINAL LESSON, MOON SHADOW

"Final lesson, Lee," Brad said to her one evening, day number 4 of the horseback riding lessons that had spanned about a month. Lee was exiting the Vista Cruiser, which she had parked next to the side stoop of Mr. Warner's house. Brad's boots made a crunching sound in the gravel as he approached the Cruiser. He tipped his cowboy hat up and back to reveal his forehead. *My god, what a handsome man,* Lee thought. She wanted to avoid him. For some reason, she was self-conscious suddenly. She was slightly nervous but could not put her finger on the reason. Maybe she thought he was much too good for her, too good-looking, too worldly. Brad took her by the hand—palm to palm. She loved the sensation of his callouses, and the warmth of his hand soothed away the desire to get away from there. He looked down at her as they sauntered toward the paddock.

"I remember the time I first shook your hand, the day we met. I was very impressed."

"Really?" She looked up at him.

"Yes, very firm. From the balance beam perhaps? I've watched you on the balance beam at times when there's basketball practice."

"I don't know what to say. I don't think I'm good at all." She blushed. She had never noticed him watching her practice on the balance beam.

"Well, Lee, I wonder if that's true. In any case, what I think would be fun is if you and I would join each other on the trampoline sometime. What do you think?"

She chuckled. "Let's practice some first."

"I understand. I can't catch a baseball to save my life unless I practice."

Okay, she thought, *let's be frank here.*

"I've seen you play many times. Almost every ball you hit is destined to leave the field. And you're highly regarded as a catcher."

"I guess you got me there," he admitted.

So serious she looked. But there were those gray-green eyes again. She possessed a speck of mirth in those eyes. She was so pretty.

He pointed straight toward the meadow. He stood behind her and put his hands upon her shoulders. He was gently pressed against her back. They both felt a warm rush throughout their bodies.

"Okay, you're on your own," Brad said to her. "Fetch a bucket of grain and fetch the roan, not the pony. That would be too easy. I want you to catch and ride the roan."

He grinned, moved to stand beside her, and put his arm over her shoulder. He looked down at her profile—soft, healthy olive-toned skin, and that gorgeous short black hair tucked back behind her ears. "You can do this, Lee. I wouldn't say it if I didn't believe it."

She grabbed the left sleeve of his dark-blue cotton shirt with her left hand and sighed. She felt his firm abdomen and felt him breathing. A warm sensation went through her.

But he had never told her she would have to catch the roan and ride him! Now what?

"Me ride Sage? Whew. Okay, this is it. Oh, gawd, I am so embarrassed."

"Hmm" was all Brad said. But that sound reverberated from Lee's head to her toes. Masculine. That was the feel of it.

She blushed. He did not blush. That made him even more attractive to her. He had control.

Small Leora trudged through the waist-high meadow in her Salvation Army thrift store cowgirl boots. Hugging the plastic bucket of grain against her tummy, she spotted the roan about two hundred feet away at the east end of the meadow. There was shade beside the fence there, and the horse was sniffing the ground lightly and exhaling, making little poofs of dust on the ground.

Sage sensed Lee approaching him. He looked up—alert, ears upright. Then he sauntered toward the grain bucket. The bucket! Lee had forgotten she was holding it. She offered the grain to Sage. He looked into Lee's eyes.

"Go on, Sage, it's yours, honey," she said to the roan. She felt a bit nervous since Sage was a tall horse, and Lee had not taken any time to get to know him. Brad had tricked her into complacency by having her ride that pony! Thinking about that for a few seconds, Lee actually smiled.

Sage was completely cooperative. The bit and bridle slid on with ease. "Sage, stand," Lee commanded. Lee swung her neck back to look at Brad, and her beautiful black hair followed the motion.

Brad gave Lee two thumbs-up.

Lee jumped onto Sage—leaped was more like it, after an actual running start—and hauled herself over so she was sitting bareback. She took hold of the reins.

"*Damn*," Brad said to himself. "She did it. She got on that giant horse."

Lee commanded Sage to gallop. The big horse took off in a jolt. He went all over the place. He was powerful. She felt free. She let go of fear and allowed herself to have a great time.

Lee went through the commands—canter, gallop, trot, and finally walk. She finally led him to Brad, who was seated on the fence near the barn, swinging his feet in the tall meadow weeds.

"This horse is amazing," she said, nearly breathless.

Brad grinned at the horse and then at her.

God, he is a beautiful man, she thought.

"You looked comfortable out there. Am I right? I think you and I should take some nice, long rides together. Do you agree?"

Lee did not know what to say. She said nothing. She was thinking of Rita.

"Hey, are you all right? I'm sorry if I'm being too forward."

She managed a smile. "I…oh no, Brad…you're absolutely fine. I think we would have a great time. Yes."

"But?"

"Don't *trick me*—she leaned over the horse and slapped one of his knees—with a different horse!"

She did not smile, but her eyes did.

"You took my joke very well." Brad chuckled. "I am really impressed. Thank you for not being furious with me."

"Not furious. Shocked at first. But I got over it. He's a great horse."

"Indeed, he is. He must like you. He was completely cooperative."

"Thank you. I do have a question though if you don't mind."

"Of course, I don't mind," Brad replied. "Anything."

"How do I say this? What about Rita? Would she ride with us?"

He frowned, puzzled. "Well, of course, she's welcome to join us if she wants to, don't you think? But it's okay if it's just you and I too. Come to think of it, maybe we could invite Darren to ride along. Catch my drift?"

"Yeah," she said with a grin, but she had no idea what he meant. She and Rita were not close friends. She did not know Rita had a crush on Darren.

He left Jim out of the conversation deliberately to see how she would comment on him.

Lee was befuddled. But she went along with it. "Those two would be a sight to see."

"Then it's a date," Brad said confidently. He looked into Lee's eyes and gave her a slight, friendly nod of his head.

He was smitten with her—*her*—not just the small, olive-skinned beauty. She was humble without being false. Her voice was just a mild, even pitch. Her smile was always even, never exaggerated. She was even-tempered. She seemed mysterious, but at the same time, she seemed to be like an open book! How could that be? But he loved her. Of that he had no doubt.

As they led the horse to the paddock, Lee held the reins. Brad walked beside her. He and Lee swayed gently in the same directions and lightly brushed their bodies against each other's. It felt natural to both of them. She felt warm and protected.

Brad asked her, "So do you have a favorite place to go to be alone?"

"Oh yes," Lee replied. "There's a little pond behind a farmhouse where I used to skate as a kid. It's a tranquil place."

"Sounds nice," said Brad.

"Yeah, I haven't been there in a couple years. I don't know if the pond is even still there."

"Too busy to go back?"

"Maybe."

"You do a lot of things, Lee—tutoring students, helping your mom at the dry-cleaner's, visiting your grandfather, working for Mr. Biology, studying. Have I missed anything? No wonder you can't get back to your pond."

"I think my favorite is seeing my grandpa. He loves the company. For some reason, he loves Jim to pieces." Instantly she thought, *I'm never that forward. Why the hell did I do that to Brad?*

"I think almost everybody loves that Stickman, don't you?" Brad said cheerfully.

"Maybe so" was all Lee could think of to say.

The straw and hay, as always, smelled fresh and clean. Lee slipped off the bit and bridle and hung them on the wall inside Sage's stall. Brad helped Lee give Sage a good brushing down. They chatted the entire time, light conversation. Then she led Sage to his stall, kissed him on the neck, and said, "Good night, Sage." She closed the stall gate and latched it. Sage appeared completely relaxed.

Lee turned toward Brad.

"Leora," he said. He gently put the palms of his hands on the top of her head.

She looked up into his kind eyes. She just then noticed it was quite dark in the barn, which meant nightfall was fast approaching outside.

"Come," he said, "I want to show you something."

He took her by the hand and led her to the south side of the barn, still inside. He led her up a set of stairs she had never noticed before then. At the top, there was a landing. They turned left, and there he turned a brass knob on a bare oak door. He opened the door. To the left, on the wall, was a light switch. He flipped that on, and there was subdued lighting throughout a large room.

"Come, look outside over the meadow," he said. He led her across the room—shiny oak floor, tan walls, and light-brown window coverings. There was a double bed on the south wall. A bathroom could be seen from across the foot of the bed.

They stood before a huge picture window that faced the meadow.

"Can you see how the light on the top of the barn casts its shadow over the meadow? The shadow goes all around the barn and outward. Isn't it something?"

Lee said, "Almost iridescent. It's so pretty."

"When it's a full moon out, the real moon shadow takes over, but it gives out the same timbre as the light above the barn. It bathes the farm in an almost silver light."

"When did you first notice that?"

"Oh, a long time ago. One night when I was putting a tractor into the barn. It can be mesmerizing to me."

"Definitely. I've seen the moon shadow over my pond too."

"How can you not pause and feel your heart settle down?" he asked.

They looked at each other.

Now what? she thought. Her heart beat a bit faster than normal. She tried to stifle a giggle but failed. She felt as if they were in the middle of a Hallmark romance.

"What?" he asked casually.

"I can't. Really. It's nonsense."

"Hmmm, I'll get it out of you some day."

"You probably will. I have no doubt," she replied.

There was a pause.

"In the meantime—" he said, and he grabbed her around her waist and pulled her up. She straddled his waist with her legs and hugged his neck. He walked her to his bed and gently lay her down onto her back. He lay beside her on his side and propped himself up with an elbow, resting his face in one of his hands. They looked at each other. She made a move, but he placed a strong leg over her knees.

She licked her lips because they felt dry suddenly. He whole being felt dry. She had imagined a different sensation in her fantasies of moments like this one. *What's wrong with me? Maybe a bit scared of letting go of feelings? Or a bit leery of him because he seems to have sexual experience?*

She looked at him shyly and asked, "Are we going to—"

He bent his face down and whispered into her ear, "I would love to. Indeed, I would."

She felt that amazing chill you can get when you've been seduced, and you know he's not going to say or do anything that will kill the moment because he's adept at this. She enjoyed herself as he gently kissed her ear, forehead, cheeks, her neck, the sides of her small nose. He opened her mouth with his tongue gently and offered her a long, wonderful kiss. She opened her eyes and met his gaze.

He rolled onto his back and looked at her again.

"This room is where I like to be when I want to be alone."

"You don't live here?"

"No."

She wondered if Rita ever visited this place. She fought back the sting of a forthcoming tear that she would not allow to appear. One small shard stung her heart, but it was gone as quickly as it had arrived.

Brad cleared his throat self-consciously. "Do you mind if I brush my teeth?"

She giggled. "Of course I don't mind."

"I know it's a weird thing to say, but I want to freshen up my mouth for you."

"Heavens," she said, "what about me?" *He probably keeps spares for his other women,* she guessed to herself.

Wrong.

"Oh, you're welcome to use my toothbrush. I always rinse it in extremely hot water. We'll be fine sharing it."

"Okay." She chuckled. He gave her a big grin. *Pray to God Rita has never touched it,* she thought.

He got out of bed and sauntered to the bathroom. He pulled a golden chain from above the sink, and a soft white light went on. He left the door open while he brushed his teeth.

Then he said, "Okay, dear, your turn."

She scooted to the foot of the bed and met him at the bathroom sink. He was handing her his toothbrush when there were two knocks on the main door to the room.

They looked at each other. For the life of her, Lee saw *nothing* in his face that indicated embarrassment or oops or uh-oh of any kind. He shed his shirt. She admired his sculpted arms and chest beneath his white tank top. She took the toothbrush and closed the door after he made his way to the main door. He reopened the bathroom door and looked at her seriously.

"I won't hide anything from you. Please leave it open so we can see who's here."

She nodded her head in agreement. She turned off the water for the time being and stood in the bathroom doorway while he approached the main door.

"Yes?" he said.

"Brad? Hi, it's Mrs. Warner. Just making sure everything's all right here. I didn't know if you were going to spend the night. Hope I'm not—"

Brad swung open the door to reveal a surprised Mrs. Warner. She entered the room.

"Ma'am, this is my good friend Leora. Lee, this is the most excellent Mrs. Warner."

"Oh, Brad," said Mrs. Warner, "such a way with words." And she said to Lee, "I'm very pleased to meet you, Leora. What a pretty name."

"Oh! Thank you. It's very nice to meet you too."

Brad said to her, "Please come in."

The dimly lit room lent a romantic sensation to the place. Wasn't Mrs. Warner aware of that? Wasn't it obvious to her?

"Oh no, that's okay. Just checking on things. Will you be staying here tonight?"

"No, Mrs. Warner," he replied. "I'll be going home in a few hours or so. Uncle Bruce is awaiting the birth of a calf, and he might need my help still tonight."

"Maureen! Are you up there bugging our young man by any chance?" came Mr. Warner's voice from the bottom of the stairs. Yeah, he was aware that his wife was being nosy. Nice, but nosy.

Mrs. Warner let out a fake moan and waved at Brad and Lee. "Good night."

"Good night," they replied to her.

Brad closed the door gently. "No lock on the door," he said with a sheepish look on his face.

"I can tell they're very fond of you," Lee said. She turned toward the bathroom sink. After her teeth felt sparkly clean again, she and Brad sat on the foot of his bed. She put the palm of one of her hands upon one of his knees. With her other hand, she gently stroked his hands, shoulders, arms, neck, face.

"That feels wonderful, you know," he said.

She did not know what to say. She merely smiled at him.

"May I touch you?" he asked.

"Yes."

"I'll stop anywhere and anytime you ask me to."

"Okay."

"Or not."

She covered her mouth with the palm of her hand and laughed. "Shit!"

He said, "This is kind of a goofy first date, isn't it?"

"But the best," she responded after removing her hand from her mouth.

"Seriously?"

"Yes, seriously."

"Okay, now I *have* to touch you. Luckily, I have permission already. If not, I'd be lying here suffering."

She chuckled.

He was kind to her. She was overjoyed with his touch as he studied every part of her with his fingers, his hands, his mouth. She was overwhelmed with lust. She retained a slow, steady breathing, which allowed her to relax and bask in the sensations. He did not demand or expect any attention in return; she was free to respond when and how she wanted to. She was shy about it, and he knew that, but he was responsive to her touch and grateful to her for pleasing him.

"I don't want to spoil this, but would you lie under the covers with me? It's getting cold in here." he said.

He held her hands and helped her stand up. They pulled back a thick comforter and two top sheets. They removed their boots. He untucked her blouse and unbuttoned it slowly. She obliged by removing the blouse. He gently unzipped her jeans and slid them from her body. Then he took off his tank top and jeans.

He whispered to her, "I'm not going to take any more of your clothes off. Keep your socks on too. I don't want your feet to get chilly."

They snuggled under the covers. He held her as she rested her cheek on his bare chest.

"Brad."

"Yes?"

"I snore sometimes."

"Oh shoot, so do I."

"Oh, good. But it's not ladylike for a female to snore, is it?"

"Believe me, you're all female."

She blushed during a short pause.

"Lee, may I touch you some more?"

"Yes, of course, please."

She sighed gently, and one tear touched her cheek. Luckily, it landed on her and not on his chest. He was unaware of it.

She felt spoiled by him. But she felt a bit nervous and admitted that to him.

"Nervous feels mighty fine over here on my end," he replied. "I'm loving this. You feel warm and welcoming. Couldn't be better."

She sighed again. "You're so kind to me."

He kissed her forehead and looked her in the eye. "We don't have to say anything right now. I have Leora Sovine in my bed with me. Talk about lucky. I can't think of a nicer surprise."

He gave her a long, luscious, moist kiss.

"Will you sleep under the covers with me for a while? I have to set the alarm for about three in the morning. I'll make sure you get home safely."

They kissed and played with each other's bodies for a while, to the point of making love numerous times, and when they were finally tired, they spooned beneath the covers. They were both asleep in a few minutes.

At 3:00 a.m., Brad's bedside alarm clock radio awakened him gradually. It had been set to play the radio softly at first and louder each minute for three minutes. It took the full three minutes to wake him up completely. He tapped the button on the top of the clock radio so the music would cease playing. Lee slept through it all. He gently woke her up with a kiss on her cheek.

"Gotta get up," he said softly. "I don't believe this particular calf is going to get born on his own. He's awfully large." He kissed her quickly on the lips. "Do you want to sleep some more? I can come and get you in time for school. You're so warm. I wish we both could stay."

"I want to go with you," Lee said.

"Honestly?"

"Yes."

"All right then," Brad announced. "It's you, the calf, and I."

He held onto her for about half an hour more, and then they got up, showered together, and dressed. After they shared the tooth-brush again, Lee asked him, "Are the horses up yet?"

"No, but soon," replied Brad. "Mr. Warner feeds them bright and early usually." He looked right at her and said, "You are so... adorable, that's the word. Warm and wonderful too. I was going to say cute, but that's not the right description."

"You can't be serious, but thank you."

"Oh, I'm serious all right. Do you have any idea what you do to me with that small body of yours? Even right now at three in the morning!"

She blushed and laughed and caressed his cheek with the palm of her hand.

He smiled at her. Together, they tossed the covers over the bed in a perfunctory manner. Then they quietly descended the steps, sneaked through the barn, walked out onto the crunchy gravel driveway—which seemed so loud, Lee was concerned it would awaken Mr. and Mrs. Warner, but it did not—under the faux moon shadow cast by the light on top of the barn, and into the Vista Cruiser.

Then they were on their way down winding blacktop roads toward Bruce's place. Lee drove carefully. She had her window down a bit for clean, fresh air while the heater kept them comfortable. Brad sat next to her and put the palm of his hand against the back of her neck the entire way there. It gave Lee a warm feeling. They chatted quietly along the way.

THE CALF

When Brad and Lee arrived at Bruce's place, he suggested she drive right up to the front of the house. She did so and then shut off the engine of the Cruiser. It was dark and silent outside. They walked around the house to one of the barns, the one that held twenty head of Angus cattle. It was quiet in the barn too, but the lights inside were as bright as daylight. They approached one of the stalls, and there was a mother cow nursing her newborn calf.

"He came out all by himself" came from behind them. It was Bruce. He was beaming. He approached Brad and Lee.

Brad said, "I'm glad it all worked out. Sorry I'm late."

"No problem."

"Bruce, this is Leora Sovine."

Bruce beamed again. He shook her hand readily. "So nice to meet you, young lady. Did you come to help out?" He winked at her.

She stammered as she looked at Bruce.

"Oh, I'm just kidding," said Bruce with another wink.

Lee looked up at Brad. She did not know what to say. Brad held her hand to make her feel comfortable.

"Well, anyway, mom and baby are doing fine," said Bruce. "I'm going to cut the lights way down. I think the calf is going to go back to sleep after he nurses to his content."

"Okay," said Brad. "We're going to head up to the house and get a couple more hours of sleep in before school starts."

"Good deal," said Bruce.

Up to the house they went in the dark, entered the house, and went upstairs to Brad's room. It resembled the room in the Warners' barn—simple, masculine, window looking out onto one of the pastures, small attached bathroom.

Brad took her into his arms and gave her a long, soothing kiss, and then he released her.

"Sigh…who needs sleep?"

She laughed. "I do!"

"I know. I do too. Come to bed with me. I promise to behave myself somehow."

They tossed back a heavy comforter and a heavy blanket and a top sheet. It was warm in the room, much warmer than it was in his room at the Warners'. Nonetheless, they climbed into bed fully clothed, spooned immediately, and fell asleep within a couple minutes. Neither one of them had thought of setting any kind of alarm. Bruce woke them up at 6:30 a.m. Brad treated Lee to a breakfast of scrambled eggs, toast, and orange juice, which she took in gratefully. While Lee was upstairs freshening up, Bruce and Brad were still in the kitchen.

"She's absolutely beautiful, Brad," Bruce said seriously. "Kind of the quiet type, but there's nothing wrong with that. You're a lucky guy."

"Thank you, but she doesn't know how I feel about her. I don't want to drive her away, seeing as I'm an ex-con."

"Some girls are attracted to bad guys gone good. That's what you are."

"Hmmm" was all Brad said. That ended the conversation. Lee descended the stairs and turned right to enter the kitchen. She and Brad left the house hand-in-hand. Then they were off, on their ride to fetch his motorcycle at the Warners' place. They did not see Bruce grinning from ear to ear for his nephew. There were few young ladies in this world as beautiful as the young Leora.

At the Warners', Brad gave Lee a wonderful kiss and a warm, firm hug.

"God, you're beautiful," he sighed.

Lee blushed and said a shy, "Thank you."

She watched his every move as he exited the Cruiser, put on his leather coat, helmet and gloves, and started the motorcycle. It was completely cooperative. It had a nice, deep hum to it. Brad drove his motorcycle carefully on the winding blacktop roads. Lee followed him at a safe distance. They drove into the school parking lot that way, and he parked his motorcycle far from the other vehicles, as usual. He met her at her car, and together, they walked onto the campus.

"See you at lunch," he said to her.

She smiled demurely. "Yes, you will."

He grazed the back of one of her hands with the fingers of one his hands, which sent an electric charge from her head to her toes. Then they parted ways. She smiled to herself.

Lee could not think of anyone with whom she could share her gladness, except perhaps Sandy, but if Sandy ever inadvertently said something to Jim, it might break his heart, and it would most definitely break Lee's heart if Jim was hurt. Lee suffered a small shard of disappointment, knowing she had to stifle her happiness. It did not seem fair. She had to keep the wondrous warmth of Brad to herself.

When she arrived home that afternoon, Sherry and Bela were already home from work. Their faces looked grim with worry and anger. A huge shard pierced Lee's heart. It had never occurred to her to tell her parents she would be spending the night with some guy, a guy they did not know, no less.

"I am so sorry, Mom and Dad," she said with complete sincerity. "I spent the night with Brad, and about three this morning, we went out to his uncle Bruce's place to watch a calf being born."

"Brad?" Bela repeated. "Bruce? I thought you were going with Jim."

"Brad's a classmate of mine," Lee explained, fearing they did not believe her. "Bruce owns Angus cattle and show horses. Brad works at a cattle ranch and lives with his uncle. He has a loft at the cattle ranch where he can sleep if it gets too late to drive home." She wondered if it made any sense.

"You couldn't call? We called Jim, but he had no idea where you were," Sherry said.

Lee's heart sank. What was she going to say if he asked her where she had been? How in the world was she going to avoid the subject with him?

"I promise, *promise* to let you know if I'll be late getting home from now on."

"Question," Sherry said. "What about birth control? I guess I never asked you about it with regard to Jim. I've been remiss big time."

"Oh, we didn't need any birth control. Jim and I haven't had sex."

"You mean you didn't have intercourse, I imagine. There is more than one way to have sex," Sherry replied.

Lee blushed. She knew she was not going to get away with even a white lie.

"Right," she said. "No intercourse. Not with Jim anyway. With Brad, it's the real thing."

Sherry asked, "Honey, do you think it's time to get you on the pill?"

Lee sighed and replied, "I guess it's a good idea. Are you ashamed of me?"

"God, no, of course not," Sherry replied, shaking her head no.

"Just worried that you were coerced into having sex with some bad guy," Bela explained, "or might get knocked up way too early in your life."

"To be truthful, I'd rather abstain," Lee said to them.

Sherry said, "It takes so little to get pregnant. You can even do it with your clothes on. Trust me, we know!"

"Oh God, please don't tell me about how I was conceived. I'd rather it be a secret."

"No problem," Sherry said, "but please take my word for it. You should get on the pill. You can't trust the guy to make the right decision. I'll make an appointment with my doctor, and he'll set you up."

"I seem so young," Lee complained.

"It's okay. You'll be fine. None of your friends need to know," said Bela. "Hell, you might be surprised to know how many school girls are taking the pill."

"How would *you* know?" Lee asked, surprised.

"They treat me like a counselor. You wouldn't believe the stuff they tell me in confidence. I always toss them over to the social worker. I never close the classroom door either when I am alone with any girls there. They could spell horrible trouble for me. I don't trust any one of my female students except you and Sandy, and Sandy has the good sense not to talk to me about boys and sex."

"Yeah, Sandy's a gem, that's for sure. I never thought of her as a girl who has sex, but I could be hiding my head in the sand. I hope she can talk to her parents about it if she needs to go on the pill."

"This is the seventies. Everybody's going wild on sex these days," said Sherry. "It's nothing new. In my day, premarital sex was practically a crime, but so was birth control, even natural methods. There were standards that got many girls into trouble with their parents and society."

"I'm glad you two aren't angry with me." Lee cleared her throat to kick back a tear. "And I'm thankful that you were brave enough to get married and take care of me."

"Well," said Bela, "I think we've all said enough. Let's all go into the kitchen so we can bother your mother while she tries to make dinner around us."

Lee chuckled. She couldn't resist him; she had to give him a hug, followed by giving her mother one too.

"You're on, you two," Sherry said sprightly.

In Absentia

Homecoming was odd for Rita this season. She was elected queen by her classmates at her high school in Boston. She learned about it from a phone call from her father after she got home from school.

"Congratulations, dear, you're homecoming queen."

"You mean at Kingston?" she asked.

"No! Here! At home!"

"Oh no! Father, what should I do? Am I even allowed to go there for homecoming?"

"Well, of course, you are, my daughter. You'll be there side by side with Paul Whitcomb. Number 1 handsome according to your little sister."

Doesn't hold a candle to Darren was Rita's response in thought. But to her father, she said, "Oh, he's a dream that's for sure." Because he was—tall, blond, handsome, self-centered. He had been Rita's type until she met Darren.

Her father said he would get her all the details as soon as possible. She was abuzz with anticipation. Homecoming no less! And her father was going to allow it—biggest surprise of all!

When Rita arrived at Kingston the next morning, her driver said, "Have a good day, my queen." Rita grinned and patted him on the shoulder before exiting the Cadillac.

During homeroom announcements, another surprise hit Rita. She was elected homecoming queen at Kingston too, with none other than Darren as her king. It was hardly a surprise. Nearly everybody at Kingston considered those two as destined to spend time together in fame of some sort. But when Rita heard her name attached to homecoming queen, she burst out laughing. Everyone else in the homeroom looked at her as if she were something odd.

"I just got chosen for homecoming queen in absentia back home!" she explained.

The room was abuzz with animated conversations.

She had to find Darren as soon as homeroom was finished. She located him at his locker. She skipped up to him and planted her arm over his shoulder. "Hey, my king."

"Oh geez, can you believe it? I mean *you belong* on the homecoming court. Me—I see it as kind of hokey, know what I mean?" For a few seconds, he wondered if he was even going to call his girlfriend in Binghamton to give her the news. Would she see it as hokey too? Probably not. Not as excitable as Rita, she nonetheless would be pleased for Darren. *Okay, I'll tell her,* he thought.

"Oh, too bad, my dear. But there's more. My dad told me I was chosen homecoming queen back home too."

"No kiddin'," said Darren, surprised.

"And he's going to let me do the whole homecoming court thing. I think he still likes me."

"Or he's being egotistical."

"Yes, there's that for sure," Rita admitted. "Nonetheless, I hope both homecomings aren't on the same date!"

They were. Bubble burst. Rita had to choose which homecoming court to be on. It was a difficult decision for her. She had grown to be very fond of the students at Kingston and vice versa. How heartbreaking and seemingly rude it would be to eliminate Kingston from her choice! She did not want receive hard feelings from them.

She left Darren at his locker. He was not the least bit surprised that she would vanish as quickly as she had arrived. Typical flighty girl. Too bad he was not able to sit at the court with someone more subdued—someone such as Sandy or Lorrie or Leora. He sighed, suddenly resigned. *It's only one night of torture,* he thought.

A Change of Heart

Homecoming week was turning out to be a nightmare. Rita had to get her hair cut and styled, her toenails and fingernails painted, and she had to purchase a gown. Her mother accompanied her to all the necessities, but Rita was not feeling excited about any of it. She was overwhelmed with the attention she was getting at Kingston, but she longed for the girlfriends at her school. Her father was going to allow her to attend the football game because at halftime, the homecoming court was announced and shown off. And Rita would be there in the spotlight, riding on the float, right next to King Whitcomb.

But how was she going to manage the same thing at Kingston if both schools had homecoming on the same night? Her father deferred to her mother, who did not know what to say.

The day before homecoming actually occurred, Rita confided in none other than Darren. She longed terribly to be at his side at the court at halftime, but she could not be in two places at once. She would be present at one court but absent at the other, where she would be just a name announced on the PA system. That would be horrid.

As much as it hurt to do so, she made her case to Darren, and while they talked, she decided to forfeit being the queen of the Kingston court, not just because she wanted to see Sara and Bonnie and her other girlfriends, but also she believed a true Kingston girl should represent Kingston.

Darren and Rita went to the school office together and had a visit with the principal. Rita made her case, and the principal admired her sense of sacrifice.

Darren was impressed with Rita. He still was relieved that he did not have to contend with her snobbery, but he witnessed a crack in that snobbery in the principal's office.

So the announcement was made. Rita Armstrong was forfeiting the queen crown to Agnes MacAllister, a very popular, pretty brown-headed girl who grew up in the Kingston school system, one of the girls on the infamous list of top 10 Kingston babes.

Lunchtime that day was a somber affair. Everyone was direct with Rita in congratulating her on queen of her own court while admiring her for her sacrifice of the additional queen assignment. Secretly, Rita was ready to burst with joy at the thought of seeing her girlfriends. She had to admit she could hardly wait to see Sara and Bonnie.

During a break between classes, Darren sought Rita out at her locker. He touched her back with the palm of his hand. She jumped and turned around.

"I admire your sense of sacrifice, even if it sounds corny," Darren said to her.

"Oh, Darren, I really wanted to be seated next to you on that homecoming float, but I think I made the right decision. What do you think?"

"Absolutely. Your loyalty should lie with your own school. I hope you're skipping school here today. You've got a long ride home and lots to do."

"Oh my god, it had never occurred to me."

That's because you're a blonde was his thought. But to her, he said, "So just go on to the office and get your absence excused and get the hell outta here."

"Oh, I hope you have a wonderful night, Darren, I mean that."

"I intend to. First, we have to kick the shit out of Utica, then our work is done, and it will be all play after that."

"Okay. Well—good luck! I'm out of here for now."

She shook his hand, and he gave her a brotherly hug. "Have fun," he said into her ear.

That shocked her. Could he really be fond of her after all? At all? No time to worry about it now. She smiled at him, and then she turned and hurried down the hallway. He watched her fade away.

"Brother, are you hassling the double queen?" came from Darrell as he approached Rita's locker.

"Nope. As a matter of fact, I wished her well. She's nervous. I told her to go home and get ready for her big night."

"That's good of you, brother," said Darrell. "Well"—he slapped Darren's back lightly—"have a great time on the homecoming court."

"Oh yeah, no problem."

"My, you're an assuming young man. Get over it."

"I'll try. Okay, I'm over it."

"All right. See you whenever."

"Yup," Darren said.

Darrell turned and left, off to get to his next class.

ONE AFTERNOON—A MOMENT AT THE LOCKER

Jim was approaching Brad's locker. Brad was in front of it, dealing with the temperamental combination lock he had been assigned. Jim spotted Lee too. She approached Brad, got up on her toes, and whispered something to him. He looked at her with what appeared to be extreme surprise. He opened his locker. Lee got back down to her five foot three, nudged him gently in the rib cage with an elbow, and went on her way, not realizing she was headed toward Jim.

Jim halted. Lee looked up just in time to see him grinning at her.

"Well, ma'am," he said, "what just transpired over there at Brad's locker?"

Lee detected a minute amount jealousy from Jim.

"Oh," she replied, "Rita told me that they were in the muddy paddock when Brad slipped and landed on his rear end. He was totally covered with mud. Rita laughed until she just about cried, but Brad didn't think it was the least bit funny. He asked Rita not to tell anybody, but Rita was naughty enough to tell me."

"Of course, Lee, everybody talks to you. You're so cute, we can't help ourselves. You know that."

Jim gave her a bear hug and kissed her on the top of her head. Then he was gone, headed toward Brad's locker.

He's serious, she thought, *Brad too. Brad really didn't want anyone to know about the muddy paddock incident. Maybe I should apologize.*

She went on her way down the hall toward the lunchroom, feeling sorry for Brad.

* * *

She found Brad alone at the lunch table. She decided to take advantage of the privacy. She sat next to him and said outright, "I'm sorry about what I did at your locker. I didn't know it would bother you. I didn't think. I should have kept my mouth shut."

He squeezed one of her hands with one of his. It lasted about a second.

"She shouldn't have told anyone because I was embarrassed and didn't want anyone to find out. You're not to be faulted, Lee. She is. Okay?"

It was as much as he was going to say about the matter, she realized. So she nudged his arm with her body and said, "I apologize anyway. *Mum*'s the word if Rita tells me anything in the future."

"That's fair, I'd say," Brad responded. He smiled at her. Then the table started filling up. Brad asked Lee to stay seated next to him, and she obliged. She felt a bit giddy being so close to Brad physically. She felt a little proud as well. Essentially happy, even though he did not speak to her during the lunch hour. Their feet talked though. Her lower legs were wrapped around his. She somehow did not care if anyone, even Stickman, saw this, but in actuality, she was relieved at the end of the lunch hour that no had noticed.

Between Jim and Brad

Jim and Brad were sitting on the side stoop of the Warners' house. The stoop was small and simple compared to the rest of the house. The house was a three-story affair with filigree soffits, three dormers, and an expansive front porch painted pale yellow, the same hue as the house.

The boys were leaning on their elbows on one of the steps of the stoop. Their legs were stretched out so their boots touched the gravel driveway. They were smoking Camels, sipping Black Label beer, and observing the changes in the sunset against the foothills.

Jim piped up, "Hey, I have news for you. Just about the entire school thinks you're Rita's boyfriend."

Brad looked at Jim. "Rita who?"

"*Rita*," Jim replied, "Rita, the rich girl, from our group."

"That's interesting. I didn't know. How did you get this misinformation?"

"Giggly girls coming out of the locker room. The school is all atwitter, and you don't even notice it. You're wearing blinders, man. Who are they for? Solve the mystery for me, would you, please?"

Brad looked at Jim with very dark eyes. He did not want to talk about it.

"Never mind, man," said Jim. "I understand your desire for privacy."

"I know you mean that, but you deserve to know, of all people."

"I'll leave that completely up to you, brother."

"Hmmm, Jim?"

"Yeah, Brad?'

"Leora."

"Huh?"

"It's Leora. Has been since the day we met."

Jim's jaw dropped. "You're serious."

"One hundred percent."

"Oh, dear Lord," Jim lamented. "I love her too."

"That's obvious. You're so solicitous of her. She depends on you. You're her protector, and she relies on that."

'Yes, sometimes I do feel as if she needs protection. But she's really not a weak person, is she?"

"Not at all."

Jim inhaled the last of his cigarette and tossed it out onto the driveway. Brad followed suit. Then they silently finished their beers.

It had gotten darker quickly since they had first sat on the stoop. The sun was a bright-orange on the horizon. The blue sky lent wisps of high cirrus clouds of pink, purple, and yellow. The light on top of the barn clicked on, but since it was not completely dark outside, the barn light did not illuminate much.

Jim said, "It's getting cold out here. Can we go inside and talk? Let me take the beer bottles."

"Thanks," said Brad. "Come on in."

Inside was a large coat room with closets and benches. The guys put their boots under one of the benches. They entered the kitchen next. Little under-the-cupboard task lights softly illuminated the large room. To the left and across the hall, Brad led Jim to the dining room. They sat at a massive walnut table, above which a small chandelier illuminated the room.

Jim put the beer bottles on the table.

"What a mess this could turn out to be."

"Maybe not. I don't intend to tell her how I feel. She deserves better than an ex-con."

"Have you ever asked Lee how she feels about that?"

"No, we don't get personal. I don't want to fall too hard for her, although I just can't see myself being in love with anybody else."

"Ditto on that, brother."

"There's something else, and I have to ask you to tell no one, not even Lee. She'll find out in due time. Due to my draft number, I've been told I'm going to Vietnam."

Jim's heart sank. "That damned war. When?"

"Within a couple weeks, I'll be at basic training. I will write to the group via you if that's okay."

"Well, yeah, that's no problem at all. What about Lee? Will you write to her?"

"For certain before I get deployed."

"This is going to break her heart."

"I actually doubt she has any romantic feelings for me."

"I believe she does. But I promise not to tell her. You have my word."

"Thanks, my friend. I'm scared shitless."

"How about Canada?"

"Yes, Bruce and I have talked about that extensively. I would have to leave my life behind—Bruce, you, Leora. It would be a true separation."

"Unless there's a pardon."

"I don't see that happening during this current administration. Maybe the next president, who knows."

Jim sighed. Shards of pain beat against his heart.

Brad said, "I need you to take care of Lee."

"No problem with that. Done."

"You're the only one who knows about Vietnam except the Warners, Bruce, and my mother. She didn't even tell my father who she lives with! I don't care. I don't want him to know anything about me anyway."

"Damn, what a night," said Jim, and he combed his hair back with his fingers.

"Indeed," said Brad.

Jim asked, "Do you think we could share Leora?"

"Possibly."

Jim was aghast. "Are you serious, man?"

"Are you?"

"Actually, I am. But how do you approach a lady about a threesome?"

"I have no idea."

"Become Mormons? I don't want to be a Mormon. I was raised Quaker. How about you?"

"Nothing. My parents were too busy bickering to bother with church."

"Sorry to hear that, man."

"Thank you."

"We must be nuts. How is the rest of the world going to behave if we succeed with sharing her? I say it's none of their damned business."

Brad mused, "I really wonder if she's the type."

"To go with two guys?"

"Yeah, two guys."

"Hard to say. She seems wholesome in a way. I don't know of her sexual experience."

Brad shrugged his shoulders.

Jim ran his fingers through his hair again.

He said, "How about we build a colosseum at school, and you and I can be pitted against each other. Lee can sit behind a silk curtain and watch. Her decision will be easy. She will rule out the dead guy."

"Oh, that would be you without a doubt."

"Whatever, Mr. Baseball. You wouldn't have a baseball in the colosseum. What else are you good for?"

"Hands on."

"*Pff!* I'm taller than you are. I could lord anything over you."

"And why is it that I wouldn't have a baseball?"

"My colosseum, my rules."

"Oh, I see. I don't want to fight you."

"I don't want to fight you either."

"So the colosseum is out."

"Okay, agreed."

"We could take about a hundred years to figure this out," Brad suggested.

"Grand idea. But if I lost her to you, I'd be crestfallen."

"You would have no trouble getting solace from all the girls who follow you around at school."

"Don't give me that crap, Brad. I have girls asking about you every day."

"Oh my," Brad said sarcastically.

"Just keep those blinders on, man. I'll keep mine on too."

"And we'll take that hundred years to figure out Leora."

They shook hands on it.

Jim said, "May we be silenced forever if we divulge our secret to anyone else."

"Deal," Brad responded.

"I'm going to get going home, Brad. It's been a pleasure."

"Likewise."

Brad walked Jim out to his car. They did not talk. Everything had been said already. Jim waved to Brad as the car headed down the road. Brad offered a wave in return.

Fort McClellan, Anniston, Alabama
November 1971

Dear Leora,

It's time for me to come clean about myself. But before I do, I must say some other things. Please be so kind as to bear with me. And forgive me for leaving you without saying goodbye.

When my mother was in high school, she got pregnant. In those days, a pregnant girl had to get married. My parents did not love each other. They were much too young and immature to raise a baby. They verbally "scrapped" constantly. My existence was largely ignored by them but for the necessary basics such as food and shelter. My father was ambivalent toward me. Mom made sure I was fed and clothed, and she made sure I did my school homework even though she never helped me with it. She saw to it that I went to school in decent clothes.

One day, when I was seventeen, we were all in the kitchen. My parents were screaming at each other. I didn't bother to ask why. My father raised his arm to strike Mom. I stepped between them, grabbed my father's arm and spun him around so his back was against my chest. I twisted his arm upward while he let out a scream. I broke his arm without trying to do so.

Mom called the police. I was arrested. I was incarcerated for almost a year. I got a GED there, but I wanted to earn a diploma.

Also during my incarceration, my parents patched up their differences and started a new life together. Mom told me about it during one of her visits. She looked happier than I had seen her in years, but it did not change the fact that my father meant nothing to me.

After a long time, my pro bono attorney and I were able to go before the judge. The prosecuting attorney repeated his assault charge, but the judge said the reason I assaulted my father was to protect Mom. The judge put me on parole and told me I had to stay away from my father. I gave the judge my word. I moved in with my uncle Bruce, my mom's brother.

I was released from parole shortly after my eighteenth birthday. Mom took me to their house. My father was there seated at their kitchen table. I told him I never wanted to see him again, and I thanked my mother for all her help.

My uncle Bruce was waiting for me outside the house. I gave Mom a kiss on the cheek and left the house for good. He did not ask for details, but a few weeks later, the two of us sat down, and I told I him everything. Bruce decided I should attend Kingston High School.

All court records were expunged as promised by the judge. Bruce and I visited Kingston High School, and I tested okay to join the senior class.

I met Mr. Warner through Bruce. Mr. Warner offered me a job on his dairy farm. I shook his hand so hard I'm surprised it didn't fall off.

On my first day at Kingston, I bumped into you, I apologized, and you were polite and smiled at me. You helped me find my auto shop class; you told me to ignore the map because it made a mess of things. You had gray-green eyes the likes of which I had never seen. You had shiny black hair. You had the most beautiful smile. You looked exotic.

When we went our separate ways, you looked back at me and smiled, and then you waved and went on your way. I watched you until you disappeared. Baby-blue sweater, black skirt—wow, you were the most beautiful girl I had ever met.

I made my way to the auto shop. I waved at those who could see me, and those guys waved back at me. I told them I had met a girl named Leora, and she pointed me toward the auto class. All the guys knew you, Leora. You are the only girl in the history of Kingston High who was allowed to take auto shop. They all mentioned how smart you are about cars and that you got the highest grade last period.

I received comments about you from Darrell, Adrian, and Jim—all great comments! I say I had to agree with them from what I already knew about you!

Adrian invited me to meet you and a group of students at lunchtime. So he found me and led me right to the lunch table. There you were listening to Connie and Sandy—you're such a great listener. In my mind, I begged you to turn and see me, and then I begged you *not* to turn around.

Adrian introduced me as Brad, his new auto-shop buddy. Everyone uttered some sort of polite greeting. But you, Leora, merely turned your head and looked at me with a coy smile.

I caught you studying me a couple times. You were more nonchalant than anything. Were you playing games? I don't know. I never asked. I just prayed that you and I would be able to become friends.

Lee, you must have figured it out already. I am nineteen years old. I will be twenty when I finally get my diploma from the Army. I tested in the 99th percentile on the Army entrance exam. I passed my physical. Now I need to pass basic training. I'm not allowed to live off-base, so most of my time won't be my own. I will write to the group via Jim as often as I can.

There is one other thing, Leora. I beg you to understand Jim's need to stay quiet about me, prison, and the Army. I had sworn him to secrecy. I see that he's the honorable man I believed he would be. He honors you too. I'm certain of that. He loves you. That came straight from the horse's mouth.

I'll close hopefully just for now. Please forgive me for leaving you without saying goodbye. I didn't know if I could bear it. I'll write as often

as I can. Basic training is grueling and time-con-
suming. I think of you constantly, Leora.

Yours,
Brad

SADNESS

The school day had ended. Leora was on her way to the Vista Cruiser. As she got closer to the split-rail fence that surrounded the parking lot, Jim—who had been jogging from quite a distance to catch up to her—called, "Lee! Hold up!"

She stopped walking but did not turn around to face him.

He approached her. Still, she did not face him. He hugged her loosely around the waist and rested his chin on the top of her head. Her beautiful black hair was warm and soft, the fragrance of ginger and lavender.

Leora rested her hands on Jim's hands.

Big honest-Leora tears flowed down from her eyes to her cheeks to her neck to her blouse. She didn't want to cry. She believed Brad didn't deserve the tears. *I owe him nothing,* she thought.

She seemed tiny to Jim just then, tiny but not exactly frail, more like fallen, weary, feeling as if her own posture was weighing her down.

"He left without even saying goodbye," she said sadly. "He lied to me. He's been in prison. I didn't even know his real age. I got a letter from him. He's in boot camp."

"I hope you can forgive him. He loves you very much."

"Oh God" was all she could say. One man would profess another's love to her and vice versa! Piled upon that weight was the knowledge that Brad had not only withheld details of his life, he had downright lied to her about it. Why had he not trusted her? Did his age even matter? The feeling was too heavy; she could not carry it. It made her heart hurt as it pounded in anxiety for a few scary seconds. Then came the tiny shards bouncing up and down around her heart.

Jim sat on the split-rail fence, swung his legs over it, and planted his long feet onto the gravel parking lot. Then he turned toward Leora. He grabbed her and held onto her as if she were a baby. He swung her over the fence as if she were as light as a feather. Then he planted her onto her feet.

Lee handed him the keys from her purse. He opened the passenger door for her and closed the door when she was seated. Then he skipped around the front of the car and got into the driver's seat— or rather *tried* to. He couldn't fit. So he pushed one of the buttons on the side of the seat, and electricity slowly moved the seat *way* back to accommodate his long, Stickman legs.

"*Damn*, I would have had my *knees* in my mouth. You're a short little lady, aren't you?" *Our small Leora,* Jim thought to himself. He combed his hair back with his fingers.

Lee's tummy felt exposed to the elements. She hugged herself with her arms.

After they arrived at Sherry's house, Jim turned the car off, and they sat in silence for a few minutes. Then they looked at each other.

"Come on," he said. "I have an idea."

"You're not going to ask me to the prom, are you?" she asked with suspicion.

He screwed up his face. "Are you kiddin' me? No way. Prom was months ago. We never go to prom anyway. Just for kicks, how many guys asked you? You aren't going to tell me, are you?"

Lee just looked at him with a straight face. The number was six, but she did not tell him.

"Didn't think so," he said. "No matter. I have a different plan. I need your phone."

In the kitchen, Sherry had an olive-green wall phone with a curly cord that was all stretched out and could extend almost all the way through the cottage.

Jim and Leora walked through the enclosed porch into the house and immediately entered the small eating area. Sherry was in the kitchen talking on the phone and looking absently out the window that was above the sink.

Lee and Jim sat on chairs that matched the red and white, speckled Formica table with silver legs. They waited patiently.

Finally it dawned on Sherry that Lee wanted the phone. "Do you need it back soon?" she asked her mom, looking up at her with tired eyes.

Sherry waved her hand in friendly dismissal. "Oh, whenever you're done, honey." Then she glanced at Jim because she sensed Lee wasn't feeling well. Jim nearly imperceptibly shook his head no to Sherry. She headed to her bedroom. He would tell her later.

He watched absently as Sherry went down the short hallway dressed in a floor-length, white cotton skirt and off-white linen blouse. She had a laid back personality with a tinge of parenthood.

Jim could not use the phone. As luck would have it, someone else was using the party line they shared with Sherry and family.

He interrupted politely, "Excuse me, Mrs. Penn, this is Jim Jones, Sherry Sovine's friend."

"Jim? Oh yeah, Jim. How are you?"

"Doing great, thanks. I wonder if I could impose upon you to let me use the line for about five minutes. Nothing major, but I should get the call done in the next few minutes. Would that prove inconvenient for you right now?"

"Oh no, I'm just blabbing to a neighbor. Give me a minute and check the line, how's that?"

They said goodbye to each other and hung up their phones. Then he dialed Adrian's number.

"Hello?"

"Hey, Adrian, Stickman here."

"Oh! Well, hey, dude. What's up?"

"Can you do the phone chain?"

"Yeah, you mean now?"

"Yup," said Jim. "Friend in distress. Must help ASAP."

"Okay. Cool. Where do you want me to start? The usual?"

"Yeah, that would be great. Everybody meet in the school parking lot at five o'clock."

Jim could see Lee lip-voicing, "No! I'm fine!" She waved her hands in front of him. But he continued to talk to Adrian. "Thanks, bud, I knew I could depend on you. No need to get back to me. Have everybody meet at the school parking lot as close to five p.m. as possible."

"You got it. See you soon. Bye."

"Thanks. Bye."

After Jim put the phone back in its cradle on the wall, he got a clear drinking glass from the cupboard and drew some tap water. While the water filled the glass, Jim gazed out the window. The western sky was brilliant blue. No clouds visible. The natural dark color of the trees was reduced by the bright, intense pre-twilight sunlight.

He returned to Lee and handed her the glass. She practically gulped down the water. It felt wonderful on her throat.

She said, "I wasn't even aware I needed that."

He replied, "I'm glad you drank it. Okay, my friendly little lady, I need to use your phone in private. Is that okay? Kinda rude, I know."

Lee said she didn't mind. She took herself down the hall to her bedroom where she plopped herself onto her back onto the bed.

He dialed Adrian again. "Hey, can you get a hold of a bunch of flowers? Corsages or something you and I can scrape together?" (Adrian's mother owned a wholesale floral company.)

"Wow, man. Have you ever arranged flowers before?"

"That's a nope," Jim replied.

"Oh heck, I'll take my chances. Let me ask my mom if there's anything leftover at the store. I think we can pull it off."

"I can pitch in some dough to pay for them."

"No need. My mom will be cool about this. I'll start the phone chain and give you a call. Where are you?"

"At Lee's house."

"Okay."

Adrian called Jim back a few minutes later. "Okay, it's the consensus that we should go cruisin' and get wasted. Is that okay? Do you think Leora will be cool with that? She hardly ever smokes or drinks. She might get bored."

"Oh, she'll be good, man. She loves having all you weirdos around her."

"We love her too," Adrian replied. "Far out. What a great small lady."

"You bet. Okay, you hippie, see you at school with flowers."

"Okay, man, see you soon. Bye."

"Yup. Bye."

After he hung up the phone, Jim carefully slipped down the hall. He peeked into Leora's room. So peaceful she looked. No dreaming. Nice, deep breaths.

He stole back to the kitchen table. Sherry sneaked into the room and sat beside him. They talked about the letter Leora had received from Brad. The letter was on the table. Jim carefully picked it up and handed it to Sherry. She read it without effect on her face. It was a mini novel to her. At the end of her read, she put down the letter and wondered, *Does Jim even know what's* in *this letter?*

"Jim, did you read this letter?" she started out.

"No, no, never will I read that thing" was his response.

"Did you tell Leora you love her?"

"No, but I told her that Brad does. She was crying after reading Brad's letter. I felt badly for her, so I asked her to forgive him because he loves her very much."

She sighed. "I'll take Lee's place here and have you read just a short statement from Brad's letter."

"Let's do this before she wakes up, right?"

Sherry located the section of the letter she'd mentioned. "You promise to read what I point out to you, and nothing else, right?"

"Of course," Jim said seriously, "I don't even want to see the small part you want me to read."

Sherry indicated the last paragraph of Brad's letter, which Jim read. He put the paper down gently and looked down for a moment. Then he raised his head and looked at Sherry. She had been studying his face.

"Whew!" he sighed. "Now she knows we both love her. I asked her to forgive Brad for telling his white lies and keeping his secrets. I had no idea she was crying in part because of *me*. I'll let her sleep as long as possible," he continued. "We're going out with a few friends for a while tonight, just to keep her company and hopefully help her feel better."

"*Pff*"—from Sherry with mirth in her eyes—"yeah, right. Booze cruisin' is more like it, with my little daughter as the designated driver."

"You looked *just* like Lee just now. It's the sparkle in those eyes. You both have it. I'll wait on the couch in the living room."

"Okay. I'll put this letter on her bedroom dresser. The rest is up to you."

"I know," he replied. He crossed over to the living room and plopped himself onto the old, plaid sofa. He put his head back. His eyes closed immediately, and he settled into a pleasant nap.

Sherry didn't think either one of the kids would awaken in time to meet their friends. She kept an eye on the clock in her room, glancing now and then to check the time while she read *Wuthering Heights*. It was peaceful in her house. When the windows were closed, no sounds could be heard from the outside. Open windows in the spring and summer invited cool, fresh air to breathe while reading, resting, sleeping. Sherry and Lee had no fear of danger of any kind up there on the bluff. Whether it was day or night, the trees gave them the feeling of being hugged by a protective wall of nature.

Sherry put down her book at about 4:00 p.m. and sought Jim first. She gently jiggled one of his feet back and forth until he awoke from his dream state and rubbed his still-closed eyelids.

"Hi," he whispered, "is this real or is it surreal?"

"Real, dear. Time to get Lee up. You're still going out, I assume."

"Yeah," Jim yawned. He stood up and gave her a hug.

She smiled. "I'll wake her up. Have fun."

"Oh, thanks. Yeah, have a pleasant night."

In about five minutes, a somber, slowly moving Lee made her way into the bathroom. She got back out in a matter of a few minutes. She had changed from her skirt and shirt to blue jeans and a long-sleeve, plaid flannel shirt. To that, she added a wool winter coat from the hall closet.

"Hey, you," Jim greeted her, "you sure you're up to this?"

Lee yawned. "I don't want to stay home all night. It will be nice to get out. I'd like to drive my car if everybody will fit."

* * *

Lee felt at home while she was driving the Vista Cruiser. It was part of her everyday life and memories of Bela. In her mind, she detected the aroma of oil and grease and gasoline, those familiar fragrances from her days of helping him work on cars in his garage, much as Sherry had helped him at the Clarks' place. He was almost magical in his ability to detect and repair just about any automotive problem. She felt lucky to spend nearly every day in that car. It was the most wonderful gift she had ever received.

It was a pleasant drive down the winding roads. All the car windows were down, and the heat was blasting to keep them warm. The movement of the car created a wind current that made Lee's hair fly every which way. Jim sported the high school baseball cap on his head to keep his hair in place. The eight-track-tape player sat in the front seat between Jim and Lee. He took a Steppenwolf tape from the glove compartment, slipped it into the opening of one of the speakers, plugged the charger into the cigarette lighter, and set the volume to a fun but not obnoxious level.

Steppenwolf kept them company on the ride. Jim did interrupt the music once to turn to Lee and say, "Lee, we can talk later if you want to. Maybe some time when we're not flying down the foothills to the tunes of Steppenwolf. Next up will be Phil Oakes, and then Led Zeppelin. Switch it up a bit, whatta ya say?"

Lee smiled. She was already relaxing behind the wheel of the Cruiser.

THE BEARS

Jim and Leora met some of the group at the school parking lot at about 5:00 p.m. They heard the crunch of the gravel as car after car moved slowly to their parking spots. Everyone piled into Lee's Vista Cruiser.

She headed east and drove for about half an hour, randomly turning—a gravel road here, a two-track there, a narrow dirt road behind sprawling farms, up steep grades on paved roads. She finally went winding down a blacktop two-lane road, actually considered a highway—curve after tight curve—with the forest and boulders, covered in moss in deep shadow, hugging the road and blending their hues of deep green in the chilled air.

Lee descended the foothill. Along the side of the Cruiser, the land was like soft edges, rolling smoothly like round, friendly ocean waves during times of sunset, one wave gently following the other… descending to rest upon a small valley. A pretty mist covered the fields and lifted its cover up into the evening sky. The Cruiser crossed a single set of railroad tracks where there was just an *X* to indicate the tracks—no lights, no electric gates.

Lee hooked a left, turning the wheel with ease with its power steering, into a stand of thick brush. The group could hear the sound of the brush scraping the sides of the car. A few people cringed at the sound. After traveling about fifty feet, the car was deep in the brush, as if it had disappeared from the road. Lee figured this was a good enough spot for them to stop and party.

"*This* will do the trick," Connie said cheerfully from her place next to the passenger front door. Sandy sat between her and Lee.

Immediately, there was the sound of half a dozen matches striking the matchbooks, and soon, the car seemed to be floating in a fog of sweetly fragrant smoke. Lee had nine friends in her car, including Lorrie seated upon the driveshaft. The Vista Cruiser had bench seats, so there was more room for passengers than there would have been with bucket seats or captain chairs or both.

"Hey, where's Brad?" Collin spoke up, seated directly behind Lee.

"He got drafted, man," Stickman replied. "He's in boot camp right now getting prepared to get deployed to Vietnam." Stickman was seated in the middle of the third seat, the seat that faced backward.

"Poor guy," said Adrian, seated to the right of Stickman.

Everyone agreed with Adrian.

"Lee, you want to smoke?" offered Collin.

"She's our designated driver," said Connie.

"Oh! Okay. Say, do you ever let other people drive your car?"

"No, Collin," Connie replied, "especially not you. You're nuts behind the wheel of a car. Pop quiz, what's a speed limit?"

"Very funny, 'Mom,'" Collin said.

"It wasn't meant to be, love."

It was twilight, and the thick brush lent even more darkness to the inside of the car. Little red orbs ebbed and glowed from the pipes and joints that were being used to smoke the marijuana. It was peaceful there. Lots of conversations floated inside the car as the fragrant smoke flowed about.

About an hour later, Darren—who was seated next to the passenger side back door with Rita on his lap—said, "Hey, Stickman."

"What?"

"Are you in the middle seat behind me?"

"Yup."

"Well, by this time, you might check to see if our little Adrian is missing, roaming about outside."

"Oh crap," said Jim, "I'd forgotten about that little hippie. He *was* right next to me."

181

Lorrie asked, "Whose turn is it to babysit him?"

"*That* would be me" came from Connie. She handed her Boones Farm bottle to Sandy and uttered a slight groan of impatience as she shoved the passenger door open against the brush. She shut the door and sidled the car, trudged almost blindly along the path the car had made, and arrived about fifty feet later to hear Adrian muse innocently, "I wonder if there are any bears around here."

Connie was the only person to hear that. Her heart seemed to drop into her stomach. Yes, the area did contain bears—big black ones.

She retrieved Adrian and led him by the hand back to the seat beside Stickman. The gate was put up, and Lee made the window go up about two-thirds of the way with the touch of a button. Adrian, as cute as a curious child, said, "Seriously, I wonder if there are bears out there."

"Bears?" some of the people in the group exclaimed.

"You mean grizzly bears?"

"You mean black bears?"

Connie sidled the car and got back to her seat quickly. She shut the door in relief. "I don't care *what* kind of bears there are out there, I don't want to see one face-to-face, ever."

"Sorry, Connie," said a diminutive Adrian.

"It's okay, honey, we're safe in the car," she replied.

About ten minutes later, someone said, "Geez, this Boones Farm tastes *terrible*!" It was Darrell, seated to the left of Stickman.

Connie demanded, "Hey, how the heck did you get ahold of my wine?"

"Sandy handed it to me. Of course, I asked for it first."

He handed the bottle back to Sandy, who gave it back to Connie.

"Oops," Sandy said.

"Why do you drink that stuff?" asked Darren.

Connie frowned. "Because there wasn't any champagne at the party store. I just wanted to see how the other half lives."

"Just ask Rita how the other half lives," piped up Darren. Everybody laughed.

"Oh, hey, everybody, I almost forgot!" came from a cheerful Adrian. "You all get corsages tonight, courtesy of my mother." He lifted a box that was in front of his feet.

Adrian passed the corsages to Stickman one by one, and soon each person in the car adorned a corsage on their coats.

There were nice comments and thanks all around the Cruiser. It was a lovely evening, a nice alternative to the prom at Kingston, which nobody in the group ever attended.

Surprise—Early December

Brad surprised the group during study hall one Friday. Mr. Jenkins had his head down and did not notice Brad entering the room.

He wore his usual attire—dark cotton button-up shirt, blue jeans, leather coat, and work boots. He looked even more athletic than ever. He put his hands over Adrian's eyes and whispered to him, "Guess who?" Then he removed his hands.

"The prodigal son is home!" cried Collin. He got up and gave Brad a hug. Brad smiled.

By then, everybody in the entire room knew Brad was there. He gave one of his handsome grins to Leora, who was looking directly at him, and said, "Hello, Leora."

She did not know what to say. She was shocked.

He went to her and hugged her for a long time, long enough to draw comments and whistles. She stayed seated, and he stood behind her, wrapping her in his arms. He whispered words into her ear that no one but the two of them could hear, words that made Lee blush, words she would never repeat to anyone. The greeting ended with Brad planting a soft kiss on the top of her head. Her hair had the fragrance of rose petals. She could barely believe he was there. How lucky could a girl be?

After he released Lee, Brad made the rounds, hugging everybody else in the group—short, friendly hugs. He and Jim gave each other a handshake, a long hug, and a slap on each other's back. Adrian invited Brad to sit beside him at the table, which he did. Brad recalled the first day he had ever sat next to Adrian during lunch. It had been on Brad's very first day at Kingston High School. Adrian had been animated and accommodating, just as he was presently. And Leora was seated in the same spot she had been on that first day. It all felt familiar and comfortable to Brad.

Mr. Jenkins made his way to the table to shake Brad's hand and say, "Mr. Adams, good to see you. You're looking well."

"Thank you, Mr. Jenkins. It's great to see you. Are you keeping this mob in check?"

The group chuckled.

"Oh, they're a great group. We all know that. Haven't had to hold up the wall since you left. That makes a record. I think they miss you though."

Brad and Mr. Jenkins smiled at each other, and then Mr. Jenkins nodded his head once to Brad and made his way back to his desk.

Rita looked around the room and took note of the large number of female students practically dropping their jaws at the sight of Brad from boot camp. The room was abuzz with conversations about him. Lee could not have cared less about any of the other young ladies. She was in heaven.

"How long are you home?" asked Adrian.

"Two days."

"Damn, that's too bad. We could use more time than that just to hang out with you."

Brad wanted to spend his time with Jim and Leora only, but he was much too kind to say that to the group. It was soon decided by unanimity that there would be a gathering of the group that evening at Lee's place. Brad consented gladly. After study hall was finished, he spent some time chatting with a throng of curious students. Thereafter, for the rest of the day, he was nowhere to be seen.

Five o'clock p.m. could not have arrived any later, or Lee would have liked to have died. She had heard nothing him since he had left Study Hall. Typical mystery man. But Lee had kept a positive face about it and had kept up good spirits all day.

* * *

At precisely 5:00 p.m. there was a knock on the door. Lee looked toward the door quizzically. Oh no, her spine went cold. Brad. It could not be anybody else. The group was expected to be there at around five, but they were notoriously late, every one of them—except Brad.

"Somebody's at the door, honey," called Sherry from her room.

"I have it," Lee replied.

"Okay."

She strode to the door and opened it with feigned confidence. Yes, it was Brad. He grinned at her and said, "Hey."

"Hey, you," she replied, sounding breathy. Brad thought she sounded sexy. "Please come in. You look very nice."

"Thank you, and you as well," he responded. He had changed into a white cotton short-sleeved button-up shirt tucked into khakis, and soft leather shoes. The stark-white of the shirt accentuated the darkness of his skin. And his eyes were more captivating than they had ever been. Lee did not know how anyone could be any more handsome than he was.

They entered the kitchen and looked toward the living room. Bela was in the recliner just awakening from a nap. "Dad?" Lee said softly. "My friend Brad is here. He's home for a couple days."

Brad and Bela had never met each other. Lee was hoping for a cordial beginning, something more positive from Brad than Bela had gotten from Jim. She was not disappointed. Brad approached the sleepy dad and shook his hand firmly.

"Pleased to meet you, Mr. Sovine."

"Oh, thank you, son, it's great to meet you too. Sherry and I hear so little about you from our shy little daughter here. You're her best kept secret." Leora looked down and blushed.

"Hmmm," said Brad.

"Say, don't let me keep you from each other's company. I'll retire to the bedroom and leave you two alone."

"Oh no, that's okay, Dad," Lee responded. "The group is on its way here anyway. Just stay put. Brad and I will sit at the kitchen table."

"Oh, nonsense," said Bela. He got up from the recliner. "Have the living room to yourselves until your friends get here. Brad, have a nice evening with Lee and her group."

"Thank you, sir."

"Our little Lee is ecstatic that you're back home." Lee blushed again.

Bela left them alone and went to be with Sherry.

Brad and Lee sat next to each other on the couch holding hands and chatting about boot camp and how glad he was to have a break, no matter how short it was. He told her he wanted to see if they could get in a little horseback riding the next day or evening.

Lee said, "Oh yes, I would really like that." She grinned like a happy child.

He kissed her on the mouth, a nicely paced one with his tongue. She was in the mood to respond with passion, but she kept cool and responded with polite femininity, which was just fine with him. Any kiss from Leora was a bonus.

Soon the group started straggling in, not bothering to knock on the door before entering the cottage. It was their home too. Many of them had had the opportunity to spend the night there during party times or just because it was too late to get back home some night or other. Sherry and Bela knew them all personally and welcomed them all into the place upon any occasion.

Since Brad knew Jim was going to arrive soon, he was polite enough to let someone sit between Lee and himself. He did not want to show Jim any disrespect by usurping Jim's place in Lee's life.

The party ended up spilling outside onto the picnic tables and lawn chairs, near a fire in the pit with which Bela had obliged them. They drank their wine and smoked their cigarettes and pot outside because it had always been Sherry's preference that nobody smoke in the house. The air was comfortable with the large fire going. Occasionally either Jim or Brad would add wood to continue the warmth. Conversations floated around for a couple hours.

Occasionally Lee heard Rita's laughter and looked her way to find that Brad had just said something funny to her. He always had a way of making Rita laugh, that was for sure. But Lee paid no mind to it that night. She just smiled at them. There were no shards. There was no pain. Just a glad heart. Brad was home.

Saturday Morning— Love Confessed

Most of the partygoers had left by 4:00 a.m. The stragglers slept in the living room—Brad, Lee, Jim, Darren and Rita—either on the couch, in the recliner, or in sleeping bags on the floor. When they were all awake, Jim asked Brad to see him privately. They met in Lee's bedroom while the others were preparing to be treated to oatmeal, toast, orange juice, and coffee.

Brad and Jim could hear the clinking of silverware on plates, along with talk and laughter. The aroma of the coffee was almost intoxicating to Jim. He promised himself a cup once this meeting was finished.

Jim said, "Lee mentioned going horseback riding later."

Brad replied, "Yeah, you coming with us, man?"

"Oh, I don't think that's a good idea. I'd be the third party. I can't do that to her knowing how damned glad she is to see you."

"I don't own her, you know. We talked about this before, remember?"

"Yeah, I remember."

"Maybe it's time we talk to Leora about all this stuff."

"I suppose you're right. Before we go riding or afterward?"

"Let's wait until afterward."

"Okay, it's a deal."

"We can find out how she feels about us."

"Right. Okay, let's get some breakfast and get going. What do you say?"

"I agree."

Thus the meeting was adjourned.

* * *

It was a cold day at the Warners' place, but the animals could tolerate it. Everyone was animated that morning. It was a pleasant time for them all. The ride lasted about an hour; after which, the blankets and saddles, bits and bridles were removed; and the animals got brushed down until their backs were not sweating any longer. Darren and Rita took their leave. Brad and Jim looked at each other.

"Are you two all right?" asked Lee.

Brad invited them to join him in the dining room of the Warners' house. When they got settled there, Brad took Lee's hands into his. She tried to pull away. She did not want to show any preference in front of Jim. But Brad held on harder. She was a bit worried. He had never been forceful to her.

"It's all right, Lee. We just need to talk to you," said Jim. "For a long time, we've been wondering if you have any feelings for us."

"Oh God" was all she could say. She had not expected this. What she *had* expected she could not say, but this was a complete surprise.

Jim looked at Brad as if he were pleading for help.

"Well," said Lee bravely, "the answer is yes. I love both of you. Now what do we do?"

"For everybody's safety, we should let each other know if any one of us has other sex partners," Brad suggested.

"Not I," said Jim.

"Not I," repeated Lee.

"That makes three of us," said Brad.

Lee, being succinct, asked Brad, "What about Rita?"

"Rita, the rich girl?" asked Brad.

"Yes."

189

"Oh, don't need to wonder about her. She's always been just a friend. By the way, can we agree that our past is the past and none of anybody's concern?" He was trying to prevent talking about Ingrid and the other girls.

"Yes," Jim and Lee responded simultaneously.

"I want both of you to give me a hug," Lee said. The guys got up. Lee got up, and she hugged them with all her might. The two guys, towering over her, hugged her and each other gently.

When she released them, Brad said, "Lee, I have a plane to catch at ten p.m. My uncle Bruce is going to take me to the airport."

The words made Lee's heart sink. She wanted to offer him a ride, but Jim was in their presence. It would be over the top in rudeness if she did so.

"After a final party at Lee's place," Jim suggested. "You want anybody besides the misfits?"

"No, just the misfits, thanks."

"Then I shall take my leave. I'll meet y'all at Sherry's."

Jim was so damn cute, and Brad was so handsome. She imagined having sex with both of them at the same time. That reverie lasted about five seconds, and she shook it off.

The party was somber. Everyone was going to miss Brad. When it was time for him to leave, Lee walked him out to his motorcycle. The weather was mild, and there was little snow on the ground. The roads were clear.

"Would you like a ride?" he asked her. She had never been on the back of his motorcycle.

"That would be nice," she replied.

He took his extra leather jacket from underneath the seat and handed it to Lee. After she put it on, he put an extra helmet on her head and adjusted the strap. He gave her a pair of extra gloves to wear.

She hugged him during the ride. It felt beautiful to be alone with him, feeling his body against hers. They did not converse. Brad took a few back roads. The ride lasted just a few minutes because it was almost time for Brad to get home to catch the jet to Anniston.

When they got back to Sherry's place, they disembarked and stood facing each other. He gently removed their helmets and jackets. He brushed his body up against hers. Her heart pounded with desire. He took the gloves from her hands and removed his gloves also. He held her face in his hands gently and kissed her for a long time. It ended with a few quick pecks on the lips.

"Tell everybody goodbye for me, would you please?"

"Absolutely," Lee replied, "I hope you stay safe over there. I'll miss you."

"I'll miss you too, more than you know."

He got back onto the motorcycle; started it up; put the jacket, gloves, and helmet back on; looked at her once with a gorgeous grin; and then he drove down the driveway.

Lee watched him leave with tears in her eyes. She waited until he was out of sight and sound before going back into the cottage.

"Brad says goodbye to us all," she said demurely. She tried to hide her sadness. Sherry and Bela could see through her attempt, as did the rest of the group. Jim approached her and put his arm around her shoulders.

"He'll be all right, honey," he said softly into her ear. "He'll stay safe over there."

She nodded her head a couple times, pretending to believe him. She wanted to cry for both Brad and Jim. *Let God keep them both in his loving arms,* she prayed.

DEAREST LEORA

As soon as Brad was back on base in his room, he plunked his duffel bag onto the floor beside the bed, stripped off his coat and boots, sat at the desk, and wrote.

Dearest Leora,

I thank God for allowing me to be in your company this past weekend. I hope you had a good time. It was fabulous seeing the group too. They are such funny, intelligent, hopeful, compassionate people.

I must tell you that you have nothing to be concerned about when it comes to Rita or any other girl for that matter. I hope you can be patient with me. It's difficult for me to open to up to people, and I must work on that so it doesn't control me.

Remember that night in the barn loft when we shared the toothbrush and I told you I wouldn't hide anything from you? I meant what I said. It feels good to be able to be honest with you, Leora. I hope you can understand that.

All right, it's getting late here. I must hit the sack. I will either stay awake all night thinking of you, or I will dream all night about you. I am

caught in the most magical kind of purgatory.
Have a lovely day.

Yours always,
Brad

POSTDEPARTURE TO BOOT CAMP—
ADAMS, BRADFORD

At the picnic tables one balmy evening in Leora's front yard, the group found itself musing on Brad and the Army.

"So since the Army says everything backward, is Brad's name Adams, Bradford?" asked Adrian.

Collin said, "I like the name Adams Bradford."

"I do too," said Darrell. "Just take the *s* off Adams, and it's perfect."

"What are some other stupid things they say in the Army?" asked Collin. "Coat, battle dress, men's."

"Ear protection, foam, one in package," suggested Darren.

"And there are actual instructions on how to put those earplugs into your ears?" Sandy asked.

"Yes, ma'am," Darren replied. "Army intelligence—the quintessential oxymoron."

Sandy said, "I understand the camouflage pattern was designed by a woman."

"That's very unusual," said Adrian, "but very cool."

Connie mentioned, "I know a veteran who says you can't see the person even four feet in front of you if they're wearing the camouflage uniform. That's amazingly effective."

"I believe it," said Sandy. "They even cover their machinery and vehicles with the camouflage material to hide them."

Brad's first letter home was written to Uncle Bruce, who in turn read it to Stickman, who in turn recited it to the group from memory. The letter mentioned physical training on hot, humid mornings, and marching everywhere—to chow hall, classes, bivouac training in the deep woods, playing "army" with live ammunition.

In his only-so-far letter directly to the group via Stickman, Brad promised to write as often as possible, but the days "are inundated with classes, ammunitions training, compass and map reading, mine-sweeping and marching, marching, marching." He told the group he would write to Jim, and Jim would "inform you all the contents of my correspondence."

"That's our Brad," said Collin, "a man of small words."

Everybody in the group laughed at that.

Despite the humor, it was hard to believe their friend Brad was now a soldier in the United States Army, being trained as a mercenary to fight in a war thousands of miles away on the other side of the planet. To the group, Brad was their friend the dairy farmer and horse trainer, the guy who wore dark clothes and cowboy boots. But they also knew him as one of the most intelligent, well-spoken, reticent young man they had ever met. But now the Army was his reality. Being back home with the group was just a dream for now.

CELEBRATING
VETERANS—DECEMBER

Brad picked up the latest edition of the *Newsflyer* as soon as the post-exchange opened. He had the weekend free. He had plenty of time to take in any festivities that might be occurring in the area. According to the *Newsflyer*, Hegnen Stables, one of the largest horse stables in the state of Alabama, were hosting a celebration of veterans that weekend. On a whim, Brad decided to take a bus to the stables. A huge banner spanned the entrance to the quarter-mile driveway.

COMING THIS WEEKEND!
GALA FOR ALL SERVICE MEMBERS, ACTIVE AND RETIRED
OPEN TO THE PUBLIC
8:00 A.M. UNTIL DARK
FIREWORKS TO CONCLUDE THE FESTIVITIES!

Brad strode down the blacktop driveway flanked on both sides by expansive horse pastures confined by white wooden fences. He made his way to an enormous red barn, perused the place, and managed to locate a familiar horse in a stall. Brad unlatched the gate, entered the stall, and greeted the horse.

"Hey there, ol' boy. It's great to see you. I hope they're giving you lots of fun stuff to do for the crowds, so you can have a good time."

"Excuse me, do you know the owner of this horse?" It was a tall, slim African American man in a dark-blue suit, approaching the stall.

Brad chucked. "Oh yes, I know the owner. My name is Brad Adams. Could you please tell me how to find—"

His mouth stopped in its tracks. There she was—Ingrid—ambling toward Brad and the horse. When she got within about twenty feet of the stall, she cocked her head to one side and eyed Brad quizzically. The last time she had seen Brad, he had worn denim and leather. He had been neat and tidy then, but currently he was downright prim and proper—khakis with perfect creases, stark-white Henley shirt, brown patent leather shoes. He looked even more handsome than ever before, if that was possible.

Brad's gaze was steadfast as she continued to approach him. When there were just a few feet between them, he broke the spell.

"Ingrid, how nice to see you."

The African American man decided it was all right to leave.

Brad shook her hand. "It's Brad. Bruce's nephew. Stallion here used to be his horse."

Ingrid smiled politely. "Yes, of course, Brad. It's wonderful to see you, but you're so far from home."

"Not so far really," he replied. "I'm in basic training at Fort McClellan in Anniston. Tell me, how is Stallion doing? He looks great!"

"Oh, he's spectacular. I'm his only rider and trainer. He'll do a fabulous job at this festival. He's just a ham for attention." She stroked the side of Stallion's neck gently.

"Has Rita ever seen you do a show?"

"Yes, she saw me on a different horse a couple years ago. That was in California."

"Well, maybe I'll stay to watch Stallion today."

"Oh, Brad, when you go back to Fort McClellan, my driver can take you back. His name is Skip."

Of course, she has a driver, he thought. "How can I get in touch with Skip?"

She managed to produce a tiny piece of paper from the pocket of her slacks. Brad handed her a pen. She wrote down Skip's number and returned the paper and pen to Brad, which he deftly stored in his shirt pocket.

Ingrid was dazzling in her tight tan spandex pants and white satin blouse. Her long braid was topped by a riding hat. She grinned at Brad as she stroked Stallion's neck again. Her teeth were bright white and perfect. She was still the beauty he had met some years ago. But he did not want any kind of a tryst with her, and he hoped she understood that. He did not want Ingrid. He wanted Leora.

"So"—the subject changed—"what brings you to Fort McClellan?"

"I was drafted, Ingrid. I cut out of school to come down here. I'm going to get my diploma before I'm discharged. I'm training to go to Vietnam."

Ingrid looked down, and when she looked up, she caught Brad's gaze.

"I'm sorry, Brad, that's not good news, is it?"

"Absolutely not, I'd rather be in Canada if you want to know the truth."

"Brad, please accept my apologies, but I have to get ready for the next show. Please stay and watch Stallion and me. It would be nice to get a picture of us afterward, what do you say?"

"Okay, Ingrid."

"You take care of yourself!"

"Have a great day."

There was a short pause. Then Ingrid instinctively reached toward Brad and gave him a perfunctory hug. He responded with a smile. After that, she turned and left the stall. Brad watched her walk through the barn until she disappeared from his sight. Then he made his way outside to the grand stands.

The Photograph—December

One of Brad's letters to Jim included an informal photograph of Ingrid and Brad at the horse stables, just outside Stallion's stall. Ingrid and Brad were merely standing side by side smiling a perfectly polite smile for the cameraman, Skip. Jim did not know if Brad wanted either Leora or Rita to see that photograph but decided they could handle it. There was almost nothing personal in the photograph; it actually appeared as if the two might not even know each other. But Ingrid had insisted on showing herself off to Rita, and Brad figured it would be all right.

That gave Leora the idea to fetch her mother's old Brownie camera from home so she could take pictures of the group at school. Lee sported Sherry's camera at lunchtime. The group had a great time exchanging places for poses. Her favorite picture was of Jim and Adrian. They were standing, leaning against each other with their ankles crossed. Jim had made a motion to kiss Adrian on the cheek, but Collin hollered out, "Don't kiss the hippie, you old queer!" Jim and Adrian put their arms around each other's shoulders instead. Adrian sported the peace sign. Lee made a copy of that picture and hung it on her bedroom wall. (She would have that photograph wherever she lived.) Everybody in the group wrote a short passage to go with the photographs. Jim insisted Lee get her face in at least one picture. He took a nice one of her grinning, sitting at the picnic table.

"You're beautiful, my dear," he complimented her.

"Thank you," she said cheerfully. He grinned at her, and his beautiful blue eyes sparkled. She gave him a loving smile in return.

Needless to say, Brad was elated with the letter and the photographs. He was especially delighted to have a picture of Leora. He had it reduced in size so it would fit in his wallet. The regular-sized photos adorned one of the walls near his bunk. He considered the pictures the best Christmas gift he could ever receive.

The Announcement—
Deployment

It was exactly 7:00 p.m. The Sovines' phone rang. It took five rings for Leora to get to it.

"Hello?" she said. She sounded a little breathy; she had been studying, textbooks and papers sprawled across her bed. She was tired.

"Leora."

It was Brad.

"Brad, oh god, how are you? Please tell me you're going to be okay."

He cleared his throat. "Are you having a pleasant night?"

"Um, just studying, trying not to doze off. Nothing important." Her heart felt as if it was in her throat. Shard upon shard pierced her chest with a mixture of fear and excitement.

"Well, I'll get right to it then," he said. "I'm getting deployed to Vietnam soon."

A pause ensued. Reality hit her rather abruptly and hard. Tears fell from her eyes and dripped down her face onto the floor. She sniffed back more of the tears and listened.

"It's a place called Saigon. Have you heard of it? I'll be in the infantry, front lines, if there is such a thing in a jungle."

"Saigon," she repeated; she felt light-headed. Yes, she had heard of the city on the news.

"Lee, I can't stay on the phone long. All the guys at the base are needing to make phone calls home and elsewhere. I am *so sorry*. But you are the first loved one I'm notifying. I'm going to call Bruce the next time there's a phone available, and then he'll call Mom. If you want to call Jim, please feel free. He's my best friend."

"Yes, yes, of course. Saigon. I'll call him right away."

"Okay. Thank you. Lee, I love you. Please don't take that with any heavy obligation. It just feels great saying it. Good night, and I'll send letters as soon as I'm able to. We fly out the day after tomorrow."

Lee's heart sank. "Brad, I love you. I love you. I'm going to call Jim right now."

"All right, dear. Please don't cry. Bye for now."

"'Bye!" she said with tears in her eyes. The very last thing in the world she wanted to do was hang up that phone, but she knew there were loved ones all over Fort McClellan waiting to make a similar call.

* * *

Jim was in his bedroom watching television when the yellow phone in the kitchen rang. He knew his mother liked to answer the phone, so he left it alone. She must have been out of earshot because after twelve rings, Jim figured he would not ignore it any longer. Slightly irritated, he ran to the kitchen and picked up the phone from the wall.

"Hello!" he bellowed into the receiver.

"Hi, Jim, it's me, Lee."

"Oh my god and to think I almost decided to let the phone stop ringing, hoping the person on the other end of the line got tired of waiting. How are you, dear?"

"Oh god, Jim," she cried, "I just spoke to Brad on the phone. He asked me to let you know. He's getting deployed to Saigon, South Vietnam, day after tomorrow."

"What unit is he assigned to?"

"Infantry."

"Ooooh, the worst besides Special Forces."

202

"He said he'll be on the front lines if there's such a thing in the jungle."

"Well, they're as prepared as they can be. They play jungle warfare for months in basic training. It's serious stuff. Live ammunition. The works. Vietnam is a very weird place, and war is not fought conventionally by the North Vietnamese. The terrain is so different from ours, and they take excellent advantage of that. But I don't want to burn you out any further. Do you need me to come over right now?"

"No, thank you so much. I'm okay. I'll let you know the minute I need you though, if that's all right with you."

"Well, of *course*, it is," he said very seriously. Then he asked her, "Should I call Bruce?"

"Brad said he was going to get in touch with Bruce as soon as possible."

"That could be hours, honey. My guess is the soldiers are being told to keep their phone calls few and brief. I'll give Bruce the heads up. Brad wouldn't mind. Okay? You know how close Brad and I are. No harm done, honey."

There was a very short pause.

"Okay," said Lee in a small voice.

"Don't cry, Lee, are you trying not to cry?"

"How did you know that? I'm not even sniffling."

"It's your tiny voice. Okay, I'm going to call Bruce, and then I'll get back with you right away. How does that sound?"

"Good, Jim, sounds good, thank you."

"No problem, little lady, talk to you soon. Bye!"

"Bye, Jim."

Jim dialed Bruce's number immediately. Bruce answered within two rings. He had had a foreboding about Brad, and he had been right.

"Hello, Bruce, it's Jim. Want to let you know that Brad just spoke to Lee. He's being deployed day after tomorrow to Saigon, Vietnam. Infantry. Front lines. Couldn't get much worse, could it?"

"Don't worry, Jim," said Bruce. "He'll never stay in Vietnam. He'll be out of there as soon as his two legs can take him."

Jim sighed. "Yeah, you know, you're right. We just need to trust him to be safe for now. And pray that we hear from him once he has hightailed it out of there."

"He's going to have to stay off the grid for a while until he's allowed to come home to the United States. So tell Lee nothing. If the FBI ever gets a hold of any of us, we have to either be damned good liars or be totally innocent. He might get in touch with me, but I'm sorry to say I won't let you know where he is, for your safety. I hope you understand."

"Yes, Bruce, I understand completely."

"I'm afraid not hearing from Brad is going to break Leora's heart, Jim, but there's no other way to handle him being off the grid."

"Yes, yes, I understand. But I'm scared for him right now on account of his place of his deployment."

"Me too," Bruce replied.

"Well, I told Lee I would call her for moral support once I got in touch with you. Sorry to cut this short, but I'm glad you were home to get my call. You will hear from Brad, but there's no way to know when or from where, stateside or South Vietnam. You take care, and let me know if there's anything I can do for you."

"Thanks, buddy, I appreciate that. Same goes for you. Talk to you later."

"Okay, bye, Bruce."

Jim called Lee immediately. She answered at the first ring. She had been sitting on the kitchen counter next to the phone.

"Hi, ol' Jim here again. You okay?"

"Yeah, I'm all right, thank you. My mom is here, and my dad is here too."

"Your dad's in town?"

"Yeah, he took some time off from teaching and driving a truck, so we have him with us for a while."

Lee always had a very good time with Bela, and Sherry took his presence as a subdued pleasantry. Nothing bad lay between Sherry and Bela, but they had known each other a long time, and what remained of their relationship was past friendship, respect, and love. The hard-charged sexual attraction had diminished, but there was no harm in that. They pledged to remain faithful to each other, and it was easy for them to do so. All in all, it was a very good relationship.

Nevertheless, Jim was not fond of Bela. Bela left Lee alone on far too many weekends. He was not always there for moral support or help with her studies. Lee and Sherry accepted his absences. Jim could not. Jim also pictured Bela as a hound dog in his youth, luring Sherry into out-of-wedlock sex, saddling her with a baby.

"Well, it seems as if you're in good hands, my dear," Jim said to Lee. "I'll let you go for now. Please call me any time you need to talk. I'll be seeing you at school too, of course. Try to get some sleep tonight. Drink some chamomile tea."

"Sounds good," Lee replied. "I'll see if Mom has any on hand."

They said their goodbyes, and Lee approached Sherry about the tea.

"Sure thing, honey, let me get you set up with a nice warm cup," Sherry suggested.

Sherry made the tea, and Lee sipped it as she sat in the living room with Sherry and Bela. They all talked about Brad and the draft, the war, and Vietnam. Lee said goodnight early that evening. She closed her textbooks and pushed them aside on top of the bed, slipped into comfortable pajamas, and crawled into bed. She worried that sleep would elude her, but she fell out fairly quickly. It was a nicely deep sleep with no dreams to remember.

THE NEW YEAR

New Year's Eve entered with a howling wind. The group was at Sherry's place drinking beer and wine and eating leftovers from Christmas dinner. They wanted to have another car party. Sherry wanted them to stay, but there was a vote, and it was unanimous. They were going. It was decided that Rita would drive because she was sober; Lee had had two glasses of wine. Sherry was only slightly relieved.

Bela took her aside, put his arm around her shoulders, and said gently, "Let them go, honey. It'll be okay."

Sherry acquiesced. Bela gave her a kiss on her forehead.

Inside the Cruiser, Jim sat next to Rita and went over all the instrumentation of the dashboard and the buttons on the door. Darren sat next to Jim, next to the passenger door. The two guys lent Rita some confidence. She figured that if they trusted her, she could manage the car just fine.

The Cruiser partially slid slowly down the steep driveway that had been plowed by the neighbor. Out on the road, snow was falling fast—fat white flakes—and the wind was creating a temperature below zero. Rita took her time getting to the desired location, directed by Jim and Darren. She parked the car. Jim and Darren traded places.

Adrian lit up his orange baby bong. Collin lit up a joint. Connie opened a bottle of red wine. All these things were passed around inside the car. The group became animated. Several conversations ensued simultaneously. Everybody stayed toasty warm with the heater blasting warm air throughout the car.

Adrian piped up, "What's going to happen next year when we all graduate? Are we going to be a storybook ending and live happily ever after with one another? And what's to become of our Rita? We all know she has to go home and graduate with her classmates there."

"Well, Rita," said Darren, "if you see it my way, you will marry me. We can go to college and live in the married dorm. We can breakfast together every morning and study together every evening. And we could stay local, not run off to some far off hoity-toity Ivy League school. Whatta ya say, Rita Armstrong, will you marry me?"

There was a short pause.

"What the hell?" Collin, seated behind Rita, said to himself.

"Darren, don't be mean to her," Connie, seated next to Collin, admonished gently.

"I'm perfectly serious, Rita," Darren said as he gently put his hand on the side of her face and made her look at him. "Yes, you're a high-class rich girl. But you also try to fit in with the group here, and you can be positively grounded sometimes. I find that dichotomy refreshing and intriguing. Yes, you intrigue me. I want to marry you. I promise to make your father look up to me as a student and as a husband. No turning back. If you say yes, you're the only one for me forever."

No one could even hear anyone else breathing. A seemingly interminable silence, even though it lasted no longer than a few seconds, commandeered the car. There was unspoken shock since they believed Darren still had the girlfriend in Binghamton, which he did. Some of the folks in the group guessed the relationship Darren had with Suzette had been waning anyway. Despite that, everyone, even Darren, was surprised by this development.

"Yes," demurely Rita replied. "Yes, Darren, I'd love to marry you."

"Are you serious?" That was Darrell, from the third seat.

"Yes," Rita said again to Darren, "to be sure."

"Oh my god," Darren uttered. He looked at Jim, who asked him, "What the hell you lookin' at *me* for?"

"She actually *wants* me," replied Darren.

"*Okay* then!" said Jim.

And the car erupted in the clapping of hands and hooting and hollering. Darren and Rita would make a happy and physically beautiful couple.

Lee merely smiled and reached out to hold Rita's hand for a few seconds. She knew they would never be the best of friends, but she also now knew for certain that Rita was not to be feared or envied because of any friendship with Brad. Lee was free from any shards on account of Rita, the rich girl.

The group continued to party until darkness fell. Then it was decided Lee, seated next to Connie, would drive home. She was sufficiently sober. Lee crawled over people and the seat back to assume her position at the steering wheel. Jim sat next to her, and Darren sat next to the passenger door with Rita on his lap. Rita was practically asleep, worn-out from the excitement.

The Cruiser made its way safely back to Sherry's place, where she insisted everyone stay there for the night so they could see what the next day would bring for snowfall. Bela was already bedded down for the night. Lying next to Bela, Sherry read *Les Misérables*, as content as she could be, until her eyes shut and the book fell onto her chest. She was asleep before midnight.

Although the group was tired from their party, they stayed awake long enough to greet the new year and toast one another with champagne. After that, they crashed wherever there was space—on beds, the couch, the recliner and the floor.

The snow continued to fall. The roads became impassable until late morning when the plow trucks made perfunctory clearing of the snow. But the weatherman on the TV issued a warning to stay home. Sherry would be glad to have the group with her on New Year's Day. She would make a huge dinner for them. Everyone would celebrate the engagement of Rita and Darren. Then they would dress warmly and go out trudging through the forest for the fun of it. Everyone would be happy, even her Leora for a while. No shards all day New Year's Day because Lee was with Jim, and she loved him very much. Brad would be mostly absent from Lee's thoughts. It was going to be a good New Year's Day.

BIG 18

Lee's eighteenth birthday was on its way. It was early February. Sherry asked her what kind of party she wanted, and Lee responded, "Just the group please."

On Lee's birthday, Sherry threw a nice, subdued party with ice cream, cake, and champagne. Adrian and Sandy gave her eighteen roses. Sherry gave her a set of pots and pans for her "hope chest." She got a variety of household gifts from the rest of the group—dish towels, silverware, hot pads, cooking utensils. Jim gave her a 1/4 carat diamond engagement ring, which made her cry with happiness while everybody else cheered and clapped their hands. Lee gave Jim a big hug and a quick little kiss on the lips, being too shy to show much affection in front of her friends and family.

Jim was happy to see Bela there. He still did not like Lee's father very much, but he kept the feeling to himself. Lee already knew how Jim felt, so she left it alone. Bela was attentive to Lee during the party, and Jim had to admit to himself that it was nice to see them together. Bela thoroughly enjoyed himself and made sure to give his daughter a big hug before the party ended.

There was a second celebration at the party that day. Sandy and Adrian announced their engagement. There were cheers and claps for them as well. They planned to get married in the summer, and everyone at the cottage was invited, "even Rita, the rich girl," Adrian teased Rita, who was there with Darren.

"Oh, whatever, Adrian, I'll be there," Rita responded.

FINAL DAYS OF SCHOOL— JUNE 1972

June was a full month for Leora. She had five exams to take, on top of doing her duties at home and at the dry-cleaning business. She decided to quit tutoring students. Her life was just too busy. One of the most involved exams to pass was the gymnastics one. She and Sandy made up routines for the parallel bars, the balance beam, the gym mat, and the trampoline. She asked Jim to be one of her spotters for the trampoline routine. He was more than happy to oblige. His presence would put her in a good frame of mind. She had a brief memory of Brad suggesting they share the trampoline sometime. But she was too busy to dwell on that memory.

Graduation night was bittersweet, heartwarming, funny, and helpful. Mr. Jenkins was the keynote speaker. Jim did the "response" because he was valedictorian. His address was short and full of clichés. Lee held back her laughter sometimes when she knew he was not even half serious about what he was saying. But he brought tears to the place when he announced, "And conspicuously absent is Brad Adams, who would have been with us if it hadn't been for his dangerous draft number. God bless, Brad, and Godspeed." Leora shed a few tears. Even good ol' Mr. Jenkins shed a tear or two. Lee would always remember Mr. Biology with fondness.

The diplomas were given out with a handshake, and when the final student was seated, they all threw their caps into the air. Then they filed out to the band playing "Pomp and Circumstance," which

Lee had played for three graduating classes ad nauseum. Was she ever glad to get out of that auditorium! Jim found Lee outside talking to Sandy. He picked up Lee and spun her around until she was dizzy. Then he plopped her onto her feet. She held onto his arm. It was decided Lee would ask Sherry if the group could party at her place. Jim took Lee home. They arrived just as Sherry and Bela had arrived from the auditorium. Sherry said it was fine to have a party. Jim called Adrian and started the phone chain. The only person missed was Darren. His father said he was with Rita for the evening at some other graduation party in Kingston.

At around midnight, a silver Pontiac GTO climbed slowly up Sherry's driveway and got parked between two trees in front of the house. Darren and Rita stumbled into the house, drunk as hobos.

"Oh my god!" exclaimed Rita. "I'm drunk! I can't go home. My dad will kill me!"

"Besides that," Darren remarked, "we couldn't stay away from you weirdos."

"Not *that* I believe," said Connie.

Everyone toasted each other with champagne at midnight. Then they all chowed down on finger food prepared by Sherry. Sherry and Bela were in bed by 2:00 a.m.; at which time, Darren was sufficiently sober to get Rita home. Everyone else left except Jim and Sandy. Sandy took to the couch. Jim and Lee jumped into her bed fully clothed. They spooned together. He whispered into her ear, "There's just one thing I want to know."

She thought, *Oh, please don't let it be about Brad.*

He asked her, "Had you ever thought of marrying me?"

"Mmm hmm," Lee replied sleepily.

"Okay, thanks."

Lee rolled to face him with a wry grin. "That's it?" she asked.

"Yes."

"You're funny."

"That's why you love me, right?"

"Absolutely. Do you want to get married right away?"

"Let's make it a long engagement. We both have college to get through. Plenty of time to consider or reconsider. Whatta ya say?"

"Yes, Jim, a long engagement makes sense to me." She rolled back over. "Now cuddle up with me. I think I'll miss you until I wake up."

"Oh, so you're a *romantic*."

"The cat's out of the bag," she said and fell asleep almost immediately.

July 1972

Dear Leora,

Lucky for me, I have the use of a typewriter. A couple of the keys stick, but all I have to do is yank them back up. It's an old black and gold manual typewriter made by the Grand Rapids Typewriter company. Grand Rapids is a city in Michigan, also known as the furniture capital. It was the first city to put fluoride in its municipal drinking water and the first city in the nation to experiment with aerial spraying of DDT on crops. I found that interesting.

I am "writing" to you from my base in Saigon. It can get crazy here with all the GIs coming and going. It's not a safe place. We have been attacked and shot at from the air and from the ground.

Forgive me for not contacting you on your birthday. You thought I forgot, didn't you? Never. You're now big eighteen. I hope you enjoyed the day.

I bought an instamatic camera. I will send you some pictures. Parts of South Vietnam are beautiful—the mountains, waterfalls, rivers (the ones that aren't polluted), and rice paddies.

I have to be off the grid sometimes. I am being transferred to Special Forces. We will perform duties that I can't talk about, and only those with Army clearance may know what they are. Sometimes we won't even know what our mission is until it's time to begin. What we will do is almost always incredibly dangerous. That's all I can say about the Special Forces. I have been promoted, so I have the distinction of leading my troops into the depths of hell.

Needless to say, I hate it here. I look at your picture and the pictures of the group countless times a day. I miss all of you, especially you, Leora. I miss your face and your eyes and your voice and your personality. I'd rather be anywhere with you than in this godforsaken land alone.

Well, my time is up. Duty calls already, and we haven't even gotten debriefed from the previous mission. Please give Jim my regards, as well as the group and your parents. I've gotten letters from Jim, Bruce, you, and my mom already. Poor woman is worried sick about me. All I can do is reassure her.

Yours,
SFC Bradford Adams
Brad

July 1972

Dear Brad,

Hello! I am using a typewriter too, an electric one. My parents bought one for me for college. I've chosen Dutchess for my associate's degree. After that, I'll decide on a four-year university or just go to work at the hospital if they will take me in the lab. Everybody in the group is talking college. I will miss them all when they go.

Thank you for your letter. I'm glad there are some folks sending you mail. I hope the pictures of the group and my parents got to you safely. I haven't heard from you since I mailed them out. Yes, I had a wonderful birthday party, thank you for remembering me.

I decided on an instamatic camera too. My Brownie is outdated. It takes better pictures, but I like the instamatic because the pictures develop right before your eyes.

Everybody seems the same except Adrian. Somehow, he has grown to over six feet tall, and he cut his thick red hair. He looks great. He has lost his little boy look. And he and Sandy have announced that they are going to get married this summer.

Rita and Darren are engaged too. It's going to be a long engagement, so they can graduate from college first. Some of us were shocked at his proposal—he proposed to her during one of my car parties!—but Darren treats her well. They seem made for each other.

Sometimes I think I hear your deep voice, and sometimes I think I see you from the corner of my eye, but you're not here obviously.

Wow, I have typed more in two minutes than I would normally speak in a week. Above all things, I pray for your safety. And I look forward to any letters from you. If you would favor me with a picture of yourself, I would appreciate it very much.

Yours,
Leora

WORKING IN THE SUMMER

During the summer of 1972, the group was busy with employment. They did not have much opportunity to hang out together except on an occasional weekend.

Sandy stayed on at the dry-cleaning business working with Sherry and Lee.

Jim kept his job as a chemist-in-training at the wastewater treatment plant. His supervisor liked him very much and invited him to stay on because he wanted Jim to continue with the apprenticeship. Jim discussed it with Lee. It was a great opportunity; he could stay close to Kingston, and he would not need to attend University of Michigan.

Connie decided to dive right in, so she started University of Michigan right after graduating from Kingston. The university gave accelerated classes during the summer, and Connie took advantage of them. She promised the group she would call and write and visit as much as she could, but the summer courses were grueling. And there were a thousand students just as smart as she was. It was very competitive. Connie did not suffer any delusions; she had visited the enormous campus three times before settling in there. It was culture shock at first—so many brilliant people from all over the world—but she pledged to herself that she could make it through the rigorous schedule. Right away, she joined a study group for a couple of her classes.

Rita's father gave her the summer off. She spent much of her time riding and racing the horses at her father's ranch. He told her she was as good as Ingrid, but Rita would never believe that.

Darren decided to become an attorney and started law school in Boston right away. He lived on campus, and Rita stayed with him often, much to the chagrin of her father. He was not pleased with her association with Darren, but he decided to wait to see if she and Darren would get married. If they decided to shack up, as her father thought of living together, he might just cut her out of her six-figure trust fund.

Darrell and Collin took daytime jobs at the Warners' cattle farm, which involved long hours and hard work. They stayed busy, always with something to do. It made the days seem to go by fast. They got along very well with each other, and the Warners were impressed with their workmanship. They were excited about starting school in the autumn and talked about their interests frequently. They joined a Renaissance study and music group that met on weekends.

Adrian and Lorrie worked at their mother's wholesale company for the fourth summer in a row. Adrian could drive a refrigerated semitruck now. He made trips all over the country to pick up flora and fauna for his mother's business. Occasionally Sandy accompanied him, with Sherry's blessings.

Speaking of Ingrid, she had called Rita just once back in April to ask about Brad. Rita had told her there had been no word from him since the past February.

Ingrid had merely said, "Odd. Okay, dear, thank you."

The sisters were not good friends. They rarely spoke to each other. It was okay with Rita. She did not miss a sister-to-sister relationship of which she heard other girls speak. She still had Sara and Bonnie. Besides Darren and going horseback riding, Rita's favorite thing to do was go shopping with her two best friends to spend obscene amounts of money without a care.

On the last Saturday in August, Adrian and Sandy became Mr. and Mrs. Auble. The wedding took place in his mother's backyard. She had a deep yard of perfect green grass, just in front of a patch of forest. There was a large attendance, mostly Adrian's extended family.

There were three large white tents put up for the occasion. Reception was a beautiful, four-tiered cake and champagne. The weather was perfect, not the typical hot and humid August of New York. They purchased a nice nineteenth-century house in Kingston's historical district, and they planned to renovate it to reflect its period in history.

On those rare occasions when the group could get together, they usually ended up at Sherry and Bela's. He would take out his accordion and entertain everybody. Some of the songs were sung directly to Sherry. She still loved him very much, and he was totally devoted to her.

SHERRY'S ANNOUNCEMENT

Sherry and Bela were already home when Lee arrived from work. She greeted her parents and met them in the living room.

"Lee, we saw the doctor today," Sherry said as Lee was seating herself in the recliner. She looked at her mother.

"I have multiple sclerosis. It's starting to affect my arms and hands and face. We don't know about my dad yet. His MS has seemed to have stalled for the time being."

Lee's heart sank. "Nothing you can do?"

"Just try to treat the symptoms. Science is years away from a cure, I'm afraid."

"I've noticed Grandpa dropping things a lot these days."

"Yes, he might need to have a helper. Or better yet, move closer to us."

"I would love that," Lee said. "I could help him even more."

"Not to the point of not having a life of your own, honey."

"I understand."

"There might come a time when I'll need help too. We can't overwork you."

"Let's deal with that if it comes," Bela suggested.

That was agreeable to Lee and Sherry.

"Just keep the faith, everyone," Sherry begged.

"Of course, Mom."

"Yes, my dear wife," said Bela.

They went into a group hug. Bela kissed Sherry on the lips.

"Okay, dinnertime. I'll see what I can muster up." She sighed.

While Lee was in her room, she heard her parents talking.

"I've signed up for life, you know," Bela was saying. "Like the day I signed on as Lee's daddy."

"I love you for that, Bela, my dear, handsome husband," Sherry replied. "And I'll forgive you if you someday bail out."

"Never. Stop talking that way. I love you now and forever, Sherry."

They stopped talking. Who knows what they were doing out there? Lee decided to stay in her room until she was called for dinner. She felt as if her head was spinning over this bad news of her mother. She sat on the end of her bed and cried.

GRANDPA ED

One bright, sunny day, Lee drove to Schenectady to pick up Ed after Sherry had notified him. He was already packed when Lee arrived at his house. He was happy to see Lee and glad to be going away for a while. The house got awfully lonesome sometimes now that his wife was gone. Cancer had taken her a few years back.

"Now what's this I hear about your mother—she has MS as well?" Ed said as they climbed into the car.

"Yes, Grandpa," Lee replied, "hands and arms and face. When's the last time you saw your doctor?"

"A month ago."

"Maybe it's time to go again."

"I'll think about it."

"Okay, Grandpa."

He could be a stubborn man. Lee saw no help in debating anything with him that day.

"I won't be a burden to my family either," he said with pride.

"Let's talk about this some other time," Lee suggested.

They had a pleasant ride the rest of the way. Lee told Ed that Jim had been accepted to the University of Michigan for chemical engineering. Ed let out a whistle of surprise. "But Jim's a brilliant young man. We all know that."

When they arrived at Sherry and Bela's place. Sherry met them at the car. When Ed got out, she gave him a hug.

"Hungry? Chicken and dumplings."

"Oh, I don't want to burden you," Ed said.

"It's on the stove already. Come inside."

It was evident Ed was having problems because when he tried to use his fork, it took three attempts before he could get a grip on it. And it took him four attempts at getting the food into his mouth.

"It's like that sometimes," he said. "It takes an eon to eat."

"Dad, I want you to move in here," Sherry announced.

"Yes, Grandpa, so do I," added Lee.

"I know your room is small, but if you can tolerate it, we'd love to have you with us."

Ed was accustomed to staying in the extra bedroom, hardly a room really. It measured twelve-by-twelve foot and had just a tiny closest. But he didn't mind.

"Okay," he agreed. "We'll do a dry run."

Sherry reached over the table and put her hand on top of one of Ed's hands and squeezed it gently.

After supper was finished, Lee excused herself to go to her room to study. After about an hour, she phoned Jim and told him that Ed was going to move in with them. She described Ed's difficulty eating that evening. Jim offered to help in any way. Lee was infinitely grateful. Jim was such a great guy.

"What are you doing right now?" she asked him.

"Watching some unknown situation comedy. It's not funny either."

"You know, you should come and visit Ed soon."

"That's a go for sure, and to see you, of course."

"I guess that would be fine."

"You *guess*!" he said in mock indignation.

"You really are the best, you know."

"Yeah, yeah, you know it."

Lee laughed.

"Well? You do know it," he insisted.

"Yeah, I do. I'm going to go bed. Happy TV watching."

"*Pff*, I'm ready to turn it off. At any rate, thanks for calling and letting me know about your grandpa. I'm sorry he's having trouble."

"Thanks, Jim. See you soon."

"Okay, dear. Good night."

It took Lee about an hour to finally fall asleep even using her breathing technique. When she did, it was a deep sleep with no dreams to recall.

YEARS FLY BY

Jim and Lee got married in 1973 in a small church in Kingston. In attendance were the group, Jim's parents, Sherry and Bela, the Clark clan, and a minister. Sandy was the maid of honor. Adrian was the best man. There was ice cream, champagne, and a beautiful white wedding cake at Sherry and Bela's place following the ceremony. Jim and Lee had requested no gifts because, together, they had already accumulated what they would need for their household. Needless to say, when the crowd had left Sherry and Bela's place, Sherry pressed a $100 bill into Jim's hand. He and Lee shed a tear of gratitude, and there was a group hug that followed.

Lee got pregnant right away. Maddie was born that same year while Lee was still in college. Krista was born in 1975. Lee took a job at the laboratory of the nearby hospital right after she graduated. The daughters were bright and beautiful blond girls with deep-blue eyes. They were spittin' images of their daddy. Jim and Lee decided two children were enough for them. They were in love with their girls. They wanted to give them as much of their attention as they could—a noncrowded family. Lee started herself back on birth control pills about six months after Krista was born, when Lee had finished nursing her. There was no specific data to warn women of the cancer dangers. Every woman Lee knew was on the pill when they were not pregnant, and there were no concerns about it. It would be many years before research would point to cancer, and by that time, it would be too late for millions of women to survive.

In 1975, Jim and Lee put money down on a nice raised-ranch house in Kingston. They were delighted with it—their first home away from her parents' cramped cottage! There was plenty of space in the raised-ranch to go around, even rooms for overnight guests.

Sherry's MS worsened in her facial muscles. She would cry out in pain in the middle of the night sometimes. She took prescription medicine, but it did not dull the pain completely. She often slept on the couch to relieve Bela of being shocked awake. Once in a while, Lee spent the night there to keep Sherry company and to give Bela a break from worrying about his wife. Sherry apologized to them profusely, but Bela always reminded her of her inner and outer beauty.

The Clark clan visited Jim and Lee a few times every year for a week at time, when Lee and Jim took vacation time from work. The Clarks took rooms at Jim and Lee's and Sherry and Bela's. There was a family reunion every evening.

One night when the girls were in bed, and Lee and Jim were alone in the living room, he said, "God, we're all getting so old! I'm going to miss our parents terribly when they go."

"Give them a few more years, honey," said Lee. "They're only in their forties!"

"Yeah, I guess you're right. I was getting ahead of myself. I feel old and out of favor sometimes."

"Oh, for god's sake, I love you so much it overwhelms me sometimes."

"Ditto, Captain. We've got it mighty good right now. We're still young enough to have a blast with our little towheads."

"Yes, honey, you're right."

Jim gave Lee a big hug and quick kiss on the lips.

"We have to be resigned to the fact that our parents might end up living here, you know," he said. "I hope it's not right around the corner. I want to raise our babies first."

Lee sighed. "That makes two of us."

Leora's Pond—March

There was a pond in the woods about a quarter of a mile north of an old farmhouse, a pond where Leora skated many times as a child. The house was closed up for the winter, the owners having gone south for a few months. But Lee had taken her chances and entered the property before seeing the house was not occupied. She had to park on the road because the driveway was impassable from the winter's snowfall.

Her trek beyond the house was across raised, bumpy, snow-covered rows where field corn was grown every year. The snow was at least two feet deep. The freezing breeze erased each of Lee's boot steps in wisps of white fog. She took her time, trying not to think about anything. The air nearly froze her face in a matter of a few minutes. She could move the muscles of her cheeks or mouth but little, despite the scarf over her mouth. It was just another brutal winter day in New York. The clouds obscured the sun. It was a rather ugly day to Lee's thinking. She much preferred sunlight and an azure sky during the winter.

She was tired all of a sudden, as if some virus had just hit her entire body. She looked back. By now, the pond was closer than the house, so there was no use in turning around. She kept trudging slowly. It was going to be so nice to just slip down that embankment and slide across the pond in her boots. She did not have her skates. She had not planned on skating that day. She just wanted the peace and quietude, surrounded by tall, giant trees that she had experienced so many times as a happy child. No other place had been so magical back then. After spending a couple hours shoveling the snow from the pond, there was maybe an hour left of energy for her and her little friends to skate. And skate they did, making up stories of wonder and rescue. They would fall on their rear ends and laugh and laugh. They built little walls of snow over which they jumped, thrilled by their abilities. At the end of their time there, they were usually too cold to take off their skates, so they made their way back by skating across the frozen field, past the farmhouse where the old couple watched and waved at them. The little girls waved back at the couple, and they skated half a mile down the snow-covered dirt road toward Sherry's place, trudged up the steep driveway, and found warmth and comfort in the cottage, where they were treated to hot chocolate with marshmallows.

Lee and her girlfriends continued to skate on that pond through their preteen years. Thereafter, Lee preferred to be there by herself. It was where she could shed worries and concerns. She could return home in a peaceful state of mind.

Back to the present day

When she got to the edge of the hill above the pond, Lee stopped and looked up so she could feel the tiny pelts of ice sting her face as they fell straight down from the sky. She made her way down to the pond carefully. The snow was almost three feet deep, but she got onto the pond anyway and trudged around it for about five minutes. She loved the sensation of her nearly frozen cheeks. The rest of her body was completely warm.

But she was so tired. *How about I just lie down for a few minutes and let the falling ice kiss my face some more?* she thought. She lay on her back and made a snow angel; after which, she turned onto her side and curled up with snow all around her. She figured the snow would protect her from cold and harm. She was completely at peace.

About an hour later, a young couple was contentedly trudging through the woods near the pond. They stopped at the top of the knoll to look at the snow-covered pond below them. Simultaneously, they furrowed their brows and bent their heads forward for a better look at the lump on the surface of the ice.

"Honey, I think there's somebody down there," she said, her voice slightly muffled by the scarf over her mouth.

He replied, "They're not moving either. You want to stay here while I go check it out?"

"No, I'll go with you. You never know what could be going on down there."

"Okay." He backed down a few feet and gripped her hands in his hands to help her start her way downward. They took long strides in the thigh-deep snow.

He was the first one to reach the edge of the pond. He slid one foot onto the ice as far as his leg would extend, to make sure he was safe. "It's solid, honey," she assured him, knowing what he was thinking. "It's been below zero for a couple weeks now, and it's a fairly shallow pond."

"Okay," he replied without looking back at her.

They walked side by side halfway across the pond. It was an idyllic place really, down in a deep gully, surrounded by the tall oaks and conifers; the wind did not reach them down there.

He got onto his knees beside Leora and took off one of his thick gloves. He reached into her hood and placed two fingers flat on the side of her neck to feel a pulse. Her face was almost gray. She lay on her right side, curled up as if sleeping soundly, hands beneath her hooded face.

He thought, *Nothing. Nothing. No. Wait. Press harder. There!*

He said, "She's alive. Shit. She's weak, but she's still alive. Okay, now what."

"Give her my coat," she said to him. "I'll warm up fast enough in hers."

"No, honey, I'll cover her with mine. Hers will warm me up okay. If it fits me. She's a tiny person."

She helped him exchange coats. Lee's coat did not fit him. The arms were short on him, and it did not zip up over his tall, athletic frame. "I can carry her." He had long arms into which he easily scooped Lee. He gently set her over his shoulder. "Okay, here we go."

She followed him closely to the top of the knoll. Although Lee was small, her weight added to his made it difficult for him to balance her because he had to take shorter steps than usual.

The couple had entered the woods from the north side. They lived in a neighborhood about a quarter of a mile north of the pond. As they got closer to their home, they hollered for help, but they did not get any response. As soon as they reached the edge of their property, which was partially wooded, the young woman ran to their house. In a matter of two minutes, their car was running, and she was helping him place Lee to lie down on the back seat. It was a 1969 light blue Buick Skylark sedan. Lee would have liked it. It probably would have reminded her of Bela. The woman sat in the back seat with Lee's head in her lap.

The young man drove like a bat out of hell through the small neighborhood and onto the main road. It was below zero outside, but the roads had been cleared of ice.

The hospital was outside the major business district. This is where the young man took Lee. He stopped his car at the entrance to the emergency department and got out of the car to meet the security guard coming from the building.

"Young lady in the back seat," said the young man. "I think she's half frozen."

"Okay, sir, we'll take it from here. Is she an acquaintance of yours?"

"No," said the woman. "We found her lying on a frozen pond in the woods of all places."

"Well, you've certainly saved her life," said the guard as two persons arrived with a stretcher. The young man gently took Lee from the back seat and placed her onto the stretcher. Inside the emergency department, he switched coats with her. He and the woman offered a silent prayer for Lee and a complete recovery.

Time to Wake Up— Moon Shadow

"She's been doing well, but she's in and out of sleep. She needs to wake up completely, eat some real food, discontinue the IV fluids, and get out of this place," said doctor number 1, who was much older than anyone else in Leora's hospital room. He meant well, but his demeanor was gruff. He was tall and bald and wore a crisp, white, calf-length lab coat with no name tag.

"She's young," doctor number 2 told Sherry. He was only twenty-five years old, a medical resident in training with doctor 1. "She looks strong and healthy."

Doctor 2 wore a dark-gray button-up shirt and a short stark-white lab coat with the embroidered name Lanning stitched above the right chest. Dark-gray wool socks, perfectly pleated gray slacks, and shiny black leather shoes completed his outfit. His black hair was neatly trimmed. He had blue eyes that appeared soft and kind. His voice matched his eyes.

After doctor 2 spoke, there was a long pause.

"Tomorrow, I expect her to be fully awake," doctor 1 said to Sherry only, looking at her with a smile on his face, but his eyes did not smile. Sherry nodded. As the two doctors turned toward the door, doctor 2 put a gentle palm of a hand on Sherry's shoulder for a couple seconds. They smiled at each other.

"Thank you both," she said.

"Our pleasure," replied doctor 1 formally.

After the doctors exited the room, Jim said, "That old fart thinks he's God's gift to medicine. He needs to retire. His face looks about a hundred years old. I wonder if he remembers anything he learned in college microbiology. He acts as if his face will crack if he even attempts a smile."

"Yeah," said Adrian. "He surely is a cranky old crab."

They all moved to the head of Lee's bed. They gazed down at her face. She was sleeping without a single worry line. The chart on the foot of her bed indicated good vitals-oxygen, pulse, heart rate, blood pressure.

Adrian adjusted Lee's sheets and blankets so that she was tucked in snugly.

"Well, I know what I have to do," said Jim confidently. "I need to leave you folks for a while. I might not be back tonight."

Sherry looked at Jim as he was walking backward toward the door. "What is it?" she asked.

Jim looked at Sherry and made a motion with his hand as if he was using a telephone.

Sherry—confused—furrowed her brow.

"Poor Sherry, you're so tired," Adrian said. He put his hands upon her shoulders from behind and nodded at Jim. "I got her, Stickman," he said kindly. "She's going to climb right into bed with Lee and take a nap. I'm going to make sure no so-called medical professionals enter this room for at least an hour." He led Sherry to the other side of Lee's bed and assisted her up so that mother and daughter were lying together. Lee was on her back, so Sherry had just enough space to lie on her side and snuggle up to Lee, putting an arm gently over Lee's abdomen. Adrian removed Sherry's shoes. After about five seconds, she was asleep, breathing gently upon Lee's shoulder. Adrian took a seat in one of the chairs in the room, a tall-backed Naugahyde thing that was very uncomfortable. He took a look around the room. Anywhere there was horizontal space available, he, Jim, and Sherry had placed vases of flowers from the warehouse of Adrian's mother.

"What we frickin' do for love," Jim said.

"Yeah," Adrian replied. "Peace, Leora. Peace, Sherry, and peace to you, Stick buddy."

"Peace to you too, my hippie friend," Jim responded. He turned and left the room.

Jim went home, picked up his phone, and dialed a long-distance number he had memorized. It was a number Bruce had given him recently. He paid for the call.

A soft, deep voice answered, "Yes."

"I'm calling about *her*," Jim said. "She's in a hospital room right now. Somebody found her lying half frozen on some pond in the woods behind some old farmhouse. There was a windchill of below zero out there. So far, the only people from the group who know about this are Sandy, Sherry, the hippie, you, and I."

"A pond," Brad responded. "Yes, she told me about a pond. Why was she—"

"She never told *me* about any pond," Jim said, annoyed. It was not lost on Brad. "We haven't heard from her what happened. She's in and out of sleep, in kind of la-la land. I think you should come and see her, whether or not she wakes up while you're there. I'll make sure you stay safe."

"What is la-la land?" Brad asked.

"She's asleep but not comatose. The doctors want her fully awake by tomorrow so they can send her home. She seems to be very peaceful. She's just so damned tired. She does so much for everybody else and nothing for herself, poor thing."

A short pause was broken by Brad. "When do you want me there?"

"Well, how long will it take you to get here?"

"Six hours at the most."

"Okay, six hours it is. Meet me under the moon shadow. Do you remember?"

"Yes."

"There's no way to for us to contact each other once you get going. I just hope you make it here. Be careful."

"All right, Jim, on my way now," Brad responded.

"Good."

"'Bye for now. Love you."

"Love you too. See you soon."

* * *

Six hours made it about 11:00 p.m. Brad walked up to the gravel driveway, surveying what he could see of the Warners' farm. He recalled the crunching of his boots on the driveway. It had been practically forever since he had seen that red barn with the bedroom in the loft. He easily recalled Leora standing at the side of his bed; he had been so happy just to have her there with him. He remembered that he had asked her, "Do you know what that little body of yours does to me?" It was 3:00 a.m., and he was on his way to help birth a calf. She had wanted to go with him. *What a wonderful girl,* he mused. He made his way to the front of the barn, the preconsidered point of meeting in case of something important.

Jim was already there, standing in front of the two closed sliding barn doors.

"How is she?" were Brad's first words to Jim.

"I think she'll be fine," Jim replied. "Thank the gods. Apparently, the people who found her live near that pond and know the area well. They picked her up and rushed her to the hospital."

"Does she still visit her grandfather on the weekends?" Brad asked.

"He lives with Lee and me part-time, and at Sherry's the rest of the time. His wife died a few years back. He has MS. He needs help with activities of daily living."

Brad looked at Jim briefly. Jim looked slightly older and more serious. The glint in the corner of his eyes was missing. Otherwise, he stood as tall and good-looking as ever.

Brad, as Jim noticed, looked a bit more stern of face. No frowns, just deeper vertical lines along the sides of his mouth. Nothing else had changed. He was still incredibly handsome.

Brad had arrived silently—neither car nor motorcycle was either heard or seen. He was wearing a down feathered winter coat, gloves, no hat. He stood at the wide, closed barn doors with his gloved thumbs in his front pockets. His cowboy boots looked experienced. *Perhaps,* thought Jim, *Brad worked with horses on some dry dirt farm far away.* Jim did not know. Jim did not ask. He sighed heavily and looked at Brad under the faux moon shadow from the light on top of the barn.

"Still hoping for a pardon?"

Brad shrugged his shoulders and said, "Never can tell if that will ever happen."

It seemed ambiguous to Jim, but he let it go. He could tell Brad had no desire to talk about his constraints.

"Okay, ready to go?" Jim asked. "I parked my truck down the street so the Warners wouldn't hear me pull into the driveway."

"Do they know about the light on top of the barn?"

"They? Oh, no. I've kept them out of the loop. They don't know where you are."

"Hmmm."

"Let's get to the hospital then."

"Right," said Brad.

They walked across the gravel driveway, walked about a quarter of a mile along the deserted road, and got into Jim's truck.

At the hospital, Brad and Jim slipped into Lee's room quietly. Lee had a roommate now, in the bed next to the window, along the far wall.

"Lee is behind curtain number 1!" Jim said softly as he slid the cloth hanging from swiveling chains.

Lee looked peaceful, and her skin had recovered its lovely olive tone. She wore the hospital-ugly cotton blue and white gown, but it did not deter from her beauty. Sherry was still in the bed with Lee, cuddled up to Lee's side, snoring slightly. Lee's breaths were shallow and even.

Brad took the ladies into his sight without emotion.

Is he jaded by all the hardships he experienced in Vietnam? Does he have a girlfriend? Children? Jim wondered, but he did not ask Brad any questions.

A tiny shard stung Brad upon his heart, just a short pang—a tiny sting of devotion perhaps—and then it was gone.

Brad and Jim stood at the side of the bed where Lee was sleeping. Jim ventured to look across the room. There was Adrian, in the uncomfortable straight-backed chair. His head had fallen back and was against the wall. He sat there, his mouth a gaping chasm of hard breathing. He was exhausted—hearing the news about Lee, getting the flowers prepped and delivered and set up in the hospital room, spending his waking hours watching over Lee and Sherry. His orange tie-dyed T-shirt was needing a wash from all the flowers, soil, and water being spilled upon it. His brown corduroy pants fared a little better than the shirt.

The other patient was a pleasant teenager. Adrian was pleasant to her in return; she actually fell asleep to Adrian singing songs from Ten Years After's first album. Not the most common bedtime music, but it worked. She did not know the first thing about Ten Years After, but Adrian gave her kudos for being a musician, clarinet player in the band at Kingston High School.

Brad's eyes surveyed the room full of flowers. In a soft voice, he asked Jim, "The flowers?"

Jim grinned and softly said, "Adrian wanted her to have some bright flowers to wake up to. He did a marvelous job." He looked at Adrian and softly said, "Isn't that right, Adrian?"

Adrian swiftly righted his flung-back head and closed his mouth. He looked at Brad and Jim and smiled endearingly. As he stretched his arms, he whispered, "Hi, guys! Hey, Brad!"

Brad stole over to Adrian and gave him a solid hug while Adrian stayed in the chair.

"You!" Adrian whispered as they hugged each other. "Welcome back! This is so far out!"

Brad whispered, "Hey, guy. You look great. Thanks for being such a good friend to our Leora. You're a grand fellow." He planted a kiss on Adrian's cheek. Adrian felt Brad's stubble and was comforted by it somehow.

Brad stole over to the head of Lee's bed and kissed her gently on her forehead, taking care to avoid pressing his stubble onto her skin. Her eyes did not change. Nothing changed.

Jim said, "They say you never can tell what they hear when they're 'in there.'"

Brad just looked down at Lee and smiled with the love he had for her. She was still so pretty. No amount of illness or age was going to erase that. He swallowed a lump in his throat. He cleared his throat quietly to kick back a tear that was trying to come from his eye. The tear did come, and it landed on his cheek and immediately disappeared into dryness—a single tear for Leora, perhaps to say "I'm sorry," perhaps to soothe away the many shards she had endured on his behalf. He had missed her so very much. He had not expected her to forgive him. And now he just wanted her to be all right.

Jim said, "We got married in '73. We have two little girls."

Brad just looked at Lee and nodded his head to acknowledge what Jim had just said. How could Brad have ever expected her to wait for him, not being able to tell her that he was still alive? Yet he *had* expected it. But Jim was there to love and protect her. Of course, she couldn't say no to Jim. She had loved him for years.

Jim suggested, "Let's let these folks get some sleep."

Adrian got up and approached Brad and Jim. They all went out into the hallway. Adrian gave each of his friends a hug.

"No more kisses from you, Brad, that was weird."

"Oh," Brad replied, "we all know what a homo you are."

"Whatever, soldier boy" was Adrian's retort. "I really didn't mind it." He winked at Brad.

Brad rolled his eyes upward.

"Can hardly wait until Lee fully wakes up to all the flowers," Adrian said happily.

Jim said, "I hope you're here when she does."

"Oh, you know this hippie will be here," Adrian responded. "What about you all?"

Jim replied, "We aren't sure yet."

"Okay," Adrian yawned softly, "it's back to the wonderful hospital chair for me. Wish I could hop into bed with Lee's little roommate here. We could fall asleep to rock songs together."

Jim and Brad smiled at Adrian.

Jim wondered if Brad was still wearing blinders for Lee. *I under-stand,* Jim thought. *Lee was my best grade school friend, my lover in high school, and now she's my beautiful wife. I wear blinders for her too.* He gave Brad a gentle pat on the back. Brad was as muscular as he always had been. No amount of age would change his physical stature.

"Okay," said Jim to Adrian. "Now it's my turn to give the hippie a kiss. I'm losin' out here."

"Oh gawd," Adrian responded as he rolled his eyes upward. "Make it quick." He pursed his lips and closed his eyes. Jim grabbed Adrian's face into his hands and planted a nice one on Adrian's left temple.

"I feel better now. Thanks, you old hippie."

"Whatever, weirdo," Adrian retorted. "Good night, you guys."

"'Night," Brad and Jim responded in unison.

Adrian went back into the room. Brad and Jim sauntered down the hallway, the way they did in high school, before there were things such as lost love and MS and Vietnam.

* * *

Jim was not at the hospital when Lee awoke at about 8:00 a.m. Sherry had vacated the bed at about midnight and had plopped her-self into the other uncomfortable chair after Adrian had moved it next to the head of Lee's bed. Lee was puzzled; she had no recollec-tion of being taken there, and she had no memory of what had led up to it.

"What's going on?" she quizzed her mother. "What am I doing here? Where's Jim?"

Adrian said, "I'll give him a call," and left the room to find a pay phone.

"Honey, you told me you wanted to visit your special pond," Sandy said to Lee. "You almost froze down there. You were rescued by a young couple who live near the pond. You might have died out there. It's been below zero outside for weeks now."

"Mom, I don't remember any of that." Lee looked over at the roommate, who was awake.

"Are we bothering you, ma'am?" Lee asked the girl.

"Oh not at all, thank you," the girl replied.

Sherry made a sweep of her hand to indicate all the flowers. "All for you from Adrian, Jim, and me."

"Oh my god," Lee said, "I don't deserve all this."

Just then the two doctors entered the room. They checked Lee's blood pressure and temperature and breathing rate. She was cleared to go home after the IV was discontinued and Lee had a bite to eat. She chose a bowl of oatmeal and a glass of orange juice. Doctor 1 cracked a smile when Lee thanked him and doctor 2 for taking care of her, even though she remembered nothing of it.

It took Jim and Adrian about an hour to load the flowers into Jim's truck and Sherry's car. Lee cuddled up to Jim on the way home. He slipped an arm over her shoulders.

"I was worried about you, my love. Please let me know next time you want to go off and be alone. I understand the need for that, but I want to be sure you're going to be all right."

"Aye aye, Captain," Lee said with a salute.

"That's good enough for me," he responded.

At home, Lee was not allowed to lift a finger. Jim, Adrian, and Sherry unloaded all the flowers. Lee watched from the living room couch, where she was seated with Maddie on her right and Krista on her left. She gave the girls an abbreviated, mostly fictionalized version of her outing.

"Say, girls, would you like to go ice-skating sometime? It's a blast. You'd love it."

"Yeah, yeah!" the girls squealed in unison.

"Daddy, guess what Mommy wants to do!" said Maddie as Jim was lugging a huge planter of colorful spring flowers up the stairs.

"Oh, some adventure, no doubt," he said the to the girls as he eyed Lee with a serious face. She understood his affect.

"Go ice-skating!" the girls squealed simultaneously.

Jim cleared his throat to let Lee know he was not fond of the idea. She understood that too.

Sandy had been in the kitchen. She entered the living room, gave Adrian a hug and a quick kiss on the lips, and went back into the kitchen to help Sherry make some lunch for everybody.

"Sandy, take as many flowers as you want," Lee called into the kitchen. "I'd be helpless without you and Adrian and Mom."

Sandy went back into the living room and replied, "I might take one, but just remember, I love you and your girls to pieces. They aren't work for me. They're a pleasure." She bent down and hugged Lee.

After a lunch of roast beef sandwiches, potato salad, devilled eggs, soda pop, and ice cream, Lee decided to take a nap. She engaged in a group hug with everybody else, and then she ventured into dreamland in her bed. She heard nothing as the rest of the adults went into the kitchen and played several rounds of gin rummy, laughing and talking and having a good time, relieved that Lee was safe at home.

THE PARDON—1977

Jim and Lee's olive-green phone rang. It was on a small table near the entrance of the hallway that contained the bedrooms. Two little tow-headed girls giggled as they raced to listen to the conversation. From high above their little selves, a hand reached down to pick up the receiver.

"Hello."

"Hey, Adrian here. Are you watching the news? President Carter has pardoned all deserters. Full pardon. They can come home now. I wonder if Brad knows."

Jim sighed. "Haven't heard. I've been keeping my eye on the news all this time though. That's wonderful for all those soldiers. Thank God, Adrian. They get to come home now."

"Will you go get him?" Adrian asked.

"I honestly don't know where he is. He went way underground after seeing Lee at the hospital. I don't think even his uncle Bruce knows where he is, although Brad will be free to get in touch with him now."

"Agreed. He'll be back, just in his own sweet time, dragging the rest of us along like little groupies." Adrian was perturbed. "All felonies from desertion will be expunged after the soldiers complete some sort of paperwork. I don't know how long that will take. He might not get back home right away."

"Don't let him do that to do you, Adrian. You're better than that."

"Daddy, Daddy, who's on the phone?" Maddie chattered. Each daughter hugged one of Jim's pant legs.

"It's Uncle Adrian, girls. You may talk to him later, okay? Right now, he wants to talk to your mom. Do you know where she is?"

"Mommy, somebody wants you on the phone!" Maddie sang.

"Right here, honey," Lee said as she approached Jim from the kitchen.

Adrian sighed. He didn't even know what to say.

"Hey, Lee," he said in a small voice.

Lee greeted him cheerfully, "Hi, Adrian, what's up?"

"Straight up, Lee. The president has given all Vietnam vets amnesty if they fled the country during the war. They are all now free to come home."

"Adrian, that's wonderful. I wondered if it was ever going to happen. I wonder though how many will actually come home. Many of them don't trust the US government, you know. And some of them might have made a permanent home up in Canada or in some other country."

"Yeah, well, I hope the government is true to its word. It would be a terrible debacle if it turned its back on the soldiers again."

Adrian wondered if Lee was thinking of Brad.

"Well, I just heard it on the news and wanted to spread the good word. Have a great night, you guys. Love ya!"

"Love you too, Adrian," Lee replied. She handed the phone back to Jim, and he hung it up. He studied Lee's face quickly for any signs of emotion attached to the news of the pardon.

"I guess that means Brad can come out of hiding," said Jim.

"If he's alive. I don't have a clue as to where he is. It's up to him to show himself or not." She sounded noncommittal. Was she? Brad had had such an impact on her in the old days, some of it full of angst. And love. Does that strength of angst and love fade away? She gave no clue in the look on her face. She remained the Leora he knew and loved.

"Hey, towheads!" Jim said suddenly. "Let's go out for ice cream. Let's celebrate one of our friends coming home. Whatta ya say?"

The Jones family made their way to a nearby soda fountain shop and had sodas and ice cream. The girls guzzled and giggled the entire time. *So much like their dad,* Lee thought, *so much humor.* Jim played along with the girls. Lee loved every minute of it. She didn't give Brad a thought…at that time. But there would be a moment later on when so much would change.

MR. CLARK

One evening, Lee and Jim got a call from Jarob. Lee answered the phone.

"Hi, Lee, it's Connor, how is everything going there?"

"We're all doing great, Connor. What's up?" She suspected trouble.

"Want to let you know that Mr. Clark suffered a stroke a couple days ago. His left side is very weak. He can't walk any more. He needs a wheelchair. The worst of it all is that he can't work on cars any longer. He's very depressed."

"Well, we can come over any time. The girls aren't in school right now."

"I think that would elevate his mood, Lee. I'd appreciate it."

"Give us a day to pack, and we'll be there."

"Okay. Thanks so much. We can talk more when you get here."

"Of course, Connor. See you very soon."

"All right, bye, Lee."

"Bye."

Lee located Jim in the kitchen and told him the news. Jim found the girls in their rooms and helped each of them pack a bag for a couple days' stay at Mr. and Mrs. Clarks'. Then he packed himself a bag as well as one for Lee. Lee called Sherry and Bela and got Sherry on the phone.

"Mom, would you please tell Dad that Mr. Clark had a stroke affecting his left side? We are all going there tomorrow to stay for a couple days. Would you like to meet us there?"

"Yes, certainly, honey. I can leave the dry-cleaning business with Sandy. Bela will be free to go too. I guess I'll see you all there tomorrow, as soon as I can get help here for Grandpa Ed."

"Okay."

* * *

When the Jones family and Sherry and Bela arrived at the Clarks', Jarob and Fulton met them outside. There were hugs all 'round, after which everybody entered the house. Mr. Clark was in the living room in a wheelchair, leaning to the left slightly. The left side of his face drooped a bit. It had been at least a year since the Jones family had seen Mr. and Mrs. Clark. They noticed that Mr. Clark's hair was all gray now and thinning. He was extremely slender. His skin was pale. He just looked old.

The girls gave Mr. Clark a hug. They did not know them as well as they knew Sherry and Bela, but they wanted to be polite. Mr. Clark hugged them with his right arm and smiled. Sherry and Bela gave him a hug too, and Bela said, "Dad, I'm so sorry."

"Oh, son, it's what God chooses to do sometimes," Mr. Clark replied. His voice was impeded by the drooping of his mouth, but he was understandable.

Bela said, "Think though—you still have your right side intact. I don't see why you can't be back in the shed with the boys helping them out with your right hand. Don't give up on it, Dad."

"I was thinking of giving up on it, but maybe I could be of some use."

"Of course, Dad," said Fulton.

"Well, if I suffer another stroke, just talk to the boys. I want them to have their freedom from me if I become totally disabled."

"That's fair enough," Bela replied.

He looked at Jarob and Fulton, who nodded their heads in agreement.

"Where's Mom?" Bela asked.

"She's in the kitchen," replied Mr. Clark.

The Jones family found Mrs. Clark at the stove. It was a newer model, electric. The wood stove was long gone, along with the wringer washer, which had been replaced by an automatic electric washer. Mrs. Clark turned to see the Jones family. Her first hug went to Bela, and it was a long, desperate one. Poor Mrs. Clark was at a loss.

"I am so glad you're here, Bela," she said. "Please have a talk with the boys. I don't really know if they want to be nurse's aides to their dad if you know what I mean."

Bela invited the rest of the Jones family to join him in a group hug, which they did. Then Mrs. Clark resumed her cooking, telling the Jones family to have a seat in the living room. The big ol' chair was still there, and when Maddie and Krista sat in it, it practically buried them. Everybody had a chuckle over that. It was standing room only in the living room after Bela and Sherry took the couch with Jarob.

"So what's the scoop here?" Bela asked Fulton. "Are you all able to handle Dad okay? Or do we need to find a helper during part of the day or at night?"

"We're doing well," Fulton replied. "We'll keep it in mind though."

"Don't let my stroke be the only reason you're here," said Mr. Clark. "There's Mrs. Clark and horses and cars to be fixed."

Sherry and Lee made their way into the kitchen to visit Mrs. Clark. She was cooking spaghetti.

"Something fast and easy," she explained. "There are a lot of folks to feed tonight."

"Grandma, do you need any help?"

"No, but your company would be appreciated."

So they chatted about many things, small talk mostly, with just a mention of Mr. Clark's stroke. Sherry asked about Mrs. Woodfield.

"Oh, she's gone to some home for unwed mothers after the poor house was torn down, a much easier job to handle than hundreds of hungry people."

"I'll say," Sherry said.

After supper was finished, the men drove to a nearby lumber-yard and bought some Wolmanized wood and quickly built a rudimentary ramp to go out the back door. Then the men widened the doorway that went into the shop so Mr. Clark could join Jarob and Fulton working on cars and other moving machinery. Jarob pushed Mr. Clark in the wheelchair out to the shed. Mr. Clark brightened up a bit. The men went to the shed and hung around there for an hour or so. By then, it was getting dark. The girls took Jarob's room and slept on his double bed. For the time, Jarob and Fulton shared Fulton's bedroom, where Jarob took a cot and Fulton took his bed. Sherry, Bela, Lee, and Jim had their sleeping bags, and they spread themselves out onto the living room floor. Mr. Clark slept in his wheelchair in the living room while Mrs. Clark took their room upstairs.

The next morning during breakfast of pancakes and syrup, eggs, and bacon—prepared by Mrs. Clark and Sherry—everyone talked about where Mr. Clark was going to sleep from now on since his room with Mrs. Clark was upstairs. Remodeling was going to be a major project, but the Clark men were capable of doing it. They got a piece of paper from Mrs. Clark and started making a model of their plans. After breakfast, the men went to the lumberyard and purchased materials. They started right away, pouring a concrete floor in a space next to the front door. The room would measure twelve-by-fourteen feet. It took them all day to lay the foundation. Two days later, it was studs and openings for two windows—one to face the front, the other to face the poor farm—as well as trusses for the roof.

"You guys want us to stay to help you finish this?" Bela asked Jarob.

"No, we've got this. We need to get drywall, insulation, and siding, and when that's done, we can bash in the wall of the house for a doorway into the new room. We've got it covered, brother. Thank you for your help already though."

"My pleasure. Now remember, there is always the option of having a helper a few hours a day. Mom and Dad can afford it."

"I'll keep it in mind," Jarob replied. "Promise."

"Okay," Bela said. "You'll call me if you need anything, and if there are any changes?"

"Sure thing, brother," Jarob said.

"Well then, do you mind if I take the girls out on the horses?"

"No problem, have fun," Fulton replied.

The older horses that Lee had ridden had passed away. The new horses they acquired were for recreational riding. Bela got the girls out of the house and saddled up the horses. He rode with Krista and let Maddie ride on her own. An hour later, three cold, happy people giggled their way back to the barn.

"You should get Mom and Grandma out here for a ride," said Krista. "That was a blast!"

"I just might do that," Bela replied. "Now you know how to brush down a horse, right? I'll help you do that, and then we'll go inside for some hot chocolate."

"Yes!" Maddie exclaimed.

Back inside the kitchen, Bela asked Fulton, "Do you have any hot chocolate?"

"Only the homemade kind!" hollered Jarob from the living room.

"Here, let me make it," Fulton said. "No packaged hot chocolate here."

"Thanks, brother," said Bela. "Say, where's Sherry?"

"Living room talking to Dad," Fulton replied.

Bela approached Sherry about a short hike across the field to the old barn still standing on the vacant patch of land with new houses all around it. Sherry grabbed her coat and went along with Bela. The barn was missing siding in some places, and the roof was hopelessly eroded. There was snow in the loft.

"Give me a kiss for old time's sake please," Bela said when they were up in the loft. So they kissed for a moment. "It's possible this is the place where Lee was conceived."

"Those were some nice times, honey."

"Right you are, darlin'. I love you even more now than I did back then. Thank you for being my wife, Sherry."

They gave each other a nice, warm hug, and kissed a bit more. Then they made their way back to the house. The girls were at the kitchen table enjoying their hot chocolate and telling Mrs. Clark about their fun on the horses.

The next morning, the Jones family and Sherry and Bela bade the Clarks their goodbyes. Jeremy and Clara showed up with Benjamin just in time to see them all off.

It took the Clark men four days to complete the new room. Mr. Clark was wholly satisfied with it. Mrs. Clark hugged each of her boys and cried tears of gratitude and relief.

Unfortunately, three weeks later, Mr. Clark suffered another stroke. This one affected his right side and his throat. The swallowing mechanism was affected. He said absolutely no to any tube feedings. He was aware that death was near, and he wanted to be home when it happened. The Clark boys got a hospice nurse to be with Mr. Clark. It did not last long. He could not eat. He grew weak rapidly, and within a week, he passed away on a mercy-filled dose of morphine that stopped his heart from beating. He was cremated, and there was no service, according to his wishes.

Mrs. Clark was very depressed. She moped around the house for a couple weeks, but she was able to cook meals for the guys. It helped her get to a new normal. It would take her a couple months to perk back up, albeit just a bit. Bela would call her every day for a month; at which point, Mrs. Clark told him his duty was over, she was going to be all right. Bela confirmed this with Jarob and Fulton.

"Well, you know if you need *anything*, you had better call us," he said to his mom.

"I promise, son."

* * *

Christmas time rolled around. Maddie and Krista decided no gifts. Instead, they asked their parents to give money to a charity that catches wild horses out west and tames them and gives them good homes so they do not live a life of misery and starvation. Lee had the girls write a little note to accompany the check she wrote for $200.

Lee was so proud of her girls! She gave each of them a big mom hug. Jim heard about what they had done, and he gave each daughter a big, daddy hug, against which they squirmed in false desire to get away from him. Then Jim grabbed Lee and hugged her for good measure, the way he used to do her in high school—gruffly, with good humor. Lee held onto Jim and laughed into his ear, "You're so weird."

"Thank you for those words of love, my darling!" Jim said.

"*Pff*, whatever," Lee responded.

HIS VOICE—1978

Leora just got home from work at the hospital. It had been a strenuous day—two lab techs were home ill and one tech at work ill. She worked harder that day than she had ever worked anywhere. She put in extra hours, and she was whipped. It was after six in the evening. She was ready for a hot bath and pajamas. Jim and the girls were visiting Adrian and Sandy's children. It was a perfect time to have some peace and quiet.

As luck would have it, the phone rang as soon as she was inside the house. She slowly slumped up the carpeted steps to the living room. She plopped her coat onto the nearby green-and-chrome Naugahyde sofa before she answered the phone. It was a familiar voice. "Leora." Years of absence were not going to take away the memory of that depth and timbre. It was Brad. Unmistakably. There was a long pause. She was stunned. She did not know what to do or say.

"Lee, are you there?" he asked finally.

She sighed softly.

"Yes, yes, I'm here, Brad. What's happening? Why are you calling me? I haven't heard anything from you in years."

"I know. I was there. At the hospital. I need to explain. Please. I need to tell you all about it. I need to see you."

Not a good idea, Lee thought. He sounded too earnest.

"You were at the hospital when I was sick?" she said, incredulous. That was *a long time ago.* And no one, not even Jim, had ever told her. How dare Jim take that away from her?

249

She felt nausea creeping up into her stomach, to think she had given up on him because of his absence, when he was actually *there* in the hospital, and he had been thinking of her all these years... She thought of her pond, that place of solitude that she had not seen since that stay at the hospital. She had no recollection of some of the events leading up to her being on that pond or being rescued. She recalled waking up to flowers everywhere in the hospital room. She had no recollection of Brad being there.

"Yes, that's when I first found out you're married to Jim. Jim didn't know where I was coming from when I visited the hospital, but I intended to change my hiding place anyway so Jim wouldn't be in any danger with the FBI. Lee, I have to see you. Please. You don't have to forgive me. I can't be that lucky. I just want to explain what happened to me—why I left Vietnam and what I've been doing all these years."

"You skipped out on Vietnam?"

Lee thought, *Did Jim know where you were? How dare he?*

"I did," Brad replied. "I was there for a one-year tour of duty. I defected the day I was supposed to go back there. I couldn't aim my rifle at innocent people any longer. I couldn't kill civilians, even under direct orders."

"You were ordered to kill civilians?"

"Yes," Brad responded, "I never did kill any civilians, but I can't say the same for North Vietnamese soldiers. Kill or be killed, that's what it was about in Vietnam. I don't think they wanted to kill us any more than we wanted to slaughter them. But this isn't why I called you. Please I'd love to see you, if only for a few minutes. I know you're with Jim now. I'm ecstatic for you. No one deserves better than you do."

"I had to forget about you, I'm so sorry. You disappeared, and Jim was there, and I loved him so much...I didn't even know if you were alive!"

"Stop, stop, I understand all that. I would never try to take you away from our best friend."

Lee let the air be silent.

Two beautiful children and a wonderful husband; a nice raised-ranch-style home; a good job as lab tech at the local hospital; friends from way back from Kingston High—Sandy, Lorrie, Connie; parents still alive and doing okay, considering Sherry had mild MS—they were enough, or were they? How could one word from Brad start the shards all over again? What was going to happen to her world if she fell in *love* with Brad all over again? If he was as dark, handsome, and kind as he had been years ago, it was certainly possible.

Goddamn it, she thought, *what the hell do I do?* But to Brad, she said, "Brad, where would you like to meet?"

There was a long pause. He could not believe what his ears had just heard.

"Lee?"

"Yes, I'm here."

"I can't believe you're willing to see me."

"It can't be here at my home. I'd prefer someplace else."

"Okay. Do you remember the Warners' farm?"

"Yes, I do."

"Would you meet me there sometime? Any time you can get away?"

"Yes, I'll meet you there. Let's do this as soon as possible please. How about tomorrow?"

Brad's eyes widened with surprise.

"Um, okay, you name the time. I'll be there."

"I work tomorrow until three p.m. Can we meet shortly after that?"

"Oh yes, that would be great." Brad sighed and closed his eyes for a few seconds.

"Promise me one thing, please," said Lee.

"Anything on this planet."

"Please let's stay away from the loft. I have such nice memories of that place. I don't want to spoil it in case we have a bad encounter." *There, I said it,* she thought. She was glad he could not see her blush.

He sighed in complete understanding. "You have my word."

"All right. Until tomorrow afternoon then?"

"Yes, Lee, and thank you so much. I'll make sure you won't regret it. I won't intrude on your personal life if you don't want me to."

If you only knew how badly it hurt to know you were gone, how many hundreds of times I wanted to talk—just talk, talk about anything that popped into our heads was Lee's thought. But she did not dare tell him that.

"Okay, Brad, I'll see you then."

"Bye, Lee, and thank you."

The next day, she begged off working overtime. She wanted to meet with Brad and get it over with. Last night, she had not told Jim that Brad had called. She was feeling a twinge of guilt. The sooner she met with Brad, the better, she thought. Then she could put him out of her mind and continue her life with Jim and the girls, her job, her friends, her parents, and her grandfather.

She punched out on time and slowly made her way out to the parking lot. She was not looking forward to this meeting. She was afraid Brad might make a fool of himself and beg her to be with him. She did not know what her reaction would be.

The Vista Cruiser hit the road and traveled from the hospital to the Warners' farm. There it was. The house had not changed, still pale yellow. The barns were still there. Cattle still roamed in the pasture. All those sights were vaguely familiar to Lee as she pulled the Cruiser into the driveway. She noticed that familiar sound of gravel crunching under the tires. She wondered if the Warners still owned the property.

To Lee's relief, Brad was there, just exiting the barn. She did not have to search for him and risk embarrassment of him watching her. He was perhaps a little rough around the edges, but it was unmistakably Brad. He smiled that familiar smile when he got closer to the car. He opened her car door, and she slid out of the seat and stood. He took her into his open arms. Friend or former lover, it did not matter to either one of them. Affection can be a thing of itself; it needs no explanation.

Lee shed some tears that landed on the front of his shirt. He hugged her a little bit harder.

It made her feel secure and sure of this moment of fate. When he released her, he looked her up and down, holding her hands with his.

"Do you work in a hospital?" he asked her.

It was then that she realized she had forgotten to take off her lab coat. She looked down at it. It was open and revealed a dark-blue A-line skirt and a light-blue short-sleeved button-down blouse. Her name tag Lee was pinned to the left side of the lab coat. She wore flats the color of the skirt.

"Oh yes, I work at the hospital in the lab. I've been there since I graduated from college with my associate's degree in chemistry. I got on-the-job training. I draw blood and look at lab cultures and specimens and report the results."

"I see. Wow, Lee, I'm impressed. I don't know what to say. Would you come inside the house with me? The Warners have passed away. Mrs. Warner died a few months after Mr. Warner. She willed this place to me. It's my farm now. I am so grateful to her."

"You're a lucky man," Lee said.

"Indeed. I thank god for this farm every day, hoping there's a god somewhere listening. Come. We can sit inside."

They entered the house, and he led her to the dining room. They sat next to each other at the massive dining room table. They faced each other.

He said, "You haven't changed a bit. Hair is a little longer, but nothing else is different."

"And you still have that black hair and blue eyes. This might sound out of place, but I can't help but wonder how many times you've captivated someone." Her words came out forced, but she felt the need to say them.

He chuckled.

"I might have attracted some ladies in my day. Nobody like you though."

She blushed. "Brad."

"Yes?"

"Why am I here?"

"I want to explain myself. I had to go underground. I came back home on leave, and I went to Canada immediately. I couldn't tell anyone I love where I was, even Bruce for a while. I feared the FBI might be snooping around."

"Jim and I got married in '73 and bought a house in '75."

"And you have children?"

"Yes, two girls. They are blond-haired and blue-eyed. They look incongruous next to me. Maddie is five, and Krista is four. They're two little peas in a pod. Quite up front with their emotions. They're in love with their father!" Lee smiled.

Brad smiled too.

Lee said, "I have pictures of them in my purse. My purse is in my car. May I show them to you before I leave here?"

"I'd be honored," Brad replied.

Lee said bravely, "I can't help but wonder what our children would look like if you and I ever had any."

"You just read my mind. Beautiful, black-haired, green-blue eyed babies."

"It's just a dream."

"Yeah," then he said, "I don't think Jim ever told you this, but he and I were seated at this very table one evening years ago, wondering if you would ever consent to Jim and me sharing you. Don't get me wrong! We both loved you very much, as I do now, and I'm sure he does too."

Leora sighed. "No, I never knew. What a secret to keep."

"Cat's out of the bag now."

"Do you have children?" she asked.

"Ah, no, sorry to say, I haven't found anyone I'd want to share kids with yet," Brad replied.

Lee caressed one of his cheeks with the back of her fingers.

He smiled at her. "Thank you."

She said, "I think I'm glad you're back. Are you willing to visit Jim and the girls and me? My mom and dad would be glad to see you too."

"How kind of you," he said, surprised. Then he said, "You must know I still love you."

"I don't know what to say. What shall we do with that feeling? I love Jim. He and the girls are my world."

He suggested, "Let's be friends, nothing more. I love Jim too much to cheat on him."

She reached out her hands to him. He gave her his hands without question. She basked in the warm roughness of his palms.

"Listen," he said, "I hope you don't mind if I don't talk about Vietnam. It was a horrible place to be. I saw and did things over there that practically kill me every time the memory comes back."

"Yes, Jim and I kept abreast of it as much as the media or the White House would allow. I never did believe President Johnson when he bragged that the US was winning the conflict. He just kept adding more and more young Americans over there to get slaughtered. I understand your need to stay quiet about it."

"Would you like to see the horses?" he piped up.

"Oh yes, of course!"

"Good. Come with me."

They were there—the pony, the roan, the mare. They ambled up to the fence once they saw Brad approaching them. "They never forgot me," he said. "I think that's amazing."

Lee nodded.

They pet the horses and the pony through the fence grates for a few minutes, reminiscing about the days of riding together.

Afterward, as they returned to Lee's car, she said, "I might have to tell Jim that I saw you. I want you to see my family. I just don't know how he'll take the news that we met in secret here."

"I already have an idea. I will call your house, and this time you let Jim talk to me. I'll invite myself over. Does that sound okay to you? I feel badly that you have to keep this meeting a secret from your husband."

"We have to keep it to ourselves. No one needs to know," Lee said sardonically. She was a little scared this visit would get out to other people somehow. "Please promise me that."

"Lee, of course, I promise."

They reached the car. He gave her a demure kiss on the cheek, and she returned the favor. He was still the dark and beautiful man she had fallen in love with as a teenager, and his love for her had not changed.

Lee showed Brad a photograph of Jim and Maddie and Krista in front of a water fountain at the local public park. Brad was amazed at their resemblance to Jim. After that, Lee and Brad said goodbye to each other, and Lee left the farm.

At home, Lee thanked God that Jim and the girls were still gone. She parked the car in the garage, got into the house, went up the stairs, and immediately went into the bedroom. She changed into fresh pajamas. She was in bed in a matter of a few minutes, and she fell asleep right away. She did not hear the girls stomping up the stairs calling out, "Mommy! We're home with Daddy!"

Jim softly told them that Mommy had been working really hard at the lab, so she was probably already asleep. He gave them their baths, helped them into their pajamas, read them a bedtime story—Maddie on his left knee, Krista on his right. The girls went to bed quietly, and they fell asleep right away. Jim stayed up for a while straightening up things around the house—a short task. He gingerly crawled into bed next to Leora and nuzzled his nose in her lavender-fragrant hair. She did not even make a move. He spooned with her anyway and fell asleep within five minutes.

THE PHONE CALL

It was dinnertime at Jim and Lee's house. The family was at the dinner table, which was in small area attached to the kitchen. The telephone rang. Jim went to answer it.

"Jim, it's me, Brad."

"Whoa, hello there! Where the hell *are* you?"

"Well, I've moved into the Warners' place. Mr. Warner passed away first, and Mrs. Warner died shortly after he did. She willed the farm to me."

"How are you? Doing the same ol' thing—cattle and horses and apple trees?"

"Yup, just getting settled. Haven't spoken to you since that night in the hospital. How is Leora? Did she come out of it all right?"

"She's right here having dinner with the girls and her grandpa."

"Jim, I'll let you go. We can talk later."

"Hell, why don't you come on over? Tonight. Be here in an hour. That will give us time to clean up the place."

"Okay, I'm a bit nervous though," said Brad.

"Oh, don't be, it's just Lee and me and our two little rug rats and Grandpa Ed. Come earlier if you're hungry. Spaghetti and meatballs and garlic bread."

Brad chuckled. "No, no, thank you. I won't intrude on your family dinner. If you're serious about a visit though, I'll be there in an hour."

"Okay, my friend. See you soon. Bye."

"Bye, Jim."

Jim sat down to eat. "Got a surprise visitor, honey. Brad's back in town and back in business at the cattle farm. Mrs. Warner left the farm to him in her will."

I know was what she wanted to say. But she said to Jim, "Wow!"

"I *know*," Jim said with admiration. "He begged off dinner with us tonight, but he's coming over in an hour or so to visit."

She felt a shard hit her heart with a big *thump* of apprehension.

"Do we have any beer in the house? I can go get some if not."

"We've got enough," Lee responded, trying to keep her heart from rising into the throat. *He's coming in an hour! I need to calm down,* she thought.

She spent the time after dinner giving the girls a bath and bedtime reading. They did the bath while Jim cleared the kitchen table and tidied up the house. It was only 7:00 p.m. when the girls were all done, so Lee let them stay up. There was no way they were going to hole up in their rooms if they weren't ready to crash out to sleep, especially if Brad was coming to visit. They did not know him and were excited to see what kind of a man he was. They asked Lee all sorts of questions about Brad, and she did her best to answer them in a noncommittal manner.

Lee's hands trembled as she finished getting the girls into their pajamas; after which, she released them into the living room. She wondered why she was so nervous. She had already met with Brad. He knew Lee and Jim were married and had two little girls. Perhaps she and Brad would look suspiciously familiar to each other in front of Jim.

I think I'll leave the two guys to hang out together, she thought. *But what shall I do with myself?*

The dreaded doorbell rang at 7:30 p.m. The girls squealed to their daddy that someone was there.

"Come, answer the door with me, girls!" called Jim. They clung to him while he opened the front door. They said nothing. The man at the door was a stranger.

"Jim" was all he said.

"Brad, please come in. Girls, this your uncle Brad."

Brad bent down so Maddie could shake hands with him. He gave her a big smile. She smiled back at him. Krista hid behind Jim.

Brad smiled at Jim but asked, "God, Jim, are you sure I'm okay here?"

"On my honor, come on in. The main living part of the house is upstairs. Downstairs are two bedrooms and a bath for Grandpa Ed. His MS is getting worse, can't use one of his arms any longer. He had to quit his job as a construction manager. Now he lives on a pension and social security disability. Anyway, welcome to our home and come with me please."

If Jim had any inkling of the feelings between Brad and Lee, he made a magnanimous effort to hide it. He reintroduced Brad to Lee. They merely shook hands. Brad looked directly into her beautiful eyes. Then Jim and Brad went to the living room to have a seat. Lee brought them some Miller beers, and the men thanked her. Maddie sat in Jim's lap. Krista did not enter the living room.

"I won't stay long," he said. "I mainly want to make my acquaintance again and invite your family to the farm to see the cows and the horses."

"Daddy, that sounds like so much fun!" piped up Maddie.

"Yes, honey, we can do that. Maybe Mom will come and ride a horse with you."

Lee was in the kitchen at the table with Ed and Krista. Lee and Ed were sipping coffee. Lee was trying not to listen to the voices in the living room.

Maddie strode up to Lee and said, "Daddy says you'll ride a horse with me. Isn't that cool?"

Lee reached out and stroked Maddie's blond hair. "Of course, I'll ride with you. Uncle Brad has *three* horses."

"Wow," said Maddie and Krista.

"So you can pick which one to ride. How 'bout that?"

"Yay," said Maddie, "thank you, Mommy. You're the best."

Brad overheard Maddie saying that. His heart swelled with admiration for Lee as a mom.

The girls went to Maddie's room to play. Lee joined the men in the living room. She sat next to Jim on the couch. She didn't hear much of what was said. She was not listening intently enough to join the conversation. Jim could sense this, so he let her sit there with his hand on her knee while he and Brad talked for about an hour. Then she excused herself to go to sleep. They all arose. Brad gave Lee a perfunctory hug. She responded in kind.

He's like a ghost, she thought, but she smiled at him wanly before she went off to the bedroom.

It was a good time for Brad to leave anyway because Jim still had to get Ed prepared for bed before he—Jim—could settle down and go to sleep himself.

Brad took his leave after shaking Jim's hand and receiving a promise that Jim would take his family to the farm soon.

INTERLUDES

Brad and Lee initiated a continuation of their love affair eventually. It was a pleasure to get together. In the spring and summer, sometimes it was a burger and a motion picture somewhere safely out of town. Otherwise, Brad drove into the country where they got out of his Explorer and found a footpath, making wonderful discoveries of trilliums and virgin waterfalls. During the autumn months, they took rides through the foothills, in awe of the magnificent abundance of colors in the trees. Sometimes it was a few hours of horseback riding. In the winter they hiked in the woods near his house or cozied up before the grand brick fireplace in Brad's spacious living room, listening to the Renaissance and nineteenth-century symphonic music.

When they restarted their affair, Brad explained the legal process by which he got permission to reenter the United States. He said that Lee had been on his mind every day of his clandestine existence outside Toronto, Canada, where he had been so bold as to approach a dairy farmer, asking if he may work on the man's farm. He admitted to the farmer that he was avoiding the draft in the United States Army. The farmer shook his hand and congratulated him for refusing to kill people. Brad started working on the farm immediately. He and the farmer became excellent friends.

Brad never told Lee about Ingrid. Sometimes he was tempted to. He preferred to be honest with her. Eventually, he figured it would do more harm than good, and it might affect Lee badly enough for her to leave him. He kept Ingrid a secret from Lee forever. He finally justified it by recalling that, many years ago, Lee had maintained that his past was none of her business.

Lee was never tired of Brad's touch. His hands offered her a wonderful sensuality any time he was holding her hand, caressing her beautiful face, touching her breasts, or exploring the softness of what he knew so well between her thighs. Sometimes when she was away from him, she ached for his moist lips and his eager tongue, recalling the control he had over her as he kissed her lips or her face, her hands, or her naked body. Sometimes she was so helpless during the climaxes he gave her so often that she could not reciprocate. He enjoyed the kind of hold he had on her during those moments. It made her even more beautiful and feminine. He spoke to her when they made love, encouraging her to feel all that she could feel, to let his love carry her as far as she wanted to go. He was a magnificent lover, and she appreciated his selfless gestures. Gradually, Lee released herself from her shyness and was happy to please Brad. He encouraged her in this and was completely satisfied with her. He answered her with honest, loving responses.

Lee felt guilt when she was near Jim, but she became good at hiding it. She was satisfied that she could get home and showered, ready for her husband to get home from work. She thought she was doing a satisfactory job of handling both relationships. Jim was always cheerful and willing to chat any time of the day or night. Despite the happiness, he was always on guard. He loved Lee so much, he was always watchful for any signs of MS.

During the Jones family vacations, far from home, Lee kept her mind on her family. It was easy to dismiss her feelings about Brad temporarily. She figured Jim did not have a clue about her affair.

Believing that, she was happy to shower her husband with personal attention and sexual favors. Jim was extremely grateful for Lee, and he did his best to return her favors. Lee had no complaints.

CANCER—1985

The house party was going well. All their invited guests were there. Lee thought it was hard to believe they had been married twelve years already. Where in the world did the time go? Maddie was a preteen! The kitchen was packed with people sampling the finger foods Sherry had prepared. The house was filled with conversation and laughter.

About an hour passed before Jim and Brad wondered where Lee was. No one knew. They searched the lower level in case she was caring for Ed, but Ed had not seen her in hours. Then Jim and Brad looked into her bedroom. There she was, under the covers, hugging herself, in grave abdominal pain.

"Honey, what's the matter?" Jim pleaded. He was shocked.

Lee shed tears but did not speak.

"Brad, I think I'd better get her to the hospital. I've never seen her like this."

"I'm going with you," Brad said.

"Let me get Sandy and Adrian and their kids to stay and watch the girls."

"Okay," Brad replied. "I think one of us is going to have to carry her."

"Yeah, I'll bet you're right. Please stay here. I'll be right back."

Brad went down onto his knees. They looked into each other's eyes. He almost shed a tear but was able to contain it. He stroked her head gently. "Jim's going to take care of you, Lee. He's going to take you to the hospital."

In about one minute, Brad vacated his spot to allow Sandy to get onto her knees. She stroked Lee's forehead. Lee tried to smile, but her pain was excruciating.

Sandy cooed, "There now, honey, Jim's going to take care of everything. I've got your babies. They're going to be just fine with me."

Jim picked up Lee and cradled her in his arms as he carried her out to the Vista Cruiser. They were at the emergency department of the local hospital in a flash.

It did not take long for Lee to be subjected to several blood draws, x-rays, CT scans, and MRIs. The doctors found a mass on her left ovary the size of a baseball.

After all the tests were performed, one of the doctors said, "I don't like to think worst-case scenario, but considering how many of these masses I've seen in my career, it looks a hell of a lot like cancer."

Jim's heart sank. He started to breathe shallow breaths. He made himself calm down, thinking, *They don't know yet. They don't know.*

Brad put his arm around Jim's shoulders for a few seconds.

The doctor continued, "So tomorrow morning, we're going to remove the mass and the ovary to be safe. The uterus looks good, so we'll leave that alone."

"How long will she be here?" Jim asked.

"She may go home tomorrow, but she must be very careful for a couple weeks. It's major invasive surgery. If the biopsy comes back malignant, she'll need to come back to get a port inserted into her chest for the chemotherapy."

"Okay, I'll get a friend to babysit her and our two girls tonight and maybe for a couple weeks."

"All right. Are you spending the night here? Do you need a cot?"

"Yes, please, a rollaway would be wonderful. I'll take one of those over the horrible chairs you have here any day."

The doctor smiled. "Okay, it might be another hour or so until we get her up into a room. She's coming back from MRI right now. Would you like me to talk to her?"

"No, thank you. I'll give her the news. She's such a brave little thing, I swear. What can you give her for the pain?"

"Right now, she's on a morphine drip. She'll be very sleepy, but the pain is gone."

Jim and Brad arose from the chairs in which they had been sitting and took turns shaking the doctor's hand. "Thank you so much," each one of them said to the doctor.

"You're welcome, Mr. Jones. Mr. Adams. Take care now."

"We will," Jim and Brad said simultaneously.

The doctor left the room.

Brad offered to get in touch with Sandy and Adrian to ask Sandy to stay with Lee for a couple weeks while Jim was at work and to take care of the girls as well. Jim thanked Brad for the effort.

Brad hugged Jim, and then he left the hospital to make the arrangements.

RECOVERY

The surgery lasted about an hour. The doctor elected to remove both ovaries. He was satisfied that he got all the cancerous tissue. That was good news to Jim, sitting in the surgical waiting room drinking cup after cup of awful hospital coffee. He was accompanied by Lee's cousin Benjamin.

"We inserted a port in her chest area where we can give her the chemo in the event the biopsy comes out malignant. She's still going to need to take it easy for a couple weeks. She can walk around the house, but no driving. No changes in her diet. The pain will subside quite well with a strong dose of codeine, but if she needs something stronger, tell her to contact her personal physician, and he will help her out."

"She doesn't have a regular doctor. She never goes to a doctor," Jim said.

"In that case, I'll set her up with one of the doctors I know—an obstetrician. He's a good guy. She can follow up with him in a couple weeks. I'll get an appointment set, and I'll let you know before you leave the hospital."

Jim and Benjamin were escorted to the recovery room. Jim gently took one of Lee's hands into his and held it gently. About half an hour later, she was awake. A nurse took Lee's vitals and found them to be satisfactory. Lee was moved to a hospital room, transferred from the stretcher onto a bed, and gently positioned by two nurses.

"The anesthesia is still in her system," one of the nurses said to him, "so she will be virtually pain free until tomorrow sometime."

266

Jim gave Lee a kiss on the lips and told her he was going to visit the girls at Sandy and Adrian's.

"Okay, are you coming back?"

"Of course, dear, to spend the night."

"All right, I'll see you soon. Love you."

"I love you too, Leora Jones." Jim left the room.

* * *

Maddie and Krista were at Sandy and Adrian's house playing with the two Auble children, Matthew and Debbie. When Adrian let Jim into the house, Jim sat down on a couch with his girls and said to them, "Mommy might be at the hospital for a couple days. After I get her home, I'll come back and pick you up."

The girls were agreeable. Maddie was more worried about her mom than Krista was.

"May I visit her, Dad?"

"Well, she'll probably be home tomorrow, but if not, I'll take you there to see her." He asked Adrian, "One more night okay for you to keep the girls?"

"Oh heavens, they're all having a grand ol' time. No problem, brother."

"We owe you so big, Adrian."

"*Pff*," said Adrian, "we'll take it out in trade sometime. I'm sure. Go on, get back to the hospital. The girls are fine."

"Okay," Jim said. He gathered his daughters in a bear hug until they squealed. Then he was gone, off to sleep beside his wife at the hospital.

Benjamin called Clara and Mrs. Clark with the latest news on Lee, after which he went back into Lee's room and said to a drowsy Lee, "Love and get well from the Clark clan," stroked her forehead, and quietly took his leave to go home to Broome County.

Following the Rules

Lee followed the doctor's instructions once she got home. She did not do any household chores except cooking, and Maddie helped out with that. *Such a good little daughter,* Lee thought to herself more than once.

Jim stayed home for a couple days, but when Lee said that she and Ed's helper had everything under control, he returned to work. He phoned Lee twice a day to check on her.

A week after returning home, Lee received a phone call from her surgeon.

"Mrs. Jones, the biopsy came back malignant. I'm very sorry. We want to start chemo right away. I'll have the hospital call you and make an appointment for ASAP. We've got it licked, I believe, but it's always a wise thing to have some chemo just in case."

Just in case what? Lee wondered but did not ask.

She thanked the doctor and waited for the call from the hospital, which occurred within the hour. She made an appointment to start chemo the next day. She called Sandy and made arrangements for her to watch the girls. Then Lee called Jim at work, and he said he was going to take her to the hospital.

"Thank you, love," Lee said to him. "You're my hero. Do you know that?"

"Of course!" he joked, and she smiled with tears of sadness in her eyes.

* * *

At the hospital, Lee was made to wear another one of those impersonal hospital gowns. She complained about it, but Jim kissed her forehead and said nothing. Once the chemo was injected into the port in Lee's chest, she was made to stay for an hour in case of side effects. A nurse told her that the major long-term side effects were hair loss and nausea. Lee's heart sank.

"I'm going to be ugly," she cried to Jim.

He hugged her hard and kissed her on the lips, but remained quiet about the subject. He knew she was just venting. He knew there was no need for him to talk.

Sandy drove Lee to the obstetrician's office two weeks after that first administration of chemo. The doctor asked her how she was feeling, and she replied, "Okay." He did a gentle examination of her abdomen to make sure there was no swelling there. He was satisfied with her condition. He removed her staples and released her from his care but not before suggesting she find a personal physician to visit at least once a year for female-related examinations. Lee listened, but she did not oblige. She felt very good about going on with her life. She promised to get the chemo treatments once a week for a month at the hospital. But she had not taken a single aspirin in the last two days. She figured she was on the mend.

When the ladies arrived at Jim and Lee's place, Sandy gave Lee a hug and said, "See you soon, love. Call me if you need anything at all. I'm going to have your mom make you some pretty scarves to wear on your head. You're still beautiful, Leora, the most beautiful woman I've ever met. Nothing will change that."

"You guys come over any time, please," said Lee. You're my best friend and my sister. Thank you so much for everything. I'll never be able to repay you."

"You are your mother all over again. So gracious. Take care, Lee."

"Thanks, hon." Lee alighted from Sandy's car carefully and made her way slowly to the front door. Maddie and Ed's helper, who were waiting and opened the door for Lee, walked behind her up the stairs, ready to catch her if she stumbled or fell.

Brad Calls

It was about 1:00 p.m. at Lee's house, several weeks after the surgery. The phone rang. Maddie answered it. Lee was in her room making the bed. She heard. "Mom! Uncle Brad's on the phone!"

Oh, dear God, Lee thought, and she felt a shard of apprehension stick to her heart.

"Coming! Hello, Brad."

"Leora." Always that deep voice, that masculine timbre.

"Yes, hi, Brad. I'm here."

"I just spoke to Jim. Are you all right? Is there anything I can do for you?"

"Oh, no thank you. They got all the cancer. I'm going to continue with chemo for another month to be safe."

"I worry about you. All the years I've known you, you care for everyone but yourself."

"But there was really no way to know I had cancer."

"I wonder about that, Lee. Regular checkups maybe? But I know you don't like to see doctors."

What don't *you know about me?* she wondered.

"No, I won't need a doctor. Don't tell Jim though. I've led him on to believe I might see one someday. I think I spoke with enough verisimilitude for him to believe me."

"Oh god, I hope so."

"*Please* don't tell Jim. You're the only one who knows."

"Of course, *mum's* the word."

She sighed. "*Thank you.*"

"When you're feeling one hundred percent, perhaps you and Jim could bring the girls over for a ride. I've got a new pony. A really nice one."

"Well, thank you, that's so kind of you. The girls would love it. They'll like the cows too."

"Lee."

Oh no, now what? she wondered. She decided not to respond.

"Do you know that after all these years, I still love you?"

"Are you sure? Can't it be an old high school crush? Wouldn't that be safer for us?"

"We can call it that if you want to. I understand."

"Do you want to see me alone?"

"Of course."

She sighed. "Okay, please give me a call sometime. I usually have the middle of the week off, you know, usually Wednesday, as well as every other Saturday and Sunday."

"Yes, I know."

"How do you know?"

"I've been your friend for a lot of years. I pay attention."

Lee blushed.

"I see. Okay, I need to get off the phone now but please stay in touch."

"I miss the hell out of you sometimes."

"Please don't."

"Can't help it. I'll let you go for now. Bye, Leora."

It was that voice!

"Goodbye, Brad."

Lee was standing at the little table where the phone was kept. She looked up and saw Maddie seated at the top of the carpeted steps. She was looking at Lee. She had heard everything.

Dear god, what have I done? Lee pleaded with herself. *Maddie heard every word I just said.*

"What did Uncle Brad want, Mom?"

"Oh, he wants to visit sometime."

"When Dad's gone?"

There it was—coming from her daughter, her very young, intuitive daughter. Lee drew a complete blank as to how to respond to Maddie.

"Mommy, are you okay?"

"Maddie, come here please, sit with me on the couch, will you?"

After they were seated, Lee hugged Maddie tightly and rocked her for a moment She still had no idea as to what to say.

Maddie filled the gap by saying, "Mom, may I go play with Krista now?"

"Of course, honey, go have fun. I'll see you later, love."

"Thanks."

Was it finished? Was Maddie going to forget all about the words her mother had said to Uncle Brad? Or would she bring up the subject at some horribly inopportune time? She sighed and looked up at the ceiling. If Jim ever found out about that phone call, Lee had no idea how she would worm her way out with an explanation. She sighed and prayed to God selfishly that Maddie would keep it under wraps, which was an incredibly tall order for a young girl.

There had always been something deep and dark about sex with Brad. He controlled her, but at the same time, he allowed her to show him her affections. Lee herself had a hard time figuring it out for herself. Sex was so compelling with Brad. With Jim, sex was fun and friendly and honest and adventurous. Sex with Brad was a crime within her marriage. And she loved Jim more than anyone else with exception of their children. She would never leave her family for anyone.

The Girls Get an Invitation from Uncle Brad

A week after a few trysts with Lee, Brad called Jim and Lee's phone number and got Maddie. She located her mother for him. Lee thanked Maddie and shyly said hello into the receiver.

"Hi, it's Brad, how are you this evening?"

"Oh? Okay. Not dandy, but okay."

"Anything you want to talk about?"

Of course, *there is!* she thought. But to Brad, she replied, "Oh no, it's all right. What can we do for you?"

"Well, I'd like to know if I may talk to Jim if he's not busy. If you don't mind."

"Of course not. I'll get him for you. I think he's a tending to my grandfather right now."

"Listen, I'll call later."

Lee was hanging on every syllable, drinking in his timbre. He sounded distant emotionally. It hurt her feelings.

"It's no problem. Can you hold for a moment?"

"Yes, Lee, thank you."

"All right, hang on."

She located Jim. He had just finished serving Ed some supper. Jim picked up the phone in Ed's room.

"Brad, hey, how's it going?"

"Oh, fine, thanks. I'm calling to invite you and the girls over to ride my new pony. She's broke and ready to go. A really nice pony. I'd enjoy your company, all of you."

"Well, I'm sure it will pass muster with Lee and the girls. Lee says she feels one hundred percent better."

Those four words—*one hundred percent better*—struck Brad hard. It evoked the memory of his most recent tryst with Lee, a most pleasurable time. It was obvious to Brad that Lee was back to her healthy self.

"Would you like to make it a social thing? I could invite Darren and Rita. They love to ride, as you know."

"That sounds nice. I hadn't thought of it. I don't know how to reach them."

"Leave it to me, brother, I'll call them."

"Do they have children?"

"Nope, not yet. Lee and I tease them mercilessly sometimes. They never did get married, so maybe that's why no kids."

"Oh, I see."

"Say, Brad, question, are you and Lee getting along okay? I wonder if something has gone south between you two."

"I just wonder if I should speak to you on the phone first, that's all. I don't know why I feel that way, but I do."

"Oh, because Maddie heard some of your conversation recently, and she said Lee was sad afterward."

"Jesus, Jim, I'm sorry that happened. I shouldn't bend your wife's ear with my woes. She might take them to heart. I won't do that again."

"Well, there's always yours truly to talk to, you know, any time, okay?"

"Perhaps I should find a woman to be nice to and have a couple children with. I think I'm living vicariously through your little family. I love all of you."

"Well, and we love you too, Uncle Brad. So let's get this get-together going, eh? I'll call Darren and Rita tomorrow, how's that?"

"Thanks, brother, for everything."

"Will you be okay with Lee being with me at your place? I don't want to bring you down. I could always stay home."

"I'll be fine, but thanks for the kind gesture. Talk to you soon?"

"You bet! Bye, Brad."

"Bye now."

Jim hung up Ed's phone and went upstairs to find Lee. She was nowhere in sight.

Jim and Leora Talk

"Damn, where the hell *is* she?" Jim said aloud to himself. He searched the house and found her in the laundry room folding a plethora of bath towels, with more in the dryer.

"Honey, you must have walked past me invisibly while I was on the phone to Brad."

"Sometimes I feel as if I need to back off and let you and Brad have your man-to-man friendship. I don't need to be sticking myself in the middle of you two all the time."

"Well, that's very kind of you, honey, but I don't feel that way, and I don't think Brad does either. I feel sorry for him sometimes, not having a partner or kids. Not that I know he wants any kids. Maybe he could catch up to Ingrid, but I guess she's not his type—born with a million-dollar spoon in her mouth and all."

"I don't know if they speak to each other."

"Yeah, maybe not. *Anyway* Brad has invited the girls to ride his new pony, and I'm going to invite Darren and Rita along. You should come along with us. Whatta ya say? Sound like a good time?"

"Surely does."

"Lee."

"Yes?"

"Look up. Look at me."

She did. He noticed dark circles under her eyes. She looked exhausted.

"Honey, are you in pain again? Are you losing sleep?"

276

"Oh, some pain and losing a bit of sleep, but I'll be fine. I think a nice horseback riding afternoon will perk me up."

"I can think of other things that can perk you up," Jim teased her as he approached her. He tickled her on her sides. She backed away laughing and bumped up against the dryer.

"Brings back memories—Mr. Biology, a beaker of water over your head. You slipped on one of those stools. All hell could have broken loose, but you saved my butt because you were so damned cute, and Mr. Biology loved you to pieces, as we all did. I recall it as if it was yesterday."

She laughed at the memory.

"Seriously, if you want me to scare the girls off to someone else for a few hours, we can have some fun. You just say the word."

"Word. Let's do it."

"Yes!" said Jim joyfully. "How about Adrian and Sandy?"

"Good choice. I'll be ready when you are."

"I need to know you're serious about this."

"I mean it. Go call Adrian."

"Yes, dear. I'll get back to you in a few minutes."

He left the laundry room. Lee continued to fold towels. It seemed as if there was never an end to them. But they felt good in her hands, and she enjoyed piling them up in neat stacks.

But about a minute later, she started crying. She just let the tears flow. She had to. This was too hard to put up with. She could not be stoic about it. She loved Jim so much. He was so cute just then with his invitation to an afternoon of privacy. How sweet of him! He had no secrets to keep from her. She trusted that he had no one else on his mind. How was she ever going to keep Brad her secret? She would not forgive herself if Jim ever discovered it. She stopped crying. She took comfort in the low hum of the dryer while she continued to fold. When she was finally finished, she sneaked a look into Ed's bedroom. He was sitting in his recliner watching television. Good enough for her.

* * *

It was early evening by the time Sandy picked up the girls. She gave Lee and Jim a big wink. She was not stupid. She knew what was going on. Lee and Jim merely smiled at her as they held hands with each other. Sandy said she would bring the girls back in the morning.

Lee and Jim had a wonderful evening of sex and love and laughter and conversation; it left them hungry. They raided the refrigerator and had cold chicken, potato chips, and ice cream. After that, they took a shower together. They put on pajamas, and then Jim attended to Ed's nighttime care; after which, he and Lee crawled back into bed and spooned together. Before she fell asleep, Lee prayed that this interlude would drive Brad from her head and her heart. At the moment, she felt whole, and she fell asleep. There were no shards. There was no guilt, just a lot of love for her husband.

WEDNESDAY AFTERNOON

Leora did it again—she used her day off to visit Brad's farm after the girls were away from the house. It became another secretive, erotic adventure. It lasted for hours and left her exhausted.

"What the hell am I doing?" she asked him. "We both know I love Jim."

"We both love him," Brad corrected her.

"I can't do this again. It will either kill me, or he'll find out, and my marriage will be a sham."

"Not a sham. Please don't say that. I am so sorry to have made you feel this way."

"You aren't at fault. I am."

"Do you recall me telling you I would never hide anything from you?"

She sighed. "Yes, way back when a schoolgirl crush was turning into love. We were practically kids."

"Are you sure you don't want to know anything?"

"The three of us made a pact that the past was none of our business, remember?"

"I do."

"I'm okay with that. I'm not your wife. I don't need to know." Her tone was pellucid.

"Let's just say there is no one now, hasn't been for a very long time. And I won't go back. I have no desire to go back. And she has no desire to come back."

What he was talking about was his time in Canada, when Ingrid had found him at a dairy farm outside Toronto after a year of wondering where he was. She had not gotten any information from her sisters. She had broken Uncle Bruce down eventually after several attempts and gotten the address and had gone right away to see Brad. He had been elated to see a friend. It had turned into a sexual affair, with Ingrid making frequent visits. But after a year, Brad had become almost frightened about being with an American woman. What would happen to him or to her if the FBI found out? So he had ended it. She had understood. Thereafter, there was no contact between them, right up until the moment Brad and Lee were having this conversation.

Brad never let on to Ingrid. But there were times in Canada, immediately after having sex with her, when Brad's body ached to feel Leora and feel her beauty and her softness. He reminisced about her willingness to let him take her as far as he wanted her to go sexually. He cried now and then, confined to the dark truth that he might never see Lee again in his lifetime, forever stretched out into a frightening doom for Brad.

They helped each other get dressed after showering together. She was not able to ignore that wonderful treasure trail she helped him cover. He smiled at her, knowing what she was thinking while she buttoned up the front of his blue jeans, looking up into the happiness of Brad's eyes.

When they were fully dressed, they hugged each other for a long time.

"I love you so much, Leora."

She cradled his face in her hands and looked into his fantastic blue eyes but did not say anything. They released each other. It was time for Lee to make her way home. She asked him to stay in the house while she left, hoping it would make it easier for her to leave. He went along with it reluctantly. At the door to the side stoop, he held her in his arms one more time for a moment and then let her go.

THE MONSTER RETURNS—1988

It was a fantastic day of horseback riding. Lee, Jim, Brad, Maddie, Krista, Darren, and Rita were all there at Brad's farm, riding and exchanging horses and ponies and doing tricks and jumping to the instructions of Rita. Lee and Jim had a blast watching their girls on horseback.

Everybody got into the action when it came time to brushing down the animals. There was lots of conversation and laughter. There were accounts of horseback accidents and adventures. Brad was ecstatic to have his friends there. He was all grins and smiles.

After the animals were groomed, there was delivered pizza and soda pop for everybody. Brad admitted cooking was not his forte, but everyone was happy with the pizza. The girls wanted to feed some to the horses and ponies, but amidst laughter, Brad said no. He found some apples for them to feed the animals later, which they did with glee. To Lee and Jim, the girls were so cute, each one gingerly holding an apple in her flat hand so the horses and ponies could grab the fruit and not bite the hand.

Rita mentioned, "Your girls have no fear. They are each a natural, Lee."

"Thank you, Rita," Lee replied. "You're very kind."

"They're beautiful girls, Lee, even if they do look more like Jim than you."

Lee and Rita smiled at each other. It was Rita's attempt at humor.

Lee had the strongest urge to ask Rita about Ingrid. Was she married? Children? Was she still traveling the circuit performing patriotic routines with horses all over the country? Was she truly a conceited rich girl, the same caliber of conceit the group saw in Rita on her first day of school at Kingston? Is it possible Brad could fall in love with Ingrid or at least have an affair with her—something that might break Lee's heart but would be good for Brad? Lee figured Rita and Ingrid were still estranged. She kept her questions to herself.

When the Jones family arrived home, Lee suddenly felt flush. She drank a glass of water and felt mildly better. Jim took a thermometer and put it under her tongue. No elevated temperature. But something was making her feel ill. Her abdomen felt sore. Was it from not riding for such a long time? Probably not. She decided to ask Jim to take her to the hospital. Jim called Sherry, and Sherry got there to stay with the girls.

Lee was not in the emergency department half an hour when she was whisked to an MRI and a CT scan. After returning to the emergency room, there was about a half hour wait for results of the scans of her abdomen. When the doctor who had first seen her reentered her room, he looked at Jim first and then at Lee.

"From what we see on the MRI, it looks like the cancer has come back, this time in your uterus. Now the doctors didn't remove it before because it was free and clear. We're going to remove the uterus and the fallopian tubes to be safe. And of course, there will be a biopsy to see if it's malignant or benign."

So, Lee thought, *the monster has returned. No wonder I'm so tired with dark circles under my eyes and sore all the time.*

"I'm sick of this," she said plainly.

"Honey," said Jim. He got up from the chair he was in and went over to the stretcher to hold one of her hands in both his hands.

"This means surgery tomorrow, doesn't it?" she asked the doctor.

"We don't want to wait. Yes, tomorrow."

"Honey," Lee said to Jim, "can you call Mom and let her know I won't be home tonight? Poor Mom. She's got her own problems." She looked up at the doctor to explain. "My mother has a mild case of MS."

"Oh, Mrs. Jones, I'm sorry to hear that."

"Thank you." Then she said to Jim, "Please call Clara to babysit if Mom isn't up to it."

"Sure thing," Jim replied.

"Okay, I'm sure you know the drill," said the doctor. "Nothing by mouth after midnight. We'll get you into the OR bright and early tomorrow morning. The surgeon will want to get every nook and cranny of cancer out of there. He's going to take his time. We'll get you up into a regular room tonight as soon as we can. We're swamped upstairs on the regular med-surg floor. We have to discharge a few patients before we can get you admitted up there."

"All right. Anything else we need to know?" Jim asked.

"Yes, press that call button if you need anything. Even food up until midnight."

"Okay, thanks, Doc," said Jim.

"My pleasure. Take care now."

Then he was gone.

"Can I get you anything, honey?" Jim asked Lee.

"Water please."

"Okay, push the button."

It took about half an hour for a response to the button. But when the nurse heard Lee wanted water, she was totally solicitous. "Are you in any pain, Mrs. Jones? We have an order for Tylenol or Percocet, which is stronger. Which would you prefer?"

"Oh dear, I'll take the Tylenol please."

"I'll be right back."

And she was, about five minutes later. Lee took the Tylenol and water and handed the water cup to Jim, who put it on a chair beside him. He dragged another chair up to the stretcher so he could sit down while holding Lee's hand.

"Do you want anyone else to know?" he asked Lee. He was thinking of Brad.

"No, not really, maybe when it's all over. Jesus, Jim, what if there's cancer all through my body? What if I don't survive this? We need to make out a will and testament ASAP."

"Well, that's a great idea, I agree. But I'm not going to concede that the cancer has spread any farther than what the doctor has indicated."

"He said every nook and cranny, I heard that."

"True. But please don't get ahead of yourself. We'll know more after the biopsy. Do you want me to stay with you?"

"I think once I get upstairs, you should go home and be with the girls and Ed for a while. Then you can come back to spend the night."

"All right, Lee."

He waited until she did get settled into a bed in a med-surg room upstairs. When she looked as comfortable as she was going to be, Jim said to her, "Now take that opiate if you need it. You won't get addicted. What am I telling *you* that for? You work in a hospital. Listen, I love you, and the girls do too. I'll be up front with them about the surgery and the biopsy." He gave her a quick kiss on the lips and caressed her forehead. "You're so beautiful, Lee. I'm so lucky to have you and our girls. You are my world."

"I feel the same way about you, go figure."

They laughed.

He gave her another kiss on the lips. Then he left the room, on his way back home where he would tell Sherry and the girls everything he had been told about the cancer and the upcoming surgery. After he finished informing them, he would return to the hospital to sleep near his wife.

BACK HOME

The surgery went well. Leora was home in three days without any pain medication.

"Too stoic to admit you're in pain, my love?" Jim teased. He was right. He urged her to take Tylenol around the dock for a couple days. She admitted it was helpful and thanked Jim for his concern.

A week later, the doctor's nurse called and told Lee the cancer of the uterus was malignant. The fallopian tubes were showing signs of precancer. Lee was informed that the hospital would be calling her to schedule chemotherapy, which would occur once a week for at least a month. The chemo could be administered through the port that was still in Lee's chest.

"I feel so old," she said to Jim that night when they were lying in bed. "I'm still in my thirties."

"You'll get over the feeling once you actually grow old. You'll feel like a girl again."

"Promise? Because I don't want to go through this damned cancer ordeal ever again. If it happens again, please just let me go in peace. Give me those opioids the doctors keep offering me, so I can slip off into forever sleep."

Jim did not know what to say in his sadness. He always wanted to be the strong one, the supportive husband and friend to his wife. He just hugged her closely and gave her a kiss on the forehead.

"Hell, I feel old sometimes too, Lee. Think of our girls. They're frickin' teenagers."

"I think maybe it's time to tell Maddie—maybe Krista too—about the birds and the bees."

"Oh, no worries, my dear. I've spoken to Maddie already. She recently told me about the life class she had to take. Believe me, she was so graphic I was embarrassed! *Ah*, those terms coming from the mouth of my child! Krista will take the class next year. Hopefully, we'll be safe until then."

"I can ask my mother to talk to the girls. She preached to me, and it was the right thing to do. I had always thought you and I couldn't conceive a child with our clothes on. We lucked out, honey, because there were times we were incredibly close to each other, if you know what I mean."

"Yeah, we were a couple of lucky, innocent kids back then. I'm okay with your mom talking to Maddie and Krista."

"Actually, I can't imagine she hasn't taken the opportunity already."

"You might be right. Your dad too. You know, when he found out you and I were engaged, he admonished me not to get his daughter knocked up before she was ready. Did I ever tell you that?"

"No, you never did. Sounds like my dad protecting his little girl. I'm so lucky to have him."

"I was frickin' embarrassed when he said that to me. But I promised him I wouldn't get you pregnant too soon, and he said that was good enough for him. I wonder if he's going to come see you soon."

"Yeah, he said he'd be here probably tomorrow night. Mom too, of course. I'll be glad to see him."

"My folks will be here soon too. Let's get out our instruments and have a jam session with Bela. I'll break out my trombone, and you can play your clarinet or finger your concertina keys."

"Sounds great. Give me enough Tylenol to last me a few hours, and I'll be all set."

"This will be fun. Let's get Maddie on her clarinet and Krista on her flute too."

"Okay, love. Now I'd better get some sleep."

"That makes two of us," Jim said. They cuddled closely and slept soundly until the morning.

And jam they did the next night after a dinner with the Jones family, Dr. and Mrs. Jones (Jim's parents), and Sherry and Bela. Dr. and Mrs. Jones were more subdued than Lee's crowd, but they enjoyed themselves anyway, and they sang when they knew the tunes. Sherry clapped her hands and stomped her feet to the rhythms.

"No offense, Sherry, but we should have Collin and Darrell over here to drum with us," Jim teased. Sherry was not offended. In fact, she kept clapping and stomping to the music.

At about 8:00 p.m., Lee announced she was in discomfort. The musicians packed up their instruments, and there were long goodbyes.

"Take care of that beautiful wife of yours," Jim's worried mother said to him on the way out the door. She had the feeling the cancer was lurking about somewhere in Lee's body, but she kept still about it.

"Oh, you have my word on that," he replied.

* * *

Lee got into pajamas and slipped under the covers of her bed. Jim stayed up with the girls for another hour or so, and after they decided to hit the sack, he joined Lee. She was not asleep.

"I'm scared, Jim. I'm afraid the pain means more cancer."

Jim kissed the top of her head. "I think you just overdid it, honey. But if you want to see a doctor, just let me know, and I'll get you there."

"I think we all had a blast tonight regardless," Lee said with satisfaction.

"Indeed. Now may I curl up against your beautiful little body for the night?"

Oh, dear God, she thought, *who else talks about me that way? Why am I even* thinking *about Brad? I don't deserve Jim. I really don't.* She asked him, "Have we ever spent a night apart since we've been married?"

"Just once, at the hospital the time you got all those flowers. I stayed home with the girls."

Lee recalled it was the night Brad had been at the hospital, and Jim had never told her about it; Brad had told her. She wondered if she should open up the can of worms by scolding him about that, or if she should leave it alone. She made the split-second decision to let it be.

"Just one night after all these years," she said. "That's a nice thought."

"It surely is."

Jim gave her a kiss on the cheek. "Good night, my lovely wife."

"'Night," Lee said in a small voice. She started snoring almost as soon as she had said it.

Worn out from having so much fun, Jim thought. *So cool.*

ED MOVES UPSTAIRS

Finally, it was time for Ed to move to the upper level of Jim and Lee's house. He had been living in the lower level. Maddie was happy to give up her room for Ed's old room. The girls had always had their own rooms, but now, they shared a bathroom with no one but each other. The bathroom sported two sinks, very convenient for them.

Within a week of moving upstairs, Ed's MS took another turn. It involved his entire trunk, and he could no longer walk. He was confined to a wheelchair. The wheelchair had a hard time navigating the house on the old shag carpet. Jim decided the carpet had to go. He called Brad one evening and asked him to help Jim, Adrian, and Darren remove the carpet on the upper level of the house. Brad was glad to help. So on the next Saturday, the three guys met at Jim and Lee's house and tore the carpet out of the living room, hallway, and Ed's new bedroom, and replaced it was a golden oak floor and trim. That night, Lee made it easy on herself and ordered pizza and soda pop for the guys and her family. The guys ate with gusto and appreciation. In the end, the upper level lent a modern touch to the house with the beautiful new oak floors, and Ed had no problem wheeling himself around. The upper level bathroom he was going to use already had tile floor, so it was easy for him to navigate it. He had that bathroom to himself since Lee and Jim had a private bathroom attached to their bedroom.

Sherry went to a medical supply company and purchased a bath chair for Ed. From then on, when Jim helped Ed bathe, Ed would sit safely in the bath chair, no more standing and worrying about falling.

When she dropped off the bath chair, she took Jim aside. "You can't keep taking care of Dad. And he's left alone all day without any way to use the bathroom safely. What if I arrange a helper for a few more hours during the weekdays? I want to relieve you of bath duties too. The helper can do that during the day while they're here."

Jim sighed with relief and appreciation, and his shoulders drooped. "What will Leora say?"

"She already has the same thoughts I do. We talked about it earlier today. We can try it with home help for a while and see how it goes. We have to give it serious thought toward a nursing home, maybe soon. At least, he can wheel himself around the house, but the physical care is another matter. I don't know when Dad will say it outright, but I know he's feeling like a burden to you and Lee, especially you."

"He never complains, and he thanks me a hundred times a day," Jim said.

"Sounds like my father. I should be able to get more help in a few days. Hang in there, hon." And she gave Jim a warm hug.

"I never do take the time to ask you how *you* are doing, Sherry," Jim said.

She replied, "All the same. No worse, thank God. I pray it will stay that way. Remission is a real thing with MS, but there's no treatment for the state I'm in right now. I'm against all those drug trials and tests. If I went through all that, I think I'd be tempted to hang it all up and steel myself to it as it goes."

"Please take your regular MS meds, Sherry. Don't stop. I don't know what Lee would do if she knew you weren't on the meds."

"Thank you, Jim. I appreciate that. Bela has decided to back me up on any decisions I make. Unfortunately, the treatment won't give me a better life span. It's just wishful thinking that it will keep advancement at bay. So far, so good."

Jim hugged Sherry this time.

"You need anything, *anything*, you had better call us," Jim said. He gave her a kiss on the forehead and then released her from his hug.

"I promise," Sherry responded.

MADDIE AND KRISTA

Maddie was an excellent student in high school. She sat first chair in the clarinet section and played first clarinet in the pep bands (basketball and football). She got straight As in all her other classes, just as her mother did years ago. She had many friends of all grades. She was very popular with the boys. Jim kept tabs on that by interrogating her once in a while to her embarrassment.

"So far, so good with Maddie and the boys," he would say to Lee. Jim actually knew most of the boys who liked Maddie because Jim and Lee allowed their girls to have friends over, male and female. The other students were jealous because Jim and Lee were the only two parents who let such socializing transpire.

Krista was so bright she was moved up one grade from tenth to eleventh. She kept up with the studies and got straight A's as well. Her instrument in the band was the flute, and she joined her sister in the two pep bands. She had her own set of followers, boys and girls. When she and Maddie had a party at home, the place was crammed with boys and girls of a wide variety of ages. Jim and Leora were proud of their girls and happy to allow them to party at their place. Much to the disappointment of the boys, they—the boys—had to leave Jim and Lee's place by 9:00 p.m. weekdays and midnight on weekends. That was fine with Maddie, Krista, and their girlfriends. They enjoyed being giggly and silly without the boys seeing them that way.

Maddie and Krista had their dad's full, beautiful, shiny blond hair. Their eyes were as blue as Jim's, although there were times when a person could swear Maddie's eyes were green. No one could figure out the cause. When she first discovered it, she went to her mother in tears, wondering if she was sick. Lee took her hand and explained it was just nature doing its thing, and to be happy that her eyes looked just like her mother's sometimes, because other than those eyes, Maddie was her father's clone! Lee told Maddie that she was elated to have Maddie look like her sometimes. After that, Maddie understood it was harmless to have eyes change color.

The girls continued the tradition of jamming with Bela and Sherry and their parents, even when there was a crowd of school friends hanging around the place. Anyone who could play an instrument was invited to join any time they wanted to, as long as the instrument could fit into the house.

Ed often stayed in the living room to clap to the jam sessions. Occasionally, there were so many musicians they spilled over into the kitchen or down the stairs into the lower level. Ed had the time of his life during those sessions. All the students got to know him, and they called him Grandpa Ed endearingly. It made no difference to them that he could not move his legs well and that sometimes he could only mumble. They all loved Grandpa Ed. Lee and Jim took Sherry, Bela, and Ed to hear the Kingston High School band concerts. Grandpa Ed was so proud, but he was simply exhausted from the trip and the sitting in the auditorium and trying to listen without letting out his occasional, uncontrollable mumbles. Sherry and Bela realized it was the beginning of the end for Ed. He hoped to be able to die at Lee and Jim's place, but there was no guarantee he would stay there that long. He still had his aides take care of him every day for a few hours, but he needed nighttime care as well, and it was getting more difficult for Jim to feed Ed and transfer him from the wheelchair to the bed. It was heartbreaking for the entire family.

When Maddie and Krista had schoolwork to study, they invited Grandpa Ed into the living room to join them. He liked TV, so they turned it on for him on a low volume so they could study. Ed seemed to really enjoy those times. He would motion the girls to him sometimes just so he could stroke their beautiful blond heads. The girls would hug Grandpa Ed in return.

One night, Lee said to Jim, "You say the word, honey, and we'll find him a really nice place to spend his last days. He's ready, and he won't mind. You've been his hero, and he knows it. He doesn't expect you to keep this up."

Jim shed a tear—one big lonesome tear. Lee hugged him hard, and they rocked gently for a moment. Then she stroked his face with her fingers, the way a blind person would study someone he or she does not know.

"You are my love and my hero too," she said to him.

Jim kept on with the hugging for another moment and then collected himself.

"I'll think about it," he said.

"Okay, honey," Lee responded.

GRADUATION DAY—JUNE 1992

Lee felt good enough to attend Kington High School's graduation ceremony. The band played the same music Lee had played with her band compatriots so many years ago. Maddie was valedictorian. She gave a short response speech after the guest speaker was finished. The guest speaker was none other than Bela Sovine. The principal was so impressed with the success rate of his math students he asked Bela to give them a short speech about hard work, endurance, and reward.

As it always happens, the final student stepped down from the podium, and the entire student body of seniors whooped it up as they tossed their caps into the air. Then they all filed out to the same "Pomp and Circumstance" Lee and Jim had played in high school. They got a good laugh over that.

The graduation party was the following Sunday. It was a warm summer afternoon. There were guests inside and other guests outside. The living room was adorned with all sorts of lovely flowers and houseplants from Adrian and Sandy. There were gifts galore in the entryway downstairs. Maddie decided to open them after the guests were gone.

Sherry had the food catered in—sloppy joes, chicken wraps, potato salad, potato chips, coleslaw, cake, ice cream, and punch. The cake was a four-layered affair with the frosting of the school colors, maroon and white. Jim offered to give some money to Sherry and Bela to offset the cost of the food, but Sherry waved a hand in friendly dismissal.

The girls chose rock and roll for the background music, but they switched to a country and western radio station halfway through the party. Many people stayed outside for the duration of the party. It started at 3:00 p.m. and went until about 7:00 p.m. Sherry helped Maddie and Krista clean up after the gathering was over, including doing dishes.

"Grandma," piped up Maddie, "Dad should buy us a dishwasher. It would be great. No more hard work for Mom."

"That would be wonderful for Lee," responded Sherry. "I'll have a talk with him about it."

"Yes!" Maddie exclaimed.

After the guests had gone, Lee decided to take a nap. "Don't concern yourselves with being quiet," she said to everybody—Sherry and Bela were still there. "I think I could sleep through a bomb under the bed."

"Okay," everybody else said in unison.

Lee made her way slowly to the bedroom. She snuggled beneath the covers because she was cold suddenly. She shivered for about half an hour and then fell asleep.

Before Jim left for work in the morning, Lee asked him if he thought they should honor the promise they had made to the girls years ago—a trip to Disney World or Disneyland. Jim said that would be cool. So he approached them as they were just sitting down at the kitchen table.

"Girls, Mom wants to know if you're still interested in going to either Disney World or Disneyland. We'd promised it to you a long time ago."

"Well," said Krista, "it would be a nice thing to do for Mom. I know she's not feeling well again. We should get the vacation going for her sake."

"Wise words," said Jim. "I'll get started on the arrangements. I think I'll just hire a travel agent so I don't miss any details."

"Good idea, Dad," said Maddie. "Is Mom still asleep?"

"Not that I know of."

"I want to go lie down with her for a few minutes."

"I'll join you," Krista said.

Jim smiled at his girls and gave each one a hug. "You girls are so wonderful."

"Thanks, Dad, you are too," Maddie replied. The girls tiptoed into their parents' bedroom and slipped into the bed, one girl on each side of their mom. Lee was drowsy but happy to see her daughters.

They spent about half an hour gabbing just about anything. Then the girls left so Lee could get a nap. Once outside the bedroom, they wondered to each other if the cancer had returned. They went into their respective bedrooms, got onto their knees, and prayed that God would let them have her at least through the trip to Disney.

Jim Knows

Leora swore this would be the final time she and Brad would get together in secret. This was ridiculous. They were adults. She was married. Brad never asked her to leave Jim for him. She suddenly felt as if she was being used for sex, and it angered her. She got onto the road one morning after calling in sick at work. She deliberately wore faded old blue jeans and an old faded red sweater and tennis shoes. She did not even attempt to hide the fuzz that was growing back on her head. No looking nice today. She was going to try to break herself from this relationship.

It did not work. She met him at the local library, where he was seated inside a quiet room reading some casual novel with ease. He looked up to see her and smiled widely. He got up from the chair and took her hands into his hands. He was so happy and so handsome. Her heart melted.

"Thank you for coming," he greeted her. "I didn't know if you would think a library is a weird place to meet. I come here once a week or so to sit and read. Just to get away from home. Does that make sense?"

"Yes, it does. Perfect sense."

"What would you like to do today? Shall we go somewhere for lunch? Somewhere out of town but not far away? Or we could go for a drive. The fall colors are very pretty these days."

"That's true, and they aren't going to last very long. Let's do that. It sounds nice."

They took off along back roads and two-tracks. They were in Brad's Ford Explorer, a perfect vehicle for sightseeing on the unbeaten paths. They went along for a couple hours, engaging in small talk, having a lovely time. Brad seemed to know every country road and byway. Leora enjoyed going slowly up the steep grades and practically flying on the way down. She sat snuggled up to Brad, and she put the palm of one of her hands upon his leg, but he was responsible and used both hands on the steering wheel. Nevertheless, they both felt romance was in the air.

"Don't put that hand of yours any farther up my leg," he said casually. "I might not be able to drive. You know how you make me feel. You're not foolin' me."

She looked at the side of his face and smiled. She felt proud of herself for being able to make him feel sexually attracted to her, even as a tiny voice inside her told her she was not good enough for him.

They stopped at a small bistro way out of town and had a pleasant lunch of chicken salad and Chardonnay. He said things about cattle ranching that made her laugh. She held her tummy a few times because the laughter hurt her. He finally settled down for her sake.

The day was clear of clouds, and the Catskills were ablaze in autumn splendor. Brad and Lee stopped at a lookout point and got out of the vehicle. They sat atop a stone wall overlooking the fantastic rolling foothills. They swung their feet and held hands and talked about many things except the fact that they were having an affair. After about an hour, he drove her back to the library. But she wanted more of him. She did not have to voice it. He knew. She followed him to Brad's farm and parked in the gravel driveway one more time.

"I want us to be in the loft," Brad said as soon as she got out of her car.

The sex they had was warm and loving. She was unaware of the time. She was lost in Brad's words and actions. This time around, he gingerly touched her as if she was in pain from the latest surgery. She felt fine but appreciated his gentleness. It was a different kind of eroticism that he gave her by being kind and gentle—her feelings were slower to emerge and more powerful in their expression.

Brad kept himself aware of the time. He got Lee back to her car in plenty of time to get home by the usual time of 4:00 p.m. As she exited the farm, Lee thought she was a fool to think this affair would last forever without being discovered by someone else. She prayed as she always did that no one would know about this pleasure that made her life so enjoyable.

She lucked out again. The girls were home at 5:00 p.m., but Jim had to work late at the water treatment plant.

"Let's go out for supper," Lee suggested.

The girls chose a pizza parlor with pinball games and lots of noise. Lee and the girls played pinball for about an hour.

Lee kept hollering, "Girls, I suck at this!"

The girls just laughed at her. It was a great evening. They got home at about 7:00 p.m. after stopping at a fast-food joint for ice cream. Jim was in the living room with Ed. They were chatting about nothing in particular. The girls gave Jim and Ed some of the leftover pizza. Maddie procured a beer for Jim and a soda pop with a straw for Ed. Jim assisted Ed with the pizza, but Ed did well with the straw. He thanked the girls for being so thoughtful.

"You're welcome, Grandpa Ed," Maddie responded. Krista gave him a hug.

When everyone was getting settled in for the night, Jim and Lee were in their bedroom pulling back the covers of the bed.

He said, "How come you didn't answer your phone today?"

"What do you mean—my work phone?"

"Yeah. Work phone. Trying to ignore me?"

"I can't tell who's calling, honey, you know that."

"True. Still you didn't answer it."

She made the motion to find the phone in the pocket of her lab coat, which was hanging over a chair in the bedroom.

"Don't bother, I checked it. No charge. Did you forget to charge it last night?"

"I suppose so. Jim, I'm sorry. I didn't mean to ignore you. Thanks for letting me know it's out of charge though."

"No problem."

His appearance was noncommittal. She couldn't tell if he was angry or not. *Should I just ask? Or will that open up a horrible, giant can of worms?* she wondered. She was frightened of the results. She decided to let go of the idea.

"I plugged it in for you. It will be fully charged tomorrow."

"Thanks, honey. So how did it go at your work today?'

"Oh, the place had to be inspected by the government for compliance of various requirements. I was drafted to give the inspectors the tour and any explanations of stuff they didn't know. And believe me, there's a hell of a lot they don't know. We passed, thank God."

"I don't doubt it. My guess is that you're always in compliance anyway."

"Right you are, my dear, makes things much easier when the government agents stop on in for a cup of coffee and a chat."

Lee chuckled.

"You look very pretty tonight, Lee, even in your old clothes. Very laid back. Kind of sexy actually."

Lee raised her eyebrows. "We went to the pizza parlor. I dressed down rather far."

"No, you look great. You should sleep in those clothes. I might want to take them off."

"Jim?" said Lee.

"I'm serious."

"Well…okay."

"You really mean it?"

"Yeah, just make sure Ed *and* the girls are all settled in bed."

Jim complied. He settled Ed into bed and made sure the girls were behaving themselves by getting ready to get to sleep. When he was satisfied there was peace, he climbed into bed with Leora and had his way with her. She giggled and laughed at first, but then they got serious. It was practically acrobatic sex that night. Lee had the time of her life.

But when Jim was asleep with his back to hers, she shed tears for a moment. She felt out of breath from guilt. When, oh, when would she and Brad get busted? She hoped it would be soon. She hoped it would be never. Just as she was drifting into sleep, she heard a voice in her head saying clearly, "It's true. Jim knows." She bolted awake and got out of bed to get a glass of water. Then she climbed back into bed to lie next to her sleeping husband. *I really blew it today. I have no excuse for that damn phone,* she thought. *Not again. Ever.* It took her about half an hour to get to sleep, but she drifted into dreamless slumber eventually.

RELEASED?

A follow-up CT scan showed no more growth of cancer.

"Maybe you're just out of the woods, Mrs. Jones," said her oncologist. "Let's go with radiation therapy for another couple months."

Lee had nothing positive to say in return. She decided to take a month away from work. She enjoyed sitting at the picnic table outside where Jim would start a fire for her before going to work. She read biographies of famous women from the silent-movie era. Many of them had committed suicide. They were beautiful women too. Their beauty could not save them from the deep depression they suffered for various reasons. Lee felt she understood some of their angst, considering she had been fighting cancer for so long. She went through her photo albums, starting when she had her Brownie camera as a birthday gift when she was ten years old. The Brownie took hundreds of photos over the years. She could not see a way to rid herself of any of them. Her favorite one was a picture of Adrian and Jim leaning against each other on a cold day after lunch at Kingston High. She laughed when she recalled that Jim had made a motion to kiss Adrian, but someone had hollered something like, "Don't kiss the hippie, you old fag!" An eight-by-ten-inch photograph of them adorned her bedroom wall.

She called Connie a few times a week to chat and give her updates on her health. The people from the group kept her busy on the phone. They all meant well, but at the end of some days, Lee was exhausted from talking and listening to her friends. For a week, Jim put a moratorium on long phone calls. It was okay for people to phone her, but he fielded the calls and made sure they were kept short.

By now, all her hair was gone from her head. She felt nauseous and had a difficult time getting any pleasure from food. Sherry sewed pretty headbands to go over Lee's head, and she pitched in and made a month's worth of dinners that she remembered as favorites of Lee and saved them in the freezer Lee and Jim had in the lower level of their house. Lee did eat small portions of those meals, with encouragement from her husband, parents, and children.

But she was weak. She no longer had a springy step. She used the rails to get upstairs and downstairs. She used a cane when she went to the hospital (she insisted on going there alone). Sometimes she was tired enough to sleep through the radiation therapy. After that, she drove herself home and took a nap. Life was not enjoyable any longer. She prayed for a fast end to the radiation in hopes of gaining an appetite and a desire to live. Around her, life assimilated itself to a new normal.

The Jones family members were not allowed to tiptoe about the house. No whispering was allowed. Any concerns that anyone had about anything would be taken up as a family. Krista was encouraged to have friends over for studying and for jam sessions, all so the family could have at least the semblance of a normal existence. Jim was allowed to call only once a day from work. He always called Lee at noon, which tended to be a good time for her for any energy. Brad was allowed to call any time, and he did a few times a week, but Lee did not allow him to see her bald and weak and sick. Jim asked him not to visit. Brad tried to balk at that, but Jim simply said to him, "It's Leora's wish. I'm sorry. I think she might be embarrassed."

"Is she embarrassed in front of her family too?" Brad asked.

"Yes, about the hair, yes, definitely. Her hair is gone, and she wears bandanas and such over her head. Sherry made some really pretty bandanas."

"Let's pray for success with the radiation."

"You got it, brother, every day, dozens of times a day."

"Same here."

"'Hey, would you mind if I brought the girls over for a horse-back ride? It's been ages since they've done that. I would be there too. Not sure about Lee though."

"You know they're welcome here any time. Maddie can even help me get the cows hooked to the milking machines. She had such a good time watching that once."

"Okay, how about this weekend then? Are you free?"

"Never from this place, but I can make time."

"Thank you, Brad, you're the best."

"I appreciate that. Come over on Saturday, say 10:00 a.m.?"

"We'll be there."

"Great. Bye for now."

"Yup. Bye."

BRAD CHECKS IN

That Saturday, Lee decided to return to work. Jim and the girls were out riding at Brad's place. Lee got a call at work. The only people who ever called her there were Jim and Sherry. Not even her children were allowed to interrupt her work.

"Lee?"

It was Brad. *How the hell did he get this number?* she wondered. *It had to be Jim.* "Brad? What's up? Are you okay?"

"I want to ask you that question. Are you all right?"

"Well, thank you, I'm doing all right. I don't know what else to say."

"You don't need to say anything else. I just wanted to hear your voice. I was talking to Jim today. He was kind enough to give me your work number. Please forgive me for calling you there. I haven't heard from you in a month. I won't call your work again."

"Brad, that's all right. It's sweet of you to be concerned."

"Well, I'll let you go for now, Leora."

Leora. Even after all those years, whenever he said her formal name, it affected her. He probably knew it would too. *Why does he toy with me?* she wondered.

"Okay, Brad."

"Yes?"

"You know."

"Yes, I do know. Forgive me. I miss you. There. I said it."

"Damn it, I miss you when you say things like that."

"That makes me glad."

"But it's the same ol' thing. You know how much I love him. It overwhelms me sometimes."

"I understand. He's always been your protector and friend. He's one in a million. Now I'm going to let you go for now. I've kept you long enough. I hope to see you soon."

"Maybe we can manage that. Give my heart some time to slow down."

"You're jesting, aren't you?"

"No, I'm not. I'm too old to be coy."

"I'm shocked but pleased. Okay, enough now. Take care, Lee."

"You too, Brad, bye."

"Bye, dear."

Lee spent the rest of the day trying to fit Brad into the back of her mind somewhere. *Life seems so right when he's not on my mind,* she mused. *Then,* bam, *here we go again. Is it wrong? Really—is it? It's love, so how can it be the wrong thing to do?* There was no answer from her conscience.

Blind Date

"Come with me please," said Brad as they approached his motorcycle one cold afternoon.

He and Leora were at his farm. It was not warm outside, but he wanted to drive his bike.

"Where are we going?"

"Oh, it's a surprise. You'll have to guess too because I'm going to blindfold you."

"What?" She was shocked. "Are you going to do something weird to me?"

He chuckled. "That's a grand idea, but no, nothing weird. Just fun—I hope. Come. Stand in front of me please."

She did what she was asked to do. He helped her put on the leather jacket. She was wearing a dark-green sweater, blue jeans, and hiking boots. The sweater made the green in her beautiful eyes deepen. He procured a neck tie from one of his jean pockets and gently tied it around Lee's head so she could not see anything. He kissed her warmly before putting the helmet onto her head. Then he assisted her in getting on leather gloves. She felt safe but very curious. Brad was not capricious in any way. It could not be something far from the realm of reality. Lee decided to play along. Brad guided her onto the motorcycle, and then he seated himself onto the front and started it.

"Hold on tightly," he said, looking back at her. "I want to feel you back there."

Lee smiled into her darkness.

"Beautiful smile," he said.

"Didn't think you'd be looking."

"Oh, I take a peek whenever I can," he replied as he lowered her helmet shield.

That made Lee's heart skip a beat. After all these years, he still affected her when he offered her his remarks that possessed a subtle sexuality.

Brad drove the motorcycle along winding roads and across stretches of dirt two-tracks. He had complete control of the bike. It was obvious he knew where he was going. Lee simply held onto him and took in the sounds and physical sensations of the evening. It was not long before the motorcycle had to make a few stop-and-go motions, and Brad slowed the speed considerably.

We must be in a town, Lee thought. *Let's see. It's late Friday after-noon, not time for everybody to go out drinking yet. I have no idea what he's going to do.* She smiled again, but he missed that one.

In a matter of just a few minutes, the motorcycle landed in a concrete parking lot. Brad alighted from the bike and put it on the kickstand. Then he aided Lee in getting down from the bike. He took her hand and led her, standing very close to her so she would feel safe. Up a flight of concrete stairs they went. He opened one of two doors. There was a *whoosh* of air from the place, and loud organ music was playing. She grinned. She knew immediately. They were going roller-skating! She had not been to a roller rink since she was in junior high school.

They stopped in front of the entrance gate where people get onto the rink. He took off their motorcycle gear, stood in front of her, and gently removed the blindfold.

Lee grinned up at Brad. "Oh my god, this is wonderful!"

Brad grinned in return. He was incredibly handsome. "Let's get some skates."

They rented skates and sat down on a bench to put them onto their feet. Brad put the motorcycle gear on a shelf nearby. He skated over to Lee, still at the bench.

"Are you ready?"

Lee stood up and nearly fell over. He caught her.

"Take my hands until you feel comfortable going alone."

"Okay," she said and took his hands. She felt so safe, slightly embarrassed but lucky to be there with her lover. Although they appeared to be the oldest skaters there, Lee felt her youth return to her. He skated onto the rink backward, holding her hands while she skated forward. He turned around and skated beside her. He was much more adroit at it than Lee was. Lee had been adept in her day, but that was years behind her. It took about fifteen minutes for her to find herself. After she did, Brad grabbed her around the waist and swung her in several circles, at which time she remembered to focus on one object to avoid getting dizzy. It worked. She was proud of herself.

There was an announcement saying there was going to be a race around the rink, four times around. Brad looked at Lee.

"No way," she said, "but you go."

"Seriously?" he asked.

She nodded her head.

"All right, darlin', here goes nothin'."

Brad won the race hands down. Someone approached him and handed him a fifty-dollar bill as prize for winning. Lee thought Brad was going to blush when people clapped for him. He usually eschewed a crowd. He merely smiled and made a circle of bows. He handed the money to Lee, which surprised her. She put the money into her jeans pocket, reached up, and gave him a hearty hug.

He held onto her, and they both laughed.

They skated and danced for another hour or so. Then they were approached by a young man, perhaps in his early twenties. He asked Brad if he may skate with Lee.

Brad replied, "Ask the lady."

Lee nodded yes to the young man, and off they went.

"My name's Randy!" he shouted over the organ music.

"Lee!"

"Nice to meet you, Lee! I think you're beautiful! When did you graduate?"

"Huh? You mean college?"

"You're not old enough for college!"

"I hate to put this to you, but I'm in my thirties!"

"No way!" countered Randy. "I've never seen anybody your age dance like that on roller skates!"

"Well, it's no secret! I just hang on and let him take the lead!"

"Is he your husband?"

A sudden pang of shock pierced Lee's heart. What if somebody actually found out where she was that night? Suddenly, she wasn't so smitten with the idea of cheating on her husband. The fear of getting caught took over for a few seconds, but she recovered. She merely smiled at Randy. "No, he's my friend!"

"Well, I think he's crazy not to marry you! You're gorgeous! Ask all the other guys who are too shy to ask you for a skate!"

Lee grinned. "Thank you, Randy, you're awfully kind!"

"I mean it!" he replied. "But I'll give you back to him now!"

They looked around. Brad was skating next to a pretty blond girl, perhaps in her late teens. Brad and the girl *whooshed* past Randy and Lee at breakneck speed. Lee grinned at Brad, but he did not see it.

Randy let her off at the gate, and then he bowed and said, "Thank you, Lee, it was a pleasure."

"Likewise, Randy, you take care now."

Randy nodded and went back to skating.

Lee looked up to find Brad skating alone toward her.

"She caught me off guard," he explained. "I couldn't say no. She was such a polite kid." He figured correctly that the girl had a crush on him, but it remained moot between Brad and Lee.

"I skated with Randy. He wanted to know when I graduated from high school. He asked me if you're my husband."

"I wish," Brad responded. "My little partner was Gloria from some place nearby. I didn't pay attention to most of what she was blabbing about."

They skated and danced together for another half hour or so, and then they headed back to Brad's place. In Brad's bedroom, they had fulfilling sex before she decided it was late and time to get home. Jim was working late that evening, but the girls would undoubtedly be home wondering where their mom was. Lee figured they already knew. She had told them she was going out, and that is all she had said. The girls had merely responded, "Okay," in unison.

Brad walked Lee to her car. Before she got the door open, he put his arms on her hips and leaned in closely so his body met hers. He still wanted her. But it was late. She would have loved to favor him with more, but she looked up at him with serious eyes, and he understood. They kissed each other, already longing for the next time they would meet. She wrested herself from his grip gently, and he acquiesced. She got into the Cruiser, started it, and backed out of the driveway. She lowered her window to give Brad a hearty wave. He returned the favor and turned toward the house.

Lee got home at about 9:00 p.m. Jim was already home. Her heart sank when she saw his truck in the garage. She parked the Cruiser slowly while racking her brain for words to say to him. She decided there were no words; this might be the night of confrontation. She stood at the front door of the house and cried for a few minutes. Would it be goodbye to Brad and I'm sorry to Jim? She had no clue. She was frightened. She sighed with resignation and opened the front door. She made her way up the stairs quietly to the living room. No one was there. Jim and the girls were already asleep. Lee considered sleeping on the couch so as not to disturb her husband. But she took off her coat and clothing, found a cozy nightgown to wear, and sheepishly climbed into bed beside Jim. He did not awaken. She figured she had some time to make up a picadillo. She fell asleep thinking about it.

Nothing untoward was said by Jim in the morning. Was it possible he did not even care that she was out last night? Her love affair had to come out sooner or later. She decided it would be Jim's call. Breakfast was normal but for Lee and her guilt. Jim went back to work; he had to work all weekend. Lee decided to ask the girls if they wanted to go shopping or get pizza at the pinball place. The girls decided they wanted to go out of town to one of the big malls that Kingston did not have. They cleared the table and put the dishes into the new dishwasher; after which, they got ready and headed out to the mall. No one mentioned Lee's absence of the night before. It would hang over her head all day. But as days passed, she figured no one was going to broach the subject. She felt a tenuous peace.

DISNEY AND THE BEACH

Florida was a three-day party for the Jones family, starting with the flight to Orlando via JFK International Airport. The girls were thrilled to see palm trees and flora and fauna they had never seen in New York. There was a shuttle bus that took them to a hotel on-site at Disney.

"I know it's kind of lame to have a hotel right at Disney World, girls, but it's so much easier than fighting Orlando traffic every day. I hear it's horrible."

"Oh, we don't mind, Dad. This is exciting!" Maddie exclaimed.

There was a hotel room for the girls adjoining a room for Lee and Jim. If the girls wanted to hang out with their parents, all they had to do was open the door between their rooms. The first day there, they actually arrived in the evening, so they splurged and ordered room service for supper. It was a grand array of fresh meats, cheeses, crackers, and fruit, along with a bottle of champagne. They all dug in with enthusiasm and gave each other cheers with the alcohol.

In the morning, there was free breakfast on the first floor. Everyone went except Lee. The rest of the family gathered food for her and took it up to her when they had had their fill of pancakes, scrambled eggs, toast, bacon, and orange juice. Lee ate with gusto, and the family cheered her for it.

It was decided that Lee was not going to tolerate most of the rides. The hotel offered her a wheelchair so Jim could push her around the grounds of Disney. She said she would have just as much fun watching as participating. She could hardly wait for old man Jim to get onto a rollercoaster with the teenagers. She wanted to see how brave he was. He would prove himself a good sport.

They spent the day waiting in long lines to get the satisfaction of ride after ride and exhibit after exhibit. They bought a load of souvenirs. Before they knew it, it was evening and time for them to get back to the hotel to get ready for the next day. Lee fell asleep early again. The rest of the family partied in the girls' room to delivered pizza and soda pop.

"Dad, you're really splurging on us. This is amazing, thank you!" Maddie said as she raised her paper cup of soda pop to cheer her dad.

"My pleasure," Jim replied. "I'm sorry we never did take many vacations with you girls."

"Oh, but we loved all those mountains out west and Howe Caverns in New York and those amazing rivers that flow underground in the Tuckaleechee caverns in Tennessee," Maddie reminded him.

"And the eyeless fish at Mammoth Caves," chimed in Krista, "and the whales at Cape Cod."

"Dad, you've made a great childhood for us. No regrets here. How about you, Krista?"

"Not a one," Krista replied.

Jim fought back a tear of happiness by clearing his throat. "Well, let's get this food finished and get ready for bed. We can leave as early as 8:00 a.m. tomorrow, but I'd rather relax and have breakfast first. What do you two think?"

"I like your idea. It was fun pigging out at the continental breakfast," Maddie replied.

"Okay, I'll see you girls at about 8:00 a.m. for breakfast downstairs. Have a good night."

"Love you, Dad!" the girls said in unison.

He hugged each girl and gave each one a kiss on the top of the head. Then he went through the open doorway into the room he shared with Lee. She looked so peaceful he hated to interrupt her. He slept on the other bed. Ironically, when he awoke in the middle of the night, Lee was in his bed curled up next to him. In her state of being so ill, she had a sallow look to her, but there was still that underlying beauty she always possessed. He lay beside her and put an arm over her waist. She stirred but did not awaken. Another night in the endless number of nights they had not slept apart from each other. It was like a heavenly dream being beside her. She meant so much to him.

The alarm awoke Jim and Lee up at 7:50 a.m.

"Crap! Sorry, honey, I thought I'd be up already. We're headed downstairs for breakfast. You just hang out up here, and we'll bring you some food again. That okay with you?"

"I feel so lazy," she said.

"Oh my god, you're kidding me. Put that out of your beautiful head. We'll be back soon. I have to get a quick shower before the girls wake up."

The girls were already awake, showered and in their parents' room before Jim got out of his shower. They had slept so well it was easy to get up at 8:00 a.m. They sat on the edge of the empty bed and chatted with Lee. She put in her order for what she wanted from the continental breakfast.

"How about some coffee too?" she said. "I rarely drink it. I'm on vacation. I think I could handle a cup of coffee with a couple sugars and a couple creams."

"Wow, Mom, you're going to have a caffeine and sugar buzz," said Maddie.

"Cool," Krista said.

Lee chuckled.

Jim got dressed. He and the girls did their breakfast scarfing again, and then they took Lee's food up to her. She was showered and dressed by then. Her light-green blouse made her spectacular gray-green eyes practically pop out of her head.

"Honey, you look nice," Jim said, and he planted a gentle kiss on her lips.

"Thanks, it's not easy to do these days."

"We all understand, Mom," said Maddie. "You're as pretty as you always have been."

Lee coughed to fight back a tear, and she hugged her daughter.

"Okay," said Jim, "let's get on the road to a new day."

Jim and the girls decided to go see a beach. Orlando is situated inland. The ocean was not nearby. The family chose Vero Beach because of its white sands. Jim hit the turnpike in a rented car at 10:00 a.m. They stopped in West Melbourne and visited the lush botanical gardens. Then they headed to Melbourne to sightsee a bit and purchase some tourist T-shirts. At last, they arrived at Vero Beach. It was a beautiful beach with the white sands the girls had seen in brochures. There was not a cloud in the azure sky. Everybody swam in the ocean. Lee relaxed on her back and let the gentle salt waves rock her to and fro. The family had lunch on a boardwalk restaurant in town and enjoyed fresh seafood to the recorded music of Jimmy Buffett and his steel drums. After lunch, they hunted for more souvenirs. Jim decided they needed one more piece of luggage to carry all the new stuff they had acquired. Then they returned to the beach and lay on the towels they had gotten at the Ron Jon Shop.

Soon, it was time to find some supper and get back to the hotel for a good night's sleep. They packed and talked and packed some more after they got back into their rooms. The girls stuffed their new suitcase with the plethora of items they had accumulated, including a sandwich bag full of the white sands of Vero Beach. They decided to have dinner in the restaurant downstairs. Lee joined them.

The return flight was smooth primarily. Maddie and Krista kept their noses to the windows of the jet so they could see the scenery far below whenever it popped out of the clouds. Maddie sat next to the window, beside Jim. Krista had a row to herself in front of her family and took the window seat.

She could converse with the family when her nose was not glued to the window. They were amazed by how small the foothills looked as the jet flew over them. They also spotted areas where deforestation was taking place, and they were saddened by the resulting bare mountaintops. But they enjoyed themselves when they experienced the occasional turbulence, when their stomachs seemed to land up in their throats. Jim and Lee got a kick out of their daughters having so much fun with the turbulence. Jim and Lee snuggled together as well as they could and held hands the entire flight—relaxed and still very much in love with each other.

Two Men Talking

A week after the Jones family was home from their vacation, Brad called Lee at work again.

"Lee, sorry for the call. This is Brad."

"I know who you are, silly. I have only a couple minutes to talk though. There's a widespread flu going around, and every doctor wants his patients tested for it."

"Are you sick?" He sounded concerned.

She smiled. "No, I'm fine, other than having a fuzzy head and a port stuck in my chest for IVs. Pretty normal other than that."

Brad sighed. "When am I ever going to stop worrying about you?"

Lee said, "How about now?"

"Never is more like it," he responded. "But what I need to know is do we need to talk about Jim at all? Do I need to have a man-to-man with him to confess?"

"I am so mixed up. Jim and I don't talk about you and me. I'll never leave him, but you already know that."

"Yes. We've never pretended anything to each other."

"It's up to you whether to talk to Jim or not. It scares the hell out of me though. I don't want him to kick you out of our lives. Because if he did, I would abide by it."

"Jesus, Lee," he said, sounding very sad. Then he said bravely, "It's coming to the man-to-man though. I can't sneak around any longer. But I'm going to be busy all day today as usual with the cattle. I have two heifers also who are ready to give birth, so I have to be close on hand. Lee, I've left my ranch hands to do all the work so far. I'm going to go help them out."

"Okay, thanks for calling. I mean that."

"The pleasure is all mine, Leora."

She *knew* he was going to do that. And a shard stung her heart—a shard of pain and joy, of suffering and love.

"Bye, Brad."

"Goodbye, Lee."

That evening after work, Brad called and got Jim on the phone.

"Just the man I'm after," said Brad. "Brother, we need to talk. Would you please come over to the farm? I'd rather leave Lee out of this."

"All right, Brad. I can be there in an hour, sound good?"

"See you then, Jim. Thank you."

"You bet. Bye."

"Bye, Jim."

Leora heard Jim but did not comment. She was in the living room watching TV with the girls. Jim took his leave about half an hour later after he told Lee that he would be back as soon as possible. Lee merely nodded to acknowledge him. He gave her a kiss on the top of her head and gave the girls a kiss on their heads as well.

"Bye, Dad," the girls said in unison.

When he was gone, Maddie asked her mother, "Where's he going?"

"To Brad's house," said Krista, "this might be the beginning of the end of that friendship."

"What do you mean?" asked Leora.

"If you hadn't been so transparent on the phone the day Maddie overheard you talking to Brad, we'd be in the dark. Maddie told me, and eventually, we both went to Dad about it. Dad knew also because you left your work phone at home one day, and it was out of charge. You never leave your work phone at home, uncharged."

"Oh, dear God, girls. I'm so sorry you all have to know about this. This is all my fault. I should never have shown Brad how much I love him. Or maybe I should have way back when we were so young. Those two guys have shared me since I was in high school. Seems as if the *affair* would have lost its luster by now, but it's still the same. And Jim, well, Jim carries me. He lifts me up and keeps me going through every adversity without complaint."

"Yeah, you are damn lucky to have him," said Krista. "Think of the way he used to kiss your bald head. He never gave it a thought. He's stayed with you through the best and worst of your life, Mom. Dad's the best. If you ever dumped him, I would never forgive you, even as much as I love you."

"Hell, he even holds your hand when you're puking your guts out into the toilet."

"True, Maddie, so true," Lee replied. "I guess we'll just have to hang out until he gets home unless it gets super late. I'm pretty tired myself. I might have to hit the sack a bit early."

"Mom, just go get ready for bed. We'll stay up for a while. Maybe it's best we're all in bed when he gets home anyway. He might not want to talk."

"Okay, Krista, good idea. I'm scared. I'll take whatever he gives me. I deserve it. He's my main man, always has been. I'll never leave your dad. Good night, girls. Please forgive me. I love you."

"Love you too, Mom," they said in unison without enthusiasm.

* * *

Jim arrived on Brad's gravel driveway in the Cruiser. He disembarked and rang the doorbell to the side stoop door. No answer. He strolled to the horse barn. Not there. He went on down the hill behind the horse barn and to the west to the cattle barn. There was Brad leaning on the wall of a stall talking to one of his helpers about Angus beef.

Jim cleared his throat to be heard. Brad, in an instant, turned his head to face Jim. "Hey" was all he could think of to say.

"Hey, Brad," Jim replied.

"Jim, this is Devon, one of my helpers, working overtime tonight."

Jim and Devon shook hands.

"Devon, we're headed up to the house. Thanks for staying. You might as well go on home now. Everybody is all set for the night."

"Thanks, boss," said Devon and took his leave.

"Let's get back to the house, shall we?" Brad suggested to Jim.

They walked in silence up the hill, through the horse barn, across the gravel, and into the house via the side door. As usual, they removed their footwear and headed into the dining room, the place that had captured heart-to-heart conversations in the past. It was a comfortable room, nonjudgmental because it did not *feel* like Brad. It still felt like the Warners because the furniture had not been replaced.

Brad sat at one end of the table. Jim remained standing opposite Brad.

"I understand you and Lee still love each other," Jim said as level-headed as he could. He did not feel like shedding tears. He just wanted to talk for now.

Brad put his head down and sighed. Then he looked up at Jim.

"She's never going to leave you, Jim. She told me that enough times for it to sink in. And I've never asked her to."

"What else do you know about me?" Jim asked in anger unfamiliar to Brad.

"She keeps you close to her vest. We know the situation sucks for me, sorry to sound so selfish, but I've loved her from the moment we bumped into each other in high school. That will never go away."

"And she tells you she loves you too, I suppose." Jim's ire was rising slightly.

"She tells me that you and the girls are her world."

"Well, I guess that's not a complete truth now, is it?"

"I don't understand."

"She's still seeing you, sneaking around when she thinks I don't know where she's going. It was her work phone that gave it away. She left it at home, uncharged, very unusual for her. That means she skipped work. To be with you. Do you remember that day?"

"Yes."

"What did you do that day?"

"Jim—"

"*Really.*"

Brad sighed lightly. "We went on a color tour and ended up at a bistro for lunch. It's not always about sex anyway. We're friends too, not to the extent that you and she are though."

"How—"

"She never puts you down or complains about you. She always compliments you. She loves you just as much as she did when we were teenagers. She can't help it if her heart feels for both of us. But I'm always on the back burner. I've resigned to be there for the rest of my life with her."

"Stop," Jim ordered in a low tone, "just stop."

Brad fell silent. He wondered if he was sounding like a wounded puppy. He did not want to sound that way. He loved Leora, and there should be no shame in that. To him, it was true love and friendship to boot.

There ensued a long pause during which neither man looked at the other.

Then Jim said, "I don't even know why I'm here."

"It's the same ol' thing. We love her. She loves us. We love each other."

"I suppose we should have become Mormons after all," said Jim sardonically. "Listen though. She's going through some very rough times. She's terminal, you know. The doctors in as much told me so. I feel like a heel keeping it from her."

"What are you afraid of?" asked Brad.

"Her tears. When she cries, I die inside."

"That would make two of us."

"Jesus, Brad, what are we going to do without her?"

"She's still with us, Jim, make every damn moment count for good."

Jim blinked back two tears that wanted to fall from his eyes.

"Why couldn't she love some other guy who's a jerk and makes her pissed off all the time, so she'll eventually kick his ass and send him home to his mama?"

Brad burst out laughing in spite of himself. He slapped the table top lightly.

"She's right," Brad said. "You *are* the best."

"Goddamn right I am. Why can't you break up with her because she has cancer and circles under her eyes all the time? And her skin is sallow. And she's weak. She comes home from work exhausted."

"I don't know, brother. I would rather die than not see her."

"All those guys chasing after her in junior high and high school… did you know that she and I have been lovers since tenth grade?"

"No, Jim, I don't need to know that stuff. It's private."

"Explain yourself to me. Why does she love you?"

Brad sighed. "I don't know. I really don't."

"Well, I can see lust for sure. You're still tall, dark, and handsome. Me—I'm losing my blond hair to half gray, half bald."

"You think she even notices that? She doesn't."

"And how are you so sure of yourself?"

"I know Leora, that's how."

A stinging shard lodged itself into Jim's heart for a moment while they were silent. It was a shard of envy.

"Jim, have you discussed me with Leora?"

"No. I just keep hoping you'll fade away. Doesn't look as if that's going to happen."

"I know her, Jim. If you ask her to stop seeing me, she'll do it. That is divine truth."

"Can I do that to her? To you?"

"She's your wife. She chose you over me, over everyone else. As I said, I'm on the back burner. If you turn the back burner off, Lee and I will have no choice but to stop seeing each other and remain just friends."

"Could you do that?"

"Yes."

"But you don't want to, do you?"

"No. You must know how I feel. She's someone a cut above the rest. And she's a phenomenal mom to those girls. And she was an amazing granddaughter to Ed. You were amazing with him as well. You are so superior to me you probably have no idea," said Brad.

"Not a lick. Tell me though. It's a hypothetical. If she were your wife and was as sick as she is now, would you stay with her?"

"I believe I would. But how could we ever know for sure? I'd love to be on hand when she's not doing well, but often, I don't even find out until it's all over with. She keeps herself to herself when it comes to me. You are definitely in the top slot with her, Jim, never, ever doubt that. I see you two together enough. She has great respect for you and always will. As will I as a matter of fact."

"I want to be angry with you," Jim said. "Why can't I be angry with you?"

"I love you, brother. Nothing will change that, even if I never see you again."

"*Not* what I wanted to hear."

"But there it is nonetheless."

"Yes, there it is."

Brad's phone rang. It was a cell phone. It was on a kitchen counter. He fetched it and answered it. Then he handed the phone to Jim. "It's Maddie."

Jim's heart sank. "Yes, honey, what's up?" he asked her.

"Mom's been coughing and throwing up essentially since you left. She tried to go to bed, but she keeps getting up to vomit. Now it's the dry heaves. Does she have meds at home for that?"

"Ah, yeah, in the refrigerator in the section where the butter goes. There are Phenergan suppositories. They work wonders. They will help her sleep too."

"'They,' you say. Should she take more than one?"

"No, just one. They work rather quickly. Listen, I'm coming home."

"Dad, Krista and I have this covered."

"I know you do. I'm coming home anyway."

When he got off the phone, he said to Brad, "Going home. The wife is vomiting. Not good. Chemo is over for now. Can't see why she would be getting sick."

Brad remained quiet about his phone conversation with Lee about the flu going around. He did not want to upset Jim any more than he was at this moment. But he felt guilty keeping the truth from his best friend. If it weren't Leora, he probably would violate the promise he had made.

They walked silently to the Vista Cruiser. Jim got in, started the engine, and said, "Good night," to Brad before he closed the car door. Brad had no time to respond. Jim put the car into gear and turned it around in the driveway. Then he was on its way home in a hurry.

MARRY ME

Jim drove as fast as he could and still remain safe. When he got home, he dismissed parking the car in the garage and opened the front door of the house, took the stairs two at a time, and hurried to their bedroom. Lee was seated on the edge of the bed. The color was gone from her face.

"I feel as if I've been run over by a freight train," she said to him.

"You have aches and pains?"

"Yeah, they started today. Maybe my stomach muscles are tired of puking. I might need some Tylenol for the pain. And I haven't brushed my teeth yet. I must smell like a sewage treatment plant."

Jim sat beside her and hugged her. "No, you don't, but if it would make you feel better, go ahead and brush your teeth. I'm right here. I'll keep my eye on you."

"Okay." Lee lifted herself with labor. Slightly bent over, she made her way to the bathroom. She brushed her teeth and returned to her position beside Jim.

"I think you should let the Phenergan work and get in a nap," he suggested. "I'll call work for you. No way you're going to work tomorrow."

"Thanks, honey, thanks for all you do for me." She shed a couple tears that she let drop onto her face. "I feel as if I've fucked up this marriage."

"*What?*" Jim exclaimed. "Why are you talking about that now? You're sick. Leave it alone and get to bed. I'll be in bed too before you know it. Right after I call your work."

"All right. You're right."

"And when you're feeling better, there's some news I have for you."

"What is it? I won't go to bed until you tell me."

Jim heaved a sigh. "It's my fault you don't know. The doctors trusted me to tell you. I just didn't want to hurt you. The doctors aren't hopeful that the cancer hasn't metastasized to other parts of your body. They want you to reconvene chemo for another month."

"No," Lee said, "no more chemo."

"Honey, you already have the port. It will be easy."

"My mind was made up after the previous bout with cancer. I'm always nauseous. I get killer headaches. My hair is gone probably forever."

"What about the girls? Have you discussed this with them?"

"God no, I don't think they would agree with me."

"Well, of course, they wouldn't!" Jim said slightly angrily.

"Please just let me go to bed for now. I'm feeling that Phenergan kicking in. Thanks for talking to me though, honey. I really appreciate it. You do so much for me."

Jim wondered how she could be so gracious when she was feeling so sick.

"I hate to tell you this," he said as Lee was snuggling under the covers. "I had a talk with ol' Brad today. I can't figure out why I can't be furious with him."

"I don't understand."

"You will when you let it sink in. We were talking about a beautiful young woman we both have been crazy about since we were teenagers."

"Well, that can't be me," she responded. "Are you in love with Ingrid maybe?"

Jim got down upon his knees and grabbed Lee's hands.

"Leora Jones, will you marry me again?"

"*What?*" She did not expect *that* to come from his mouth.

"Marry me, Lee, please."

"Well, I think we'd better hurry it up. I don't feel as if a long life is in my future."

God, she understands, Jim thought. He cried—hard. He sobbed. She let him get it all out without interfering.

"Just marry me for as long as we both last," he said finally.

"Yes, of course, I'll marry you. There's something I'd like to talk to you about though. I've been thinking it would be cool if Brad started Maddie on breeding Angus cattle. She takes such an interest in his venture. He could get a cow for her, and she could raise it and sell it. Or breed it. What do you think?"

"I think it's an excellent idea," Jim replied. "I'll get her in here." He left the room and fetched Maddie, who returned with him to see Lee. Jim proposed the idea to Maddie. Maddie was thrilled with the idea.

Jim asked her, "Shall I call Brad?"

"Yes!" Maddie responded, wanting to jump up and down.

"Okay, I'll be right back." A few minutes later, he was back. "Brad's going to find you a heifer to raise. You can pay him for it once it's been butchered. Sound cool?"

Maddie hugged her dad and gave him a kiss on the cheek. "When will I know?"

"Well, he'll give you a call once he's obtained the heifer."

"Call *me*?"

"You're in the cattle-raising business now, honey," said Lee. "Consider breeding the heifer though. That way, you can continue your business indefinitely. It's up to you. I'm so proud of you, Maddie."

"Thanks, you two!" said Maddie with a grin on her face. "I guess it's time for me to hit the sack for now. Good night."

"Good night, honey," Jim and Lee said in unison.

Jim said to Lee, "We're going to have to find something for Krista to do, something fun and exciting."

"Sure thing, dear. But it's time for me to get some sleep. Maybe we can talk about your extramarital love sometime later."

"I'm not going to bed until you understand we were talking about you."

"*Me?*"

"You might as well know that Maddie and I figured it out before Krista did. Your uncharged phone gave you away. And then there was something about Maddie overhearing a phone conversation you had with Brad."

Lee cried, "Oh, dear God, you do know, don't you?" A shard of guilt and shame stung her, making her heart feel bruised.

"Yes, of course, I know. Brad confessed as well. It's all out in the open now. But I love him so much, how can I be angry with such devotion? He told me he accepts being on the back burner for the rest of his life. What kind of existence is that for a handsome, intelligent guy like him?"

Lee said nothing. At this moment, she was not worried about Brad.

"He wants to be your friend if nothing else. Can you cope with that?"

"If you make an ultimatum, I will honor it."

"Oh, dear God," Jim sighed. He felt tremendous pressure pushing him down upon his shoulders. "Just marry me. We'll figure out the rest later. I just want you to be my beautiful bride once again."

"Beautiful is out of the question."

Jim left the room and fetched Krista, who followed him to see Lee. "Honey, I've asked your mom to marry me again, and she said yes. Can you and Maddie do some makeup for her to give her a nice pallor, and maybe some lipstick?"

"Of course, Dad. Maddie and I can work our magic. Cool! This is going to be fun!"

And it was fun. A week after that conversation, Jim and Lee were married in one of Kingston's small churches by a nondenominational minister. Maddie was the maid of honor, and Krista was one of the bridesmaids. Adrian and Lee's cousin Ben were the groomsmen. Jim and Lee looked wonderful. They wore their previous wedding clothes. In attendance were the Jones family and Jim's parents, the Clark clan, Sherry and Bela. There was a pretty white two-layered cake and champagne at Sherry and Bela's place afterward. It was a perfect day for Jim and Lee.

Brad did not attend the wedding. He was not invited. He did not even know that Jim and Lee had the ceremony.

ED AND HIS MS

Ed started losing interest in eating. His helper could not get him to eat much food for a week and finally called Jim at work to let him know.

Jim said, "Okay, I'll get him to eat when I get home. Thanks for letting me know." He then called Lee at work and gave her the news.

At home that evening, Jim and Ed had a conversation. Ed wanted to go to a nursing home to relieve the pressure on Jim and Lee.

"If you're serious, I'll start looking," Jim said to him.

Yes, he was serious. It had to be quick because he refused to eat much food, even when Jim was home. He needed a feeding tube if he was to survive.

"No feeding tube. I just want to go somewhere and die. I'm ready to be in heaven with my wives."

Jim was not shocked. Ed's bladder and bowel control was practically nonexistent, and he had such nerve pain in his legs. There was no medicine that would take it away entirely.

"I'm just sick of being alive," he mumbled to Jim. "Please take me somewhere so I don't have to burden my family by dying at home. I'm ready to vacate this sore, old body."

Jim and Lee took a couple days from work to locate a nice nursing home. They were hard to find. The nicest ones were too expensive. They finally found a decent place in Albany where he would have a roommate. Ed was satisfied when Jim described the accommodations. He was transferred there by an ambulance. The room at the nursing home was small with just enough room for one small dresser for each resident, one bed per person as well as one small closet for each person. Lee arranged hospice care since Ed decided he wasn't going to eat any more meals. Ed signed a do-not-resuscitate order so he could die in peace.

Jim, Lee, Sherry, Maddie, and Krista visited Ed on a daily basis. He lasted about a week. He slipped into a coma. The family got to the home before he passed away. Each of them took a turn holding his hand and telling him they loved him. There was no response. The next day, Ed started the Cheyne-Stokes breathing so common in persons in a coma. The hospice nurse called Lee and Jim. Ed passed away that evening before the family could get there. When they did arrive, they encircled the bed and prayed for Ed's safe journey to heaven. There were many tears shed by Lee and the girls and Sherry. Sherry had gone through so much with her dad, had put him through some rough times. She asked him for his forgiveness.

Ed was cremated, and the service was a private one with immediate family, a pastor, the helpers who had taken care of him at home, and the hospice nurses. He was buried at one of the cemeteries in Kingston on a bright, brisk day.

WATCHING SHERRY

After Ed passed away and was buried, Sherry's family started watching her with hawk eyes for any change, even a tiny one, in her MS. She did admit that at the end of the workday, her arms were very weak and could hardly lift anything over five pounds. And she continued to have the flare-ups of the facial pain. But for the most part, the MS had leveled off. She continued to refuse experimental tests and medication. If she had to die the way her father did, that was all right with her. Bela did not like hearing her talk like that. He knew he was going to miss her terribly if she passed away before he did. She kept her thoughts from Maddie and Krista because she did not want to scare them. She was extremely worried about how they were going to handle the death of their grandmother. Maddie and Krista cried about Sherry often. Finally Jim took them into the living room and gave a full explanation of MS and how it can progress.

"Your grandma's in pretty good shape right now, girls," Jim said. "And your mom shows no signs of MS. Keep praying for both of them, and I will too."

"I miss Grandpa Ed," Maddie complained. "He loved to jam with us with our music. He could barely talk, but he tried to sing and clap his hands. He was fun."

"He surely was," Krista agreed.

But as the weeks went on, the pain of missing Grandpa Ed faded. Life started its new normal. Brad called them about a month after Ed passed away. He spoke to Jim first. They had a brief conversation, and then Brad asked to speak to Lee.

"Hello?" she said into the receiver.

"Lee, it's Brad. I'm calling to offer my condolences on the death of your grandfather."

"Yeah, he was a great sport. But eventually being alive was too hard for him to manage. He just gave up. But he seemed to go peacefully, starting with a coma. We didn't get there in time for his passing, but we encircled his bed and prayed for his safe journey to heaven."

"That's beautiful, Lee."

"Thank you. What else can we do for you?"

"Oh, I thought I would impose upon your family to have a cookout with me at your place. I called Darren and Rita about it, and they're in. Adrian and Sandy want to join us as well. I know it's intruding, but I feel like it's the best way to get everybody together."

"You know what? I'm going to see how many people from the group I can locate. I haven't spoken to Connie in ages. I'll see if I can find her, as well as the rest of the group. Family reunion time."

"That's gracious of you, Lee. Thank you. I'll provide all the charcoal and meat from my farm. We can ask each person to bring a dish to pass. Does that sound okay? I'll have the beef already cooked overnight in the barrel roaster."

"Sounds great to me, Brad. And you said cooking's not your forte! Thank you very much for thinking of us. This should be fun. It's October now, so now's the time before November rolls around."

"All right, Lee. When you have the RSVPs all in, would you let me know?"

"Of course."

"Lee, one other question. How's your mom doing?"

"It's status quo. No changes. We keep close watch over her all the time. Her arms get weak at the end of the day."

"Well, please give her my best, will you? She's a very strong woman, always has been from what I have seen."

"Indeed. I love her and worry about her, but I don't let the girls see me worry. They have their own feelings about Mom, and they are very sad about the MS sometimes. I guess they're actually old enough to hear the whole truth about MS, but I just keep thinking of them as little girls, know what I mean?"

"Yeah, I understand. Well, I'll let you go for now. Have a great evening. I've got cows to take care of."

Lee smiled. "All right, you have fun out there."

"Oh yeah, it's a blast. I have a couple good helpers though, makes life easier."

"Great! Okay, talk later?"

"You bet. Any time, you know that."

"You're very gracious, Brad. I appreciate you in more ways than one."

"Ditto, young lady."

She chuckled. "Okay, bye, Brad."

"Bye, Lee."

What a relief she felt to know the conversation had not been cloaked in secrecy.

THE REUNION

The next Saturday afternoon, the reunion took place. It was a success, attended by everyone who was invited, including their children if they had any. Maddie and Krista were given permission to invite a few of their friends too. Even Brad's mother was there. Absent was Brad's father. Brad had make it plain to his mother, as soon as he had moved into the Warners' house, that Brad's father was not welcome anywhere Brad was. Brad's mother did not balk at that, and his father had no desire to see his son anyway. The relationship between Brad's parents was strained; his mother felt free to open up with Brad and his guests at the reunion.

Brad stayed at his station of the roaster he had pulled there with his Explorer. He had started it the previous night at Jim and Lee's, and he had slept in his Explorer so he could be near it. While Brad tended to the roaster, he and Bela spent time chatting about farming. When the meat was finished being cooked, Bela helped Brad serve it to the guests. After eating, several of the guests started a game of croquet on the front lawn.

The place was loud with conversation and animation. Lee was delighted to have all her friends there having fun being together again. Everyone looked almost the same as they had in high school, with the exception of Connie who had lost a good deal of weight so her face and her figure were slimmer. She looked even more like her cousin Collin.

Eventually the young people found their way to Maddie and Krista's bedrooms to play board games or watch movies. Some of them were virtually strangers to the girls, but they all acted as if they had known each other a long time. It was a perfect melding of personalities.

Some of the group wondered about Darren and Rita—where they worked and where they lived. Darren had taken a job as an attorney for the State of Massachusetts. They lived near Boston. Rita did not work. Darren provided an excellent way of life for her. He spoiled her with horses. And she spoiled him by cooking him dinner every night and tending to his personal needs to his "great satisfaction," according to Darren, right after he swung his mallet and won the first croquet game.

"Okay, enough said about *that*," said Jim, right behind Darren. "You're embarrassing me." Jim finished in second place.

Brad was the only single adult male from the group. The group teased him about it.

Connie said it most clearly, "You are so handsome. There's no way you haven't been chased and pursued, Brad. I know you don't like to talk about such things, and you don't have to, but I hope you're happy being single. Otherwise, I'm going to have to go shopping for you. I hear the women in Russia are extremely beautiful."

The group howled at that. Nobody wanted Brad to have to lower himself to purchase a bride. But many of them did wonder why he had neither a girlfriend nor a wife, seeing he *was* very handsome and personable and successful with his dairy farm.

Brad kept his mouth shut. He was thinking of Leora and Ingrid, but he guessed that nobody knew about either one of them as they pertained to his life. He was lonely; he admitted to himself, but Lee kept him from being sad about it. On this day, he actually wondered if he could tolerate Ingrid enough to have a romantic relationship with her. Brad would have to ask her father of her whereabouts, which did not thrill him at all. Besides that, he feared he would lose Lee forever. Could he live without Lee? They rarely got together, but when they did, he was the happiest he could be. They were both getting older. Was once-in-a-while good enough for Brad? He did not worry about Lee because she had Jim and loved him very much. Brad assumed they had an active sex life. He figured Lee was satisfied with infrequent encounters with Brad. He would love to have her all to himself, but it was impossible. Her relationship with Jim was a forever one. Nevertheless, Brad had a great time at the reunion. It rolled on into the evening. At 8:00 p.m., Bela took out his accordion. Darrell had his recorder, and Collin had his Renaissance drums. There ensued a fun jam session. But by 9:00 p.m., everyone was ready to head home. They left en masse after long goodbyes and lots of hugs and kisses.

Brad was the final person to take leave. He and Bela talked while Brad hooked the roaster up to the Explorer. Brad sought Jim and gave him a big brotherly hug and a pat on the back. Then Brad found Lee and hugged her as well, making it a friendly gesture, which is what he was good at when necessary. He gave her a secret kiss in her ear though, making sure nobody was looking when he did it. Just that little kiss warmed Lee from her head to her toes. *Look how old he is, and he still turns me on with a little kiss,* she thought. She looked up at him with her beautiful eyes. He smiled at her.

It took a good hour to clean up the picnic table and the inside of the house. Sherry and Bela stayed to help, and the girls did their parts at well. Then Sherry and Bela took their leave. Sherry's arms were feeling very weak. By then, the girls were tired out from the fun and went to bed right away. Jim and Lee sat in the living room on the couch talking about the party and promised each other to have another one as soon as the weather got better, which was months away. Winter was knocking at New York's door. Another party had to wait until spring or summer.

BRAD'S PLACE

In May, there was a break in the weather. It felt like summer instead of spring. The temperature outside went up to the seventies. This gave Leora copious opportunities to sit outside and bask in the sunshine. Within a couple days, her complexion improved, and her eyes were bright again.

One evening, Jim approached Lee about taking the girls to Brad's place for a ride. Jim asked Lee to go along. She felt well enough to say yes, and Jim was pleased. He wanted to give her a good day at Brad's place, even if she did not ride.

On the second Saturday in May, the Jones family packed a picnic lunch and headed to Brad's place at noon. To everyone's shock, Brad had built a gazebo for Lee. It was a beautiful cedar gazebo, and the fragrance pleased Leora. It was situated near the front of the barn so she could see some of the meadow and some of the orchard. It had a built-in round table in the middle of it and built-in benches that went all the way around the table. There was plenty of room for everyone. They ate lunch out there. Brad provided beer for the adults and Faygo grape soda pop for the girls. The girls had never tasted Faygo before, and they both decided it was one up on Nehi. Brad was pleased to hear that the girls liked his choice of beverage.

Lunch was cold chicken, pulled pork sandwiches, potato chips, and raw veggies with Sherry's delicious homemade dip. After everyone had their fill, they relaxed for about half an hour in the gazebo. Lee felt self-conscious about her looks, but Brad told her she was just as lovely as ever, knowing—but not caring—that his words would make Jim either angry or jealous. Lee ate with gusto and no nausea. Jim praised her for her fortitude.

"You're intrepid, my love," he said to her. Everyone else repeated the sentiment in his or her own way. Lee was not used to so much attention at one time, and she blushed at all the compliments.

It was finally time for Jim, Maddie, and Krista to ride. They stayed out about an hour. Brad and Lee watched the girls take on their dad in a race.

Near the end of the ride, Lee said to Brad, "I apologize for being a bummer. It's a drag, this cancer stuff."

"Lee, my god, don't apologize. You've been through the ringer. Right now, you look beautiful to me. I hope you like the gazebo. I built it for you so if you want to be outside, you're covered. It's yours, so come any time at all if you want to sit out here or even if you want to be in the house. If you just need a break from reality and the family—I know they love you to pieces—please feel free to drive over. If I'm busy, I'll stop what I'm doing to make sure you have everything you need. Please let me be kind to you. You mean more to me than you will ever know."

Lee held his hands in hers and squeezed them lightly.

"Please don't tell Jim, but I won't take any more chemo treatments. I'm going to let God take me when he's ready. And I believe I've caught the flu from one of my patients. That's why I have been coughing and vomiting so much. The hospital is inundated with flu patients right now."

"I pray for you every day and every night, Lee. Jim is puzzled about your sickness, but I never told him that you thought you had the flu."

"Thank you. I don't know what else to say."

"Nothing is okay with me. Oh, look, the girls seem to be on their way back."

Maddie, Krista, and Jim took the animals to the paddock and into the barn for a good brush-down. It took about half an hour, after which Jim and the girls joined Brad and Lee.

"Thank you, Uncle Brad," said Maddie. "We had a blast."

Krista said, "Dad's a better rider than we are. We had a race, and he beat the pants off both of us."

Lee said, "Yes, we noticed." She smiled at her girls.

The girls approached Lee. Each girl gave her a kiss on the cheek. Maddie decided to sit next to her mother. Krista sat across from Lee, and Jim sat next to Krista. He was perturbed to see Brad and Lee sitting so close to each other, but he fought off the shards of anger and jealousy for her sake. She was his wife after all, and she never mentioned divorcing him to be with Brad. Jim would always be her only husband. He wondered what would have happened with this lovers' triangle if Brad had never been drafted, or if he had never fled to Canada. Jim was in a quandary as to how to handle the situation. Lee was not shy about sitting snuggled up to Brad. Didn't she know she was showing disrespect toward her husband? Wasn't Brad exhibiting the epitome of disrespect as well?

Lee decided she should go home and rest.

"It's been great to see you, Lee," said Brad. "Have a good rest at home."

"Thank you. I will. Jim and the girls are so kind to me. They stay quiet when I need my rest. Sometimes they can get me to play a board game or a card game, but I get tired so easily. I feel like a poor sport."

"Oh my god, Mom," Maddie scolded Lee. "Think about yourself in a positive way. You're the rock of the Jones family and the reason we're here on earth. And you're dynamite at Twister!"

Lee smiled weakly at her beautiful daughter.

Jim packed up the leftovers, and Brad cleared the table. He took the tableware into the house and loaded the items into the dishwasher. Jim followed him into the house and told him that he had bought Lee a new dishwasher. Brad was glad to hear that.

It was time for the Jones family to go home. They climbed into the Cruiser and said goodbye to Brad. They waved to him as the car approached the road, and Brad waved back. He felt lonely all of a sudden. He knew Lee still loved him. But she always went home to Jim. That would never change.

FADED LOVE?

Brad and Jim were seated on the steps of the side stoop of the Warner farm, aka Brad's place. They had their ankles crossed. Their boots were touching the gravel of the driveway. It was the start of a beautiful summer sunset in the Catskills.

Brad said, "What will we do without her?"

Jim replied, "Die, I suppose. She's been at my side for more than twenty years. I can't imagine even one day without her, let alone the rest of my life. It will kill me."

"Then I shall die too," Brad said. "I have loved her since the moment I met her. It sounds corny, but it's the truth."

"Maybe now is the time to come clean with her if you know what I mean."

"Not exactly. Please explain."

"We've discussed love with her before. Remember? It was in this house, in the dining room. The two of us confessed our love to her. And she reciprocated to both of us. But then you went away, and I nabbed her. But your love didn't fade with the years, did it?"

Brad shed one tear. It dried upon his cheek. Jim did not see it.

"No. Not one shred. But I must confess, and you're the only man who knows about this. I had a sexual relationship with one other woman while I was in Canada. The woman has been out of my life for years. I don't want to see her again, and that's okay with her. I just feel as if I've cheated on Lee with this woman. I never told Lee about her."

"I know who it is. You don't have to tell me."

"Well, then you know why I can't be with her. She could be a friend but not a wife."

"Well, you can't have my wife. She's mine, brother."

"Yes, I know. I just want you to know I still love her very much. And life for me as it is will die if we lose her."

Jim put his chin in his hand. "Hmmm, I wonder…would she perk up if we went in there together and confessed our love once more?"

"Or would it be way too much pressure?"

"Exactly."

"There's no way to practice it. We'd have to just do it. What do we have to lose?"

"I'm up for it. You?"

"All the way," said Brad.

"I'm going there to spend the night. Will you meet me there sometime tomorrow in the morning?"

"I'll be there come hell or high water."

"Good man," said Jim. He stood up and faced the sunset.

"Mighty nice sunset, isn't it? Maybe I can catch the end of it from the hospital."

"Only one way to find out."

"Okay, I'm outta here, brother. See you tomorrow."

"Right."

Brad slept fitfully that night, but he was awake at 8:00 a.m. ready to go. He showered and shaved and ate a bagel with cream cheese. Then he was off on his motorcycle to the hospital to see Jim and Lee.

What had happened was another attack of pain. This time it was underneath her breasts. Jim had rushed her to the emergency department, and there were ultrasounds and CT scans and breast exams. A few hours later, it was announced the cancer had returned in her lymph nodes in her underarms. The breasts were okay.

"Surgery again?" she had asked the doctor.

"Yes, I'm afraid so. We will know within a week if it's benign or malignant. Let's cross our fingers. I'm afraid there will be chemo and radiation this time around. We need to keep this cancer from coming back."

Crossing their fingers did not work. The cancer in the lymph nodes was malignant. The doctor had gotten all of it out, but her figure was changed. Her arms hung limp and mottled. Lee did not cry. Jim did not cry. He had simply asked her, "Who do you want to know about this?"

Her answer had been "Brad. Mom and Dad. The group. Connie. The girls."

For three days, the girls stayed at her side in the hospital unless they went downstairs for a bite to eat. They ate little because they felt nauseous on behalf of their mother. Sherry had visited every day for several hours a day. Connie had stayed for a couple days, sleeping in the hospital chair at night and conferring with the doctors during the day. Lee was in a private room in the intensive care unit.

Jim had slept at home. Lee had wanted this experience to be among her female friends. He visited her in the evenings after work. So on the fourth day, Jim drove over to the Warner farm and had the discourse with Brad. Now he was back at the hospital waiting for Brad to arrive.

Brad showed up at 9:00 a.m. in a quiet manner. Jim was standing at the head of Lee's bed. Lee's eyes were closed, and the girls were seated in chairs against the wall beneath the window. They looked up simultaneously when Brad entered the room. Jim nodded a greeting at Brad, and Brad nodded back.

Jim said, "They gave her some Tylenol. She's not in much pain. But she had her first round of chemo this morning, and she's worn out. Please stay though. We'll talk when she wakes up." Then he whispered to Brad, "Please help me. I love her so much. Maybe your love can make her stay."

Brad shed a single tear again and felt shard upon shard of guilt stab his heart. Why was this woman's husband begging for Brad's help? Jim's love was as steadfast and complete as ever; surely, it was capable of keeping her alive.

Lee awoke about fifteen minutes later. The girls arose, and each girl held one of Lee's hands for a few moments. Then Jim turned to

Maddie and said, "Honey, we need to speak to your mom. Can you give us a few minutes?"

"Of course, Dad. See you soon, Mom," Maddie responded. The girls left the room.

Jim sighed. Brad did not sigh. Jim smoothed Lee's hair back from her forehead. It had been growing long, and she had not cared about it. She had started not caring about things about a month prior, when the pains had returned.

"Honey," he said to Lee, "Brad's here."

Lee opened her beautiful eyes widely and held out her arms for Brad. Brad practically fell into her embrace. She was warm and small and weak. She gave him a kiss on the lips that lingered for a few seconds. Then she released him and beckoned to Jim, who swallowed her up in his embrace. There was no kiss, but she whispered into his ear, "I love you. You have always been my world."

Jim's heart sank. He had a dreadful fear that she was going to speak a death-bed message. She cleared her throat and said very clearly, "My lovers, my men, how I love both of you. Surely you must know that. I can't live any longer without telling you so. And it's not meant to hurt either of you. And it's not just getting guilt off my chest either."

Brad was shocked, from the kiss through the confession.

Jim was shocked as well. He felt a shard of anger and hatred toward Brad. But he made himself bury the feelings because this was Leora's moment, not his.

She asked Jim, "Do you recall when I said I didn't want to go through this damn cancer shit again? I meant what I said. This is the last chance I'm giving modern medicine. My hair is going to fall out. I'm going to feel like puking all the time. And there's no guarantee any of the chemo will stave off another attack. I will be the judge as to whether or not the chemo will continue. I hope you understand. I do hope you understand."

"We want you to live, Leora," Jim pleaded. "We've both decided we'll want to die if you go."

"You can't die. You have to raise our girls until they're ready to leave the roost and find their own lives and loves. Promise me that." She looked at Brad too. "Promise me you will help him."

"Anything on this planet you want, I will do," Brad replied.

Lee nodded her head once. "Now I want to sleep. I'll tell the girls I'd like to be alone today. It's a day of introspection for me. I need to assess my life as it stands. And please call Mom and Dad and Connie to let them know they can stay away today. They all need a break. I feel as if all I'm going to do is sleep anyway."

Jim cried. "I'm afraid to leave you. I'm afraid."

She held out her arms for him to hold again. "Not afraid. Brave. The girls need their daddy. They have always favored their daddy. Now's the time to admit it and be happy about that."

"Okay," Jim said, and he sniffled.

"Leora," said Brad, looking her in the eyes, "we're going to stay until you're fast asleep and don't need us for anything."

Jim looked at Brad and frowned at him in anger, but Lee said, "That's fine."

So Brad and Jim took the chairs vacated by the girls. When the girls returned, Lee beckoned them to her, and she spoke softly to them. Brad and Jim did not hear the discourse. Then the girls walked to Jim and hugged him and cried. He hugged them in return but stayed steady for them.

Maddie released herself and said, "Uncle Brad." To his surprise, she gave him a hug and a kiss on the cheek. "You're family." Brad returned the hug.

Krista stayed connected to her dad. But soon enough, Lee asked the girls to go on home and relax for the day. They obeyed her but stayed by the phone in case they would get a call from Jim.

FINAL DAYS

The next week, Jim took Leora out for dinner in Skaneateles. It was in a beautiful Victorian house converted into a restaurant. They enjoyed a four-course meal topped off with champagne to celebrate the renewal of their vows. Jim bragged to all of those people attending to them. He and Lee received polite congratulations.

But after that, Lee took another turn for the worse. Those aches and pains never went away, and she was just so tired all the time. She coughed so hard the sputum that came up was sometimes tinged with blood. She refused to see a doctor and took cough suppressant instead.

"It's the flu," she said to her worried family. "I've had to test hundreds of patients for this flu at work. Somehow it keeps getting to me. It's viral and can't be cured. We just have to ride it out and see if I'm strong enough."

Jim and the girls sat up at night sometimes, worrying as Lee coughed as if she had the croup. Her rib cage was sore, so she took Tylenol for that. She kept up with the Phenergan and the cough suppressant as well as copious amounts of water. But she was in a weakened state. She did not last a month after the renewal of their vows. She spent the last three days of her life lying in bed talking to whoever was there to visit. She had many friends stop by, and the entire Clark clan and Jim was at her side almost constantly. He cut out of work. He would not go back until after Lee passed away.

Brad was left in the dark about the graveness of Lee's illness. Finally she asked Jim to invite him to their house, which he did right

344

away. Brad was there in less than an hour. Jim led him up to the bedroom. It was bright with lights and sunshine, and Lee was wearing a white cotton nightgown. But Brad was shocked. Her face was pale and gaunt. She had lost a profuse amount of weight, and her bones protruded from beneath her gown. Jim left the room, and Brad got onto his knees and put his hands into her hands. He sobbed, sniffed, and looked at her when he was finished with the tears.

"My god, how I will miss you."

"Take good care of Maddie and her cows. She just loves working with you."

"I invited her to take up residence in the loft. It's all hers if she wants it."

"Make sure to show her the faux moon shadow and the real one. She will appreciate that. She's such an outdoor girl."

Lee bent over a facial tissue and coughed blood into it.

"Sorry about that."

Brad kissed her on her forehead.

"Will I need to take care of Jim too?"

"I don't think so. He has the girls. They will be okay after a while. Jim's young enough to find another woman and start all over again."

"I don't see that happening, Lee," said Brad.

"Stranger things have happened. I for a while thought he might have had a thing for Ingrid, you remember her?"

"Surely do. Rita's big sister. Horse trainer."

"Jim and I used to wonder if you ever saw much of her. She seemed like an impressive woman to me. We even thought she might be a good mate for you." Lee smiled.

"I don't know where she is. We were friends a long time ago. We parted in a friendly way."

"Oh, so you did see her for a while?"

God, here it comes. She knows, thought Brad. *Now what to say?* He decided upon a little white lie, even though he felt guilty about keeping the entire truth from his dying lover.

"We met before I was at Kingston. She was out of school by then. She was at Uncle Bruce's with her own uncle, looking to buy a stallion. Then I bumped into her in Anniston, Alabama, of all places. She was doing a show at some stables when I was at Fort McClellan. She invited me to watch her perform a show on one of Bruce's stallions, which I did."

"I see."

"I didn't want to be with her."

"Okay."

"I wanted to be with you."

"You're with me now."

"Yes, and I don't have it in me to figure out how profusely I can thank Jim for giving me this moment. We had a talk recently, you know."

"Yes, I know."

"After you renewed your vows, did he ask you to stop seeing me?"

Lee frowned as she tried to recall.

"No, I don't think so. He probably thought you'd fall apart if you never saw me again."

"He's right. I'm falling apart right now."

"Oh boy. Jim's got everything covered. Anybody who makes a fuss over me or makes me cry or feel sick isn't allowed to stay with me. You have my permission to fall apart, but you won't have Jim's."

"How you talk—why aren't *you* falling apart?"

"You think I'm not?" she replied. "Physically I'm already there. Mentally comes next. My body is taking all my strength from me. Yes, I'm falling apart."

"God, Lee, please forgive me for saying that. You're such a strong little thing. We all have depended on your strength all these years."

"Got to find your own now, my dear. Remember *Harold and Maude*? Harold said to Maude, 'I love you.' And Maude replied, 'That's *wonderful*, Harold. Go and love some more.' Good advice I think. Now kiss me please, my love. I shall miss the hell out of you."

Brad got up and bent over Lee and kissed her on the lips. He did not care that she was contagious with the flu virus. He thought it would be okay if he lay down beside her and died when she did. He could not fathom loving another woman in his lifetime.

"Thank you," she said in a weak voice.

"Leora." Brad burst into tears.

Jim walked into the bedroom. "All okay here? Oh, shit, Brad, go into the kitchen and get a nice glass of water or a nice cold beer."

Jim patted Brad on the back as Brad made his exit.

"You okay, honey?" Jim asked.

Lee nodded her head a couple times. She reached for another tissue and coughed into that one. "I'd like to be cremated."

"Yes, babe, we discussed that."

"Really? When?"

"About a month ago. You insisted on talking about it over dinner, which wasn't really so bad. The girls and I were there and heard it all."

"They're okay with cremation?" Lee asked.

"Yes, of course, honey, do you recall their agreeing with you?"

"No."

"That's okay. It was a quick conversation."

The next day, the coughing got worse. Lee refused food but did continue with the cough suppressant and small amounts of water. She asked Jim to have Bela and Sherry over for supper, and Jim said it would be done. Supper was a little more animated than everyone expected it would be. There were jokes and laughter and small talk. Bela and Sherry asked to stay until the end. Jim gave them his permission. They took over Ed's old room.

A couple days later, just before dawn, as Jim was lying in bed beside her, a weak Leora turned to Jim and said, "I love you the best. I always have and will forever, my wonderful best friend and husband."

He gazed into her eyes and replied, "I love you too, Leora Jones, my one and always," and kissed her on the cheek.

She held one of his hands, gave a light sigh, and then she was gone. She was thirty-eight years old.

The coroner listed her cause of death as complications from viral pneumonia. Jim was satisfied with that. He and the girls decided against an autopsy. It could have been the cancer too, but they saw no need in tearing her body apart.

Jim called Adrian right away, and Adrian did the phone chain to notify the group. The mortuary put Lee's information in the obituary. It was a short, simple announcement. Lee was never one for accolades.

The funeral home held a great mass of humans for Lee's funeral. People kept arriving and arriving. The funeral home attendant had to open the door to the adjoining room to accommodate all the guests. Jim vacillated between being good ol' high school Jim to being the serious widower with two children to see off into the world. Maddie and Krista made the rounds. They were quite busy talking to friends, coworkers, family, and former high school and college buddies.

When the Clark clan arrived, Clara and Jeremy took turns hugging Jim. The five of them chatted for a few minutes. Then Jim was whisked away by some friend for some reason. He returned to them with an apology, which Clara and Jeremy said was wholly unnecessary. He continued to make the rounds.

Brad showed up almost late with his mother. He and Adrian and Adrian's mother delivered half a pickup truck full of bright, vibrant summer flowers. Brad said to Jim, "I thought they should be bright and sunny."

Jim and Brad shook hands.

"I've got to help Adrian spread these flowers around. Good thing we have two rooms."

"Yeah, she surely had a lot of friends, Brad."

"Yup, and you are her best one."

Jim cried.

Brad put his arm around Jim's shoulders for a moment, and then he went to work on the flowers with Adrian.

The pastor who helped them renew their vows was on hand for a short, nondenominational devotion to Leora. There were no other speakers.

She was interned in the small cemetery in Kingston where Ed was buried. A huge crowd of guests followed the hearse to the opening and watched as the beautiful rosewood urn was gently laid to rest. Jim cried so many tears he could not even see. Maddie took over his care with tissues and an arm around his waist. When the dirt started filling in the space, Jim just bawled and bawled, burying his face in his daughter's neck while she hugged him.

Brad had been put in charge of the headstone, which had images of a clarinet, an accordion, and a pony engraved upon it. Jim told Brad that was a nice touch.

Everyone left before the burial was complete. Most of them retired to Bela and Sherry's place for finger sandwiches, vegetables, and dip and punch or coffee. The house was overpowered with people. Bela had gotten a couple extra picnic tables recently, so people made use of them.

The next day, there was a crowd of folks gathered at Jim and Lee's place. There was love and laughter. There were memories and plans for the future. Maddie was handling herself with amazing teenage grace. Krista tried, but just that one-year difference was noticeable. Nevertheless, she came across as a charming young lady.

Day 3 was quiet. No visitors arrived. Jim was relieved. He took half a dozen naps that day and got up in time to eat meals that had been left by well-wishers. There were wonderful homemade dinners dropped off at Lee and Jim's as well as at Bela and Sherry's. There was no need to cook for a long time. Sherry had no idea how to thank all those food preparers because most of them did not leave their names with their wrapped food items. Nonetheless, the food was greatly appreciated. Later, she sent thank-you notes to those whose names were attached to the food bags.

Brad stayed away for several days, but he called every afternoon to get report from Maddie on how everyone was doing. During one of their conversations, Maddie said, "This might sound morbid, but I wish we would have buried her in her Vista Cruiser, Uncle Brad. That car doesn't belong to anyone but her."

"I think she would want you to drive it. It's coming apart at the seams at long last, but the engine just purrs along. Why don't you ask your dad? I think Lee would be proud to give you that car."

Jim was elated when Maddie approached him about the car. "Let's get the title changed, and it's yours. Grandpa Bela will be proud. It was his pride and joy too, you know."

"I know. They worked on it together."

"Yup. Hell, take the keys and go for a ride right now."

"Okay! Hey, Krista! Let's go for a ride in Mom's Cruiser!"

She was out of sight somewhere. Krista came running. "I'm *ready*!" she announced. They took a ride to Uncle Brad's farm to look at Maddie's cow. They got into the fenced area with the heifer and pet her and cooed to her.

"What's her name, Uncle Brad?" asked Maddie.

"That's up to you, Maddie," he replied.

"Oh man…"

"I know," said Krista. "Let's name her Indigo. I know her eyes are brown, but who cares."

"Indigo it is," Maddie agreed.

JIM

Jim went back to work within a week of Lee's death. He kept long hours there because he hated going home. He seriously considered selling their house and finding something else. Too many memories lurking about in their house. Too much of no Leora. The girls did their best for their dad. They had supper waiting for him every evening. They ate with him to keep him company. They asked about his work. Jim obliged and was very grateful for those two young and beautiful daughters of his. The girls did the laundry and housekeeping so Jim would not have to be bothered with it. Sometimes they had good laughs. Other evenings, Jim was silent and let the girls do the talking. Maddie and Krista talked to each other about Lee, but they kept quiet about her in Jim's presence unless he broached the subject.

Maddie took a job as one of Brad's farmhands immediately. She wanted to learn everything there was to know about animal husbandry. She loved her job and got along very well with Brad. The more she got to know him, the more she understood Lee's attraction to him. Maddie allowed Brad to speak of Lee whenever he wanted to. He never fell apart talking about her. He seemed resigned to the loss.

Krista took a part-time position in the human resources department at the water treatment plant, courtesy of her dad, the day Jim went back to work. She enjoyed the job. She got to talk to people a lot. Jim told her she had the gift of gab.

Sandy stayed on at the dry-cleaning business. She kept Jim and Bela apprised of Sherry's condition, which was worsening. By midday, most of the strength was gone from her arms, and her hands were almost worthless by 5:00 a.m. Jim contacted Bela, and the two of them planned a powwow with the girls and themselves and Sherry. About a month after Lee's passing, the powwow was assembled at Jim's house. Sherry did not know the details until they were spelled out to her by Sandy. Sandy was apologetic for spilling the beans, but Sherry was actually grateful that Sandy cared so much about her boss. Sherry would work from 8:00 a.m. until noon. Sandy knew everything about dry-cleaning by now. She was the perfect choice to take over the duties.

Bela asked Sherry, "Now is this a good choice for all of you? What will you do after you're finished at noon?"

"I don't know yet," Sherry replied. "I have to establish a new normal for myself. I'm not accustomed to just sitting around."

"No, you've worked hard ever since I met you when we were in our twenties. It's okay to slow down. Give your arms and hands some rest. Maybe they need just that."

"It's possible," Sherry said to placate Bela. She knew Bela worried about her every day. She pledged to try to get better so he could have a break from an invalid wife.

"You know I love you," Bela said to Sherry. "I'll back you up with any decision you make. Just think of yourself for once, please, and don't worry about the rest of the world."

Sherry smiled at her husband. How well he knew her! He was her biggest worry. She was afraid he would lose all interest in life if she died at a young age. She never said as much to him, and she did not plan to talk to him about it. They knew each other extremely well. They could read each other's minds as well as they did when they were young.

Sherry took on her part-time position at the dry-cleaning business right away. After the first day, she decided to go to the library and get out as many books as she could carry. She took out fiction, nonfiction, and biographies. She settled into the recliner chair and started reading. When Bela got home from work at about 4:00 p.m., Sherry was asleep with a folded book on her chest. Bela tiptoed around the house until dinnertime, which was about 5:00 p.m., when he took a couple steaks out of the refrigerator and seasoned them. He knew how much Sherry enjoyed cooking. He woke her up at about 6:00 p.m. She smiled and stretched her arms and got up to make dinner. When dinner was finished, Bela broke out his accordion and serenaded Sherry with little Romanian ballads. She sat in the recliner and took in the beautiful music being made by her handsome husband. His looks had not changed over the years. He still had a youthful countenance despite his salt-and-pepper hair, which he kept short. Sometimes Sherry felt sorry for Bela being the husband of a disabled woman, but she learned to keep the pity to herself. Bela never showed anything other than love and respect for Sherry. He had many times pledged his life to her. She did not want to be whining all the time. It was not her style. But always there was a shard of doubt pinching her heart, doubt of his loyalty, wondering how bad it had to get before he would leave her. Sherry was still a very pretty woman, in spite of her dishwater-blond or gray hair, and she was smart and a wonderful cook. Bela was not shy in reminding her of such things often. Yet the shards took up residence around Sherry's heart.

KRISTA GRADUATES— SUMMER 1992

It was time for Krista to graduate from high school. She was salutatorian. Sherry, Bela, Jim, Adrian, Sandy, and Maddie cheered for her as she crossed the stage to receive her diploma and handshake from the principal. Krista looked out into the audience and spotted the cheering section. She beamed a shy smile at them. She joined the other students at the conclusion of the ceremony by tossing her cap into the air. It was a bittersweet moment for her. Lee was not there to enjoy Krista's success.

Krista was so sad she decided not to have a graduation party. That did not stop people from dropping off gifts and flowers to Lee and Jim's place. A week later, there was a party with the Clark clan, Jim and Brad, Sherry and Bela, Maddie, Devon, and Krista. It was a subdued affair, but Krista was glad to take part in it. She felt that she might regret it if she passed on having a celebration.

She continued the job at the waste water treatment plant, but she started looking for full-time employment. Brad offered her a job at his farm, and she considered it seriously. When she asked Jim what his opinion was, Jim replied, "Brad's the best boss you could ever have, honey."

She also had grant and scholarship money available because of her high school GPA. She thought about going to college to study business management. Jim and Maddie told her they would back her up 100 percent with any decision she made. She finally decided to keep her current job until the autumn and then attend Cayuga Community College to study business, perhaps to continue at a university to get her bachelor's degree. Jim was happy and sad at the same time. His baby was growing up. How was he going to finish raising her without the help of her amazing mother? Sherry was certainly going to have to help in any way he needed her to. He asked Sherry to be open to talking to Krista about anything she wanted to discuss, and Sherry said, "Of course, honey, both my beautiful granddaughters are welcome to come to me with anything." Jim thanked God for Sherry.

REUNION TIME AGAIN

About three months after Lee passed away, Brad called Jim one evening. "I haven't heard from you in way too long. How are you doing?" asked Brad.

"Well, not that great, Brad. As you can imagine, it's hard to believe I have to pick myself up and carry on without her."

"Well, I have an idea. I'd like to host a reunion of the group at my place, and I need your help getting in touch with them. Are you up for making some phone calls?"

"Yeah, it would give me something to do," Jim replied. "I'd be glad to help. Just tell me when and where."

"How about the Saturday after this one? Say noon? I'll have meat for everybody. If they would bring a dish to pass, it would be great. I'll supply the drinks and the tableware also. The gazebo fits about twenty people, so I'll have lawn chairs out too. I really miss the group, Jim. I never hear from them now that Lee's gone. I'd love to have everybody get together again. You never know what could happen to any one of us any day."

"I know exactly what you mean, brother. Sometimes I'd like to take myself out and leave this wretched planet, but my girls keep me alive. Thank God for them and for you too. I'm sorry I've been remiss in talking to you. Maybe it's high time I join the real world once again."

"I like hearing that from you, my friend. Let's get this reunion going, shall we?"

"Okay, will do. I think everybody is still living where they were the last time we had a reunion. Should be easy to get in touch with them. I'll keep you apprised as I get responses. How's that?"

"Great. Thanks for your help. And by the way, Maddie is doing great with the heifer. She got the heifer bred, so soon, she'll have another cow to take care of. I'm proud of her, Jim. She's a natural. And a wonderful young lady. I think I need to keep an eye out though. I believe my helper Devon is sweet on her."

"Shit, she never talks about him. Is he a great guy? He'd better be if he's going to go out with my Maddie."

"Top of the line, Jim. I trust him completely. You can too."

"Okay, I'll take your word on that. I might have to meet him again though. My introduction to him was perfunctory."

"Indeed. I remember."

"All right, Brad, ol' boy, let me get started on the phone calls."

"Okay. And thanks again."

"You bet. Bye, Brad."

"See you, Jim."

"Who were you talking to, Dad?" came from Maddie in the kitchen.

"Brad, honey. We're planning another reunion. I'm going to get in touch with everybody. Brad's going to host it. We all need to stay in touch with one another before we're all in the grave."

"Well, let me know if you need help."

"Okay, dear. By the way, Brad tells me that his helper Devon is sweet on you. Tell me, what's up with that?"

"He's adorable, Dad. I could fall in love with him in a heartbeat. We're just friends for now. We've gone out on a couple dates. We've agreed to take things slowly."

"Smart man, honey. And you're doing the right thing for yourself. Just let me know if he needs a kick in the pants for any reason."

Maddie chuckled. "Will do, Dad. I love you. You know that, right?"

"Ditto, my beautiful child. Now it's time for making some phone calls."

Jim was successful in getting in touch with everyone in the group, and they all were happy to hear from him. Everyone said yes to the reunion. Jim was actually happy after getting all the positive responses. It had been ages since he had been happy about anything. After he had gotten in touch with everyone, he sat down on the couch and sighed. He tried to empty his mind because he was thinking of Leora, and she would be conspicuously absent during the reunion.

When does the pain ever go away? he asked himself. There was no answer to be had.

The next Saturday rolled around. Jim and Krista were the first guests to arrive. Maddie was already there helping Brad with the cattle. Jim went to the cattle barn immediately to reintroduce himself to Devon. They shook hands again. *Devon is indeed a decent fellow,* Jim thought. He stood about six feet tall in his work boots, a few inches taller than Maddie in her own boots. He had blond hair and medium blue eyes. He and Maddie seemed very comfortable around each other. Jim felt a slight shard pinch his heart, knowing that if Maddie married Devon or somebody else someday, Lee would not be there to enjoy the moment. It made Jim shed a couple tears while he turned his head away from Maddie and Devon. He went back up to the house to help Brad greet the group. They filtered in, and by noon, almost everyone Jim had invited was there. They kept Brad and Jim busy at first, taking a tour of the farm in small groups. None of them had ever been to the farm, and they thoroughly enjoyed the place. They were all very impressed with the success Brad was enjoying.

Brad started up the grill at about 2:00 p.m. Sherry and Bela showed up shortly after that, and Bela stayed at the grill with Brad. They chatted about farming and a host of other things. They enjoyed each other's company. Brad would have loved to talk to Bela about Leora, but Bela did not know about the affair. Bela did mention her a few times during their conversation. Brad felt the shards—shards of a broken heart. He missed Lee terribly, and the only person with whom he felt safe talking was Maddie. He knew Krista would disapprove. He never said a word to her about Leora.

About an hour later, Jim went to his truck to fetch a dessert. He noticed a car that had not been parked nearby earlier. He looked toward the house. There was Rita hugging a beautiful young blond lady, more like a girl actually, maybe in her midtwenties.

"Is that Ingrid?" he said to himself. "Can't be. Ingrid is taller. This young girl is maybe five foot five. Besides all that, Rita and Ingrid were never close enough to give each other such warm hugs as Rita is giving this young beauty, as my memory has it."

Jim checked out the car. It was a late model Mercedes Benz, black, with a vanity license plate of EJA. Something began to click in Jim's head. Ingrid, Rita, and what was the youngest girl's name? Jim snapped his fingers a few times to help his memory. *Enid!* It had to be her. Jim hurried across the driveway to catch the two young ladies.

"Rita!" he greeted her. "May I have the pleasure of being introduced?"

"Oh, hi, Jim. Yes, of course, this is my younger sister Enid. Brad invited her, but she's a bit late. She was giving jumping lessons to a group of kids at my uncle's farm."

"Enid Armstrong? I'm ever so pleased to meet you," Jim said as he shook her hand heartily.

"So pleased to meet you too, Jim. Brad says such kind things about you. I'm sorry for the loss of your wife."

A shard stung Jim right in the middle of his heart. What the hell did this young girl know about Jim and Leora? Weird.

"Thank you, Enid. Please make yourself at home."

What a stupid thing to say. She's obviously been here before, Jim thought.

"I'm going to get this pie up to the gazebo," he said. "Perhaps we can chat later."

"Okay," the two beauties said in unison.

But Jim was curious. He found Enid and Brad in an embrace in the gazebo about five minutes later. *Okay, I must know,* he thought. He sauntered up to the couple, who obviously knew each other well. "Brad, are you keeping this young beauty a secret?" he said as humorously as he could be, which was not very.

Brad grinned at Jim. "Brother, meet my friend Enid Armstrong."

"I've already had the pleasure. Enid, you are a spittin' image of your sister Ingrid."

"So I've heard," Enid said with a grin. "Not so bad to look like Ingrid. She's a sight for sore eyes, I think."

Brad said, "We met through Ingrid, sort of. I had been trying to get in touch with her just to talk and see how she's doing. But she never returned my calls. So I got brave and tried to reach her at her father's house. Enid here answered the phone. We chatted for quite a while, didn't we?" Brad looked down at Enid, and they smiled at each other. "Anyway, I decided to see if we could be friends."

Enid said, "He told me about a dear friend who had passed away recently. I guess it started from there."

Jim's jaw dropped. He could not help it. *She's been gone only three months.* Jim's heart was pounding. He had to take a few deep breaths to get over it.

"Jim, are you okay?" Brad asked as he put his hand on Jim's shoulder.

What does she know? Jim wondered. *I can't ask. I just can't. Maybe when Brad and I are alone sometime. But I won't spoil his day.* He said, "Yeah, I'm fine. I think I could use another beer though. I've had only one so far. I think I can indulge."

Brad grinned at Jim. "Help yourself. Enid and I are going to saddle up a couple ponies. She and Rita are going to do some jumping and barrel racing for everybody to see."

Yes, I remember, Jim thought. *When we first met Rita, Enid was in 4H. God, I think I'm going to be sick.* He excused himself and sought out Maddie. He felt as if she was the only person in whom he could confide. He found her and Devon in the kitchen of the house. He was by then crying. Maddie instantly reached out and gave her dad a hug.

"This is hard for you, isn't it?" she asked. "For me too. I miss my mom so much. It hurts my heart."

Shards. Now Maddie was subjected to them.

"I'll leave you two alone," Devon suggested.

"Thank you" was all Maddie could say.

Devon went outside.

Jim righted himself and sniffed away the tears. "Brad's got a girlfriend. Your mom's been gone only three months. And this Enid girl is probably half his age. She seems as smitten as a schoolgirl. I don't know if I should tear his eyes out or be happy for him."

"Neither, Dad, let it go. We don't want to ruin it for him by divulging anything about Mom to little Enid. Who knows—the relationship might not even last. It never did with Ingrid."

"Maddie, Maddie, this is too much for me. All of it."

"Do you want to go home?"

"Yes, I do actually."

"I'll go too."

"No, please stay. Devon is here. The girls are going to put on a horse show you might want to see. I just want to go home and be alone. Please stay."

Maddie gave her dad a long, warm hug.

"I'm sorry you found out about Enid. I was hoping he would have dumped her by now. Maybe it's just a thing to help him transcend his sorrow about Mom. I don't know. I forgive him. Maybe you can too. You were always number 1 to Mom. Don't ever doubt that—ever. She passed away exactly where she chose to be—right beside her husband and best friend. I know it smarts to see Brad with some young thing so soon. I understand how you feel. We have to try to let it go. For our sakes, know what I mean?"

Jim released himself from Maddie's hug. "Thank you, honey. You're the best. For a while there I was worried you had a crush on Brad because you spend extra hours over here."

"No, Dad, he's my uncle!"

"Okay, okay, I get it. Thanks."

"I might stay awhile afterward and help Brad clean up though. Is that okay?"

"Of course, yes. Would you send my goodbyes to everybody?"

"No, problem, consider it done."

"You're a gem. So much like your mother."

"I'll take that as a high compliment. Okay, Dad, call me if you need me. I have my car phone."

"Thank you, dear. I'll sneak out the front door."

"Okay. Love you."

"Love you too, Maddie, very much."

Brad was too happy with Enid and the group and the pony show—which was a great success—to notice that Jim had gone home. After the party was over, he looked around for Jim. He approached Maddie.

"Oh, Dad left a long time ago. He meant to say goodbye but couldn't find you," Maddie lied.

"I'll give him a call in a day or two. I think he misses Leora."

"Damn right he does. He just couldn't be here without her. I understand that."

"I do too," Brad responded.

Enid, ever at Brad's side, piped up, "If I may—who is Leora?"

Brad and Maddie looked at each other. Maddie's eyes said to him, "You get yourself out of this mess. I'm not helping." Brad understood.

"She was Maddie and Krista's mom. Jim's wife. She passed away a few months ago."

Now if Enid doesn't get the connection, she's a moron, Maddie thought.

"I'm sorry for your loss, Maddie."

"Oh, that's kind of you, thank you. My mom and dad spent a lot of time here. Dad's still feeling the pain. He'll be fine. It just takes a lot of time for some folks to get on with life." That was a little dig at Brad. She could not tell if he took it as such or not. She did not care. She had to get away from Brad and his little blond babe.

Going South

Jim just could not see Brad the way he used to see him. Their relationship went south. They were still friends, but Brad sensed Jim pulling away, and he did not attempt to bring Jim back. Jim could not get past Brad and the young Enid being lovers after only a few months—perhaps even fewer—after the death of Lee. He saw Brad as a user of women, a handsome man's man who could attract women young and old. Jim was so disgusted about it he did not even want to take it up with Brad or anybody else.

The Jones family still visited Brad's farm occasionally to get in some horseback riding or a lunch or dinner. Brad proposed to host a reunion of the group every year. He so enjoyed showing off Enid on the jumping and barrel racing he expected her to put on a show at every reunion.

One evening, Maddie decided to talk to Jim about Brad. "Dad, what's up? You and Brad are so distant. Is it because of little Enid?"

Jim decided it was time for him to talk about this. "You cut to the chase, my dear. Yes, it's little Enid. Actually, it's Brad. I will never know how much he actually loved my wife, not that it matters any longer, but I just feel as if he used Lee the way he seems to be using Enid as a pretty lady on his arm."

"Well, they don't live together. I can tell you that. Her father would never allow it. I just don't see him being in a hurry to get married either, if ever."

"We really don't know what kind of relationship he had with your mom, do we?"

"He loved her a lot, I know that. But she kept her emotions distant from Brad. She loved you far more than she did him. He was an almost infinitely distant second. She didn't pursue him. He was the assertive one. But I don't think she would allow herself to be used for Brad's selfish satisfaction. That doesn't sound like Mom. I miss her like hell sometimes. I know you do too. We're all lucky to have had her as long as we did."

"I agree with all my heart about your mom, honey. I just don't want to be Brad's best friend any longer."

"I think he knows that, Dad. He respects your feelings, whatever they are. And don't concern yourself with Enid. I'd be totally shocked if he ever asked her to marry him. He might be past the point of wanting babies, for one reason. I imagine he would be furious if Enid ended up pregnant."

"How do you know him so well?"

"We used to talk after Mom passed away. We haven't done much talking since Enid has come onto the scene though."

"Can he lust after Enid and still feel love for my wife?"

"Oh yes, certainly he can. Enid wasn't in the picture when Mom was alive though. I know that for certain."

"Okay, my darling daughter, enough of the heavy talk. Shall I help you girls with dinner tonight?"

"Yeah, would you set the table? Let's use our best dishes, shall we? Get out the china plates and the crystal glasses. Let's make this a nice meal tonight."

"Maddie, my love, I'm happy to oblige."

It was spaghetti, homemade meatballs, homemade garlic bread, and chianti for dinner. Jim, Maddie, and Krista got a bit tipsy on the wine, and they got quite giggly. It felt fantastic to all three of them to be having a good time with each other. Jim went to bed early to ward off a hangover headache, and the girls sat on the couch chatting for a few minutes before hitting the sack themselves. They all slept soundly and had pleasant dreams.

Connie Checks In

About a month after the reunion at Brad's place, Connie called Jim to check on him.

"I missed you when I was leaving. I didn't see you or your truck. You must have slipped out."

"I did exactly that, Con, how astute of you."

"Anything you want to talk about?"

Connie had no knowledge of the Brad-Lee love affair. Jim quickly racked his brain to come up with an answer.

"To tell you the truth, Con, I missed Leora so much I couldn't bear to be around couples. And I might as well tell you that it grosses me out to see Brad with such a young thing hanging on him as if she were a schoolgirl and he was her high school teacher."

"I get you on that one all right. He doesn't seem totally happy, although it's hard to tell with ol' Brad. He keeps his feeling close to his vest."

"He's really none of my business. I just can't help but wonder why he chose little Enid. With his looks and success, he could find a wonderful adult companion, I would think."

"Maybe he's actually shy," Connie suggested. "But I want to make sure you're all right. I'm not going to worry about Brad. He's a big boy."

"True," Jim responded.

He could have given Connie a mouthful about Brad and Enid, but it had all come from Maddie, and he figured it was hush-hush. He would not break Maddie's confidence, even for Connie.

"I miss her too, honey," Connie said. "She was a big part of my life, particularly during her cancer and chemo. She let me call her and bug her any time to find out how she was feeling. She was a special person, Jim, to many people."

"Especially to me if I may brag a bit," Jim said.

"Of course, you may brag. I recall days in high school when you would make her laugh so hard I thought she would stop breathing."

"Yeah, she was good for that. I loved her, you know, way back in high school." He did not want to tell her the entire truth. "Tenth grade is when I fell in love with her."

"I can see that now. It wasn't apparent to me back then when I figured the group was a bunch of buddies until Darren proposed to Rita during one of our car parties, that is."

"Yeah, I think he was as shocked as we all were when she said yes. She said yes, and Darren turned and looked at *me*."

"I remember that!" said Connie. She laughed. "He couldn't believe his ears even after he shot his mouth off and proposed to her."

"And still together after all these years," Jim mused.

"Yup. They surely are."

"And hopefully forever."

"Well, dear, I won't keep you any longer. Hope you're doing okay. Please, please call me if you ever need to talk or have some company. I'm safe. I've sworn off men forever."

Jim chuckled. "I just might take you up on that sometime soon. I think the girls would like to see you too."

"Your girls are amazing, Jim. You and Leora have done a fabulous job raising those two. Be proud of yourself."

"Thank you, Connie, that's very sweet."

"Well, I mean it. Thank God Brad didn't try to snatch up Maddie or Krista. I would have had to get out my pistol!"

"Truth be told, Connie, I did wonder about Brad and Maddie for a while because she has to spend so much time at the dairy farm. But she set me straight in a hurry."

"Good to hear," Connie said, "I'll put the pistol back in the gun case."

Jim smiled. "You're just the greatest, you know," he said.

"Ditto, my buddy. We'll stay in touch with each other, okay?"

"Absolutely," Jim replied.

"Okay, dear, bye for now."

"Yup, bye, Connie."

Jim cheered up a tiny bit after talking to Connie. He sought the girls and asked them if they wanted go out for dinner. They chose the pizza place with all the pinball machines. Jim was actually very good at pinball and air hockey since he had spent time playing the games when he was a teenager. "I'll beat the crap outta both of ya," he said while he was driving to the restaurant.

The girls laughed.

Boy, was he right. He did a tilt after he had won half a dozen pinball games. He beat Maddie and Krista at air hockey two times each. He did not go easy on them. The girls had a great time anyway.

While Krista was chowing on some mediocre pizza, Maddie said, "I haven't been here since Mom took us here. Remember, Krista? She kept telling us she sucked at pinball."

"And did she?" asked Jim.

"Oh hell yes," Maddie replied.

They all chuckled.

Thankfully, Jim did not recall the connection between the pizza restaurant and Lee and Brad going on a date when she was still alive. It was the day Lee had forgotten to charge her phone, and she had left it at home, and Jim had found it and put two and two together. But on this night, that was not on his mind. He was having a grand time with his girls.

JONES FAMILY VACATION—1993

Winter proved itself to be another brutal one in Upstate New York. Maddie and Brad and Devon moved the cattle from the open dairy barn to the enclosed barn with heat. Brad turned on the heat in the horse barn as well. Instead of being grass fed, the cattle and horses were fed hay and grain during the winter. It was all organic. All of Brad's and Maddie's animals were extremely healthy.

Maddie's heifer Indigo gave birth to a healthy male calf. Maddie was on hand for the birth, but neither mother nor baby needed help. Maddie was so proud of Indigo. She got into the pen right after the calf was born, and she hugged Indigo and stroked the sides of her neck. Then Maddie left Indigo to feeding her new baby. She named the calf Jimmy after her dad.

* * *

A new normal was long time in coming for Jim, but he carried on with pride and humor as he always did. He started joking around at work again, and the women who worked there hung on his every funny word, the way the girls had done in high school.

"You've still got it, Dad," Maddie said when he told her he was making his coworkers laugh. "I'm so happy for you."

"Yeah, Dad"—Krista spoke up—"I'm proud of my old dad too."

Jim smiled at his daughters and decided they were his only soulmates, so he thanked God then and there for Maddie and Krista.

"We need to go on a trip," Krista suggested.

"Yeah, back to the caves and caverns. They were my favorite places," said Maddie. "Or we could to out west again but where we haven't been. I hear the Grand Tetons are a sight to see."

Maddie called Brad and asked if it was okay for him and Devon to care for Indigo and Jimmy for a couple weeks. Of course, Brad said yes.

Jim and Krista put in for a two-week vacation. Within a week, Jim bought a small Airstream and hitched it to his pickup truck.

The Jones family camped along the way on a spontaneous basis. The all took turns driving. By evening times, they were already in their camper playing cards or cooking a meal or just talking.

They reached the Tetons in four days. The Jones family was speechless when they had the chance to view them in their entirety. They camped in a campground that had full view of the Tetons.

They went on a couple hikes up to the Tetons on horseback. The horses were very tame. They would have taken to the trail and back again without any coaxing, but the family enjoyed the hikes anyway. Krista told the guide about the family having experience with horses, and the guide looked at her and winked at her. She beamed a grin. The guide was a Shoshone American Indian, extremely handsome with his dark eyes and short black hair. The guide decided to have Krista ride beside him so they could talk. They talked about just everything under the sun. Krista was enthralled with this young man, who appeared to be in his midtwenties, and he stood over six feet tall on his long legs.

On the day they decided to head out of Wyoming, the horseback guide found the Jones family and approached Krista about taking a real hike on real horses. Krista looked at Jim immediately.

"Oh, go on," he said. He asked the man's name. It was Ben.

"I want her back in three hours. We're packing up and heading out soon. But have fun and be good!"

Ben nodded. He shook Jim's hand with a firm grip. Then he and Krista headed out in Ben's Jeep convertible.

"What have I just done?" Jim asked Maddie.

"Oh? You just gave Krista some freedom! She'll have a great time. She has a hell of a crush on Ben."

"Yeah, I know. I'm sure he's safe."

"We'll know in three hours."

"Maddie!"

"Just kidding, Dad. Now let's get this camper packed up so we can get going when Krista gets back."

Needless to say, Krista had an amazing three hours with Ben. He told her about the history of the Shoshone Indians. He talked about his love for horses. She told him about Maddie and her Angus raising business. They rode real horses, which meant when they wanted to go faster, the horses responded to "Canter!" and took right off. Krista was in her glory. She kept up with Ben. She was every bit as good on a horse as he was. It surprised and pleased her. It surprised and pleased Ben as well.

By the time Krista and Ben returned, the camper and the truck were all set to leave. Krista shook hands with Ben and thanked him from the bottom of her heart for the day. He nodded his head in recognition of her thanks. Then he shook hands with Jim and Maddie and told them he had had a wonderful time entertaining Krista. He suggested she take some time to work out west at one of the campgrounds. Krista had to think it over. It was a long way from home.

As the Jones family was leaving the Tetons. Krista had lots to say about her hike with Ben. Jim and Maddie let her rattle on as long as she wanted to. It was a memorable adventure for Krista, and she was a chatterbox anyway; there was no way to stop her.

They visited the Badlands in South Dakota and camped where there was a view. Then they traveled through Iowa and its seemingly endless landscape of corn, even growing in the highway medians. After they left Iowa, the Jones family decided to visit Chicago. Jim did very well pulling a camper through Chicago traffic. They paid a fortune for parking so they could go up in the elevator of the Sears building to get an aerial view of Chicago. It was truly amazing. Chicago spanned way out to the horizon in every direction including stretching out toward the vast waters of Lake Michigan.

They went home by way of Michigan, then Canada, then back into New York. Jim decided since there were three drivers, they could travel cross-country without any more campsites to find. Jim took the wheel first, followed by Krista and Maddie. It worked out that there was one person sleeping, one person driving, and a third person keeping the driver alert. This was the way they made it home, the exceptions being fueling up the truck and stopping for meals. Happy but tired when they got home, they decided to unpack later and take an immediate nap.

The next day, life started its new normal. Jim and Krista went back to work, where Krista told everyone about her adventure with Ben and where she watched her dad goof off and make the office people laugh. Maddie went back to work and told Devon all about the vacation, including, "I missed you guys, Devon. I should have sent you a postcard, but we were so busy all the time."

Devon gave her a hug and a short kiss on the lips, which shocked Maddie.

"I forgive you. I'm so glad you're back. Brad and I missed you so much. It's no fun not having a pretty young lady like you to work beside."

"Thanks, guys," Maddie said to Brad and Devon. "Now it's back to work for me."

WINTER—1993

The winter in New York passed as most of them do—a few monstrous snowstorms, then a few weeks without snow, followed by spurts of snow and perhaps one or two more storms. Jim and the girls hunkered down in their home, did not go out much except to visit Sherry and Bela, or spend some time at the Clarks' place. Lee's cousin Benjamin found a bride, and they eloped to Hawaii for their private wedding and their honeymoon. He took her home to the Clarks', and Jim and the girls were there to meet her. They had been living together already in a large farmhouse not five miles from the Clarks' place. That left Jarob and Fulton as the single males in the family. Fulton was satisfied with that situation. He no longer went into town to chum with the girls. He had outgrown that. Jarob contended he would never grow up. He took young women to the farm to meet his mother and brother occasionally, but none of the ladies suited his fancy as far as forever went. He and Fulton continued on as automotive mechanics, and they continued to raise hay.

Mrs. Clark was keeping up with good health. She had no medical concerns. She continued to keep house and cook for Fulton and Jarob.

Adrian and Sandy had about half a dozen dinners at Jim's place during the winter. While they visited, Sherry and Bela were there to make music. Maddie and Krista joined their grandparents. Jim was too rusty to play his trombone, but Adrian did fine on his drums or his baritone saxophone.

Lorrie and her husband, Rich, paid a few visits to Jim's place as well. They had decided long ago not to have children, and they appeared to be a very happy, loving couple. When it was time to jam, Lorrie added music to the mix with her alto clarinet.

Darren and Rita moved from Massachusetts to Kingston to be closer to the group. Enid's father encouraged her to go on the road with Ingrid, partly because of Enid's talent and partly to get her away from Brad, the darky who was not good enough for his daughter. Enid considered going on the road with Ingrid, but that would have to be Ingrid's choice, and the two girls did not correspond much with each other. Enid continued teaching jumping and barrel racing at her parents' horse ranch.

Collin and Darrell were still fast friends and spent a lot of time together. They and their wives and children visited Jim and the girls a few times during the long winter. It was always hours of fun and games and laughter with Collin and Darrell. Their wives and children just shrugged them off in good humor. Collin and Darrell added to the music with their Renaissance flutes and recorders.

Connie and Jim talked on the phone a few times a week. She was a refreshing friend to have after long days at work during the long winter and the absence of Leora, the pain of which started to finally ebb. One evening after talking to Connie, Jim realized he had not mentioned Lee during the conversation. He felt weird about that, but immediately he felt as if a new normal was beginning for him at long last.

When the winter finally broke and the spring weather gave them temperatures in the fifties and sixties, Maddie, Krista, and Jim started riding horses and ponies again at Brad's place. Enid was usually there, not helping Brad out but just being nearby. The Jones family decided she was a permanent fixture that they could ignore if they wanted to.

Indigo and her calf weathered the winter extremely well. Maddie made the decision to butcher Jimmy—or rather have Brad take him somewhere to have the job done. Jim bought a freezer for all the meat they got. Maddie decided to sell the next calf to make money and finally pay Brad for purchasing Indigo for her. Brad gave Maddie a calendar to mark down the date on which she could document the breeding process and mark how it was going along. This she posted on the outer wall of Indigo's stall.

Brad gave Maddie a hug when the butcher called him to tell him the meat had all been delivered to Jim's place. "I'm so proud of you, Maddie."

"Thanks, Uncle Brad," she replied with smile as she looked at Enid. Enid blushed a bit and cast her eyes downward. Perhaps jealous? No one asked her. No one seemed to care.

"Enid had better behave herself," Maddie said to Jim and Krista when they were all together at home. "Brad won't put up with the jealous type."

"Oh well," said Krista, "she's his problem."

"I don't see it lasting much longer. She's just a baby. What the hell do they even talk about? She's never out in the barn unless she wants to be near him. Weird relationship," Maddie said.

"Oh well," Jim and Krista said unison, "she's his problem."

They all laughed.

Second Reunion at Brad's—Summer 1995

It was reunion time again. Everybody who was invited was there with the exception of Enid. None of Brad's guests knew where she was, and nobody asked him. Thoughts rolled in their heads though—busy at her job, broke up with Brad, Brad broke up with her. As soon as the crowd gathered together for the meal, nobody cared any longer. Brad asked Maddie to join Rita in the pony jumping and barrel racing show, and Maddie graciously accepted the offer. She was not as good as Rita. She and Rita set up the barrels and fences to accommodate Maddie. The show was a hit with everybody. After Maddie dismounted the pony, Brad was there to give her a big hug and a big thank-you kiss on the cheek.

"No problem, Uncle Brad, anytime," she responded to his kiss.

"You're every bit as good as Enid, I must say," he said to her.

"Yeah, but not as good as Rita. She's got years on me."

"True, but just remember you were very good on that pony today."

"Okay, thanks again, Brad."

"I'll take her in and give her a brush down. You go join the group," Brad said.

Maddie gave Brad the reins and walked out of the meadow into the yard to join the party.

Connie kept Jim close company during the reunion. Maddie and Krista could often look over to see them talking and either smiling or laughing. They thanked God for such a good friend as Connie.

"Maddie," Krista said during one of those laughing moments, "do you think Connie and Dad are sweet on each other?"

Maddie replied, "Not sure. They don't get together like this as far as I know. They do talk on the phone a lot though."

"Wouldn't it be cool if they got married?"

"Krista, it's been a long time, but I don't think it's been long enough for Dad. You never know though, do you?"

"Exactly," said Krista, "I think I'm going to ask him when we get home."

"Ah! Krista!" Maddie exclaimed. "Are you sure?"

"Hell, why not?"

"Okay," Maddie said doubtfully.

"Are you going to want to know?"

Maddie sighed. "Yes and no."

"Well, that isn't going to help me at all," Krista complained.

"Okay, yes, please let me know."

"Tonight?"

"Whenever you want to, as long as it isn't at a party or a reunion."

Krista sauntered away a happy young lady. She passed by her laughing dad and a grinning Connie on the way down the steps of the gazebo.

A few moments later, Darren and Rita approached Maddie, who was now in the gazebo picking at Sherry's delicious finger foods.

Rita said, "Thanks for joining me, Maddie. You did a wonderful job."

Maddie looked up at Rita.

"Oh, thanks, Rita. I know I don't hold a candle to you, but Brad was nice enough to say I was as good as Enid. That surprised me."

"It didn't surprise me," Rita responded.

The three of them looked over at Connie and Jim at the steps to the gazebo, chatting with Collin and Darrell and their wives.

"By the way," Darren said, "how's your dad doing?"

"Do you mean with Connie?"

Darren nodded his head once.

"I really don't know, but Krista is going to ask Dad about Connie when we get home. I'm a bit nervous about it."

"Why is that?" Darren asked.

"I don't want him to think he's disappointing us if they're just friends."

"Do you want your dad to get married some day?" asked Rita.

"It doesn't matter to me. But I hold whoever it might be to an awfully high standard. You knew Mom. She was one of a kind."

"I agree," said Rita.

Darren nodded again.

"But I would love to see my dad happy again. Actually, he looks quite happy today."

"I'm sure Collin and Darrell have some to do with that. They're such clowns," said Darren.

"That's true," Maddie admitted. "But he hasn't left Connie's side since we got here. I think that's adorable, even if they're just friends."

"I agree, Maddie," said Rita.

They parted ways.

The gazebo was empty except for Maddie and Brad now. He approached her carefully and sheepishly asked her for a moment of her time. Maddie was confused, but she said, "Of course, Uncle Brad, what's up?"

"I still miss your mom," he stated succinctly. "I loved her. I still do."

Maddie sighed. "We do too, Uncle Brad. How do you carry on when someone so awesome will never be in your presence ever again?"

"I miss her lovely skin, that hair, those eyes, her sense of humor…How could I ever start again?"

"Uncle Brad, you have to. You're young and handsome and successful, you know that. So many people have told you that, including my mom, I'm certain. We all miss her, but we have to live on and make a name she would be proud of, maybe is proud, if heaven is a real place."

Brad hugged Maddie and shed a couple tears that she did not see. But she could feel them on her neck where he had his chin buried as she hugged him.

She wanted badly to ask about Enid and Ingrid but told herself not to. It was really none of her business. She separated herself from Brad and dried his cheeks with her fingertips.

"This was our conversation, right? Nobody needs to know," Maddie suggested.

Brad nodded his head.

"Let's go join the party, shall we?" said Maddie.

She took Brad's hand—one of those warm, calloused hands Leora used to adore (and Maddie could understand why!)—and left the gazebo. They parted ways and enjoyed the rest of the reunion.

The end of the party was one long goodbye, so many people to talk to before parting ways. When most of the guests were gone, Jim helped Brad hook up the grill to his Explorer so Brad could put the grill into the garage. Maddie and Krista cleaned up the gazebo. Jim and Brad sat in the gazebo afterward and talked for a few minutes.

While in Jim's truck, just before they left, Maddie said to Brad, "See ya Monday, boss."

Brad cracked a grin.

"Boy, is that a nice thing to see on your face," Maddie said to Brad.

He reached into the pickup truck and tousled Maddie's hair. She was seated in the middle.

After Jim took off, Maddie sighed. "If he wasn't so old, I could fall in love with that guy."

"Maddie!" said Jim and Krista in unison.

"Don't worry. I have a huge crush on Devon. I'm ready to take it to a higher level. I just don't know how. I think I'm too old-fashioned to ask him out. He kissed me. He should make the move."

"It's 1995, honey," said Jim. "Go for it. It's a modern age now. If he feels less of you when you suggest going out, you'll know he's definitely not the one for you."

"Okay," Maddie piped up.

After they arrived home, Krista checked the answering machine they now had.

"Maddie, call from Devon!" she hollered to her sister.

Maddie bounded up the steps and grabbed the phone. She happily waved Jim and Krista away, and they obliged.

JIM AND CONNIE

That night, Krista sat on the couch beside her dad. She smiled brightly at him and dived in.

"Dad, Maddie and I saw you cracking up with Connie today. You wouldn't believe how happy you two made us."

"Well, thanks, honey, she's a dear, dear friend. We've known each other as long as I've known everybody else in the group except Brad and Rita."

"Well," Krista said, "how dear a friend is she? You see, we all miss Mom terribly at times. There's no way around it. But as the cliché goes, 'Life must go on.' I'd be happy for you if you married Connie."

There was a lengthy pause. Krista wondered if she had reached too far into her dad's personal business.

"Let me say this," Jim said. "She knows me back and forth, inside and out. She accepts my pain when I talk about Leora. To use a phrase Adrian used to use, we jive together."

"Yes?"

"I've been thinking of asking her on a real date, just the two of us."

"Do it!" Krista said as she nearly jumped up from the couch.

"What does Maddie feel?"

"The same as I do. Do it, Dad. There's only one way to know if Connie feels the same way you do."

He did it—the next night. He asked Connie to have dinner with him at a nice place in Binghamton the following Friday night.

She said she would be delighted. Jim hung up the phone and gave Krista (who had been listening to the conversation) two thumbs-up.

Krista did jump from the couch this time to give her dad a big, glad hug. "You are so lucky to have her in your life," Krista said.

Krista sought out Maddie and told her the news. Maddie grinned a big one and said, "Thanks for putting him up to it, Krista."

The next Friday rolled around. Jim dressed up in a new brown suit, white shirt, matching tie and brown patent leather shoes. The girls told him he looked handsome. He was nervous, but it would be okay because he could tell Connie how he felt, and she would understand.

* * *

The dinner was a resounding success. They ate a four-course meal, drank champagne, talked, and laughed the night away. When he dropped her off at the house of a friend in Kingston where she was staying for a week, he gave her a good night hug. She responded by finding his mouth with hers and gave him a nice, long kiss. Jim sighed. He was on cloud nine.

Many dates, lots of time spent together, and a couple months later, and Jim and Connie got engaged. Connie was invited to live with Jim and the girls, and she gladly accepted the invitation. Jim wanted to remove the few photos of Leora that he had on various walls of the house, but Connie suggested they stay up. She was an understanding woman. Jim cried openly when she made her suggestion. She gave him a nice, long hug and talked him into peace. They decided they would look for another place to live, but they would take their time, maybe wait until the girls had moved out.

The wedding took place a few weeks later at Brad's gazebo. The minister was one of Brad's customers, and he led the crowd in a pleasant, nondenominational service. Adrian was best man, and Sandy was the maid of honor. The reception was right there as well. The group was there, as well as Jim's parents, Connie's parents, Connie's daughter Cindy, many of Connie's friends, many of Jim's friends, the Clark clan, and Sherry and Bela. Bela played his heart out on his accordion to the delight of all the guests. The reception was porter-house steak, redskin potatoes, salad, and champagne. The cake was a four-layered affair—white cake with white frosting. Connie wore a beautiful off-white gown with no trail or veil and white heels. Jim wore a black tuxedo, white shirt, black bow tie, and black patent leather shoes.

There was no honeymoon planned for the near future, but the Jones family stayed busy moving Connie into the house. (Connie had been living in Michigan. She left her practice there and decided to start one in or near Kingston.) The family conferred about the bedrooms, and Jim decided to give his and Leora's room to Maddie. She would have a bathroom of her own. Krista took the other bed-room upstairs and used the family bathroom. Jim and Connie took the large bedroom on the lower level. They used the bathroom down there, which was quite private. They had a phone installed in their new room for private conversations.

As the months went on, less and less talk of Leora took place unless it was a fun memory of some kind. Jim and Connie got along famously. He was thankful to God for such a kind, supportive woman.

CHANGES

In August 1996, a few things happened. First, Devon asked Maddie to marry him. They planned on an engagement of a couple years so they could save money for a house. Second, Krista received a postcard from Ben from the Tetons National Park in Wyoming. He invited her out west to work at the park. She had no idea at first what job she would have, but she had Ben's phone number on the post card, and she called him. There were lots of jobs available, he told her. The pay was not very good, but the experience was. Krista conferred with Jim, and he gave her his blessing.

Krista took a jet plane out to Wyoming. There was one layover. She was a bit shy of the large crowds at the airports, but she read the overhead signs and found her second flight just fine. Ben met her at the airport in Jackson Hole, Wyoming, and drove her in his Jeep to a cabin that would be her home for the rest of the summer and the autumn. Ben told her he would take her to the camp office the next day to find her a job. She was ecstatic. She was so happy to see Ben she could hardly believe it.

The next day arrived, and Ben picked her up. At breakfast at a nearby restaurant, he told her there was a horseback riding guide opening for her if she wanted it. She jumped at the chance. She rode with Ben's pack until she learned the lingo she had to give to the park guests. Ben told her she was a quick study.

Needless to say, in a few weeks, Ben and Krista were an item. He asked her if she would consent to being engaged to him. She readily said yes. They enjoyed the summer and autumn, and then it was time for Krista to go home. Ben promised himself to her, and he told her he was planning on moving to New York to be near her. Krista nearly cried with joy.

By winter 1996, Ben was living in an apartment in Albany. He and Krista decided to live together and attend Auburn University together using her grant money to pay tuition and rent. Jim and Connie pitched in and paid the rest of the rent and the utilities.

* * *

What became of Brad? He had stayed single for another year. Then he met a nice woman at a state fair in summer 1997. Her oldest (ten years old) daughter was showing a horse. He happened to watch the girl doing her routine. He was seated near the mother and complimented her. The woman grinned at Brad and nodded her head in thanks. Brad got brave and visited the horse in the stable afterward, as well as visiting the girl and her mother. The horse was completely at home with Brad. The mother was a widow of three years, a stay-at-home mom keeping herself busy with four children, two boys and two girls, the ten-year-old being the oldest. Brad told her about his cattle businesses. She seemed impressed. He asked her if she would favor him with her company sometime. She took him up on his offer right away. Their first date was horseback riding at Brad's farm and grilled steaks from his beef, with baked potatoes. She was forty years old, stood about five foot five, had light-brown hair down to her shoulders and soft, kind brown eyes. Her name was Cathy. Her children's ages ranged from ten down to four years old.

By autumn 1997, there was another wedding at Brad's place. The group attended, of course, as well as some of Brad's friends and his mother, colleagues, and customers, and many of Cathy's friends and family. Devon was best man, and one of Cathy's friends was maid of honor. Brad looked absolutely handsome in his black tuxedo, white shirt, bow tie, and black patent leather shoes. His hair was now slightly peppered with white, but it did not take away from his looks at all. Cathy wore a pretty, silk cream-colored layered dress with no trail and no veil, and cream-colored pumps. When Brad's customer-minister told him to kiss his bride, Brad did not waste a second to embrace her and give her a nice, long one. All the guests hooted and hollered and clapped their hands.

"Brad, married after all this time!" Maddie said to Jim and Connie. "I hope he stays happy. He's got four stepkids now, all of them into horses. He's going to be a busy dad. And he has five more mouths to feed."

"I'll bet he'll hand over a major portion of the cattle businesses to you and Devon and hire another helper," Jim said. "He needs to have some fun."

Brad and Cathy did go on a vacation to Alaska that autumn, without the children, and spent ten days there. They had an amazing time. There was a bit of culture shock; the only way to get to where they wanted to go was by float plane. Danali was by far their favorite place on earth. They returned from their honeymoon refreshed, in love, and eager to start their life together.

* * *

Maddie and Devon got married and honeymooned at the Gulf Coast of Florida for a week. They bought a small brick ranch-style house in Jim and Connie's neighborhood, in a lot full of trees. Krista married Ben a couple years into their engagement. They backpacked to the bottom of the Grand Canyon on mules and slept in a tent. Back home, they stayed in their apartment until they graduated from the university and then started a search for a house. Ben's parents visited occasionally from Wyoming. Jim, Connie, Maddie, and Devon got the opportunity to meet them and host them at dinners.

* * *

What became of Sherry? She lost some control of her legs. She was often weak, and she used a walker to get around the house sometimes, and she used the walker to go out. Bela was very patient with her, even when she got angry with God and herself for putting Bela into such a negative lifestyle. Bela helped her do leg and hand exercises to try to maintain a bit of strength and control. One evening, Maddie and Krista were staying with Sherry because Bela was out with some friends. Sherry became frustrated with her inabilities and began to cry. Maddie and Krista looked at each other.

Maddie said, "It's time for Wonderful Wanda."

Wonderful Wanda was a middle-aged African American woman who helped out with chores now and then. Maddie decided it was time for Sherry to hire Wanda for help with personal care such as bathing and dressing for the day, as well as household cleaning. Wanda was an excellent worker.

Bela was all for it if it would help Sherry feel good about herself. He decided he would help Sherry make meals, and he decided to stop taking the overnight trucking jobs he was offered once in a while. He was happy to help Sherry get into her pajamas at night. He still enjoyed sharing their bed with her, where they might talk for hours or make love or just fall asleep in each other's arms.

Bela and Sherry had saved up enough money to pay for Wonderful Wanda and the other helper. But they had wanted that money for a rainy day for themselves or Leora. Maddie talked them into going on a cruise before Sherry got worse, God forbid. They chose a Romanian river cruise. They joined a tour group of ten other people and toured the country during the day, mostly on a bus that stopped in prearranged destinations, ate fantastic food, and heard wonderful music. Bela seemed to be in his element. Sherry was amazed by the beauty, antiquity, and music of Romania. She commented on the beauty of the Romanian women.

Bela responded, "Maybe they are beautiful, but nobody here or anywhere else holds a candle to you, my darling wife." Bela purchased a brand-new accordion from a factory. He played it for Sherry in the evening when they were reposing on the cruise ship. She loved him so much. They returned home happy, well rested, and ready to tackle the elements of MS that kept Sherry from enjoying everyday life. She took experimental medicines in the name of her beloved Leora, who would have wanted her to at least try them for a while.

Once in a while, either Brad, Jim, Maddie, Krista, Sherry, Bela, or Connie would see someone or hear someone who resembled

Leora. It always gave them a double take to see it was not Lee. There was a shard of disappointment for a few seconds, but then life continued the way it was laid out for them. Leora would always be a part of their lives.

ABOUT THE AUTHOR

Mary Rodenburg was born in 1957. She grew up in the countryside of Kent County, Michigan, the sixth of seven children. Her father was an automobile mechanic, and her mother was a personal aide to numerous clients. Mary has an associate's degree in arts. She worked in medical clinics and hospitals around the area of Grand Rapids. She was a French horn player in the 126th US Army Band for twenty years. She traveled overseas with the band a few times and enjoyed her time wherever they were taken. She has two adult children. Mary lives in Grand Rapids, Michigan, in the Riverside Gardens neighborhood, where she has resided for twenty-one years. She enjoys spending time with her one-hundred-year-old mother. Her favorite animal is the cat, and one of her most enjoyable activities is walking along the shoreline of Lake Michigan during the winter. She has written poetry for leisure.

CPSIA information can be obtained
at www.ICGtesting.com
Printed in the USA
BVHW080010180323
660664BV00006B/162

9 781662 482793